Chasing Justice includes material some readers might find difficult, including violence against women, drug and alcohol use, and discussion of suicide.

CHASING JUSTICE

Kathleen Donnelly

carina
press

carina press®

Recycling programs
for this product may
not exist in your area.

ISBN-13: 978-1-355-62393-5

Chasing Justice

Copyright © 2022 by Kathleen Donnelly

For questions and comments about the quality of this book, please contact us at CustomerService@Harlequin.com.

Carina Press
22 Adelaide St. West, 41st Floor
Toronto, Ontario M5H 4E3, Canada
www.CarinaPress.com

Printed in U.S.A.

For my mom and dad,
with much love.

CHASING JUSTICE

Chapter One

A black truck with an old camper shell whipped around a switchback in the distance. Driving too fast for the dirt road, the vehicle fishtailed on the washboards. A plume of dust swirled behind it.

Maya Thompson, a U.S. Forest Service Law Enforcement officer in training, sat in the passenger seat of the patrol Tahoe studying the truck speeding their way and debating if the driver might lose control. Her FTO, or field training officer, Doug Leyton, didn't seem bothered about the vehicle careening toward them.

As the truck flew by, it kicked up a rock that smacked the windshield and bounced off onto the dirt road. Maya startled, but Doug's hands sat steady on the steering wheel, completely unfazed while her heart pounded. Nothing about rocks hitting windshields or trucks passing on dirt roads had been the same since returning home from Afghanistan.

Give it some time, everyone said.

Time healed everything.

Maybe.

Maya took a deep breath and pulled her long red hair

back in a ponytail, securing it with a hair band. "How far out are we?"

Doug shrugged. "Maybe another five minutes."

In the back of the SUV, Juniper lay on the seat specially designed for K-9s, with rubber mats and a vent for air-conditioning or heat depending on the time of year. With her eyes closed, the Malinois rode with the relaxation of an experienced veteran, despite being two years old and new to the job. A black fur mask crossed her face, mixed with a light brown coat over the rest of her body. A white spot splotched her chest.

Juniper opened one golden eye, then closed it again, the picture of contentment.

"Wish I could chill like that," Maya said.

"Me too. Although she's not always like that at home. When she's not working, she can be difficult." Doug glanced at Maya. "How've you been doing?"

"Fine."

"No, I mean, how are you really doing? You can tell me. I'm your best friend, right?"

"Seriously, I'm fine. There's no need to worry about me."

Maya turned her head to watch the trees passing by in a blur—a mixture of green and brown from the pine beetle kill over the last few years. The pine beetle was about the size of a grain of rice and native to Colorado. The beetle infestation had impacted over 3.4 million acres of forest. The trees had been dying before Maya left to join the military, but at that time, the damage wasn't as widespread. Now she was back and the beautiful, lush forests she loved so much were partially dead, with trees cut up into slash piles waiting for winter snow to burn. The forest looked like Maya felt inside.

"You know if you ever need to talk, I'm here for you."

Doug reached over and took Maya's hand, giving it a squeeze. Maya interlocked her fingers with his, appreciating his strong and reassuring grip. Doug was right—not only was he her FTO, but he was her best friend. They'd grown up together and she was grateful for his help.

"I know you're here for me. Thank you." Maya released Doug's hand and undid her seat belt as they pulled into the trailhead parking lot. She wanted out of the vehicle to breathe the fresh air and stop her chest constricting from panic rising through her body. The feelings came so often now, but she had learned to control them, or maybe ignore them, and keep going. Or so she told herself every day. *No more war zone.*

She had thought about telling Doug more. Without him she wouldn't have this job as a Forest Service officer. Maya would probably still be drinking herself to death at the cabin her grandmother left to her.

But despite how much she wanted to, Maya couldn't fully open up to Doug. She didn't want him to know how much of her had changed from the war. Most of all, she didn't want him to know about the feelings she had stuffed deep down and shut off. When she was in Afghanistan, Maya heard other soldiers talking to their loved ones. She'd stopped calling home—it was too difficult to speak with those she loved, especially her grandmother. Nana had had a way of knowing when Maya wasn't telling the truth and sensed she was struggling. Now that Nana was gone, Maya wished she could go back in time and talk to her.

Maya knew she was broken, but Doug had stayed

friends with her and for that, she was grateful. She feared she would never be the same again, but working with Doug helped her move forward. Someday she would talk to him more, but for now, she kept herself closed off.

Doug opened the back door and Juniper bounded out of the vehicle. She shook and then stretched, her brown fur glistening in the sun. A part of Maya wanted so badly to reach down and run her hands through her beautiful coat. She could imagine the feel of the soft fur that would dance through her fingertips, but even worse, she could hear the ringing in her ears from a bomb exploding. The yelping of a dog in pain. Brown eyes begging for help. The memories from Afghanistan that haunted her dreams every night.

Maya stared off into the horizon to gather herself. She never wanted to feel the pain of losing a K-9 partner again.

Maya's love of dogs came from when she was a little girl. Her grandparents had adopted a Great Pyrenees German Shepherd mix puppy named Bear. Together, Maya and her grandmother trained Bear. Maya loved the loyalty and how Bear waited for her after school at the front door. They'd hiked together and Bear always slept with her, which helped with her childhood nightmares.

When Maya joined the military, she applied to be a K-9 handler, but while deployed in Afghanistan, she'd lost her military K-9, Zinger, and the pain cut deep.

Especially since she was at fault for Zinger's death.

After discharging from the military, Maya resisted working alongside a K-9 again, but knowing she was desperate for a job, Doug had convinced Maya she could suck it up and work with him and Juniper. She would only have to ride with him for a short time and then she'd be out on patrol on her own, with no dog reminding her of the past. Maya had debated the choice. In the end having a job where she was supporting herself and acting like an adult who made money for essentials like food and clothing won out.

When she joined Doug and Juniper, Maya couldn't help but admit there was still a draw. Deep down she wanted to take the leash and feel the vibration, the dance, the power, and most of all the partnership, where a handler gave the dog the lead and they trusted each other. This animal was bred for their job and their instincts were superior, but Maya had killed a dog through handler error. She vowed to never put another dog in danger.

I'll never take the leash again. Only a worthy K-9 handler like Doug should work a dog.

Low-hanging clouds from a morning rainstorm rolled in off the mountain peaks, crawling down the valley, pushed by the wind. She caught Doug studying her and smiled at him. *Reassure everyone that you're okay.* That was the only way to survive. Maybe someday it would be true.

"We'll head out toward the old Baker homestead. The call to dispatch came from a hiker near that area," Doug said.

"All right. Let's go." Maya put on her green Forest Service jacket. The panic from the rock hitting the windshield was already leaving her body. The mountains had a way of calming and soothing her. Doug made sure Juniper's leash was secure on her collar along with her Kevlar K-9 vest before the trio headed out toward their destination.

Maya traipsed over the rough trail, dodging fallen logs and stepping over rocks. Doug hiked ahead of her ducking under thick tree branches. His light brown uniform blended in with the surrounding forest.

Sudden movements to the north of the trail made all three of them stop abruptly. A mule deer leaped out from behind a tree, her large ears flipping back and forth. A fawn with white spots followed. Juniper sat by Doug and cocked her head to the side. Maya saw the curiosity cross the dog's face, but obedience overrode her predatory instinct.

"She's a good dog. Amazing to see a Mal that relaxed," Maya said.

"She's a *great* dog. I feel lucky to have her. Maybe one of these days you should try working her. Or even take a bite from her in training. Just get the feel again."

Maya shrugged in response. She hadn't told Doug much, just that she'd lost her K-9 partner, Zinger, due to an IED.

It was my fault. I didn't trust my dog. I didn't listen to my dog.

Watching Doug and Juniper's partnership ripped open painful wounds.

They waited for the deer to continue on their way, their hooves softly hitting the ground until the mother and baby disappeared into a grove of fir trees. The trio started hiking again and the sound of Juniper's sniffing cut through the quiet forest. The dog jogged back and forth in a zigzag pattern, working a scent.

"She enjoys the trails, doesn't she?" Maya said.

"Yeah, she's always up for getting out here and doing

her job. Loves tracking work the best, although bite work is a close second for her. Your grandfather offered to do some decoy work a while back," Doug said, with a laugh.

"Pops? Decoy? Does he even know how?"

"Yeah, I think he does, but I wasn't able to connect with him. How's he doing? You talk to him lately?" Doug asked.

"I think he's good. Haven't you caught up with him? Don't you boys get together for poker night and beer?"

"You need to call him, Maya."

"Why? Is he okay?" Maya stopped.

"He's fine. He misses you. With your grandmother gone now, he's lonely. You should at least stop in and say hi."

"I'll think about it." Guilt washed over Maya. She and her grandfather had kept things cordial, but Maya knew he had every right to be mad at her. The thing was, she was mad at him too. Her grandfather was the Western River County sheriff, and with Maya's job, she had to work with him and at least pretend to get along. To add to her frustration and anger, Maya had wanted a job as a deputy, but her grandfather ripped up her application. He'd told her to find a different job—one with less danger. He didn't want Maya following in his footsteps. She would have been an asset to the department and her grandfather knew that. He also knew she desperately needed a job. *Not to mention, if he'd hired me, I wouldn't be stuck working with a K-9 and reliving my nightmare.*

Juniper sprang to attention, cutting off Doug from continuing the conversation. The Malinois stretched her nose in the air and scented off the slight breeze that came through the trees.

"Let's keep going," Doug said. "She's air scenting in the right direction. Maybe she's smelling a good marijuana grow."

"Did the reporting party give you information about a possible grow?" Maya asked.

"No. They just said suspicious activity at the Baker cabin. Saw a person lurking."

Juniper put her nose to the ground and picked up the pace. Her body became tense and her tail was straight up in the air. Doug and Maya increased their pace to keep up. Every now and then Juniper would pause and change direction.

Maya started to feel the burn in her legs from going uphill, dodging rocks and hopping over fallen logs. Pine needles cushioned the ground, but made it slick too.

Juniper took a sharp right and pulled on her leather leash, dragging Doug into a clearing, where they finally stopped. Doug grabbed a map out of his pocket and checked their location.

"I thought the Baker cabin was abandoned?" Maya asked.

"It was. But a few years ago, the Forest Service came in and restored it enough that someone could stay the night if need be. Gave us a place to get out of the cold when we had to be out in the winter, or get out of a storm in the summer."

"Wouldn't it be locked?" Maya asked.

"Since when do locks keep people out?"

Juniper tilted her head back and forth, listening to Doug and Maya. The dog seemed to grasp what they were saying. She nudged Doug and gave a sharp bark.

"Okay, girl," Doug said, rubbing Juniper's pointy ears. "Let's keep going. We'll get to the area by going up the trail and coming around the backside."

"But I thought…"

"I know the cabin is that way, but look up at those trees. Beetle kill is bad around here and these pines have lost branches. There's a bunch of widowmakers through that area."

"The forest has changed a lot since I left," Maya said, staring up toward branches that lay across other trees at odd angles. If the wind picked up or the ground was soft from rain, a tree might shift and at any time one of those branches could come crashing down and kill a person. Widowmakers had become much more prevalent in Colorado due to the pine beetle kill.

The trio wound their way around heading back to the northwest. They rounded a grove of aspen trees. The brown wood of the cabin contrasted against the white of the aspen bark.

Maya took in the scene little by little. The door to the cabin was jimmied open, but they didn't have a clear view inside. Juniper put her nose up in the air, taking in the scent, when her body language changed. She crouched down and a low growl rumbled in her throat. Maya saw the dog step in front of Doug, positioning herself to protect her handler.

Maya didn't see anyone in the cabin, but the phrase *trust your dog* went through her head. You always trusted the dog.

From around the corner of the cabin, a person popped out and strutted toward Maya. Chin up and their chest puffed out, the person had one hand closed and the other hand open with their fingers splayed out. Were they clutching a knife? Trying to distract her with the open hand?

Maya wasn't going to take any chances. She unholstered her Glock.

Chapter Two

"Freeze, U.S. Forest Service Law Enforcement!" Doug yelled. "Put your hands up and get down on your knees."

Maya aimed her Glock towards the suspect. The person wore shredded jeans, a plaid long-sleeve flannel, a handkerchief over their mouth, sunglasses, a camouflage ball cap, and gloves. Based on size Maya guessed their suspect was a skinny man. As the person put their hands up in the air, she noticed the object wasn't a knife, but rather something about the size of a small cell phone.

Doug yelled instructions for the person to lie down on the ground. Juniper strained at her leash. Maya provided backup with her gun drawn. Doug wouldn't be able to pull his gun since he needed to hang on to Juniper.

Juniper started to bark and lunge at the person, hitting her leash until the suspect complied. "Keep your hands where I can see them!" Doug yelled.

Maya wondered why he wasn't making the person drop the object in their hand. She moved to her right as Doug and Juniper stepped forward. Maya needed to make sure she stayed in a position where she wouldn't put Doug or Juniper in danger if she fired her gun.

The different angle provided a new view of the cabin. Humps of dirt lined the front.

The suspect suddenly leaped to their feet. Hands slithered into their pockets, and even though Maya couldn't see the person's face, there was a moment where she could almost feel a smile. A change in body language. A split-second decision where you didn't know what the person would do next, but it wasn't going to be good.

Their suspect had the upper hand. Or so they thought. Was there a gun in the person's pocket? What was the device they were holding? Juniper might be their only hope to get the situation back under control. The presence of the dog barking and the threat of a bite sometimes helped convince suspects to comply.

"Stay down!" Maya and Doug yelled in unison.

"Get back down and drop what's in your hand!" Maya screamed, stepping closer toward the suspect. "Get back down."

As Maya approached, flanking from the other side, the person started to back away. Then it hit her. Lumps of dirt. The person was drawing them closer. They held some sort of radio remote in their hand. Probably not a cell phone—there'd be no reception up here.

Everything happened in slow motion. The suspect pulled their other hand out of their pocket, showing a knife. That was enough of a threat to allow Juniper to apprehend the suspect.

Doug released Juniper, who sprang forward as he told the dog to "go get 'em." Maya yelled at Doug to get down, get back. Find something to get behind. Shield himself.

Maya dove behind some large logs lying nearby. Distance and shielding could mean life or death surviving a blast. She had learned that the hard way in Afghanistan.

As Maya scrambled to the ground, covering her head, the IEDs exploded.

There was a deafening roar as the gunpowder ignited and dirt flew around her caking her eyes. The ground shook. Windowpanes on the cabin rattled and shattered as the pressure from the explosion rocked the giant log she hid behind. In the distance she thought she heard a yelp but didn't know if it was real or a flashback. Dirt and debris rained down.

Then a calm quiet came back over the forest. A raven cawed in the distance. Or maybe it flew overhead. Maya couldn't tell because her ears were ringing from the explosion, but she was alive.

She wiggled her fingers. Toes. She could move. Her legs worked—barely.

Shaking, she grabbed the giant log, an old pine tree that had come down and probably saved her life. She pulled herself up, feeling the rough, rotted bark. Some of the wood gave way and crumbled to the ground. Maya stumbled to her feet.

"Doug. Doug." Maya scrambled over the log, shredding her uniform. She didn't care as she pushed forward. The ringing in her ears seemed to intensify. She tripped and fell to the ground, but then pushed herself to her feet. Debris scattered in the breeze and Maya thought she saw a medicine wrapper flutter by like a bird, but she couldn't trust herself. Not at this moment. The aftereffects of an explosion included confusion.

Where were Doug and Juniper? They had to be okay. Maya scanned the area for the suspect but saw no one.

She forced her legs to work and sprinted to the cabin.

Doug.

Juniper.

Where are they?

She stopped and thought through their last location. Her mind flipped through what seemed like pictures on a high-speed slideshow. The blast would have thrown them away from the cabin, but Doug had released Juniper to apprehend the suspect, so Maya didn't know where she had ended up. For all she knew Juniper could have found the person and still be holding onto a bite. Maya doubted it, though. Not after an explosion like this.

In answer to her thought, Juniper came limping out of the woods.

"Juniper. Come, girl," Maya said softly, trying to hold her voice steady and calm the dog. Maya ran her hands over Juniper's sides and down her legs. Despite the limp, Juniper seemed okay. The K-9 Kevlar vest had probably helped along with being farther away from the blast. "Where's Doug, girl? Where is he?"

Juniper put her nose up in the air and then trotted over to some bushes, still lame on one of her hind legs, until Maya could see Doug's boots. She cleared the area looking for any signs of the suspect, but the person seemed to have left.

Maya rushed over to where Doug lay and started taking his vitals and assessing him. Juniper whined again and licked one of Doug's hands.

"It's okay, girl. I'll help him."

Maya knew Doug could have internal injuries, but the explosion had ripped into one of his legs. His calf was slanted at an odd angle and blood was pouring down from his thigh. She took out a tourniquet from her trauma kit and tied it above the injury pulling down as hard as she could. She wished she had the medical kit in the car. And that they were parked closer.

Doug was still breathing. Barely. He had a faint pulse.

Maya had always relied on Doug's strength, and it was hard to see him lying here bleeding and injured. She loved him like a brother. Everything from his humor to his ability to understand her made him someone she wanted to hang out with. The thought of losing Doug made her stomach churn and her chest hurt. *Why didn't I tell Doug about how hard things have been and that I haven't been able to escape the nightmares of war? I should have let him know how much he's helped me.*

Maya fought back her feelings and focused on saving him. She needed to get ahold of dispatch and request a helicopter to airlift Doug. Juniper too. And put out a BOLO for the suspect.

Maya carefully examined Juniper, going through the same first aid checklist you would use with a human. Her breathing was fine, and respiration seemed normal. There was no obvious hemorrhaging.

The dog snarled for a moment as Maya hit a sore spot around her ribs. Broken? Maybe. Or perhaps some internal bleeding or lodged debris. Maya wasn't certain. She carefully pulled up the dog's lips and looked at her gums. They were still pink but starting to lose color. Juniper's respiration and pulse were strong. Pieces of shrapnel from the bomb had peppered her leg, but somehow the dog seemed to have escaped the worst of the explosion. Maya took some bandages out and did her best to wrap and protect the wound until a veterinarian could examine her and remove the debris.

She didn't want to move Doug or make Juniper walk, but to bring a medevac chopper in would require a location that was safe for landing. Maya remembered a meadow she'd seen not too far away. If she could get Doug moved, she could radio dispatch, but she needed to be farther away from the cabin. Her radio could spark any undetonated explosives.

Juniper had protectively put her head on Doug's chest.

"Okay, Juniper. We have to move you two. Come on, girl, help me out." Maya kept talking to the dog as she moved behind Doug and gently lifted up his upper body. She crossed his arms and pulled him from behind.

At the edge of the tree stand around the cabin, the wind picked up and whistled through the mountain hillsides. Maya peered up and saw that to get to the meadow she would have to take Doug through a stand of evergreen trees that all had widowmakers. The wind shook the treetops and as they swayed, the broken branches that had fallen at odd angles creaked and shifted. At any time one of them could crash down.

Maya could drag Doug the longer way and avoid the widowmakers, but he didn't have much time. Or she could go the short route and risk one of the branches falling on them.

The wind died down almost as fast as it had whipped up.

Maya chose the short route.

Chapter Three

Blood spread onto Maya's hands as she pulled Doug along.

Behind her, Juniper limped along with them, whining at times but keeping up.

"Come on, girl," Maya encouraged her. *The last time a dog made that noise…* She stopped her thoughts there. She couldn't go there. Not now.

The breeze once again whipped up and gusted to a steady thirty miles per hour, indicating a cool front moving in. The trees creaked and swayed in protest. Behind her, a branch snapped, the crack echoing like a gunshot. The tree limb crashed to the ground. Maya's heart pounded as she flashed back to Afghanistan, pulling her fellow soldiers out of harm's way as bullets flew around them. She stopped and closed her eyes, listening to the wind whistle as another branch shifted above her.

I'm in Colorado, not Afghanistan.

If she didn't keep moving, it was likely that branch would fall right on top of her.

Don't stop now. Keep moving. Don't quit.

Maya's breathing was short and hard, the exertion getting to her. She could see the meadow up ahead, the sun streaming in and illuminating the grass. She thought Doug stirred, but she held her grip and continued dragging him.

I love him. I have to save him.

"Just a little bit farther, Doug," Maya said, not sure if he could hear her. "You're going to make it. I promise."

Just as Maya stepped into the meadow, a final gust of wind shook the trees, and behind her a limb collapsed down. Damn, where was Juniper?

Maya situated Doug on the grass. The tourniquet was doing its job, but more blood flowed from somewhere else. Maya examined Doug, only stopping to try to radio dispatch. There was no signal. *Dang it. Figures we're out of radio range.*

A whine interrupted Maya's thoughts. She stood and stared back at the forest.

"Juniper?" Maya said. Her chest constricted at the silence. From behind the trees came a faint cry.

Maya pushed the fear down, knowing that later all the emotions would hit her. Paralyze her. She didn't care. She sprinted in the direction of the fallen branches. What if the dog was stuck under a tree limb? What if she was dying?

The high-pitched whine continued. Maya looked around the dark forest, her eyes taking a moment to adjust from the bright sun of the meadow and back to the dark from the canopy of the trees. She waited. The whimper came again. Over to her right.

Marines never leave anyone behind, no matter the cost.

Maya picked her way through the forest, dodging stumps just high enough off the ground to trip her, branches lying across the path and pine needles thick like carpet but slick enough to make her fall… But the real danger could collapse from above.

Another wind gust picked up, throwing dirt into Maya's eyes. Wiping the grit out of her eyes, she searched the area desperately seeking the light brown of Juniper's coat. The cries came again, and Maya followed the noise.

A widowmaker had missed Juniper, but the dog was trapped behind branches. Juniper held up her hind leg in pain. Maya didn't know if Juniper would try to bite, but she didn't care. Tears streamed down her face as the image of her old K-9 Zinger lying on the sandy ground again stampeded into her mind.

"You're home. You're safe." Maya didn't know who she was trying to reassure more—her or the dog. She hiked over to Juniper, staying quiet and calm, knowing this would help the dog more than anything else.

Maya rubbed Juniper's head, massaging the triangular ears. She received a groan in response. Maya's tears landed on Juniper's soft coat, like trickles of rain.

"You have to trust me, girl," she whispered.

She squatted down and ran her arms underneath the dog's front end and hind end. With all the strength Maya had left, she lifted up and cradled the animal. Maya held Juniper close to her body, put her head down, and picked her way out of the forest.

Sunlight streamed into the meadow, and Maya saw Doug's shadow. She had to climb to higher ground and get radio signal. Juniper remained limp in Maya's arms, but Maya felt the in and out of Juniper breathing. The dog was still alive.

Now save Doug.

Maya laid Juniper down by Doug. The dog whined and moved closer to her handler, nuzzling him with her black nose. She licked Doug a couple times. Doug's hand stirred and found its way to Juniper's head. He stroked it gently.

"Doug?" Maya said.

He turned and looked at her.

"I'm radioing for a chopper. You're going to be okay."

Doug smiled but didn't say anything, continuing to pet his dog. Juniper looked back at him, and every now and then, she licked Doug's hand.

As hard as it was to leave, Maya pushed herself back to her feet and strode a few feet away. She kept testing the radio, but still, there was no response.

"I'm going up to the top of the hill to see if I can get a radio signal," Maya said.

Doug gave her a weak thumbs-up and Maya sprinted off, ignoring her own aches and pains as she moved up the hill, checking in to see if she had a signal. The mountains often messed with the ability to get radio signal or make a cell phone call.

Maya reached the top of a nearby hill, out of breath, and radioed dispatch. "This is FS 28. Need immediate assistance. Officer down. Needs medical due to explosion."

Letting go of the button, Maya waited. To her relief, static came through and the dispatcher at the local sheriff's office answered. Maya confirmed her location and the need for a medical helicopter for Doug and Juniper. She told the dispatcher the suspect had escaped and deputies in the area needed to be on the lookout. She also let the dispatcher know she would lose signal down by Doug and Juniper. Then she scrambled back down the hill.

Juniper's long brown tail thumped in the grass as

Maya approached. She crouched down to check Doug's vitals. Doug grabbed Maya's hand and tightened his grip, surprisingly strong for the injuries he'd sustained.

"I need to… I need to tell you something," he said.

Maya clutched Doug's hand. "There's something I need to tell you too."

"You? Saying something?" Doug tried to chuckle. "Never."

Maya clung to Doug's hand and sat down next to him, reassured that he was teasing her. That was a good sign. Could she get the words out? Let him know how much he meant to her?

Instead, she said, "You need to try to stay quiet. Save your strength. There's an air ambulance coming for you and Juniper."

Doug shook his head and struggled to speak. Maya ready to tell him to be quiet again when he squeezed her hand and said, "Listen to me. This may be the only chance I get—"

Maya tried to cut him off, but he continued, "Please promise me you'll take care of Juniper. Be her handler. You can do it. I don't trust anyone else."

"I don't know—"

"Promise me," Doug said.

"Okay, I promise, but you'll be fine. She won't need me as a handler."

Doug reached up and took a piece of Maya's hair that had come loose and tucked it back behind her ear. "Thank you. You're my best friend, you know."

"Ditto," Maya said. "You're my best friend and you're not leaving us."

"Listen to me. Your grandfather knows the truth.

About all of this. The explosion. Everything that happened here today. Go talk to him."

"What are you talking about? You're not making sense."

"Just go talk to him. Talk to him about your grandmother too, Maya. He knows more than he's telling you."

Maya froze.

What about my grandmother?

Her grandmother had taken her own life when Maya was deployed. What information could her grandfather be holding back?

"You're going to be all right, Doug," Maya said, choking back tears. Doug was probably delirious from his injuries. What did he know about her grandmother's death that she didn't? Frustration and grief coursed through her body. Maya took a deep breath. "But if you know something, you can tell me."

A smile slid across Doug's face. He gazed at her and said, "You're beautiful. I love you. I'm sorry, this is all my fault."

Then he closed his eyes.

Maya rubbed his chest. "Doug. Doug?" She leaned over him. He was still breathing, but his pulse was slow and weak.

"I love you too," Maya whispered.

Did she feel his hand squeeze hers or was she imagining it?

The wind gusts had died down, making it easier on the helicopter to get to them. In the distance the sound of rotors echoed off the mountains. The *whop, whop* noise disturbed the quiet meadow as the blades cut through the thin mountain air.

The tourniquet was holding, but Doug was getting pale. Juniper kept her head on Doug's chest. Maya flew to her feet and helped direct the helicopter to a landing zone. The giant bird sat down on its skids, the grass flattening as the blades thumped and the engine roared. Small branches and other debris skittered across the ground.

The side door opened, and two flight nurses hopped out. They went over to Doug and went to work. Maya helped them lift and secure Doug on the gurney that fit into the tight quarters of the helicopter.

One of the nurses examined Juniper. "We have a special kit for dogs. Here, help me get this on her."

Maya secured a basket muzzle on Juniper. Under stress a dog could try to bite, and the muzzle would help keep everyone safe. Together they loaded Juniper into the helicopter. The other flight nurse had already started an IV for Doug.

"What about you?" the nurse asked.

"What about me?"

"You look like hell."

"I'm fine," Maya said. "I need to secure the scene. Promise. I'm good."

"Okay, I don't have time to argue with you." The nurse shut the door to the helicopter and Maya stood back covering her eyes so that debris wouldn't hit her. The chopper took off and within a few minutes the sound was distant.

Then silence.

Maya collapsed to the ground. Her hands shook so bad she had to place them on the earth to stop the vibrations. Each breath in and out came short and harsh.

What the hell just happened?

Death?

The very thing she'd been trying to escape.

Doug had to be okay. Juniper had to be okay. Death didn't happen at home. Death happened in war zones.

With her chest constricting, Maya let out sobs. Sobs she had kept in since Zinger died. The day she messed up and messed up her dog. She hadn't cried once. She'd been strong and tough, never showing any emotion, but now it all came rushing out and Maya sat in the grass, letting the mountain air surround her as she cried for her dog. Her grandmother, and now Doug and Juniper.

Chapter Four

Maya wiped her nose with the back of her hand. She'd lost about thirty minutes crying—valuable time she should have been using to secure the scene. She needed to get herself together. She rubbed her palms on her thighs to get rid of the dirt stuck to them. Her pants were torn and tattered, and her auburn hair fell around her shoulders, stringy pieces sticking to her face. She was a mess.

Maya stood up, her moment of emotion done. *Over.* But she knew tonight the nightmares would come. Although with everything going on, she wouldn't be getting sleep anyway.

Her legs were stiff and tight. Her shoulders were sore from dragging Doug and carrying Juniper through the woods. Maya didn't care. Pain and soreness meant you were alive.

She picked her way back to the cabin—the long way this time, avoiding the pine trees, since the wind was blowing again.

In the distance she could see what was left of the cabin. One wall still stood and appeared normal. Glass littered the ground, the smell of gunpowder still hung in the air. She would secure the scene until the sheriff's department could come help with the perimeter. Then she would contact her boss and wait until the FBI showed up to investigate. This time Maya stayed farther back. A bomb squad would need to check out the cabin and clear the area to process the scene.

A scrub jay screeched in the distance while a chipmunk scurried up a tree, chirping its disapproval at Maya for approaching its territory. Everything seemed so normal. Surreal. As if nothing had happened. Maya needed to tape off and secure the scene, but the supplies were back at the patrol vehicle. She would have to wait for one of the sheriff's deputies to arrive. Due to the remote location, that could take a while.

Who had done this? And why? Why hadn't Doug stuck to normal protocol? He didn't get behind anything to protect him or his dog. He never asked the suspect to drop their items.

Maya crossed her arms and took in the wreckage around her. Someone knew their explosives, but parts of the cabin still stood, leaving the crime scene techs plenty of evidence. They would be able to piece together the bombs and find fingerprints or even DNA.

They would catch this person. No, they *had* to catch this person.

The sound of a vehicle lurching up a logging road behind the cabin broke the silence. Maya took out her Glock and held it pointed down, finger off the trigger but ready, just in case.

The front end of a white sheriff's vehicle appeared and then parked near a grove of aspens. Maya relaxed and holstered her gun.

The thought struck her: why hadn't she and Doug

driven up here? Why did he insist on parking at the trailhead and hiking here?

The deputy unfolded out of the vehicle. His tall frame and broad shoulders gave him an intimidating presence. At least to most people. But not Maya. She put her hands on her hips.

Great. Josh Colten.

Just what she needed today.

Colten was new to town and every woman around, single or not, liked to check out the deputy. Maya had even overheard some women at the local café discussing how they would love to get pulled over by him. One giggled about being handcuffed too. Maya was only annoyed by him because he seemed like such a Boy Scout. He always did everything perfectly and by the book, and for some reason, that drove her nuts.

As he walked toward her, Maya noticed Josh had a swagger, as if he knew every woman thought he was good-looking.

That just irritated her even more.

Carson Ray sat atop a horse on the hillside, peering through his binoculars as a sheriff's deputy parked at the crime scene.

His horse snorted and started pawing. Carson reached down and stroked the liver chestnut's neck, soothing the animal. The horse was probably picking up on Carson's frustration.

"Damn it," he muttered under his breath. This couldn't be happening. The feds would not leave this alone, and the last thing he needed was the government meddling in his business. It would only spur on what they started a year ago, taking over his land and his cattle, shutting down the logging company and forcing him out of a job, all while his wife was dying from cancer. No one cared.

Someone from the damn government was always messing with him and his livelihood, but not this time. From his previous work, Carson knew the forest well. He figured it was payback to the government to manufacture drugs in the Baker cabin, and tracing the drug production back to him would be damn near impossible. This was his own business. He'd made something of himself, and for the first time in years he had extra cash.

Someone was going to pay. No one would take this business away from him.

He turned the horse around and asked for a lope. Carson needed to get back to his hunting cabin and make some calls. Navigating the mountainside, the horse lowered his haunches and trotted up to the cabin that had been in Carson's family for over one hundred years.

The horse stood still as Carson dismounted. He looped the reins around a tree branch and found a water bucket, giving the horse a few small sips. "You did well today. I'll get you home soon. Sorry for the workload today, big guy."

Satisfied that the horse would be okay, Carson marched toward the cabin, thoughts of the lost revenue running through his mind. The cabin was where he came to think. To get away from everything. It had been in his family for generations, and with the money he'd made recently, he'd completely renovated it. He'd saved the original windows, though. They were so old the glass wasn't clear anymore. It was like looking through a kaleidoscope, but even with the lack of clarity, Carson saw the outline of a person inside moving from the table to the kitchen sink.

He wasn't expecting anyone here. Carson pulled his pistol from his shoulder holster and crept around by the window to peer in.

Jenna.

His daughter could be difficult to say the least, but he had to give her credit. She'd come home when he needed her most and nursed her mother until cancer took her from them. Jenna had also helped with the new business.

Carson holstered his gun. Still looking through the old window, he saw another person inside the cabin. He'd recognize that grungy baseball cap anywhere. His son, Cody. He was worthless in Carson's opinion. A spoiled brat his mother had let get away with anything he wanted. But the flip side was Carson could make his son do anything *he* wanted. The stupid kid was always trying to please him.

Carson opened the door so hard the hinges creaked, and the door hit the wall behind it. He stepped inside and shook his head at his kids. He'd been hoping for five minutes alone, but he guessed it was family meeting time.

"What's up, Dad?" Cody asked.

"What's up? What's up? Are you serious? Did you not see the giant black cloud that used to be our drug lab?"

"That poor animal out there," Jenna piped up. "I know you love the horses, but you're asking too much of him."

"Can you cook another batch?" Carson asked, ignoring Jenna's comment about the horse and furious that she blew off what had just happened. She needed to appreciate him and his efforts more. She didn't understand what he'd been through just to keep food on the table over the years.

"Not very easily. I need a lab and more materials. You're going to have to call Lana and let her know what happened," Jenna said, standing up and pacing around. Her boots clunked on the wooden floor.

"I know. She'll be pissed, but I can handle it," Carson said. "How much codeine do we have?"

"Not enough. You need to get more."

"All right. I'll do it."

Jenna stopped pacing. "Do you know if anyone was there? Did the feds find us? Or was it someone else? Like the cartel?"

"I saw someone getting airlifted, and maybe a dog, and someone else stayed on scene. Couldn't see who."

"Maybe Sheriff Thompson, or his granddaughter. Heard she got a job with the Forest Service and is in training," Jenna said. "No one else would be in this remote area of the forest. We'll figure it out, but we need to get out of here before anyone comes asking questions. I'll take the horse home. You take my Jeep. That way you can get home faster."

Carson waved her off, frustration building.

"Hey," Jenna said. "You better be nice, or you won't get anything from me. I'll head back to school in the fall."

"Oh, you'll cook no matter what."

"Why do you say that?"

"Because you need this as much as I do. Plus, I know you need your cut of the money if you ever do want to go back to school. Go home and figure out how we're going to finish this order out."

Jenna shrugged and headed out of the cabin. Carson

watched her talk to the horse and rub him on the neck, soothing the animal. Then she mounted and walked off, giving the horse enough rein so he could stretch his head down.

"Now that she's gone, what's your plan, Dad?"

Carson turned around and assessed his son from head to toe. Small and wiry like his mother's side of the family, the kid wasn't bad looking—if he would shave and get a haircut. He was a slob. Sitting at the table with his legs propped up, Cody had on ratty cowboy boots, torn and tattered jeans, a camouflage shirt, and had sweaty hat hair. He'd thrown his sweat-lined baseball cap on the table.

"My first plan is to get you to start looking respectable. You can't dress the way you are and expect to run a business. Why are you so dirty?"

Cody shrugged. "Chicks love me all rough and cowboy."

Carson sighed, knocked Cody's legs down from the chair, and flung the cap at him. "You need to come with me and get the men together. We need to figure out who did this. Who wanted us out of business?" After striding to the door, Carson stopped and turned around. "And then we need to get revenge."

He thought he saw a bit of fear creep across Cody's face. It was good for the kid. It was time for Cody to grow up and become a man.

Chapter Five

The bomb squad had arrived to make sure there were no more surprises. Once the scene was cleared, the crime scene techs moved in. Maya stayed back. Her job right now was to help create a perimeter. A forest was always a hard place to decide where to run crime scene tape because the crime scene could literally be acres.

Camera flashes created a strobe light effect in the late afternoon shade. Maya watched, numb, all of this bringing back her own horrors and nightmares. *I won't be sleeping tonight.*

"You look like crap."

Maya narrowed her eyes. "Yes, you told me that earlier. You know how to make a girl feel good about herself."

Josh wasn't just another deputy. He was the chief deputy sheriff, or her grandfather's second in command—something that many of the other deputies had questioned. Maya could see why. She had heard through the grapevine that Josh came with baggage. Josh had been a Chicago cop, but something happened, he had lost his job, and now he was here. Her grandfather, the sheriff, had given him a second chance because Pops had served with

Josh's grandfather in the Marines. And yet Pops wouldn't give Maya a second chance.

Maya stood tall. "What are you still doing here? Weren't you just going to help me secure the scene and then leave? Don't you have something important to do?"

"Just saying you should maybe get checked out by a doctor, Thompson. The sheriff's office is here to help. You wouldn't have crime scene techs without us."

"Yeah, I know we have a partnership with the sheriff's office, but the FBI is going to investigate the bombing, just remember that."

Josh held up his hands like he was surrendering. "I know. I know. I'm staying out of the way. And it's not like we haven't helped before with investigations. It's that whole work together thing. You know?"

"Then why are *you* here? Doughnut shop closed?"

Josh laughed. "Nice. No, I told your grandfather I would come see what needed to be done up here."

"Where is my grandfather?"

"At the hospital waiting to find out more about Doug. You talk to Wayne lately?" Josh asked.

Maya shook her head. How the heck was he on a first-name basis with her grandfather? She supposed it made sense since he was the chief deputy sheriff, but everything about this man made him difficult to work with. Not to mention, his question only reminded her of the conversation with Doug earlier. Maybe he'd be less annoying if he could give her an update on Doug and Juniper.

"Do you know anything about Doug? How he is?" Maya felt a catch in her throat. She would not cry again. Not in front of everyone anyway.

Josh's face turned serious. "No. I'll see if I can find out more."

"What about Juniper..." Maya heard herself almost whispering.

"I don't know. Look, when you're done here, I can take you home, you can get cleaned up and then we can go to the hospital," Josh said.

Maya stiffened. "I can take care of myself. I need to get our Forest Service vehicle. And I need to stay here to oversee this investigation. Someone has to keep watch over the crime scene."

"I have a deputy here who can take over." Josh nodded in the direction of a man standing off to the side. "He'll keep watch over the crime scene. It may take all night to process this. I think your boss would want you to get checked out and make sure you're okay."

"I look that bad?"

"You do. I mean, actually, for surviving a bombing you look pretty good, but I still think you should have a doctor examine you."

Maya sighed. "Thanks for being honest. I think. I still need to get our patrol vehicle."

"I can give you a ride to where it's parked."

"Fine. I'll take you up on that, but I'm not going home first. I'm going straight to the hospital."

"Suit yourself," Josh said.

They hiked a good distance to stay out of the way and get to where Josh's SUV was parked. Maya got into the front seat, and as she sat down, exhaustion washed over her. She didn't want to admit it, but Josh had a calming presence. He didn't seem to get flustered by anything. His demeanor was helping her out. She'd worked with men before in the military and in law enforcement and she'd never had an issue with any of them. Josh was the first person that calmed her down and yet made her want to punch him at the same time.

"You're going crazy," Maya muttered to herself.

Josh got in and put the car in Drive. They jostled and bounced on the rough dirt road. "I called your grandfather."

"Why?" Maya didn't mean to snap at him, but it came out that way.

"To let him know you're okay."

"Great, that'll go over well. He's already certain I'm in the wrong career."

"He loves you, Maya."

"I don't understand why he loves *you*."

That shut Josh up for a moment and Maya closed her eyes. She had to start being nicer, but sometimes with the way the anxiety weighed on her, it was hard to not be edgy.

"Wayne is a good man."

"We don't see eye to eye."

"I can tell."

Josh pulled into the parking lot where the Forest Service vehicle sat. Maya stared at it. Earlier today, everything had been fine. And now…she didn't want to think about now.

"Why did Doug park here?" asked Josh.

"I don't know. I was in my last week of training; tomorrow was my last day. I didn't question him since he was my field training officer."

"Okay. Not questioning your FTO is probably good."

"You think?"

Maya stepped out of the vehicle and mumbled a thanks, but not before glancing back at Josh. She could see what the women around town were talking about. He wasn't hard to look at. He was nice. She needed to get over her annoyance because she had to work with him.

Or maybe she just needed to have a doctor examine her and tell her if she was crazy. Maybe she was the one with a problem.

Chapter Six

Maya floored the patrol SUV, taking deep breaths in and out. She rolled down the window and took in the sweet, cool mountain air. The temperature was dropping as the sun started setting behind the mountains, casting its rays up through the clouds. How did such a destructive day end so beautifully? A few times she thought she'd have to pull over, but she took some more deep breaths and calmed down.

Arriving at the hospital, she parked next to Josh's sheriff's SUV. The scene with Doug and Juniper replayed in her mind. The mounds of dirt. Maya yelling. Doug hadn't seemed to hear.

She stepped out of the vehicle and the keys jingled as her hands shook. Her legs felt like jelly.

"Thinking about what happened?" Josh strode up behind Maya, startling her.

"Maybe." She worked to compose herself.

"You can tell me about it if you want. I know you'll have to write a statement, but if you, you know, need to talk."

"I'm fine. I'm just thinking through what I'll have to write up."

"All right."

An ambulance sat near the ER doors, back doors open, the patient inside somewhere. On the top corner of the hospital was the chopper that had come to rescue Doug and Juniper. The blades were tied down, but the bird shook a little in the breeze.

The cool summer air stung Maya's arms. She rubbed her hands up and down her arms, hoping to warm herself up. She'd have to get home and have a good hot shower, but not before she saw Doug.

"Here." Josh held out a sheriff's windbreaker.

She hesitated, then grudgingly took the windbreaker and slipped it on. "Thanks," she muttered.

"What was that?"

Maya shook her head. "You heard me."

"Well, you must be cold if you're desperate enough to put on a sheriff's jacket. Cross jurisdictions here. What will we do?"

Maya ignored Josh and headed for the sliding doors leading into the ER. As they strode through the parking lot, an old green Chevy truck caught her eye. It was missing a few letters across the back and instead said *Chev let*.

Her grandfather's personal truck.

Other than when work forced their paths to cross, she had avoided Pops since their last fight. Maya knew her grandfather had every right to be mad. Not coming home for Nana's funeral and lying about where she was hadn't been her best moves, but at the time it was the only way Maya knew how to cope.

Take a deep breath and face him. He's not that bad. Just your grandfather.

Maya continued into the ER waiting area. Pops was surrounded by other law enforcement officers concerned about Doug, including Deputy Sam King. Sam had started with the sheriff's department the same year as her grandfather. He had been like another father to her. She hadn't seen him since she had returned home, and in the years Maya was gone, Sam's hair had completely grayed. Always a fan of the cliché doughnut, he had a belly that protruded over his duty belt. He had to be nearing retirement.

Maya held back, observing the group, feeling like a kid who'd snuck downstairs after bedtime to spy on their parents. Her grandfather chatted with the other men. He looked tired and worn and had aged about ten years since her grandmother's funeral…maybe she had too.

Sam spotted her first. "Maya," he exclaimed, coming over and squeezing her shoulder. "How ya holding up?"

"I'm good, Sam," Maya said. "It's nice to see you."

"You too. Been too long. Come join us—we're waiting on news about Doug."

Maya's grandfather turned her way and their eyes connected. They had the same green eyes that her grandmother said could look through anyone. It always felt like a pissing contest with Pops to see who could outlast who.

She stepped forward and joined the group, noticing that Josh hung back. "Pops," Maya said.

"Maya."

"I'm going to get a cup of coffee. Anyone want one?" Josh asked, escaping the tension.

"I'll go with you," Sam said.

The two men scrambled away towards the coffee machine. Maya stood taller. *Never back down.* That was the Marine way. Semper Fi and all that crap. Once a Marine, always a Marine… Maya didn't know if she bought into that anymore.

"Hey," Maya called over her shoulder at Josh. "Get a cup for me too, please."

Josh waved in acknowledgment. Maya had to admit he wasn't hard to look at walking away. *You're as bad as the women in town.*

Maya turned back toward her grandfather, pushing her thoughts aside. "Might be a long night. You need a cup?"

"No." Her grandfather shook his head. He appeared defeated. Gray stubble dotted his face. A twinge of guilt swept Maya.

"How's Doug?" she asked, trying to break the ice.

"In surgery."

"He lost a lot of blood out there."

"He did. We were told you did a lot to save him. He would have bled out without the care you gave him and without calling in the helicopter."

"I did what I could."

Silence again. The clock on the wall ticked away. Maya shifted back and forth on her feet.

After what felt like an eternity, but was probably only thirty seconds, Pops said, "You look like you need to see a doc."

Maya narrowed her eyes. Here's where it started. When her grandfather would tell her why she shouldn't be doing what she was doing. Don't join the military, you won't be able to handle it. Don't become a law enforcement officer, you'll see things that will haunt you. Don't do this. Don't do that. "I'm fine."

"I didn't ask how you were. I said you need to see a doctor."

"I heard you." Maya crossed her arms.

"You should see yourself. Good thing Josh gave you that windbreaker."

Maya smelled some of Josh's cologne on the windbreaker. Even that was perfect. Why had she let him give her the jacket anyway? She had her own coat in her patrol vehicle. "I'll go home and clean up. I'm fine, Pops."

"Well, you don't look fine. And at our last poker night, Doug said he was worried about you. Dealing with that mind stuff, that PT, whatever you call it. You should get help."

"I'm just fine. Doug doesn't know what he's talking about."

"Look, Maya, I want you to take care of yourself. You're not doing that."

"Pops, if I have to say I'm fine one more time, I'm going to…" Maya couldn't come up with a good threat. She sounded like a toddler. What was she going to do? Throw herself on the floor and have a tantrum? "I'm taking care of myself. Look, this has been a long day. Let's just see how Doug is doing. Do you know anything about Juniper?"

Her grandfather shook his head no.

"Then I'm going to call the vet hospital and find out more."

Maya marched back toward the doors outside. The fresh air would be better and out in the dark parking lot it would be harder for someone to see the tears that threatened to fall again. She needed to pull herself together. Now.

Chapter Seven

The phone rang for what seemed like an eternity. Maya paced around the outside of the ER, making the glass doors open and close. She moved farther away to avoid the sensor. The vet clinic might be closed because it was after hours, but someone had to be there taking care of Juniper. Her heart raced and her throat was dry. Would the dog be okay?

"This is Dr. Asher."

Maya gripped the phone. She tried to talk, but words wouldn't form. A part of her wanted to hang up. Maybe she didn't really want to know how Juniper was doing.

"Hello?"

Maya forced herself to speak. "This is Officer Thompson. I'm calling for an update about K-9 Juniper. How is she?"

"She made it through surgery well. She was sore in the ribcage, but no major injuries. Her leg is stitched up and will need some care, but that wasn't too bad. Infection is the biggest concern. We're keeping her on IV antibiotics and sedated, but she should be able to go home in a day or so and actually return to work soon."

"Okay, thanks."

"You can come see her tomorrow if you want. Might help for the dog to have someone she knows visit her."

"Juniper."

"Excuse me?"

"Juniper, the dog's name is Juniper."

"Ah yes. Well, please come see Juniper tomorrow. I think it would be good, especially for these high-strung breeds. They need some consistency, and waking up in a vet clinic might put her on edge."

"Okay, I'll think about it. Thanks, doc." Maya hung up. She didn't want to see Juniper. She just needed to make sure Juniper was okay. That was all.

Maya strode back inside. The fluorescent lights seemed harsh after being outside in the dark. Several more deputies and friends of Doug's had shown up. The sound of the coffee machine drowned out some of the conversations.

Several of the men, including Pops, turned toward her with expectant gazes. Maya filled them in on what the vet said. She was interrupted by a doctor coming into the ER. He wore blue scrubs and the surgical hat over his head accentuated his tired face.

"You all here for Officer Doug Leyton?"

"Yes," Maya's grandfather answered.

"Are you family?"

"Yes."

The doctor shrugged and sat down. "Mr. Leyton came in with a lot of trauma and internal bleeding. We were unable to get the bleeding stopped. I'm sorry. He passed away."

Dizziness swept Maya's body.

She grabbed the back of a chair to steady herself.

Josh moved closer to her, but she shot him a look

and he stopped. She didn't need help, just a moment to gather herself. Sadness turned to anger, and Maya clutched the chair harder. He couldn't be gone.

Her best friend.

Her only friend.

Maya's knuckles began to ache as her fingers dug into the back cushion. She strode over to the vending machine. Without thinking, she made a fist, pulled back her arm and punched the machine as hard as she could.

"No, no, no" came out of her mouth, but the sound seemed distant. Like it wasn't coming from her.

All she'd succeeded in doing was leaving a small dent, while her knuckles hurt like hell. People in the waiting area stared at her.

A hand grazed her elbow, and Maya turned to see Josh. He had ignored her moment of anger against the vending machine and braved coming over. "You need to rest. Why don't I take you home?"

"I can drive myself."

"Take your grief outside, Maya," Pops said. Maya hadn't noticed that he had joined them.

With Josh and her grandfather flanking her, she strode outside as anger and grief churned up inside her like a brewing storm.

"You're making a scene," her grandfather said.

"I thought you'd be more worried about Doug and less about your granddaughter embarrassing you," Maya said.

"I'm just as upset as you. He was like a son to me. But I'm handling this like an adult."

"And I'm not?" Maya started pacing, knowing that she wasn't being reasonable, but unable to stop herself. "I'm going to figure out who did this and make them pay."

"Be careful what you say," her grandfather said.

"I am being careful, and I will figure out who did this. End of story. I'm heading home now."

Maya marched toward her car, glancing over her shoulder once to see Josh and her grandfather watching her. The clouds had cleared out and stars shimmered— the only light in the darkness. In Afghanistan Maya would sit and watch the stars, wondering if her grandparents would be sitting out on their porch doing the same thing. The stars connected her to home.

Maya opened the car door, got in the front seat, and sank into the cushion. She pulled down the visor and looked in the mirror. Her face had small cuts and was smeared with dirt. Her hair was snarled. Nothing a good shower and couple beers wouldn't fix.

She slammed the steering wheel with her palm. Despite her grandfather's warning about being careful, she would catch who did this and get justice for Doug.

Chapter Eight

Carson paced around the barn that had been remodeled into a bunker. The only sound came from his boots thudding on the wooden floor. From the second round of business profits, he had redone the outbuildings to better fit his new vision—a gathering place for those like him. Those the government had screwed over. Those who had lost their jobs because of federal regulations and cuts.

The first round of business profits he'd used to pay off his wife's medical bills after her death. He thought doing that would bring him peace and a sense of pride.

It hadn't.

Carson then decided what would bring him pride was the power of being in charge. He was tired of being run over and treated like dirt. It was time to prove his worth and that he was a legitimate leader. He wanted the men he commanded to know they didn't need the government. They could do whatever they wanted because this was a free country. Screw federal regulations.

Men from all walks of life filled the room. Most of them had been ranchers. Many of them had worked at the logging operation with Carson. Some sat, some stood, some chewed tobacco and spit into old Styrofoam coffee cups, waiting for Carson to tell them what was going on. Behind Carson was a large room full of rifles, handguns, and ammunition in case anyone threatened their way of life or their new business.

Carson had everyone's attention. He needed to start with a punch. Something to make sure these men stayed on his side and continued doing what he wanted.

"This is war," Carson said, continuing to march back and forth. "We need to know who destroyed this drug lab and why. Who took these profits from us?"

"My money is on the feds," said a man named Roger. He had also been a rancher, dependent on his cattle grazing on federal land. Then someone had spotted a rare bird and his cattle were no longer allowed on the land. Was it an owl? Grouse? Carson couldn't remember and he didn't care. All he cared about was that Roger was angry enough at the feds to do what Carson needed. When Roger had to sell his cattle and lost the income, it was easy to get him to realize they had a way to make money. They just had to work together.

"I agree, could be the feds. They've always had it out for us," Carson said. "They certainly need to be on our list. We should also look at the cartel. Even our Russian friend Lana who thinks we're working for her. Whatever the reason, whoever it is, we cannot allow someone to come in and take over our business. There needs to be revenge. Now."

Some of the men agreed and nodded, a murmur of voices throughout the room. Carson had them wrapped around his little finger. While he still had no idea who blew up the lab or why, at least having the men on his side would help him get what he wanted—getting drugs back into production and making money.

"How are we going to find out who did this?" asked Roger.

"Good question. Get out there and question everyone. When you're out riding fence, keep your eyes open. Keep an eye out for more feds. The FBI. ATF. Even our local sheriff. Whoever is investigating the explosion could potentially lead us to the answer. Then we can take matters into our own hands. Solve this problem our own way."

Carson banged his fist on a coffee table that sat in the center of the room. "We trust no one, not even the person we have on the inside giving us information." He stared around the room at all the men nodding in agreement. "Keep reporting back to me."

Carson's girlfriend, Bobbi, strutted over and started to rub his back. "Stay calm, babe," she whispered in his ear.

Carson saw Jenna staring at them, a flash of anger on her face. He knew Jenna didn't like or trust Bobbi. He didn't care. What right did she have to judge? So what if he had met someone who made him happy again? Sure, it was only a few months after his wife had passed, but everyone needed to move on. Bobbi had helped him, and he was grateful.

Roger spoke up again. "I think we should look at the feds and the sheriff. I think they all blew up the drug lab."

"Why would they do that?" Jenna asked, rolling her eyes.

"I think it's something we should consider," said Carson, stepping in before any of the men could answer and his daughter started a riot.

"I saw that Forest Service fed, what's his name—

Doug—and the sheriff having a heated conversation last week," Roger continued. "I saw them when I was at the sheriff's office to pay off a ticket. Damn bastards. I should be able to go whatever speed I want when I drive on these back roads. If they couldn't prove the lab was ours, I could see our crazy sheriff deciding to blow it up to get rid of it. I bet that fed discovered the lab and told the sheriff about it."

Several men around the room chimed in agreement. Carson needed to keep the meeting on track. "I think then we should look into the sheriff and see what we can find out and what he knows. I believe he's been investigating our business."

"How would the feds or sheriff benefit from the lab blowing up?" Jenna spoke up again. "I mean, seriously. Think about it."

"You know something we don't, Jenna?"

Jenna sat down on a tattered couch and crossed her legs. She studied a fingernail and glared back at Carson. "No, Dad. I don't."

"Then all of you keep your ears and eyes open. You see anything suspicious, like what Roger saw at the sheriff's station, report back to me. Until then, Jenna will work on production and we'll meet again next week to figure out distribution."

Carson watched the men file out of the room one by one. He had eyes and ears where he needed them. The tip about Doug and the sheriff fighting was good information. As far as he knew, Doug and the sheriff were all buddy-buddy. In fact, when Carson recently struck up a conversation with Doug, he told Carson he was the only officer around for miles and he had mentioned how busy he was with summertime activities like checking up on campers and making sure camp-fires were properly put out.

So then, if it was the fed, Doug, being taken away by chopper, why had he been at the cabin, far away from any campsites, with the other officer? The sheriff's grand-daughter no less. Carson needed to find out.

Chapter Nine

Maya drove up into the foothills toward Pinecone Junction, the small mountain community where she lived. But when she reached a picnic area, she pulled off the road and parked, letting her forehead rest against the steering wheel.

Maya couldn't name all the emotions hitting her at once—anger, numbness, sadness. She supposed they all added up to what the counselor at the VA would call grief. She had tried one support group, but in the end she'd left. The counselor had attempted to talk her into staying, but Maya ignored her. A group of veterans telling their stories made things worse. Everyone had a sob story. That was the reality of war.

That was why she didn't reenlist. She had thought at the time that discharging and coming back to Colorado was the answer, but if going home meant that more people she loved would die, then she was ready to escape. Problem was, she needed a job and she didn't feel qualified for anything except what she was doing. If Doug hadn't helped her out, then she'd probably be sitting in her cabin, drinking nonstop. She loved and owed Doug. And the only way she could think about paying him back was to figure out who had done this and why.

Then there was the promise of working Juniper. Doug knew that not everyone could handle a K-9. They were high-energy, high prey-drive dogs. The partnership you earned with one of these working dogs was hard to put into words. There was nothing else like it in the world. You became a team, feeling each other through the leash, communicating with each other from the slightest change in body language and trusting the dog to do their job.

Trust.

Could Maya trust herself to do her job? Could she keep a dog safe?

With Zinger, she had become cocky as a handler. Maya accidentally pulled him off a scent, which meant they had missed an IED. Zinger had turned around to go back and show her where the scent was. She had tripped and fallen. Somehow that trip saved her life, but Zinger rushed forward and the IED went off, killing him.

Maya closed her eyes and leaned her head back against the headrest. That night haunted her dreams. Sometimes she could only sleep three to four hours. The counselors at the VA had tried to give her meds to help her out, telling her that over time things would get better.

"You never get over PTSD, but you learn to manage it," they had said.

Maya tried to believe them, but she couldn't because the nightmares continued. If she drank enough beer, she could sometimes sleep. That was her way of managing.

Doug had helped her more than the counselors. He never asked too many questions. He'd take her out fishing and they'd sit there in silence. Occasionally Maya could talk to him, and eventually Doug coaxed her out of her shell. She found over time she could talk to him a little more and a little more until, somehow, she'd been able to function again. When there'd been an opening with the Forest Service for another law enforcement officer, Doug had talked her into it. She had the training. In the Marines to be a K-9 handler you also had to train and work as a military police officer.

Maya had hesitated at first, not sure if she wanted to get back into law enforcement, but Doug had told her that most of her days would be hiking in the woods, enforcing a few violations, and talking to people here and there. Nothing too dangerous. Maya needed to do something, so she'd accepted the job.

And now Doug was gone.

Maya sighed and put the vehicle in gear, feeling calm enough to drive. Before she could merge back onto the empty road her cell phone started ringing, lighting up the cab. Her boss, Todd Davis. Maya put the vehicle back in Park and answered. If she drove and talked, she would probably lose signal heading back to her place.

"Hello, sir."

"Thompson. Glad I got you. How are you doing? You okay?"

Maya shrugged and said, "Honestly, with everything that happened today, sir, not great."

"I understand. Dumb question."

Maya liked her boss. Todd was relaxed and easy to talk to—something you didn't always find in government bureaucracies. She didn't see him much because he was the patrol captain and lived in Wyoming. Todd was in charge of six law enforcement officers in several national forests. Because he had so much on his plate,

Maya and Doug checked in with him weekly by phone but only saw him about four times a year.

"I'll get right to the point because I'm sure you're tired and ready to go home. I'm officially ending your training. You're now an officer. Congratulations. With that comes the fun of paperwork. I need your report about what happened ASAP. I'll be coming into town the day after tomorrow. We can go over the investigation then. Also, I'm assigning you Leyton's patrol vehicle."

"Okay, I'll start working on my statement tonight. And glad you've assigned me the patrol vehicle because I'm driving it." Little things around the vehicle reminded Maya of Doug. His sunglasses were still clipped to the sunshade. The mirrors weren't set in quite the right place for her. It was as if at any moment Doug would show up and get into the vehicle, like this nightmare had never happened. Instead, the end of Doug's life would come down to a statement to be filed away while everyone else went on with their lives.

"Great, and one other thing. Since you have Leyton's patrol vehicle, which is set up for a K-9, I would like you to be Juniper's handler."

"Excuse me, sir?" Maya said. She rubbed her forehead and sighed.

"I talked to the vet and it sounds like K-9 Juniper will make a full recovery and quickly. She's going to need a handler. You have the experience, and I would like you to work her."

"With all due respect, sir, I'm not sure I am the best person." Maya knew she had made a promise to Doug, but her boss didn't know that. She hesitated as guilt took over and then said, "But I could do a trial period with her. See how it goes. See if she'll work with me."

"I'm willing to give that a shot. How about a six-week trial period? Take her to work with you. Start some training with her. Honestly, Thompson, this is one of the reasons I hired you. You are a highly decorated K-9 handler and your CO from the military has nothing but great things to say about your ability. He said you're one of the best, so I'm sure you will do fine."

Maya didn't know how to answer. Wouldn't her commanding officer have said how she screwed up? She felt a giant headache coming on—something that could be solved with a cold beer can against her head. "I'll take her on a six-week trial period. We can stay in touch about how she's doing, but no guarantees."

"Okay, I'll get the paperwork going. I'm also thinking you should take some leave time."

"What? Sir, with all due respect, I don't need to take any time off. I've come home from being deployed. This isn't my first rodeo."

"Heard, okay. If you want to keep working, you can, but at least take a few days off when you pick up the dog. And you still need a doctor's evaluation. Get that done ASAP."

"Where do I go for that?" Great. Another counselor telling her how to deal with her issues, but she had to do it if she wanted to work.

"I'll give you the information. Do you have a pen and paper?"

"Hang on, sir. There's paper in the center console." Maya popped open the console and began rooting around for the notebook she and Doug carried in there. She noticed a tiny black-velvet box stuck in the back corner of the compartment. Maya picked it up and flipped the top open. A diamond ring glittered in the cab light.

"You still there, Thompson, or did I lose you?"

"What... Uh, yes, sir. Just a minute. I'm having trouble finding a pen." Maya put the box with the diamond ring down on the passenger seat and found a pen.

She wrote down the words, but her mind kept going to the ring sitting on the passenger seat. She assumed it was an engagement ring, but for who? She and Doug had shared everything. Well, almost everything. She had to admit that she held back a lot about her military experiences with Doug and of course how the nightmares and PTSD affected her, so why would she expect Doug to tell her he was dating someone, much less going to ask her to marry him?

Chapter Ten

Sunlight glared through the curtains, blinding Maya as she struggled to open her eyes. Sitting up, she heard cans clattering to the floor. *Guess I had a few beers last night.* As she stood and threw her blanket back onto the couch, beer cans crunched under her bare feet.

"Ouch, son of a…" Maya muttered, gimping her way to the kitchen to start some much-needed coffee. Her head pounded and she closed the curtains to keep light from coming in. After starting coffee, she popped a few ibuprofens to stop her headache.

Grabbing the trash, Maya picked the empty cans up from the floor and couch. Maybe she did need to cut back a little bit. Pops had told her that, but she had blown him off at the time. Maya bagged the cans and set them by the door to recycle.

Promising herself she would get her act together, Maya poured herself a steaming cup of coffee. She opened the fridge for some creamer and discovered there was none left. She grabbed the milk, but it smelled sour, so she poured it down the sink. Her fridge looked like a bachelor lived there, with old pizza and a few more beers in the back. That was it other than some moldy cheese that Maya added to the trash.

Taking in the cabin, she had to accept the whole place looked like a disaster. She had unpacked the basics, but moving boxes littered the floor. Her battered couch was once plaid and now had coffee stains and probably beer stains. The small room adjacent to the kitchen had her bed—when she made it there to sleep. An old rug with bear and moose designs lay over the wooden floor. It need cleaning—vacuuming at least.

Maya sighed and flopped back down on the couch, sipping the coffee and hoping the ibuprofen would kick in soon to diminish her headache. She closed her eyes. She had about a half hour before she had to start getting ready for work. Maybe a shower would help her feel better.

She remembered coming home last night and cleaning up her wounds. Nothing serious, just some scrapes and scratches. Her pants were in the trash and she would need a new shirt, but she could bring that up with Todd when he came into town. Josh's windbreaker was draped over a kitchen chair. She supposed she needed to return it, but didn't feel like dealing with him today. Her statement was strewn all over the table. She'd started it, but stopped after her third beer.

After draining her first cup of coffee and starting to feel a little human, Maya gingerly stood up to get another. She noticed her cell phone had a voice mail. She must have slept through the call. Maya typed in her security code and saw the voice mail was from Juniper's vet.

"Hi, Officer Thompson. This is Dr. Asher. I have some great news. Juniper is making a quick recovery. We see no reason to keep her here for much longer. I wanted to let you know you can pick her up tomorrow. I talked with your supervisor and he told me you would be taking Juniper. Please give me a call and we'll figure out a time for you to come get her. I'll give you instructions for her home care."

Maya sighed and threw the phone across the room. What was she thinking? She couldn't take this dog. She could barely take care of herself. But at this point, she couldn't go back on her promise to Doug or to Todd. How the heck would she pick the dog up tomorrow? She didn't even have a crate for her. Everything would be at Doug's house. The last thing Maya wanted to do was to visit Doug's empty house; it would be another reminder that he was gone forever.

But Maya would have to go there today and pick up all of Juniper's supplies and dog food. She also needed to build a solid fence and kennel. Working dogs were not treated like pets. You didn't want the dog to like staying home more than going out to work. You never gave a young working dog the run of the house, not if you valued your possessions. They needed kennels, crates, and structure—something Maya didn't feel like she possessed.

People often assumed that because K-9s were so well trained, they were perfect pets, but in reality, the dogs were high-energy and would entertain themselves. That usually involved chewing, ripping, and digging. Yep, she had a lot of work to do to get ready for a young Malinois to move in. Or Maligator as Maya called them.

Hopefully, Doug kept his spare key in the same spot he always did—a fake log in his woodpile. He'd done that for years, and Maya had given him crap about it, telling him he never changed.

Now she knew he did change. Like buying an engagement ring and not telling her who he was dating.

Maya forced herself to get off the couch and go take a shower. She had to get moving if she was going to answer all these questions.

Chapter Eleven

Maya climbed into what was now *her* Forest Service Law Enforcement Tahoe specially designed for *her* K-9. Last night she'd taken out every reminder of Doug in the vehicle and bagged the items up. She adjusted the mirrors and the seat. If Maya was going to do this, she had to make this vehicle hers and not Doug's.

Behind the passenger seat was a special insert in the vehicle for the dog that had a rubber horse stall mat, dog bed and water bowl. Because of the fluctuating temperatures in Colorado, the insert also had air conditioning and heat as well as a system that monitored the temperature. The door was equipped with a special system that would pop open if a handler needed their dog to assist them since a K-9 was often the best backup available. Along with all the other equipment that law enforcement carried there were special K-9 first aid kits and even a K-9 carry litter.

Maya clung to the steering wheel, apprehensive about picking up Juniper's items from Doug's house. What would it be like going through his residence? Even though he had died yesterday, it already felt like years ago.

She felt numb inside.

Doug lived at the edge of town, and it took Maya about twenty minutes to get there. The small town of Pinecone Junction wasn't much to look at, but the main street was paved. Beyond that there were gravel roads. Small shops lined the street including a local diner and bar called the Black Bear Café, a hardware store, antique store, and a chamber of commerce inviting visitors to learn more about the surrounding area. The Forest Service office was located on the edge of town and painted in the usual brown color. Maybe there had been a sale on brown paint for the government.

Doug's house was on the east side of town, and as Maya pulled up, she admired how well he had renovated the place. She hadn't been over since she'd been home. The last time she was at Doug's house she was on leave and at that point it was still a fixer-upper. The house now had a fresh coat of forest-green paint with white trim, a new front porch with two Adirondack chairs and hanging baskets with marigolds. Maya hadn't suspected that Doug would be the hanging basket type, but the orange flowers contrasted nicely with the green paint. Maybe she should take a few pointers and think about her cabin. Flowers would help spruce her place up. So would completely moving in.

Maya opened the car door and went around to the side of the house where the woodpile sat. The fake log was tucked in with the other pieces of timber.

"You're predictable," Maya said out loud. Somehow talking to Doug made her feel better. She slipped open the compartment with the key.

She opened the front door and stepped in, surprised by what she saw. In the past Doug's house hadn't looked too different from hers—a cliché bachelor pad. Instead, these floors were clean and new rugs decorated various areas. A vase of bright yellow sunflowers sat on the coffee table in front of a new couch with stylish pillows at each end. Maya peered in the kitchen and saw new hardwood floors and granite countertops.

Not only did the place look immaculate, but some good money was spent on the remodel. Where would Doug get that kind of money? While their salary wasn't terrible, it didn't allow a top-of-the-line remodel. Not to mention, Doug was a typical guy and Maya was expecting not only a bachelor pad, but also a couple mounted deer or elk heads. She suspected the mystery girl had something to do with the decor.

To confirm her suspicions, Maya went to the bedroom where a down comforter and more stylish pillows adorned the bed. She peeked in the master bathroom and saw a hairbrush with some blond hair. Doug's hair was dark brown. There were two toothbrushes. Maybe she should have knocked before coming in. She didn't even think about someone else being here, which was silly considering the ring.

Maya retreated toward the kitchen looking for where Doug stored Juniper's items. As she gathered Juniper's things, she thought through every single woman she could think of with blond hair—about half of the town. A couple were natural blondes and the others had help from the local hairdresser.

Did it matter who the mystery girl was? The only thing that bothered Maya was if Doug and this girl had such a serious relationship, why wasn't the town talking about it and why wasn't this person at the hospital? Doug had gone to great lengths to keep this relationship quiet, and yet he had bought a ring, which would eventually make the relationship public.

"Get on with it, Thompson," Maya muttered to herself.

In a mudroom off the kitchen leading to the backyard, she found Juniper's food dishes and other items like extra balls, Kongs, and a fire hose to play with. A large crate sat in the corner of the kitchen. Maya would need to take that today.

After a couple trips to the car with dog food and other items, she stopped to gaze at some pictures. There was one of her and Doug when they were about twelve. They'd each caught a rainbow trout and proudly held up the fish that glittered in the sun. Maya remembered her grandfather snapping the photo. Then they both released their fish back into the river.

Maya grabbed the picture to take with her.

There were a couple of other snapshots with Doug and Juniper together. Juniper stared lovingly up at Doug in all the photographs, her pointy ears alert as she sat back on her haunches. Maya stuffed those prints in the box she had with all of Juniper's toys. She didn't care if the mystery girlfriend came in and found her stealing. She needed something to remember Doug.

Looking around, she realized there were no pictures of Doug with another person. Curious, Maya decided to snoop. She felt guilty, but not enough to stop what she was doing. Obviously, someone else was living here, but who?

Maya went to the closet back in the master bedroom and opened it, but there wasn't much to reveal as far as female clothing. There were some jeans with blinged-out back pockets and western-patterned shirts, but everyone wore this style around town.

On a snooping roll, Maya went into Doug's office and flipped through his papers. They were all bills, some marked paid, some weren't. She opened drawers and poked through them one by one, but there was nothing exciting. The last drawer contained letters—two stacks. She recognized one stack.

They were from her.

She'd written home about once a week when she was deployed. It was old-fashioned, but time to call was limited and she didn't have kids or a spouse, so she'd often given her phone time to soldiers with families. It earned her respect with her unit and it also meant she didn't have to talk to anyone and lie about how things were fine when all you heard was bombs in the distance, jets taking off, and soldiers talking about friends not returning home.

Maya grabbed the letters and shoved them in her pocket. She wanted them back. She didn't want to share them with anyone else—especially not the mystery girlfriend.

The other stack, Maya realized, were from Doug addressed to her. He'd written back but never mailed them. She'd always wondered why he hadn't sent letters back.

Maya snatched that pile and shoved them in her other pocket. That was the last drawer, and she walked back out of the office feeling frustrated. If Doug was so in love with someone, why wasn't there something indicating who that person was? Why was he being so secretive?

Maya took one more look around the kitchen both to snoop and to make sure she didn't leave something important that she'd need for Juniper. A box of dog treats sat in the corner, and Maya decided she might need all the bribes she could get. Switching handlers was not easy for a dog.

She also needed to get the crate. Maya grabbed the crate from the front to pick it up, but it didn't budge. She wiggled it, thinking maybe it was stuck somehow. Crates were awkward to carry, but not heavy. It didn't move. Maya crouched down and inspected the sides and back. Why wasn't this thing moving?

She realized it was bolted to the floor. "Great, thanks, Doug. Hope this isn't a sign of what Juniper is like when kenneled."

Maya stood back up and rummaged around for a wrench. She found one and started to undo the first bolt. When she loosened the bolt, she heard an echo beneath her. Did Doug have a crawl space under the house? She couldn't remember. She continued getting all the bolts free and pulled the crate out. The same echo came from underneath her.

She felt around the flooring, trying to find a loose board, but there was nothing. The wooden floor was new and smooth. Why would you bolt something down through a new wooden floor?

Maya knocked around on the flooring and every time, she heard an echo beneath her. Curiosity driving her, she tried pulling up on the bolt holes. Nothing moved. She jiggled the flooring. Nothing moved. She was about ready to go get a crowbar and then decided tearing out flooring was going a little too far. She sat down on the floor and leaned back against a cabinet.

That's when she noticed the space under the trim. Maya got on all fours and peered under.

The gap was barely noticeable, but there was enough room to slide about a foot worth of flooring. Maya took ahold of the holes where the bolts had been and pushed back. The board slid underneath the trim. Down below was a dark space. She grabbed a flashlight.

A safe. What the heck was Doug hiding down here?

Maya tried entering Doug's birthday. The safe didn't open. She tried other number combinations, including her own birthday. Nothing worked. She couldn't give up now. She had to know what Doug was hiding. Maya thought about numbers she had used for combinations. She often used her badge number, so she tried Doug's badge number and heard a click. The door opened.

Stuffed in the safe were multiple stacks of cash.

Reaching down, she grabbed one of the wads. All hundred-dollar bills. She couldn't see how much cash was down there, but if they were all hundred-dollar bills then there could be thousands of dollars. Damn. What the hell was going on? Maybe Doug didn't trust banks anymore. But this amount? With their paychecks, not likely. Maybe this was an inheritance from Doug's father who had died when they were kids. Or maybe the mystery girlfriend was loaded.

Maya set the money back and slid the board back into place, grabbed the dog crate, box with toys, pictures, and treats, and left. She locked the door behind her, wondering who else had a key and knew about Doug's secret.

Chapter Twelve

The next day flew by, and around 5:00 p.m. the urge to have a beer overwhelmed Maya. She could go to the Black Bear and have a couple beers and then head home. That way she wouldn't drink an entire twelve pack and would be able to get out of bed the next morning to pick up Juniper. Two or maybe three beers at the most, Maya promised herself. Plus, the bar would give her a place to think. She was still bothered by what she'd found at Doug's house.

Since she was done with work, Maya changed into her civilian clothing. The Black Bear Café served breakfast, lunch, and dinner, and was also the local beer joint. The café, which had been open since Maya was a little girl, was constructed from large logs. The inside had western paintings and deer, elk, and moose head mounts, as well as other western-themed items. There was a wood carving out front of a black bear standing up on its hind legs. Maya patted the bear's nose as she walked in.

The bar was in the back and looked like something out of the 1800s. Maya sat down on her stool. She'd heard through the small-town grapevine that her old sixth-grade teacher, Mr. Williams, was the bartender.

She saw him down at the other end of the bar. His hair was now gray, but he had the same handlebar mustache that curled up on the ends. He always smiled. Maya couldn't think of a time she'd seen him angry—even when they were misbehaving as kids.

Mr. Williams saw her and nodded in her direction while he finished up with another customer. Then he came over and put a small drink napkin in front of her. "Maya Thompson, good to see you. How have you been?"

Maya felt like she was back in sixth grade and needed to raise her hand before speaking or to order her beer. "Good, Mr. Williams. Nice to see you. Heard you retired from teaching."

"Yep, coming up on two years now and started working here not long after. I needed to do something with my time other than drive my wife nuts."

Maya laughed thinking of his stern yet softhearted wife who had taught math at the high school. "How is your wife?"

"She's good. You should stop in sometime and see her. She'd like that. What can I get you to drink?"

Maya thought for a moment and then decided to be decadent. "I'll have a Fat Tire."

"You got it." Mr. Williams paused and then said, "I was sorry to hear about Doug. I know you two were good friends."

"Thanks," Maya muttered, playing with her napkin. She didn't want to talk about Doug. The entire day had been spent working on paperwork that had to do with the explosion and figuring out when she could go get an evaluation from a doctor.

Mr. Williams nodded and went over to the cooler,

grabbing a bottle with the telltale Fat Tire label, took off the top and set it down on her napkin.

"If you need anything, anyone to talk to, let me know," Mr. Williams said.

"I appreciate that. I guess things have changed a bit since I left," Maya said. *Everyone thinks talking will make things better, but it doesn't. Or maybe I just can't talk because who would understand?*

"Only thing constant in life is change. Only thing that's different is that you came back. Most people leave Pinecone Junction, and they don't ever want to return." Mr. Williams gave her a wink and headed to the other side of the bar to take care of another customer.

Maya let the cool, smooth liquid slide down her throat. She closed her eyes, enjoying the taste of the cold beer.

Someone stirred in the booth over to Maya's right. Jenna Ray was drinking a Coors Light and staring at Maya. Maya turned her attention back to her beer bottle. She and Jenna had grown up together and were in the same grade. Nothing like a class reunion at the Black Bear with one of their teachers bartending.

Maya figured she and Jenna had the same idea— come into town to get away. Ranches around Pinecone Junction were spread out, but like cattle, everyone showed up at the same watering hole. Some of the ranchers came to socialize. Others—like Maya and, it seemed, Jenna—came to be alone with their thoughts and get away from the demands of their work.

Maya glanced at her again and noticed Jenna was still glaring at her. She and Jenna had been friends, and for a while they played together at school, but then they drifted apart. Jenna had started hanging out with a tougher crowd in high school and was one of the smokers and drinkers. Maya knew at that point that she wanted to join the Marines and that there was no time for smoking and drinking.

Of course, that changed. Maya took another swig of beer. One more and then she should be going, call it a night. But the truth was a night without more beer terrified her and meant nightmares would invade her sleep.

As Maya was lost in her thoughts, the door behind her opened and closed. She peered over her shoulder, not really liking the fact her back was to the door, but there was no other way to sit with the design of the bar. The person behind her was silhouetted with the sun shining through the door. They walked with a swagger and had a skinny stature. Not too different from the suspect from the explosion. Maya tried to look discreetly, but she locked eyes with the person and realized it was Cody Ray.

Cody Ray was an ass. There was no other way to put it. While Jenna had hung out with the tough crowd and been a partier, Maya knew that she was an okay person. Cody, though, had been obnoxious and mean. Maya had never liked him. She had caught him torturing a dog once, and had punched Cody out and saved the dog.

She should finish up her drink and get out of here.

But then Cody opened his mouth and said, "Who let the damn feds in here?"

Maya tightened her fingers around her beer bottle, the condensation making it slick. She worked to not make any eye contact. Ignore the jerk. Plus, as a federal employee, she had to get used to people saying obnoxious things. The Forest Service had made enemies over the years with grazing restrictions, logging restrictions and other forest management practices that people didn't like. Cody's father, Carson, had been on the losing side of those restrictions and there was a lot of animosity.

Maya went back to sipping her beer. Cody sauntered up to the bar and ordered a shot of cheap tequila. Mr. Williams brought the shot over and said, "Behave yourself, Cody."

"Always do." Cody smirked. He rubbed a lime on the back of his hand between his thumb and index finger, stuck it in salt, licked his hand, then threw back the shot and sucked on the lime. He grinned at Maya and said, "Lip, sip, suck, fed. Does tequila make your clothes fall off?"

Maya rolled her eyes and said, "Check, please." She pulled a twenty out of her wallet and waited for the bill, irritated that Cody had ruined her night.

"Feds are worthless pieces of crap. Why did someone hot like you decide to become one?" Cody asked.

Maya continued to ignore him. Nothing good would come from engaging Cody. Ninety-nine percent of the time, she would try reasoning with a person who was being hostile. Cody, though, was that one percent where talking wouldn't work.

She stood up while she waited for her check. If she remained sitting, she was at a disadvantage if Cody engaged her.

"Shut up, Cody," Jenna said from the booth. "Leave her alone."

"You're friends with this fed, aren't you? I forgot about that," Cody said.

Maya continued to grip her beer and stare straight ahead. She slugged back the final bit in the bottle and

Mr. Williams came over with the check. "Let it go, Maya," he said.

"I know," she said. "I'm doing my best."

As Maya was setting her twenty on the counter to pay, Cody asked for another shot.

"Go sit with your sister and I'll bring it over to you," Mr. Williams said to Cody, as he went to the cash register to get Maya's change.

Maya hoped that Cody would listen and go sit with Jenna, but of course he didn't. Instead, he came closer. Maya could smell a mix of tequila and chewing tobacco on his breath. A little bit of brown spit lined his lip. Disgusted, she stared straight ahead, focusing on all the bottles up on the bar. She began reading them one by one—Jack. Knob Creek. Maker's Mark.

When she got to the high-end whiskey, Cody opened his mouth again. "You and your pig of a grandfather better watch out. We don't like your kind."

Jenna stood up and marched over to the bar. "Stop being so stupid, Cody," she said, grabbing his arm and then saying to Maya, "Sorry, he's just being an ass. He's drunk and looking for a fight."

The door behind Maya opened and closed again. Someone else had walked in the bar and was now strolling their direction. She peered over her shoulder and saw a small blonde lady. She wasn't anyone Maya knew. The lady focused on Cody and Jenna. She wore jeans similar to those at Doug's house, but didn't look like someone who fit in with the Rays. Her clothes were ranch-style, but new and clean. They didn't have the wear and tear that came from hard work wrangling cattle, moving hay and all the other labor that came with owning a ranch. Her boots were new and spotless. She seemed more like a tourist trying to fit in. But based on Jenna's and Cody's body language and annoyed expressions, the Rays obviously knew her. And she knew them.

If this person was connected to the Rays, Maya was now outnumbered three to one. She needed backup. Now. "Mr. Williams, can you call 9-1-1 and ask for a deputy to come?"

Mr. Williams nodded in agreement and headed for the phone.

Cody staggered back over next to Maya's bar stool and grabbed her forearm. His hand was smooth and soft, not the rough callused feel of someone who did ranch work. It showed he was spoiled and never lifted a finger. Maya's reflexes kicked in as Cody grabbed her and spun her around, grabbing onto the front of her shirt. "You need to look at me. I'm talking to you."

"You better back off, Cody. Think this through. You really want to start a fight with an officer?"

"Screw you," Cody said.

"Just remember, you asked for this," Maya said, as she blocked his arm with her left hand and then made a fist with her right hand, punching him as hard as she could in the solar plexus to knock the wind out of him. She wanted to create space between her and Cody for her safety. And his.

With a grunt, Cody staggered back and fell on the floor littered with peanut shells.

"You were saying?" Maya asked, staring at Cody's thin body. Yes, he was definitely the same size as the suspect at the cabin.

The new blonde and Jenna rushed over and grabbed Cody, heaving him to his feet. They stomped toward the front door, dragging Cody between them. Maya could still hear him whining, but before going out the door, Cody yelled, "You'll get what's coming to you, fed! You and your asshole grandfather."

Maya didn't answer. She stood her ground, making sure that they were gone before she turned back around. Maybe she could have one more beer in silence, but Mr. Williams handed Maya her change and said, "I think you should head home too. The Rays won't forget this. I don't need that headache tonight."

"He grabbed me first," Maya said, wanting to make sure she had a witness on her side just in case the Rays called her boss.

"I know. I saw that, but I also think it's time for you to go home."

Mr. Williams's expression was serious. Maya grabbed her cash and thanked him. As she walked out the door, the sun was setting, and the light bounced over the mountain peaks. Maya put on her sunglasses and saw Cody, Jenna, and the mystery woman at a black truck that looked exactly like the one that had passed her and Doug yesterday. The one that threw the rock on the windshield and made her startle.

Maya pulled out her cell phone and took some quick pictures. She changed angles and made sure she had the license plate in one so she could run it later. Maybe the truck was connected to the explosion. It wouldn't surprise Maya if Cody was running drugs, but he wasn't smart enough to make them. Was he smart enough to set bombs?

Maya's view was suddenly blocked by a white Tahoe that said *Western River County Sheriff.* The window rolled down and Josh was inside. He grinned.

"What?" Maya snapped.

"So, I was called to a bar disturbance where an off-duty officer needed backup. I was just down the road and said I'd respond."

"Figures," Maya muttered, noting that once again everything about Josh was perfect. His uniform was clean and crisp, his dark hair was styled in just the right way to show off his natural waves, and the inside of his vehicle appeared immaculate. Damn him. Why did he make her notice these things? And why did she care?

"You still need backup?" Josh asked.

"No, thanks. I'm good now. I supposed we could ticket or arrest him, but I think that's more trouble than it's worth."

"I agree," Josh said.

Josh and Maya stared at the Rays. Jenna and the mystery woman shoved Cody in the back of the truck cab. Maya could see he was still running his mouth off, but they were far enough away that she couldn't hear what he was saying—which was probably good. It would probably only piss her off and then she'd change her mind about arresting him.

"I take it he was trying to start something with you?" Josh said, breaking their silence.

"He apparently doesn't like feds or law enforcement." Maya unlocked her cell phone screen and said, "You mind running some plates for me?"

"Nope, give me the plate and I'll run it."

Maya handed Josh her phone and he called into dispatch. While they waited for dispatch to respond, Maya said, "Have you seen that truck around town a lot?"

"Yeah. I've seen it. Never been a problem or had any reason to pull it over." Josh's radio crackled and the dispatcher gave him the vehicle's information. Josh wrote it down. "Registered to a Roberta Lind," he said.

"Okay, thanks." Maya jotted down the information on a small notepad that Josh handed her.

"You think it has something to do with yesterday?"

"Doug and I passed it on the road," Maya said. "Driver was definitely speeding and erratic. If we hadn't been on the other call, we might have pulled it over. But the fact it's connected with Cody Ray is interesting."

"Yeah, he's a real winner."

"Since I saw that truck yesterday and Cody was just loaded into it, I thought maybe I should find out who it belongs to. Maybe I need to go talk to Roberta Lind."

"If you do that, let me know. I'll go with you for backup," Josh said.

Maya was about to blow him off, but the look on Josh's face had changed. It was serious. "What makes you think I should have backup?"

"Your grandfather and I have been watching the Rays. We have nothing yet to arrest them or even get a search warrant, but we suspect the Rays have illegal weapons, and the old man is starting his own militia. Ever since Carson Ray was laid off, your grandfather has been concerned about what's been going on out there. For someone out of work, he seems to have lots of money. The property has changed. All sorts of stuff."

"Maybe he's dealing drugs too," Maya said. "Might be more money in that than guns."

"True. If you go out there, let me know."

Maya reluctantly agreed. Josh was right; she needed to be careful. "I'll let you know then when I go. For now, I'm headed home."

"Need a lift?"

"Why?"

"You were drinking. You okay to drive? I'd hate to have to pull you over in a Forest Service vehicle."

Maya rolled her eyes. "I had one beer and we've been standing here talking forever. I'm fine."

"How's Juniper?"

"She's doing well. Vet wants me to pick her up in the morning."

"That's good. You ready for a psycho dog?"

"She's not psycho."

"I helped with the K-9s in Chicago. They're not sweet little pets either. Let me know if you need anything. I'm happy to help."

"Okay. Oh, and I still have your windbreaker. I need to get that back to you."

"Sure. Maybe we can meet up for coffee when you're in town. I can get it from you then," Josh said.

"Yeah, or I can just drop it by the office."

Maya pushed back from the vehicle and waved goodnight. She hated to admit it, but Josh was easy to talk to, and she could see why her grandfather liked him. She realized she wouldn't mind seeing him again and having him help her with Juniper, especially if he had K-9 experience. Or having coffee with him.

That bothered Maya even more. She'd worked with men in the military and now law enforcement. They were friends. Brothers. They weren't someone who you had coffee with. And yet, there was a part of her that wanted to.

She hadn't felt this conflicted about anyone in a long time, but Maya had learned the hard way with the one serious relationship she'd had in the military that it was better to not mix business and pleasure. She would definitely drop the windbreaker off at the sheriff's office.

"Stop these thoughts, Thompson," Maya muttered. "You're as bad as the other women in town."

Now she really wanted to stop by the liquor store, but instead she headed home. She had to make her house as dog-proof as possible because Josh had a point. She wasn't bringing home a sweet little pet. She was bringing home a dog capable of tearing up everything in her house.

Chapter Thirteen

The next morning Maya was up early drinking coffee and watching the sunrise. There was a sweet time where the sun kissed the mountain peaks and for a moment, they appeared to be a combo of orange and pink. All seemed right with the world.

Then the sun moved, and the day started. Maya had to go pick up Juniper and face her fear—working another dog. Seventy pounds of pure energy would be living with her. Maya remembered the head officer and K-9 trainer in the Marines saying, "When God made the Malinois, he took a bunch of rubber bands, strung them together as tight as possible and then released it." That pretty much summed it up.

Maya took her mug to the kitchen sink and picked the smooth leather leash off the counter. She had a huge job ahead of her if she took on working Juniper. You didn't just become a dog's handler overnight. There would be good and bad days. Maya didn't want the bad days to mean that she was risking her dog's life or someone else's life. With handling a dog there was responsibility.

Her clock chimed the top of the hour and Maya headed out the door. About thirty minutes later she pulled into the empty parking lot. The vet clinic wasn't open yet. Dr. Asher had mentioned that she thought it best Maya pick up Juniper when no one else was around.

She approached the doorway and stood outside, hand poised to knock but not letting herself follow through with the motion. The glass read *Pinecone Junction Veterinary Clinic. Hours M-F 8-5 and Sat 9-12*. Maya read the hours over and over. If she went in, she would take Juniper. Care for her. Fall in love with her. Feel that special vibration through the leash. That dance. That partnership. Did she want all that again when there was so much to lose?

Her chest tightened and her breath came in shallow gulps. She closed her eyes and made a fist, fingernails digging into her palm. Her body shook. She had loved Zinger. He had been her partner, but because of her mistakes, he was dead. Could she risk loving another dog again?

Maya opened her eyes and rapped her knuckles lightly on the glass.

The door creaked open and Dr. Asher said, "Good morning. Sorry it took me a minute to get here. I was checking on some of the other animals who were left overnight. Come on in. I'm so glad you're taking Juniper today. She's ready to get out of here."

"Thanks," Maya said, stepping into the vet clinic. The familiar smell of disinfectant mixed with dog and cat odors stung her nose. When she was in middle school, she had thought about becoming a vet. She had come and helped Dr. Asher for a summer, and that had convinced her that she didn't want the job. Maya had always loved animals and she'd found it difficult to see animals in pain with injuries. "How's Juniper doing?"

"Really well. The wounds are superficial. Give her a

few days and she can probably go back to work again. She's lucky considering the trauma that happened. Follow me. Juniper's in the back. I want someone who knows her to get her out. To be honest, she's been full of herself, not resting the way I would like."

Maya started to answer, but words wouldn't form. She didn't know what to say. Juniper was Doug's dog. He should have been the one to take her home. Should have. That was the problem.

With a heavy sigh, Maya followed the vet back to the kennel area. The spotless kennels smelled of disinfectant. The tile floors were hard and cold. A few of the crates housed other animals. A cat lay in one with an IV attached. Another dog whined, the cone of shame on his head.

"Over here," Dr. Asher said to her, waiting patiently. "I had to put her in a separate room because she was not fond of the other dogs."

Maya hesitated. She remembered Zinger at the vet, tubes coming out of him and the blanket laid over him. The vet saying there was nothing more he could do and shutting Zinger's eyelids. Zinger was then covered with an American flag and Maya petted his fur, wishing she were the one who had died, not her dog.

Maya shivered and rubbed her hands over her bare arms. She stopped at Juniper's kennel and stared in. There was a bandage around the leg, but otherwise Juniper appeared to be feeling fine. She had a muzzle on, and when she saw the humans outside her crate, she began to growl.

"She's been feisty without her handler. Understandable," said Dr. Asher. "I muzzled her this morning to make it easier to change her bandages. You can take the muzzle off if you want."

Maya didn't move. She and Juniper locked gazes. Juniper's golden eyes reminded her of Zinger. Then Maya averted her gaze. Not a good idea to stare down a dog like this.

Could she explain to Juniper that Doug was gone? That they now had to try to make a team? Would Juniper connect with her and switch to a new handler or have PTSD like Maya and never make it back? Maya had to give her a chance.

"Do you have some treats?" she asked.

"I do." Dr. Asher went to the cupboard and pulled out a box of dog cookies, handing it to Maya. "Take your time. I have paperwork to do and the first client won't arrive for about an hour, so you can let me know when you two are ready to go."

"Thanks." Dr. Asher left the room, leaving Maya alone with Juniper. Her feet felt heavy as she walked over to Juniper's kennel. "Do you remember me, girl?"

Maya knelt at Juniper's level and looked at her intelligent eyes and the black mask covering her face. The dog picked her head back up and gave a low, guttural growl. "That's why you need that muzzle, but we can figure this out."

She sat down by the kennel and opened the door. Could be a mistake, but right now Juniper didn't look like she wanted to go anywhere. She looked as sad as Maya.

"I miss him too. A lot," Maya said to the dog. "Doug was my best friend and…now he's gone. I can't believe he won't be back."

Maya rolled around one of the treats in her fingers—

if she could get the dog interested in her, that would be a start to bonding.

Juniper tilted her head and then sat up. Her long frame looked thinner, but Maya knew that despite what the dog looked like, she was still strong. Mals were amazing that way. Lighter boned than a German Shepherd, they could run faster and bite harder. They were machines and nothing much stopped them. Except bullets and bombs.

Maya closed her eyes and tears trickled down her face. "I lost someone else I loved too. You two would have made a good pair, only he was a brindle. Not light brown like you. I made a mistake. A handler error that cost him his life. Doesn't matter how much an investigation clears your name, you know you made a mistake, and you have to live with that the rest of your life."

Tears fell quicker and Maya buried her head in her arms, knees drawn up to her chest. "I should have been the one to die. Not Zinger. Not Doug. Why am I always the one who lives?"

A cold hard nudge came against Maya's arm. Juniper had crawled over to her and wanted the treat Maya held in her hand. "Enough of my sad story, huh?"

Maya reached toward Juniper's head to undo the muzzle. Over the past year, pulling away and shutting off her emotions had been the only way she knew to deal with her pain. Once she touched Juniper, it would all be over. She would care for the dog again. Become a handler, which meant a partnership that you couldn't explain to anyone. You knew what each other was thinking. You became a team and you relied on the dog. Juniper would be her eyes. Her ears. Her nose. She needed

Juniper as much as Juniper needed her. Now she had to hope that Juniper took to her as a handler.

"What do you want, girl? Do you want to come home with me? 'Cause if you don't, now's the time to tell me. I don't know if I can take any more heartbreak."

Juniper answered with a sigh and crawled a little bit closer, nudging Maya's hand, poking around for the treat. Maya took a deep breath and gently unbuckled the muzzle. Warm and bristly hair tickled her as Juniper pushed her head in Maya's hand.

Maya slipped off the muzzle. She opened her hand and let the treat rest on her palm, feeding it to the dog almost like you fed a horse—fingers out of the way. She expected Juniper to gulp the treat, but instead the dog surprised her by taking it in a dainty fashion. Juniper slapped her tail on the floor and stared at Maya.

"Want another one?" Maya pulled another treat out of the box, and this time Juniper took it a little quicker, her warm tongue flicking across Maya's palm.

"So, what do you think? Are you coming home with me? I come with a lot of baggage. Not to mention I'm rusty as a handler. I don't remember the last time I thought about which way the wind was blowing so a dog could scent better or working a grid pattern or making sure I directed you to areas with good air flow on a vehicle. I don't even have a good place for you, you know. But you can come home with me if you want and we can figure this all out."

Juniper climbed into Maya's lap and rested her front end across Maya's legs. She rooted around, her nose quickly finding the treat box. Maya laughed, wiped away her tears and gave her a couple more.

"I have a new partner, don't I?"

Chapter Fourteen

Juniper remained draped across Maya's lap as they sat on the cold floor. Maya stroked the dog's head concentrating on the feel of the fur—stiff until her undercoat, which was soft.

"Let's go before the vet thinks she has two new patients today," Maya said.

Juniper raised her head and leaped to her feet. She stretched and then shook her whole body. She danced around, jumping up and down, smacking Maya with her front paws.

"I think I see what Dr. Asher meant by full of yourself."

Maya hoisted herself to her feet, avoiding Juniper as she moved around the kennel area. She clipped the leash to Juniper's collar, taking note of the bandage covering the leg where the shrapnel had been lodged. The injuries could have been much worse. Footsteps came across the tile floor and paused as the vet opened the door. Juniper's triangular ears perked up.

"Sit. Relax," Maya said, using a hand signal with the command. She hoped Juniper would listen to her. Juniper eyeballed Maya and Dr. Asher and then she listened, sitting down by Maya's side.

"Looks like you two have bonded," Dr. Asher said. Maya shrugged. "At least for the moment."

"I have her paperwork and care instructions. Come with me and then you can take her home."

Maya put Juniper back in her kennel. The dog lay down and placed her head between her paws, her golden eyes staring at Maya. She yawned and a squeak came out followed by a sharp bark letting Maya know her displeasure at being left behind.

"I'll be right back. I promise."

Dr. Asher gave Maya care instructions. After signing off on the paperwork, Maya went back into the kennel to retrieve Juniper. This time she was greeted by the wag of a tail and slurp of a tongue. She clipped the leash on, and they strolled out of the clinic together. Maya loaded Juniper into her special K-9 area of the vehicle. She was getting ready to head home and continue the process of bonding with Juniper when a sheriff's vehicle pulled into the parking lot. Josh. Great. Not the distraction she needed right now.

Josh pulled up next to Maya's vehicle in the typical cop window-to-window fashion. Juniper circled around her back area. She whined and then gave a sharp bark.

"Quiet," Maya said, rolling down her window. "He may not be our favorite deputy, but you still have to be nice."

Juniper cocked her head to one side, listening.

"Of course, I'm not sure I have a favorite deputy," Maya admitted to Juniper. "It should probably be my grandfather, but technically he's the sheriff, not a deputy. I'm sure you'll meet him at some point too. Or maybe you already have."

Maya's window finished rolling down and she said, "What's up?"

"You talking to the dog?"

"Maybe. Why? Jealous?"

"Just curious if it was a good conversation," Josh said. Maya didn't answer. Her heart rate increased and she had to look away. Why did he have that effect on her?

"Your grandfather heard about the call at the bar. Just FYI. I thought you'd want to know," Josh continued. "Don't shoot the messenger."

So, to add to his other duties, he's my grandfather's messenger too.

"Did you pull up to harass me or did you actually have something important?" Maya leaned her arm on the window. In the back Juniper started panting out of excitement. She poked her nose on the door that opened between the cab and her K-9 area, making a wuffling sound as she sniffed.

"No, I do have something else to tell you, although harassing you is fun too," Josh said, grinning.

"Get on with it. I need to get Juniper home and start getting her settled in."

"All right, all right. Had an arrest last night. Domestic. When we got there the guy had calmed down probably because he had decided to take all the drugs the couple were fighting over."

"Okay," Maya said, noticing that Juniper had decided to circle in the back now and, based on a ripping noise she heard, the blankets she'd put in there were being shredded. Typical for a young working dog. Maya should have known better. Hopefully, Juniper wouldn't eat the blankets.

"When we arrested him," Josh continued, "I noticed that he had sores all over his body, mostly where you would inject the drug. We had to take him to the hospital and have him treated. The wife also had the start of some sores in injection sites. They were both having trouble speaking."

"Are you thinking it's infected heroin injection spots? Or are you thinking of something different?"

"We're having them tested for Krokodil."

Maya sat back in her vehicle. Krok was a drug that she had only run across in Afghanistan and was popular in Russia. Users of Krok had large sores, which was how it got its name. According to the DEA, the drug hadn't made its way to the United States because the main ingredient was codeine. That was available over the counter in Russia, but the United States was strict about codeine prescriptions. "You really think that's what it is?"

"I'm not sure. Tox reports will take a couple of days to come back, but I was wondering if the lab has let you know what kind of drug was being manufactured up at the Forest Service cabin."

Maya shook her head. "No, but my boss and some FBI investigators are coming into town either later today or by tomorrow. They should have some more information. Krokodil would be unusual. I keep thinking whoever had the lab was producing meth or something along those lines."

"Yeah, that would make more sense, but when I was working as a cop in Chicago, we arrested some Russian mobsters. It was a big raid with a lot of three-letter agencies. They had been starting to produce Krok to sell in the U.S."

"I guess it makes sense. If they can get the codeine here, it's cheaper to make than meth," Maya said. "Better high for the user, stronger addiction, everything you'd want to gain a good drug clientele. I saw it in Afghanistan when we would raid buildings. People were oblivious to us coming in. They were off in their own world. The high only lasts about two hours so they would need a fix right away. Didn't see it often because it's more of Russia's problem, but our medical guys would try to help them because often the sores were gangrene. Not that we could really do much."

"Yeah, according to the doc at the hospital, the guy we arrested may lose his foot to the sores. Said the same thing, looked like gangrene."

"Let's keep each other in the loop," Maya said.

"You mean work together?" Josh raised an eyebrow, faking surprise.

"Yeah, work together." Maya sighed, noticing that Juniper had lain down in what appeared to be the shredded remnants of the blanket.

"Then you'll need to put my number on speed dial. And I need yours."

"You have mine. Or at least the sheriff's office does."

"Yeah, but do you have my personal number?" Josh asked, taking out one of his cards and jotting down his number on the back. He handed it to Maya. She took it reluctantly.

"Thanks," she muttered.

"You know, I have some K-9 experience. If you need some help with training, let me know."

"You said that yesterday. What do you consider K-9 experience?" Maya asked.

"I helped decoy for the Chicago PD. Helped with

tracks, hid narcotics. Things like that. Went through all the proper training."

"My dog taking a big bite out of you would be something I'd like to see," Maya said. She had to admit, she and Juniper needed to train together before they went to certification. Good agitators were hard to come by because they had to be willing to put on a bite sleeve and have the dog run at them, latch on to the sleeve, hopefully not another body part, and then absorb the dog's energy correctly. They also needed to know how to encourage and entice the dog to stay on the bite. If you did it wrong, you could hurt the dog as well as discourage them from biting. Maya had taken the bite sleeve from Doug's house. "I don't have a full bite suit, just the sleeve."

"I'm fine with that."

"You know that dogs have been known to not attach to the sleeve, but sometimes go for other body parts. Especially those important to guys." Maya laughed, thinking about how in their military training a dog had bit a guy in an extremely sensitive area. They had all given him a hard time about speaking an octave higher.

"I'll take my chances."

"Okay, when Juniper gets medically cleared, I'll give you a call." Maya held up Josh's card. "But if you get bit somewhere else, don't say I didn't warn you."

"Sounds good. I'll be in touch about the tox report."

Maya put her window back up. Once again, she realized Josh was easy to talk with, but she reminded herself not to trust him. She didn't know him that well.

She glanced in the back where Juniper was now curled up in a little ball, golden eyes staring at Maya.

"Well, guess I better get you home. You're supposed to stay quiet for a couple more days, but somehow, I don't think that's going to happen."

Chapter Fifteen

Carson stomped his way to Cody's room. The worthless kid had really made him mad now. Jenna had filled him in about Cody harassing the fed. Not just any fed either. He had to pick the sheriff's granddaughter. They didn't need anyone on their back right now, least of all any type of law enforcement. His son was screwing things up.

Throwing open the door, Carson wished he hadn't barged in. The smell of feet permeated the room and Cody was asleep in his boxers on top of the covers. He reeked of stale alcohol.

Carson kicked Cody in the butt. "Wake up."

Cody startled, drool coming out of his mouth, turned over and, seeing his father there, shut his eyes. "What?"

Carson went over to the window, avoiding boots, jeans, and other things littering the floor. He opened the curtain and allowed the sunlight to hit Cody in the face. "I need you to get up, get dressed, and try to look respectable for a meeting in a half hour. We need to get some things in order before Lana arrives to discuss business."

"Why do we need a meeting?"

"Because I say so, for starters, and because we have

a situation." Carson booted some items out of his way as he navigated through the room.

"A situation?" Cody asked sarcastically.

"Yeah. A situation, like one of our members was arrested last night. Appears he might be sampling a little bit of the local flavor we're producing. I want to know how he got it. We all agreed that no one around here would sell or use our product."

"I don't know anything about it," Cody whined. "Let me go back to sleep."

Carson marched back over to Cody's bed and said, "You get your butt out of bed now. This is a problem for everyone."

Carson picked up Cody's jeans and flung them at him. As he threw them, some cash came out of the pocket. A couple of Ben Franklins landed on the floor.

"Where'd you get this cash?" Carson asked.

Cody shrugged.

"Are you the one selling to people around here? You better not be using." Carson started to look around the room, opening dresser drawers and seeing what else his son was hiding. Lately, Cody seemed more like a teenager, not a young man in his twenties. Carson had noticed Cody sleeping more and having some nosebleeds along with bloodshot eyes and some shakiness. All signs of someone using and staying irresponsible rather than growing up.

When Carson came to the top dresser drawer, he found some paraphernalia—a couple pipes, needles, and syringes.

"What's this?" he demanded.

"Nothing."

"This cash is now mine. And these items here are now mine."

Cody sat up, a look of anger crossing his face. "That's not fair. I do my share to help you."

"Yeah? Well, I'm thinking about our future. I've worked hard to get this business going. I've worked hard to pay off bills from your mother's illness and to give you a better life than what I had. You can have what you want and not work in godforsaken jobs like I did. But if you use this stuff—" Carson held up the paraphernalia "—you won't get anywhere. And I'll kill you before you can kill yourself with this crap."

The anger on Cody's face turned to fear. Carson felt satisfied that he had made his point. "Now get dressed and meet us in the bunker in ten. We've got things to discuss."

Carson left the room. He'd kill that kid if he screwed around anymore. He wouldn't let anyone take him down—not even his own son.

Chapter Sixteen

Maya pulled up, and as she parked at her cabin, Juniper stood and started making tiny circles in the back. Maya had Juniper's crate inside, ready for her, but she had a bad feeling that Juniper wasn't going to relax and stay quiet like the doctor ordered. "Okay, okay. If you can behave yourself, maybe in a little bit we can go for a short walk."

Juniper stopped spinning and sat down.

"Good girl. Let me get you out." Maya took the leash and climbed out of her vehicle. The previous night a thunderstorm had come through, leaving behind puddles. She stepped over a few and made her way to the door.

"Wait," she told Juniper as she opened the door and snapped on the leash. Maya tried to help Juniper out of the vehicle, but Juniper was ready to escape. She launched herself past Maya, landing directly in a puddle. Juniper shook and then danced around splashing with joy.

"Great," Maya muttered. "Heel."

Instead of heeling, Juniper decided to test her new-found freedom by leaping around in the water. Maya shortened the leash and was about ready to give her a correction when Juniper came up to her, sat for a moment and then jumped up, slapping her paws all over Maya's shirt.

In a firm tone, Maya asked Juniper to sit. Juniper's ears drooped and she grudgingly sat.

"Good girl," Maya said through gritted teeth. "Heel."

Juniper listened and stayed by Maya's side as they went into the cabin. In many ways Juniper was still a puppy, but Maya knew that Doug had worked on obedience. She would do the same. Right now, the dog was ready to get out and run around, oblivious to the wounds that needed time to heal.

Juniper air scented, taking in her new surroundings. Then she placed her nose to the floor, sniffing all the different smells.

"You'll be happy to get back to work, won't you?" Maya said, knowing it was a silly question. "Here, kennel."

Maya opened the door to the crate and Juniper tucked her tail, stopping for a moment to look at Maya with an indignant expression. Maya waited her out, and when Juniper realized that Maya was not going to back off, she slunk into the crate. Maya praised her and gave her more treats.

"We'll try going for a walk in a little bit," Maya promised.

Juniper's tail thumped in response. Maya breathed out, realizing that she was holding a lot of tension. There was always stress when a handler was getting to know a new dog. Having a new K-9 partner was a little bit like going on a first date. A good handler knew how to be alpha, but there was also a balance of allowing the dog to be who they were and learning their personality.

Maya wanted a beer, but she knew better. She needed to be on her game for Juniper. Instead, she got herself a cup of coffee and settled down on the couch to look over some of the letters Doug had written. She wanted to know why he hadn't sent them.

Just as she started to read, Maya heard a cry from the crate. The noise started soft and then escalated. Maya ignored her. She couldn't get Juniper out while she was still whining. That would only teach her a bad habit.

The whine turned to a yowl, and then Juniper was quiet again. Maya started to read the first letter when howling started along with the sound of paws scratching and clawing. Leaving Juniper in the crate wasn't going to be a good idea. If Juniper stayed this active, she would open the wounds that needed to heal and delay getting back to work. Maya could get her out and practice a down-stay. That might keep her quiet, work on obedience and help them bond.

Maya waited for Juniper to stop her whining. Once Juniper was silent, Maya strolled over to the crate. Juniper's tail made a thumping sound. She gave Maya a soulful look, her head down and eyes staring up, pleading to come out.

"Wait," Maya said. She was pleased when Juniper listened, and Maya managed to snap on the leash. She stepped back and was about ready to give the command for Juniper to come out. Before she could get the words out, seventy pounds of muscle and fur came bounding at her, then started leaping around.

Maya gave Juniper a quick correction, had her kennel back up and then wait until Maya told her she could come out. This time Juniper listened, and Maya praised her.

"Good girl. You're supposed to stay quiet, remember? Let's go read some letters. Maybe it will make both of us feel better."

Maya grabbed the notes from Doug off the couch and had Juniper heel with her over to the kitchen table. She asked Juniper to lie down and the dog responded. Maya gave her another treat and stepped on her leash, making it short enough that it would be difficult for Juniper to get up and walk around. Juniper put her head between her paws and then rolled to one side, content to be with Maya. Maya reached down and scratched Juniper's belly, realizing how much she was enjoying the company. Usually Maya was alone with her thoughts, which would lead to heightened anxiety. That led to drinking and then being disappointed in herself that she couldn't control things better. That maybe when Pops told her she wouldn't be able to handle things, he was right. But Juniper brought out a calm in her—a newfound patience and purpose.

Glancing back at the table and the letters, Maya saw the small black box that sat on the other side of the table. The engagement ring.

"You know who that belongs to? I bet you do, but you're not going to say a word, are you?" Maya said. Juniper thumped her tail and her golden eyes stared back. "Okay, I'll read this first letter to you. We'll see why Doug didn't send these. Maybe he'll tell me in the letters who this ring belongs to."

Maya picked up the first letter and started.

Dear Maya,
I received your letter the other day and was glad to hear from you. I miss you. I'm not great at

writing, but since you mentioned you don't want to call, I'm going to do my best.

Things here are good. The job with the Forest Service is going well and someday, when you get home, I'm going to talk you into working with me.

I want to be with you. Not talking face-to-face might make what I'm going to say easier. I love you, Maya. And not in the way you're thinking. I know you'd say you love me like a brother, but that fact is, when you left, I felt like a piece of me left with you.

Maybe someday you can love me like that too. I can only hope. Until then, stay safe and know that I care deeply.

Maya set the letter down on the table. She'd always thought of Doug as family—the brother she never had and the friend she could count on to go fishing, hunting and hiking with her. She'd had no idea he felt something more.

Before enlisting, Maya had asked Doug if he wanted to join the military with her. Her grandmother had encouraged her to see the world and she thought the Marines would give her that along with a sense of pride to fight for her country. But he hadn't wanted to leave Colorado. Maya understood, but she knew she had to see the world before she could settle down.

Juniper sat up and draped a giant paw across Maya's arm.

"Did you know about this?" Maya asked her. Juniper stood up, gave her a big lick, and then, feeling the pressure from the leash, lay back down.

"Good girl," Maya said, petting her head and rubbing around her body, being careful to avoid her injured spots. She flipped through more letters with Doug filling her in about stuff happening at home and a couple more where he talked about their future. Then Maya found a letter where Doug's tone started to change.

Hey Maya,
I want you to know that I do love you, I really do, but I met someone, and I think she's pretty special. Right now, I can't tell you who it is, so I'll keep it to myself and at some point, when you come home, I'll fill you in.

I hope you are doing well. Saw on the news that things in Afghanistan are, as usual, unsettled. I look forward to you returning and telling me about your experiences.

"Why didn't he say who this mystery girl was?" Maya asked Juniper. Juniper whined and put her head between her paws. "Maybe he thought I couldn't handle it. Wish he would have said who this person was so I could get her the ring...and see who stole my best friend's heart."

Maya knew she was a little bit jealous, but also happy that Doug had found someone. Although that someone didn't care enough to show up at the hospital. Or maybe she was scared for some reason. Maybe the person was already in another relationship or even married. That would be a good explanation.

Juniper crawled forward and put her head on Maya's foot. "Was she married? Is that why Doug didn't say anything? Maybe waiting for a divorce to go through?"

Juniper lifted her head, cocked it to one side and

then turned so her back was facing Maya and returned to resting.

"Okay, I get it, you don't want to talk about it right now."

Maya rummaged through more of the letters until she found one that was close to when she had returned home. She pulled out the letter and started to read:

Maya,
I still miss you every day. I love you, but I see now what you meant by we should just be friends. I'm very much in love with this person who walked into my life a couple months ago. I hope you will understand. I also hope someday when you meet her, we can still hang out.

While I'm in love, I miss having you to talk to. In fact, right now I wish you were here because things in my relationship seem so complicated. I went and talked with your grandmother today. She was helpful. Told me I'd always do the right thing. I wish I could believe her, but somehow, I can't.

Maybe it would have helped if I had sent all the other letters. Your grandmother is worried about you. She said she can tell you are having a tough time. I don't want to burden you with my troubles, so I'll make sure you never see these letters.
Love you,
Doug

Maya set the paper down on the table. The room seemed to spin as shock washed over her body. What was complicating Doug's relationship? Was this mystery girlfriend pulling him into something he didn't want to do? Maybe even something illegal? Did it have anything to do with all the cash she found?

Maya thought back to Doug's last words. That her grandfather knew the truth and that Doug wanted her to go talk to him.

She needed to know the truth about her friend even if it was something Maya didn't want to hear. It could be the start in finding justice for him.

"Come on, Juniper. We're going to take a little trip."

Juniper sprang to her feet.

Chapter Seventeen

Maya loaded Juniper into the back of the SUV and sat for a moment in the car. She hadn't been to her grandfather's place since they'd fought. Should she call him, let him know she was thinking about stopping by? Or just surprise him? She wanted answers to Doug's letters and what he had told her, and she wanted them now, but that philosophy didn't always work with her grandfather, and patience wasn't one of her strong suits.

Maya knew she'd been the one who created the problems. She had to admit that he had every reason to be mad at her. She had lied to him—something she had never done before, at least not at this level. She had told him she couldn't come home for her grandmother's funeral, that she was still in Afghanistan, but that wasn't true. Maya had been stateside in San Diego.

After Zinger died, she had been under investigation. Eventually she was cleared. Maya began her discharge process, and then she'd found out about her grandmother taking her own life. Maya couldn't believe it and wasn't ready to handle that after everything else she had been through, so she'd lied and gone to a bar.

She couldn't handle seeing her grandfather's sorrow or more death, and she had grieved the way that worked best. Maya had toasted to her grandmother. Over. And over. And over. Then she'd made the mistake of drunk dialing Pops and spilling her guts that she was in a bar in San Diego and she could have come home. As the saying went, that's how the fight started.

She couldn't explain to her grandfather and he didn't understand. Even after she'd decided to move home, she and Pops continued to fight. Maya now realized that while she had told herself she moved home to find peace and normalcy, she also needed her grandfather. Admitting that was hard. Maybe talking to him today was the first step.

"Ready to go?" Maya asked Juniper.

Juniper barked and hopped up and down in the back.

"Remember, you have medical restrictions."

Juniper barked again. As they drove, the mountain peaks hid behind low-hanging clouds. Dew clung on tree leaves. June could be warm in Colorado, but this year the nighttime thunderstorms and rain made everything feel like spring. The summer heat had stayed away up here so far.

Maya wound her way through the back-mountain roads, finishing up her coffee and wishing she had more. The lack of sleep was catching up to her.

"Don't get in a fight," Maya muttered. "Try apologizing for once in your life."

Juniper whined in answer.

Her grandfather's driveway appeared after a sharp curve. Maya, out of habit, had already slowed down. She turned in and stopped the car. She could still change her mind. There was still a chance her grandfather hadn't seen her.

Juniper let out a loud woof. "Quiet," Maya corrected in a firm tone.

Juniper whined and circled around the back seat, panting in excitement.

"You're not working right now, but I'm glad you're feeling better. You need to take it easy for a while. Doctor's orders. Remember?"

Maya put the car in gear and continued down the drive. The house sat about a quarter mile off the road. The old log cabin had been restored by her grandparents and had a fresh coat of varnish on it. Pops had been busy.

A wave of guilt swept through Maya. She should have been over helping him with stuff like that, not sitting at home feeling sorry for herself. A pile of leftover wood from winter was stacked on the front porch between two pillars. Two rocking chairs sat on the other side of the porch near the bright red door.

Maya fought back tears. Only one of those chairs was being used now. She missed Nana so much.

Maya parked near the house and got out of the car. Juniper made small circles in her car kennel. Maya ignored her as she climbed the steps to the house. The second step still creaked. She picked up her hand, ready to knock, but instead it fell by her side. Peering in the window, she could tell the kitchen was empty, which meant her grandfather was probably out in the barn.

The old red barn, built in the early 1900s, had also been restored and had provided years of refuge for Maya. She could escape and go read up in the hayloft, Bear snuggled in next to her. It became her own secret place to think or be alone. Her thoughts would wander from wondering what life would be like if her mother had lived and dreaming about traveling the world while serving her country.

Maya stepped back off the porch and headed toward the barn. A round pen sat nestled back in the trees, and as she came closer, she heard hoofbeats. Coming around the corner, Maya caught sight of a cute little sorrel filly trotting around the pen in a nice rhythm.

Maya's grandfather stood in the middle, looking all cowboy. He wore brown leather chaps, a Carhartt vest, and his favorite worn brown cowboy hat with sweat stains. He had a lasso rope in his hand, and when needed he would tap his leg with the rope to encourage the filly to keep trotting. He clucked and let the rope slap his thigh and the filly obediently went into a soft, steady canter. Then Pops shifted slightly in front of the horse and the filly picked up on his cue, coming back to a trot.

Her grandfather could dance with an animal. He knew how to help them overcome fear. He was one of the best horsemen she knew. Working dogs was similar. Maya knew her abilities had come from both of her grandparents. Nana had taught Maya so much about patience when she helped her train Bear.

Pops walked in a slight diagonal across the round pen and drew the filly's eyes in his direction. Then he stepped back, and the horse blew out her breath, walked, and turned toward him, joining him in the middle of the pen. He sat and stroked her face, his fingers massaging around her ears. The filly relaxed, licking and chewing and allowing Pops to rub all over her head.

"Hello, Maya."

Maya had been so engrossed watching the beautiful partnership that she realized she hadn't said anything. Not even a hello.

"Cat got your tongue?" her grandfather asked, continuing to massage the filly's head, his hands now massaging down the horse's face and jaw.

"No. Hi. Nice filly. How old?"

"She's three. Last foal out of Daisy."

"Really? I didn't think the old girl had it in her to have another foal."

"I wasn't sure, but Doc said she was good for one more. Since I'd sold her colt, I thought I'd give it a try. She gave me a good one here. I think I'll be able to use her for some mounted patrol work." Maya's grandfather went to the edge of the round pen and picked up a halter. The filly followed him, sniffing at his elbow. She stayed in place as he put the rope around her neck.

"Who's the sire?" Maya asked.

"A nice quarter horse in the Parker area. Poco Bueno breeding with some Doc Bar on his mother's side. Typical quarter horse breeding, but I thought it would cross well with Daisy's racing bloodlines." Pops opened the gate and led the filly out. The filly stepped her hindquarters over as he turned and shut the gate. "But something tells me you didn't come here to ask about Velvet's breeding."

"Velvet? Really, Pops?"

"What's wrong with Velvet?"

"I just didn't peg you to pick such a girly name." Maya had been the one who had named Daisy long ago. Pops had given her a hard time about the guys taking him seriously when he rode a horse named Daisy with the mounted patrol.

He started to lead the horse into the barn. "Did you really stop in to give me crap about what I named my horse? Plus, she's named after *National Velvet*."

Maya shoved her hands in her pockets. That had been one of her favorite movies growing up. As they walked into the barn, scents of hay mixed with manure and shavings hit her nose and brought her back to her childhood.

Her grandfather led the filly into a grooming area and tied her up. He started to untack her, carefully loosening the back-cinch and breast collar first.

"I didn't stop in to give you crap, Pops. I wanted to say hi."

"I'd like to believe that."

Maya's face flushed. "Why can't you believe that?"

"After what you did, lying to me, I can't believe anything you say."

"I know. I understand. I hope you can start to trust me again."

"That will take time."

Maya bit her tongue. *You're not here to fight.* "Pops, I'm sorry. Maybe someday we can talk about that. When we're both ready. There's things you don't understand."

"You're right. I don't understand." Her grandfather pulled the saddle off and placed it on a saddle stand. He began to rub the filly with a currycomb. The young horse started to paw and dance a little in place. Pops put a hand on Velvet's neck and spoke to her until she settled.

"Look, I didn't come here to start a fight. And you're right. I have a question," Maya said, watching him calm the horse. When she was a little girl, he'd come into her room and had done much the same thing after her nightmares.

"What's your question?"

"Do you want to finish putting her away? Maybe we can have some coffee."

"Yeah. Sure."

He brushed down the filly and led her over to an open stall. Warm breath came on Maya's neck and she turned to find herself face-to-face with Daisy. Maya stroked the old mare's face, cupping her soft muzzle in her hand. Her whiskers tickled Maya's palm as the mare nuzzled her, searching for treats. Contentment filled Maya—Daisy was beautiful and a piece of home Maya missed.

Her grandfather hung up Velvet's halter and started marching toward the house. Maya followed him in silence, stopping to check on Juniper in her climate-controlled area. She had curled up and fallen asleep, so Maya left her in the vehicle.

Pops hung his hat and vest on the pegs inside the door. Maya took off her boots out of habit. Nana had been a stickler about not wearing boots in the house. She noticed Pops left his boots on.

Maya saw Nana's touch everywhere from the curtains to the watercolor mountain-scene paintings hanging up on the wall. Nana had loved artwork and learned to paint when Maya was in high school. She'd given Maya several of her paintings, but she had left them in boxes. They were too painful to look at.

She couldn't breathe for a moment. She closed her eyes, thinking of one of her favorite memories of her grandmother.

Maya followed Nana out to the chicken coop to collect the eggs. They opened the special door to the nesting boxes. The hens looked like little feathery bundles sitting on their nests.

"*Do you want to get the eggs today, Maya?*" *Nana turned to her with the smile that made her wrinkles curve up. The wind blew some strands of long, dark hair loose from her grandmother's ponytail and they fluttered in the breeze.*

"*Yes, Nana.*"

"*Okay then. Be careful. You know how these hens can be.*"

Maya giggled. The hens would sometimes try to peck her, but it didn't hurt. Nana taught her that if she stroked the soft feathers first, the hens were a little less grumpy about her taking the eggs. She reached under the first hen, who puffed her feathers, but Maya extracted the egg and put it in the basket. She repeated the process with the other five hens.

"*Perfect. Now we can make Pops his favorite omelet for breakfast,*" *Nana said.*

"*I want a ham and cheese one,*" *Maya said.*

They walked back toward the house together and Maya slipped her hand into her grandmother's.

"*Are those scary dreams still happening at night?*" *Nana asked.*

Maya stayed quiet at first. She hated the dreams Nana was talking about. The fire. Her mother lying still and not moving. And the bad man. The person who had tried to take Maya away. The dreams happened a lot, and Maya used to wake up screaming. Her grandparents would come running, and Maya would cry. Nana would hold her and comfort her on those nights. Pops would often read Maya a story to help her get back to sleep.

"*Yes, Nana, but they aren't as scary as they used to be.*" *Maya supposed that was a little bit of a lie since they actually* were *scary. Especially the bad man with a gun who shot her mother and then was searching for her. But in the dreams Maya hid so well the man never found her.*

"*I'm glad to hear they're not as scary,*" *Nana said, giving Maya's hand a squeeze.*

They went up the steps together and into the kitchen, where Maya helped put the eggs in the sink to be washed. The dreams had sparked a question for Maya, though. "*Nana?*"

"*Yes, Maya?*"

"*Do you miss my mom too?*"

Nana dried her hands on a towel and went over to a rocking chair in the living room, gesturing for Maya to come sit with her on her lap. Maya loved sitting with her grandmother. Just the two of them. She climbed up and snuggled into Nana, smelling the fresh lavender from her soap.

Nana sighed and then closed her arms around Maya even tighter. "*I miss her so much, but Pops and I are so lucky to have you. Your mother loved you very much and so do we.*"

Maya closed her eyes, enjoying the feeling of being loved. Nana never just said it, she always showed it. "*What about my father? Does he love me?*"

Nana paused again, like she did when she was thinking hard. "*Your mother never told us about your father,*" *she said.* "*But I'm sure if he knew you, he'd love you too. What's not to love?*"

"*Is my daddy a bad guy? Is that why she never told you about him?*"

"*I'm sure he's a good guy, Maya. What I know for*

sure is Pops and I would never let anything happen to you. And we'll always protect you, no matter what."

"Even when I'm grown up?"

"Even then." Nana released her hold and said, "I think you're old enough for me to give you something. It belonged to your mother."

"Really?" Maya hopped off her lap.

"Really. Follow me."

Together they went up the stairs to her grandparents' room. Nana went over to the dresser Pops had made from pine trees. She opened the top drawer and pulled out a necklace and a picture frame. She came back over to Maya and crouched down in front of her.

"This necklace belonged to your mom. I think she'd want you to have it."

Maya opened her hand and Nana placed the necklace in her palm. The pendant was a key with numbers engraved on both sides.

"That's your mother's birthdate," Nana said. "And on the other side is your birthdate. Your mother used to tell me that you held the key to her heart. Here, let's try it on you."

Maya grinned and turned around, picking up her long curly hair so her grandmother could put on the necklace. "There," Nana said, closing the clasp. "It fits you perfect."

Maya let her hair back down and fingered the key. "I'm never taking this off, Nana."

"Good. And this is a photo of you and your mother. You look so much like her. This is one of my favorite pictures, but it's time that you have it," Nana said, handing Maya the frame.

Maya always had a hard time remembering what her

mother looked like. She studied the image, staring at it. She couldn't remember her mother, this person with a large smile, hugging her, but somehow the picture made Maya feel better.

"Thank you, Nana."

"You're welcome. Now, we need to go make some omelets before Pops gets home."

"Maya?" Pops's voice interrupted Maya's memory. "You okay?"

"Yeah. I'm good. Just remembering Nana," Maya said. Her fingers went to the smooth necklace that, true to her promise, she had never taken off. The Marines allowed women to wear necklaces as part of their dress code and in Afghanistan it brought her comfort.

I miss you, Nana.

Maybe coming here was a mistake.

Chapter Eighteen

Her grandfather prepped the coffeepot and hit the power button. As the machine started to sputter and percolate, Pops leaned back against the counter, crossing his arms. He appeared tired and worn. How often had Maya only thought about herself and her feelings from her grandmother's death? Had she ever stopped to think about her grandfather's feelings?

"So, what do you want to know?" Pops asked.

"I want to know about Nana and a few things Doug told me."

"What about her?"

Maya sat down at the family dinner table. She ran her fingers over the grooves and nicks created from years of family meals and activities. "Do you really think Nana took her own life?"

"What makes you ask that?"

"Do you?"

"You're not answering my question."

"And you're not answering mine," Maya shot back.

"I don't know."

Maya hesitated, then blurted out, "Doug said you knew the truth about Nana's death. What did he mean by that?"

Her grandfather stared at her. Maya's face flushed. Maybe that was too much. Barking came from outside, and he turned to look out the window. "You have the dog with you?"

"Juniper."

"What?"

"Juniper. Her name is Juniper. I'm tired of everyone calling her 'the dog.' You're trying to get out of my question."

"My honest answer is I don't know." Her grandfather pulled down two mugs and poured coffee into both. He added cream and then asked, "Sugar? You can bring the…uh, Juniper in."

Maya shook her head no. "She'll be okay out in the car. I need to get to know her better, so we don't destroy your house."

"Okay. When did he say that?" he asked, joining Maya at the table. The chair scraped the wood floor as he pulled it back and sat down.

"After the explosion. We were waiting for the helicopter to come. He told me you knew the truth about Nana's death, and that you knew the truth about the explosion. I'm trying to figure out what he meant. Is he saying she didn't commit suicide? That she was murdered? Are you looking into it? And was Doug in trouble? Why would you know about the explosion?"

"Maya, slow down. I think you're jumping to conclusions. He was injured. Delirious. He probably didn't know what he was talking about."

"Maybe, but I think Doug was into something he shouldn't have been."

"What makes you say that?"

Maya hesitated. She didn't want to tell her grandfather about the letters. She wasn't sure why. Somehow, they felt private, like a last conversation between her and Doug. There was also the money. She'd been snooping so did she need to share everything? Was not sharing information the same as lying? "I don't think the explosion was an accident. I think that call to dispatch was made deliberately to get us out there. Someone was waiting for us. Doug knew something he shouldn't have. Maybe Nana knew about it. Like he went to talk to her or something. I also believe he was in a secret relationship."

Her grandfather didn't answer. A thoughtful look crossed his face and he stared out the kitchen window. The curtain fluttered in the breeze and the smell of pine trees wafted in. A magpie chattered in the distance, its distinct call answered by a mate. Maya took a sip of her coffee and noticed the mug had the Marine emblem.

"One of my favorite mugs," Pops said.

Maya leaned back in her chair and took another drink of coffee, her hands trembling. Pops was avoiding answering her. "Are you investigating Nana's death on your own, Pops?"

"Maybe."

"Come on. It's me."

"All right, yes, I'm investigating on my own. Your grandmother's death, that is. Doug, well, he came and spoke to me in confidence. I listened and I'm not at liberty to talk about what he told me."

Maya decided to try to find out one thing at a time. "What have you found out about Nana?"

"Not much so far. I can't figure out motive. Your

grandmother wrote the suicide note. That was her hand-writing."

"So, someone made her."

"Maybe. Maya, I don't know. We both know that we don't want to believe your grandmother did this, but maybe we need to accept the fact that she did."

Maya reached across the table and took her grand-father's hand. "Or maybe she didn't take her own life, Pops. I want to help with this. Please. Let me do this with you. I need to know about Doug too. I want to fig-ure out what happened and put away the people respon-sible for both of their deaths."

"I don't know, Maya. We might not ever figure any-thing out. Maybe I missed all the signs. Maybe I was so engrossed in my career and took her for granted that I never realized she wasn't happy."

"I can't live with that. And I know you can't either. There's something bugging you about her death. Give me the file. Let me look it over and maybe I'll see some-thing you didn't."

Her grandfather paused and then said, "I don't want you to see the pictures. That's not how you want to re-member your grandmother."

"I can handle it. You forget that I served. I've seen lots of things. Things that most people don't want to. I can handle it."

"I'm sorry, Maya. I will keep you posted if I find anything out, but I need you to stay out of this. Let me handle this. My way."

Maya pulled her hand away and sat back. "I'm not a little kid anymore. You don't have to protect me."

"You'll always be my little girl. I can't help it."

Maya changed tactics. "So what about Doug? What did he mean about talking to you because you would know about the explosion?"

"Doug came and talked to me. He let me know about some troubles he was having, but he wasn't specific. I listened, didn't ask much. I stayed out of his business. He was asking me for some advice. That's all."

"What about?"

"Nothing important."

Frustration built up in Maya. She sighed and stared out the kitchen window at the grove of aspen that had recently sprouted green leaves. In a couple months they would turn a beautiful gold color. Her grandmother had planted some columbine wildflowers under the trees. They were about ready to start blooming.

Maya allowed the frustration to drain a little bit from her before she spoke. "I hope someday soon you can forgive me. Accept my apologies. Then you can start treating me like an adult. You don't have to hide anything from me. I know that will take time, but if there's anything, anything at all that you know about the explosion, please tell me. Maybe we can catch Doug's killer."

Her grandfather leaned forward and said, "Nothing he told me would help you. It's best to leave things alone. Let the FBI and your investigators work on it."

"Fine," Maya said, standing up. She should leave before her anger and frustration made her pick another fight. *Why does Pops always have to be so stubborn?* "I need to go. You know my number."

Maya started toward the door when she heard her grandfather say, "Maya." She turned around, expecting some sort of lecture, but all he said was, "Thanks for stopping in."

"Yeah. See you around, Pops."

Maya closed the door behind her, descending the porch steps. She paused at the bottom and shoved her hands in her pockets. Her grandfather was holding back, but why?

Chapter Nineteen

Maya sat in her SUV in Pops's driveway. The keys were in the ignition, but she hadn't been able to leave. She'd stared off at the mountains in the distance; some early afternoon thunderheads were building. It was that time of year when storms would roll in bringing much-needed rain and dangerous lightning.

Juniper woke up from her nap and stretched in the back. She put her nose up to the door that opened between her compartment and the front of the vehicle. Maya unlocked the door, giving Juniper a couple treats and rubbing her head. She thought about the conversation with Pops. What would it take to get him to open up to her?

Maya glanced down at the center console and saw her phone was blinking. Her boss, Todd, was calling so she immediately answered.

"Thompson, I know it's your day off, but can you come to the office ASAP? An FBI agent will be there along with Coleman. We need to talk. We have a situation."

"Sir?" Maya said. Coleman was the special agent in charge of criminal investigations for their region. His job would be to help investigate Doug's death and present the case to the attorney general when they found the bastard who had done this.

"Just get here ASAP. No uniform needed," Todd said.

"Okay," Maya said, hearing the click on the other end of the line as he hung up. In the short time she'd known Todd, she had never heard him this upset. It had to be something with the investigation. But what?

She thought about the hidden cash, the letters where Doug mentioned a complicated relationship, and the fact Pops was holding back on information. Was Doug somehow involved in all this? Had she done something? Maybe they had changed their mind about Juniper and had decided to give her to another handler. That thought made Maya feel sick. Thinking about it made her realize that the trial period was bullshit. She wanted to be Juniper's handler.

Maya floored the SUV and peeled out of the driveway. She took the curves as fast as she dared, glancing every now and then at Juniper, who had flattened herself up against one side of her enclosure, giving Maya a look that said she didn't appreciate the speed.

After passing a couple vehicles, Maya made it to town in good time. She grabbed Juniper's leash and went around to get her out of the back. While Juniper was supposed to stay quiet, she needed to move around a little bit and Maya had to admit that whatever Todd was about to tell her had her nervous enough that she wanted the support of Juniper by her side.

Maya noticed two more vehicles with government plates parked by Todd's car. She recognized the special agent's car and figured the other belonged to the FBI. There would be many different organizations helping with this investigation since the crime happened on federal land, but the sheriff's office would also be involved. Maya wondered why her grandfather wasn't called in too.

She opened the office door. Todd was sitting at her desk and the two other agents sat facing him. "Sir," Maya said, clearing her throat.

"Officer Thompson, thanks for coming so quickly. You know Coleman, and this is FBI Agent Kessler."

"Gentlemen," Maya said, shaking their hands. Coleman was all business and nearing retirement. She had heard through the law enforcement grapevine that Agent Kessler was a recent Quantico graduate and new to the Fort Collins field office. He had a baby face with slicked-back hair and fiddled with his wedding ring, making Maya suspect he was a newlywed. She supposed you had to start somewhere, but she had hoped there would be a more senior agent assigned to the case.

Juniper pushed her way between Maya and the two men. "Nice to meet you," Maya said. "I'm Officer Thompson and this is K-9 Juniper."

Maya sat down by Todd and asked Juniper to lie down. Much to her relief, Juniper listened. "We have some results from the investigation," Todd started. "Before we talk any further, I need to know if you know anything that you'd like to tell us."

Everyone stared at Maya. She felt her face heat up even though she hadn't done anything wrong. "Sir? Like what?"

"Anything. Did Officer Leyton ever tell you anything that we need to know? I know you were good friends, so it would be natural to protect him," Todd said.

"I'm not sure what you mean," Maya said. Juniper

swiveled her head back and forth, taking in the conversation. Maya reached down and scratched Juniper's ears.

Coleman cleared his throat. "What we mean is that we were able to get fingerprints and DNA from the bomb pieces as well as parts of the drug lab."

"Good. Do you have a match?" Maya asked.

"Yes," said the FBI agent.

Maya didn't like the way he was looking at her, as if she were the one who was being interrogated. *Maybe I am being interrogated.* She decided to play their game for now. She didn't care about the agents, but the look on Todd's face bothered her. There was a mix of mistrust, frustration, and resignation—something she'd never seen from him before. "That's great. Have you arrested the person?"

"No," said Coleman.

"Why not?" Maya asked.

Todd leaned forward on the desk, set his hands down and interlaced his fingers. "Because the prints and DNA belonged to Officer Leyton."

Maya's stomach constricted and her shoulders tightened. *Dang it, Doug. I don't want to believe you would do something like this, but the evidence is piling up.* She stopped scratching Juniper and took in the three men around her. She wanted them to tell her they were messing with her, that this was some sort of sick rookie hazing deal, but she knew that wasn't the case. This was different. There was the cash, the letters and something Pops wasn't telling her. Maya had to admit, if she were the investigator, she would come to the same conclusion.

"I don't understand," she finally said, hoping to draw more information out of the agents. Juniper nudged her hand wanting more attention, but Maya couldn't move.

"We don't either." Coleman spoke up. "We know you were close with Doug, so we were hoping you could shed some light on all of this. I'm also going to need a statement from you."

"I've already started working on my statement," Maya said. "I can finish it tomorrow."

"Good," Coleman said. Maya didn't appreciate the way he was staring at her. She knew from her military and law enforcement training in interrogation techniques that he was studying her for signs of lying or withholding information.

Maya let out a sigh. She had to tell them about the money and maybe the secret girlfriend. She couldn't believe that Doug would be involved in anything bad, but DNA evidence didn't lie. She also knew what Doug wrote about being in trouble in the letters he never sent. *How could he change so much?*

Her grandfather had been withholding information when she talked to him, she was sure about that. She would tell them everything that seemed important, but it felt like betraying Doug. But maybe Doug had betrayed her.

"Doug didn't say anything to me that would make me think he was involved in something illegal," Maya started. "But…"

"Yes?" Coleman asked.

"I don't know if this is anything or not."

"Spit it out, Thompson," Todd said.

Maya had never heard him speak like that before. She wasn't put off or offended. After living the life of a Marine, it took much more than that to rattle her, but she had never seen this side to her boss. "I went over to Doug's house to get Juniper's things. When I was there,

I found a hidden floorboard. Underneath it was a safe. In the safe I found cash. Lots of cash. I couldn't estimate it, but there were bundles of hundred-dollar bills. I thought it was odd Doug would have that amount of cash hidden."

"You think?" muttered the FBI agent.

Maya gave him her best stare-down—the one people didn't want to see from her. The men in her unit called it the battle face, and it meant get out of her way or else. "Yes, I did think it was odd, but on the other hand, don't we all do odd things? I'm sure even you do, Agent Kessler," Maya said.

He squirmed for a moment in his seat and Maya took satisfaction in that. She redirected her gaze back to Coleman and Todd. "I also think he had a secret serious relationship, but he never told me about it, which I also found strange since we've been best friends for a long time. I figure he would have told me eventually… *if he was still here*," Maya said, deciding to leave out the fact that she'd removed the letters from his house. They would probably now be considered evidence, but she didn't want to give up one of the last memories she had of her best friend. From the sounds of it, there were plenty of other things that made Doug the prime suspect, so they didn't need the letters anyway. Maya tried to convince herself that there had to be a good explanation. If Doug was involved, why did they go to the drug lab?

"All right," Coleman said. "We'll get some crime scene techs to go over and process his house. I was planning on that anyway, but I'll tell them about the cash. Maybe we can trace it."

"What about the other person? The one who detonated the bomb?" Maya asked. "There had to be more fingerprints than just Doug's."

"We didn't find any evidence of another person being there," Coleman said. "I know what you said, but there were no other fingerprints or DNA. Maybe you hit your head when the explosion happened."

"I know what I saw," Maya said, annoyed that Coleman didn't believe her. She took a deep breath. Getting angry wouldn't help her cause. "And what about the cabin? It was converted to a drug lab. A local sheriff's deputy told me he arrested someone the other night. It appears they were using Krokodil. Maybe we should investigate with the sheriff's department on this one."

Coleman shrugged. "Yeah, okay, good idea. We should have the identification of the product from the lab soon. If you think of anything else, call me."

"Yes, sir," Maya said, standing up as Coleman and Kessler also stood. They all shook hands again, and then Coleman and Kessler left.

Maya turned to Todd. "Sir, I really don't know anything else. And there was another person there."

"I believe you. Sit back down and let's talk some more."

Maya plopped back in the chair, exhaustion hitting her. She rubbed her forehead. The urge for a beer came on strong. Juniper stood up, pushed her head into Maya's hand, then smacked Maya with her paw.

"Okay, girl. Lay back down," Maya said.

Juniper sighed and then listened. Maya rewarded her by scratching her head.

"Looks like you two are getting along," Todd said.

"Yes. She's a great dog."

"Good. Glad to hear that. You want to skip this trial

period and plan on going to the next certification? It's coming up soon starting in July."

Maya hesitated. She wanted to be Juniper's handler, but what if she wasn't ready? What about her past mistake as a handler? Did Todd know about that?

"What are you thinking, Thompson?"

"You know that I was a K-9 handler for the Marines."

"Yes, that's why I thought you'd be good to step in. It's a big reason why we hired you. We wanted to get another K-9 for this area when you were ready. Doug told me you were the best. Your CO told me you were the best. Hell, don't you have a bunch of medals? The achievement medal? Your dog did too, right?"

Maya nodded. "Yes, but what they left out was that I screwed up as a handler. It's my fault that he died. No medal can make up for that."

"Hell, Thompson. It's war. You didn't screw up—you were just lucky to get out alive."

Maya wanted to believe Todd. "You ever serve?"

"No. Thought about it, but went into law enforcement instead. That's war too. Just in a different way. Look at what happened to you and Leyton."

"I know." Maya hesitated again and stared down at Juniper. Her golden eyes stared back with a mixture of intensity and contentment. Her ears pricked up, waiting for Maya to give her the signal that they would be doing something that wasn't as boring as lying around and discussing the past.

Maya owed Doug. She'd made him a promise.

"I'll do it," she said, turning her gaze from Juniper back to Todd. "I'll be Juniper's handler and go to certification."

"Good. You think she'll be ready? Vet give her clearance?"

"The vet wanted her to stay quiet for a couple more days and then said she could get back to work. Keeping her quiet hasn't been easy. She needs to do something with her energy."

"Keep in touch with the vet, but go ahead and start working her when you think she's ready. I trust your judgment."

"Okay. There's one other thing," Maya said.

"What's that?"

"I really did see another person at the cabin. They detonated the bombs. I know what I saw, and I know that person had the bombs set up to go off. We walked into a trap. I can't explain Doug's DNA or fingerprints, though."

"I believe you," Todd said. "But evidence doesn't lie."

"No, it doesn't. When Juniper is ready, I'd like your permission to go back up and do an evidence search with her. I know we're not certified yet, but I also can't believe that Doug would have done this. There must be another explanation. And maybe it'll give us a lead on the drug product being made there."

"Permission granted. I agree with you—Leyton was a good officer. I was as shocked as you to get the results. Just keep me in the loop. It'll be a couple days for Juniper to be cleared to work, so the evidence will probably lose its scent."

"I know," Maya said, "but I think it's worth a try. And there's one other angle I'd like to investigate."

"What's that?"

"I was in the bar the other night. Off duty," Maya added quickly, seeing Todd's eyebrows rise. "Some locals came in. The Ray family. I grew up and went to school with Cody and Jenna Ray. Cody was spouting off about feds and how much he hated them. They left in a black pickup. Doug and I passed that pickup on our way to the cabin."

"Why didn't you say this when Coleman and Kessler were here?"

"Because the Ray family is full of crap most of the time. They've always been troublemakers around here. Cody especially. I thought he was just trying to make me mad, start a fight. I'm wondering what he knows. I'd like to go talk to the Rays at some point, although I'm not sure when. Do you think we can work with the sheriff's office and get a search warrant?"

"We need more evidence for a search warrant. A local redneck wanting to start a fight with you isn't enough. If that was all we needed, we could have tons of search warrants. You know that."

Maya shrugged in agreement.

"See if you can find out more and keep me in the loop. If you go talk to them, make sure you have backup too. Take Deputy Colten with you. He's been really good about working with us. And please, be careful."

"I can go on my own if I'm just asking questions," Maya said. "I'll have Juniper with me as backup."

"No. This is a dangerous situation. If this Ray family is involved in drug production and running, they won't think twice about killing you. I agree with you that something is off here with Doug, the evidence…and the lack of evidence of the second person at the scene. If you go there, I want to make sure you have backup to help keep you safe and also as a witness. Work with

Deputy Colten. You'll need to foster these relationships as you take over Doug's area."

"I'll make sure I take someone with me then, but I can't guarantee it will be Deputy Colten."

"No. Connect with him. He's the person we're coordinating with for operations in this county. Do you have an issue with him? Something I need to know about?"

"No, sir."

"Good. Then start working with him. I'll see you tomorrow."

"Yes, sir." Maya swallowed hard.

Tomorrow was Doug's funeral.

Chapter Twenty

Maya stepped up to the front door of the church, Juniper by her side. She took a deep breath and smoothed back a couple strands of loose hair that had escaped her bun. Her dress uniform seemed stiff and uncomfortable only adding to the stress of the day. Some dog hair stuck to the front, and Maya brushed it off as well as she could.

Deciding she couldn't procrastinate any further, she grabbed the large iron door handle, opened it, and stepped inside. The sun shone through the stained glass, reflecting different colors onto the wood floor.

"This isn't going to be fun, girl," Maya said to Juniper. "But I think we both need some closure. Or at least that's what I'm telling myself. Does that work for you?"

Juniper wagged her tail but didn't look excited either. Maya knew Juniper needed to get back to work. They all did. Nothing helped grieving like throwing yourself into your job. That was one of the ways Maya made it through her time in Afghanistan. Go out and find the bad guy. Make them pay.

I just have to make it through today. Having Juniper by her side would help.

Maya and Juniper slipped into an area in the back where they could stand and not bother anyone. The pews were too close together for Juniper to lie comfortably. Maya saw Pops sitting near the front. He turned around and scanned the church and, seeing her in the back, gave a nod, which Maya returned.

"Hey there," Josh said. Maya hadn't seen him come up, and to her surprise, Juniper gazed up at Josh and began wagging her tail.

"I think she likes me," Josh said. "Mind if I pet her?"

"No, she's off duty, so you're good. And it looks like she likes you."

"I have that effect on women," Josh said, with a wink.

Maya gave him her best Marine stare. *Can you be any more arrogant?* Not to mention she would have to add Juniper to the list of women who flirted with Josh.

"I'm really sorry about Doug," Josh said as he scratched behind Juniper's ears. A hind foot started twitching and the sound on the wooden floor sounded like someone knocking at the door. A couple people turned around to see what the fuss was about. "I know you two were friends. I didn't know him very well, but I know he was a good guy."

"Thanks," Maya said. "Maybe you better find a seat because we're disturbing everyone."

Josh shrugged and then said to Juniper giving her a final scratch, "I'll come see you again later."

Maya nodded, once again having trouble finding words. She'd worked with good-looking guys before—why should Josh be any different? She hated to admit it, but there was a pull with Josh. Something that made her want to be with him, but that scared the crap out of her, so she had to make sure she set some boundaries. She didn't need to be in a relationship right now. Plus, what made her think that he felt the same way about her? Was she also that arrogant? It was better to just leave things alone.

A couple more deputies came in, and Josh went with them up front and sat by Maya's grandfather. Everyone had solemn looks on their faces, some people already dabbing at tears. Doug had meant a lot to many, especially Maya.

Her chest constricted as she fought back her own tears. She wouldn't cry. Not now. Not here. She hadn't been comfortable showing emotion since she came home. It was easier to be shut off, ignore others and give the impression of a tough Marine.

The preacher arrived and started the service. Maya gazed around the church looking for a blonde she didn't know. If Doug and his mystery woman were that serious, wouldn't she be here?

Juniper let out a small whine, and Maya was getting ready to hush her when she followed her dog's gaze and saw a person back in the hallway that led to the restrooms. The hall was dark, and the person stayed in the shadows. Maya couldn't make out who it was. She'd have to interrupt the entire service to head that direction. Suspects would often show up at funerals.

Juniper sat back down and continued to gaze at the person standing there. The shadow must've felt Juniper and Maya's eye contact and turned toward them. Maya thought she caught a glimpse of blond hair, but the person spun around and headed toward the bathrooms. There was also a back exit down that hall.

Maya gathered up Juniper's leash and they snuck out the doors, although there were a few heads that swiveled around, including Todd's. He gave her a *what the hell are you doing* look and she pointed to Juniper, hoping he would guess that the dog had to go to the bathroom, and mouthed *I'll be right back.*

They strode around to the back of the church. Juniper air scented, catching odors coming off the slight breeze. Maya thought about asking her to track, but she didn't have the tracking harness and she didn't want Juniper to exert herself that much yet. She did give Juniper slack in the leash and let her follow her nose.

They walked to the corner of the church near the road. Suddenly Juniper stopped and tilted her head, her pointy triangular ears pricked and alert. Then a low growl rumbled from Juniper's throat.

"What is it, girl?" Maya asked, stepping in front of Juniper to see the road better.

Just as Maya stepped forward, the black truck flew by. The driver floored the vehicle and sprayed gravel toward her and Juniper.

"What the…" Maya grabbed Juniper's leash and hauled her back, getting them both clear of the vehicle as it fishtailed on the dirt road by the church. Brake lights came on and the truck slammed to a stop. The tinted window rolled down. Maya couldn't make out the person driving, but she could see the hand pointing at her gesturing as if it were a gun and Maya and Juniper were the targets.

Then the window rolled back up and the truck sped off again.

Maya checked over Juniper to make sure she was okay, but the dog seemed fine.

Now I really want to find and question Roberta Lind. Threatening me just makes me mad, especially when my dog is involved.

"We're going to find that truck the next time we're on duty," Maya said to Juniper. Juniper tilted her head and made a soft humming sound. "And when that happens and we pull it over, we're going to figure out exactly who Roberta Lind is and why she just threatened us."

Chapter Twenty-One

Maya and Juniper went back inside the church and a few people gave her disapproving glares. She ignored them. The preacher was elaborating on how Doug loved this community, hunting, fishing, and keeping the national forests safe. He died doing something he believed in.

Then he ended the service by inviting folks to come up and give speeches about Doug. Maya knew she should, but she stayed put. She wasn't ready to get up in front of a crowd and spill her feelings—especially after Doug had kept so many secrets from her. For the first time since Doug's death, she was furious.

Todd went up front, looking uncomfortable in his official dress uniform. He tugged for a moment at his shirtsleeves and then pulled out some cards and started reading. Maya tuned him out too. She didn't want to remember Doug by all these people making speeches. They didn't know him like she did.

The speeches came to an end and everyone started to go up and pay their final respects. Maya and Juniper stood at the back of the line and waited their turn. When Juniper got up to the front of Doug's casket, she lay down and whined.

Maya fought back tears. She gave Juniper a moment and then touched the casket, cold and hard. It was closed, of course, because after the explosion no one would want to see what Doug looked like. It was better to remember him as he was.

Maya didn't want to remember him from the day of the explosion, so she closed her eyes and focused on the past, when the sun had highlighted Doug's hair while they were fly-fishing. The look of contentment on his face as he cast out and then reeled back in.

She heard someone behind her clear their throat, and Maya picked up Juniper's leash. The dog climbed to her feet and nudged the casket. She stared at Maya inquisitively, gave a sigh and followed her down the aisle.

Maya's breath came in short gasps. She walked out the back door and took in the fresh air. The sun penetrated through the clouds feeling warm and harsh against her skin. She hadn't put on sunscreen, and with her light complexion and freckles, it was much needed.

Sunscreen. It had always struck Maya in Afghanistan how someone would die and then the rest of the soldiers would go on worrying about stupid things like the movie that would be shown that night or if the chow hall would serve the god-awful spaghetti and meatballs or delicious burritos. Such simple things that make everyone's day and helped you move on from thinking about death.

"You okay?" Josh asked.

Maya hadn't realized he'd followed her out. "What do you think?"

"Good point. I don't know why people ask that at funerals."

"Neither do I." Maya took a deep breath. Josh was only trying to be nice. He was courteous and kind. He'd been nothing but friendly toward her. Just because she had issues being around him didn't mean she had to be mean. "Sorry. It's been a tough day."

"Yeah. I know what it's like to lose your partner."

"Oh yeah?" Maya said. "How do you know about that?"

"Another story for another day. I'll tell you sometime if you'd like, but not today. Today is about Doug. Speaking of which, are you helping to carry his casket?"

"I am," Maya said, reaching down to scratch Juniper's ears. Juniper gave another sigh of pleasure and pushed her head into Maya's thigh.

"Then you better come soon."

"Okay, I'll need to put Juniper in the car."

"I can hold her or walk with her. Seems like she should be part of this too. I mean, if you want." Josh shrugged.

"She doesn't know you and you don't have that much K-9 experience."

"Actually, I think she likes me because she keeps wagging her tail when I'm around. I'll be right by you with her, so you can save me from her jaws of death should she decide to not like me, but it's up to you."

Maya nodded and stared off toward the high peaks still dotted with snow, then glanced back to her dog, whose tail wiggled from side to side. "Okay, let's try it. If Juniper isn't happy, we can switch places."

"Works for me."

The procession went as well as expected. Juniper behaved for Josh. Maya kept one eye on them as she helped move the casket out to the waiting hearse. After her part was over, she went and took Juniper back from Josh.

"See?" he said. "She does like me."

"Yeah, well, you survived this time," Maya said, although a smile crept across her face. She didn't know what to say. She fidgeted with the leash and then blurted out, "Did you really do agitation work?"

"Yeah. I went through all the training."

Maya did need to start Juniper back into training and thought she was ready for some light work. "Would you be willing to come to my cabin for a simple training session? Just to see how she does? Maybe tomorrow?"

"That works. What time?"

"How about nine?"

Josh grinned. "I love getting bit by seventy pounds of fur missile first thing in the morning. I'll see you there."

"Okay, it's a plan." Maya was about ready to turn and walk away when Josh stopped her.

"So, uh, you going to give me your address or do I need to go ask your grandfather?"

"I'll text you. I think I still have your card," Maya said. She saw Todd waving at her from his vehicle. "Gotta go. Boss is calling."

"Okay, but don't forget to text me," Josh said. "Or I will ask your grandfather and let you explain that one later. Oh, and I'll get my windbreaker from you then."

Maya shrugged, relieved that she wouldn't have the smell of his cologne permeating her cabin anymore. "Works for me."

She headed for her vehicle and glanced over her shoulder. Josh was still watching her and waved. She smiled and waved back. *Why am I smiling?* Maya hated to admit it—while she found Josh annoying, he was nice too…in an annoying way.

Todd pulled his vehicle up by Maya and Juniper.

"Thompson, hurry up. There's some news on the investigation," he said. "Meet me at the office ASAP."

Maya and Juniper hurried to the patrol vehicle. As Maya was opening up the door to load Juniper, she glanced off to a side street. Sitting back in the shadows was the black truck. She still couldn't make out the person, but they appeared to be watching her.

Chapter Twenty-Two

After arriving at the office, Maya and Juniper took the stairs two at a time and rushed in the front door. Agents Coleman and Kessler were there, looking solemn. Todd sat at Maya's desk.

"So." Todd took charge. "What's the news?"

Coleman crossed his arms and sat back more. "We sent crime scene techs to Doug's house. We couldn't find the stash of cash."

"But I know it was there," Maya blurted out, then added, "Sir," as an afterthought.

Coleman glared at her and she shut her mouth. She knew from the military when she needed to be quiet. "We did find the space under the kitchen floor," he explained. "Only there was nothing there. We finger-printed everything and got back Doug's prints. There was a print we couldn't match, and of course your prints, Officer Thompson. Actually, your prints were all over the house. I was wondering why."

Maya felt herself turning red from the neck up. Not from embarrassment, but from anger that Coleman was suggesting what she thought he was. "I went to pick up Juniper's things."

"Well, it appears you were quite nosy then, unless

Doug was in the habit of keeping Juniper's things in his desk, on bookshelves and in the master bath."

"I stopped to look around. I was remembering Doug."

"Any idea what happened to the money?"

"No, and if you're asking if I took it, I didn't."

Coleman gave her an icy stare. "I'm not suggesting anything. I just simply want to know where the money might be and why there's an empty drawer with your fingerprints all over it on Doug's desk."

"I didn't take the money. If I had, I wouldn't have told you about it. As for the desk, I was looking for some letters I had sent Doug when I was in Afghanistan. I didn't find them," Maya said. Coleman didn't need to read the letters with Doug professing his love for Maya or that he was in a troubled relationship. There was already enough evidence linking him to the bombing.

Coleman nodded; his arms remained tightly crossed. "We also found drug residue in the safe where you said the money was stashed. We tested that and it came back positive for Krokodil. This is unusual in the U.S. We have called the DEA and let them know what's going on too. They will help with the drug trafficking investigation. We now believe that Officer Leyton was involved in drug trafficking and blew up the cabin as a possible suicide."

"Doug would never kill himself," Maya said, anger building. First Nana supposedly killed herself, and now Doug? *This can't be happening.* "What about the other person at the cabin?"

"We've found no evidence that there was anyone else. Perhaps you hit your head, or maybe you're making up a story to protect your friend. We're not sure, but just know that if you have anything to add, now is the time to tell us. Not later."

Maya took turns looking at the three men in front of her. It was hard enough to stomach that Doug was involved in this mess, but did they really think she was too? When her gaze arrived at Todd, he looked away. "I have told you everything I know. I do believe that Officer Leyton had a girlfriend, but I don't know who it is. Maybe if you can find her, you can get more answers."

"We did find some blond hairs at Leyton's house." Kessler spoke up. "The DNA belonged to two different people, but it was hair that fell out naturally and there wasn't a root with it, so the only DNA we can get from it is mitochondrial, which just tells us it was two different people who weren't related. We can't get an ID from the hair. Maybe Leyton didn't have one girlfriend, but rather two."

"He'd never have two girlfriends, he wasn't that kind of guy…" Maya said. But apparently he had become involved in drug trafficking and taking bribes, so she could see why they thought he might have more than one girlfriend. She clenched her fists by her side. If Doug were still alive, she'd arrest him herself. This was not how Maya wanted to remember her friend. Juniper stood up, her eyes staring intently at Maya, reading her feelings. "Doug was a good man and I'm sure there's an explanation for this."

"Look," Coleman said. "We believe Leyton acted alone for the bombing. We believe he was using the national forest to traffic drugs and that part of the investigation will be turned over to the DEA and your local law enforcement, although I will get reports from them for our part. We believe Leyton set the bombs and detonated them to take his own life. Maybe you are involved. Maybe not. But we're closing the investigation with the FBI since we can't find any evidence pointing to you or any evidence pointing to another person. The only evidence is what I just told you. So, for our part of the investigation concerning the bombing, case closed. Leyton did it and we can't prosecute a dead man."

Maya unclenched her fists and sat down in a chair. She rubbed her forehead, hoping to relieve some tension. *How could you do this, Doug?*

Opening her eyes, she said, "I can assure you I wasn't involved and there was another person at the explosion. I ask that you keep this case open for now. We passed a black truck that day. It belongs to a Roberta Lind, who I believe may be involved with the Ray family. The Rays are under investigation by the sheriff's office. As you mentioned, we can work with the sheriff's office because this seems connected to our case. And Roberta Lind is a blonde."

"At this point, Thompson, we're calling it done on our part. We can't just go around serving search warrants to people because they're blonde," Coleman said.

Maya slumped back in her chair. There was more to this case than just Doug. She knew that, but how could she prove it without the evidence? She gazed down at Juniper, who was lying calmly on the floor by Maya's feet. She had the best tool for gathering evidence. When she went back out on patrol, she would start her own investigation. *They can't scare me away from finding out what really happened.*

Coleman and Kessler shook hands with Todd and then left. Maya heard the door close behind her. "Am

I under any type of investigation or suspension?" she asked Todd.

"No. There's no evidence supporting you being involved. Coleman is just covering his ass," Todd said.

Maya wanted to add that Coleman was also a jerk. "I know that officially this investigation is closed, but with your permission, I'd like to see if I can find out more about the Rays and what the sheriff is investigating. It may not pertain to this case, but the Ray Ranch backs up to Forest Service land. If there's another illegal operation going on, we should know about it."

"Agreed," Todd said. He sat down in a chair with a thump. "And for what it's worth, Thompson, I believe you."

"About what?"

"About the fact that there was another person."

"Thanks."

"I just can't believe this. I completely missed the warning signs. I thought Doug was a good officer. One of my best."

"If it makes you feel better, I was his best friend and I didn't see it either."

"I wish Doug would have talked to me," Todd said, banging his fist on the desk. Juniper jumped to her feet and Maya settled her back down. Todd started to rub his temples. "I feel a headache coming on. Okay, if you see something, look into it, but there's two stipulations."

"What?" Maya asked.

"You keep me in the loop. If Doug was keeping something quiet, he shouldn't have. That was a mistake. And be careful. I know you're not certified with Juniper yet, but if you need her for backup at any point, use her if it means keeping yourself alive. I can't find another officer out there anytime soon."

"I'm touched, I think," Maya said. "But copy. I'll be careful and I'll keep you posted."

"Okay." Todd tapped the table with his fingers. "We're going to take a lot of shit about this. I mean with the investigation saying Doug was at fault, but we'll deal with it."

"Yes, sir," Maya said. "Wouldn't be the first time the Forest Service took shit about something."

Todd laughed. "No, it isn't."

Maya stood up and Juniper was instantly by her side. "With all due respect, sir, I'm tired and ready to go home."

"Me too," Todd said. "Get out of here. I'll lock up. I'll be heading back to my office tomorrow."

She nodded. "Have a safe trip home."

As Maya left the office, exhaustion washed over her. She stopped at the liquor store on the way home. She wasn't supposed to in her Forest Service gear and vehicle, but she slipped in and out fast before anyone saw her. She was definitely going to need help sleeping tonight.

Chapter Twenty-Three

Maya woke up the next morning with sunshine glaring into her eyes. She'd left her curtains open. Her tongue felt like a cotton ball stuck to the roof of her mouth. Her head pounded. She couldn't roll over.

She reached out, trying to figure out why she was stuck, and her hand landed on fur. She felt up and down the fur until she reached pointy ears. A groan came from Juniper.

Juniper.

Shit.

Maya sat straight up. Juniper lay on her side, taking up most of the bed. The dog had a content look on her face and stretched her legs, toes splaying apart.

"You're supposed to be in your crate," Maya said, throwing back the covers. "You're not a pet and you don't get the whole bed."

Maya stepped down, her feet hitting the cold floor. She felt a little nauseous, and memories from the previous night flooded back. She'd bought a large case of beer and toasted to Doug—all night long.

Maya put her head in her hands. At least she was off today. That gave her time to sober up. How did Juniper get out of her crate? Or had Maya in her drunken stupor forgotten to lock the door or even put her in there?

"Time to get up, officer," Maya said to Juniper, who now had edged over where Maya had been lying and taken up more of the bed. Juniper flicked open one golden eye and then shut it again.

"Really? Fine. Stay in bed. I'm going to start some coffee."

Maya stood up. Her head throbbed. She shuffled her way to the kitchen, where she found a war zone-like disaster. Apparently, Juniper had decided to use up some energy while Maya was passed out. No wonder the dog was sleeping so well. Maya's couch cushions looked like a bomb hit them. Stuffing was torn out and littered all over the floor. The one rug she owned had been chewed and ripped apart. Maya's box of stuffed animals from her childhood had been broken into. Each animal looked like it was tortured by a serial killer. Except for one—a teddy bear.

"Great," Maya muttered. If she couldn't even take care of herself, how could she take care of a dog like Juniper? She was spiraling out of control and had no clue how to get things together.

As Maya took in the mess, Juniper slithered her way out of bed and sat by Maya, observing her masterpiece. Juniper strolled over to the teddy bear, gently picked it up in her mouth and went to her crate. She slunk inside, turned around, put her head between her paws, keeping the teddy bear in her mouth.

"This is my fault, not yours. I obviously didn't lock you up last night. And I guess you can have Teddy as long as you don't destroy him too."

Juniper sighed and closed her eyes.

Maya made her way through the destruction, just wanting coffee. She couldn't be too mad at the dog when she looked at her kitchen table, where beer cans littered the entire area.

"Looks like we both partied hard last night," Maya said.

The only answer was dog snores.

Maya started the coffee and was in the process of picking up beer cans and putting them in the trash when she heard the crunch of tires outside. Juniper woke up, grabbed the teddy bear in her mouth and shot out of the crate to see who had arrived. She put her giant paws up on the door and peered out the window, tail wagging.

"Who the hell is here now?" Maya asked, going to the window to peer out. "Oh crap."

Josh. Did I text him my address? Or did he have to get it from Pops?

She had forgotten that she had discussed having him come over to help work Juniper today. She turned away from the window and leaned back against the wall, closing her eyes. She better get over her hangover real quick.

She turned back and looked out the window again. Josh stepped out of his sheriff's vehicle. Unlike Maya, he looked ready to tackle the day. Juniper tried to give a happy bark, but it came out muffled with the teddy bear in her mouth.

Josh strolled up the worn path to the door. Maya opened it, hoping she didn't look too terrible. On the other hand, why did she care how she looked?

She didn't want to admit it, but around Josh, she kind of did care.

"Hey there, sorry, running a little bit late," Maya said. Josh raised one eyebrow and Maya turned red, realizing she still had on her pajamas, which didn't cover much. She crossed her arms as if that would hide her lack of bra and loose-fitting shirt.

"Yeah," Maya said. "So come on in. I'll be just a minute. Keep an eye on Juniper."

Josh stepped inside and was about ready to say something, but Maya turned and took off before he could. She sprinted to her bedroom, slammed the door shut, threw on different clothes and then brushed her teeth as quick as she could. Her hair looked like a bird's nest, red curls tangled and sticking out every which way. Maya solved the problem by pulling it back in a ponytail and throwing on a Marine baseball cap. She stepped out of her room like she had planned this all along.

"I'm going to grab a cup of coffee and then I'll be ready to train," Maya said, noting that Juniper had herself leaning up against Josh's leg and was giving him lovey eyes. "You want any?"

"Sure. Thanks. Nice place you have here. What a great location. I love your view."

"Uh, thanks." Maya marched over to the coffee maker. She pulled down two mugs and poured coffee, handing one to Josh. "You take cream or sugar?"

"Cream would be great."

Maya opened her empty fridge. There was no milk or cream. "Um, sorry, all out."

"That's fine. I'll drink it black. Looks like you do have a pyscho dog after all."

Maya shook her head, embarrassed by the mess. "I think it's good Juniper's going back to work. I'm not sure my cabin will live. I also need to get an outside kennel built."

"You need help cleaning it up?" Josh grinned, still scratching Juniper.

"No, that's okay. But thanks," Maya said, gulping her coffee. The coffee hit her stomach and made it churn.

"Did my windbreaker survive?"

"Oh. Yeah. No teeth marks on that." Maya set her cup on the counter and handed Josh his jacket. "After you put that in your car, are you ready to hide some dope and maybe get bit? I know Dr. Asher wanted Juniper to have more time off, but based on how my cabin looks this morning, I think she's ready to go back to work."

"Sure, hiding drugs and getting bit are my favorite things to do on my day off," Josh said.

"K-9 handlers, we're all a bit psycho too," Maya said with a laugh. She liked how Josh didn't seem to judge her and brightened things up. *Stay focused.* "All right. Let's do it then."

She showed Josh the lockbox with the narcotic training aids. Inside the box, there were jars with different contraband that included marijuana, meth, heroin, and cocaine. All of the drugs were evidence that had been released to use for training. Maya had to keep everything secure and make sure that she could return the exact amount and weight of each narcotic.

"Let's give her three hides," she said, using the slang for concealing drugs. "I don't want to overdo it, but I do want to see if she'll keep searching after her first alert. Juniper and I will go back inside and wait until you tell us that you're ready."

"You got it," Josh said, putting on latex gloves so his scent didn't transfer to the training aids.

Inside, Maya had Juniper's reward, a squeaky ball with a rope tied through it, in her cargo pants pocket.

Juniper knew the toy was there and had gone from a destructive house dog to a well-trained narcotics dog. She sat and stared at Maya, waiting for the command to go to work.

Maya heard Josh yell, "Okay!" Juniper's body shook with excitement.

"Let's go find the dope," Maya said. Juniper's ears pricked straight up, and she leaped forward in front of Maya. Maya opened the door and Juniper shot out in front of her. Maya began to direct her dog's search pattern.

"Check over by your driveway and the small ditch," Josh said.

Maya knew he wasn't giving her the location of the hide, but rather helping Juniper not tire herself out by narrowing down the area to search. Maya and Juniper ran a grid pattern alongside her driveway. A slight breeze picked up, but they worked into it. Directing Juniper into the wind would help her find the hidden narcotics.

Maya allowed Juniper to have the freedom to follow her nose. Juniper's body tensed up; she air scented for a second and then put her nose back down in the grass. Maya knew she had the odor and quit asking the dog to work the back-and-forth grid pattern, but instead followed Juniper, feeling the vibration down the leash.

Juniper shot forward, passed a large rock, stopped, whipped around, and went back to the boulder. She sat and stared at the rock, waiting for her reward.

Josh nodded that her alert was correct. Maya flung the ball in front of Juniper, who joyously latched on to the toy. Maya played tug for a second and then let go, allowing Juniper to chomp down on the toy and fling it around. Sometimes Juniper would deliberately drop it, letting the ball bounce different directions before snapping it back up in her mouth.

"She did well," Josh said. "Looks like she loves working narcotics."

"She did do well. I think she's happy to be back to work," Maya said, taking out her notebook while Juniper continued to play. "What did you hide?"

"That was cocaine," Josh answered.

Maya recorded the drug and amount for the logbook she was required to keep. Down the road, when they would go to court, Maya would need proof that Juniper could indeed find narcotics.

After making her notes, Maya went to take away the toy from Juniper. She had lain down and was now aggressively chewing on the ball, making it squeak in quick staccato tones. She flicked one eye toward Maya. Knowing that Maya was going to take away her toy, she deliberately turned her body away.

"I see how you are," Maya said. She pulled another toy out of her pocket and started to squeak it. Juniper stood up and flipped around, cocking her head. Maya squeaked the toy again until Juniper dropped the ball in her mouth. Maya rewarded her by throwing Juniper the other ball. They played the game until Maya was able to get both toys back. Juniper glared at her, obviously annoyed.

"Let's go find some more dope," Maya said. If the dog could have shrugged and said "okay," she would have. This time Juniper wasn't quite as energetic, but she found the hide of marijuana in Maya's personal vehicle. Maya praised her again and played with her.

The third hide, Juniper became a little distracted by

an animal scent. Maya reminded her to "find the dope" and Juniper went back to work. They played again, and after Maya got the toy back, she made sure Juniper had some water and rest.

She and Josh sat down on her front porch while Juniper lounged in the shade.

"Ready to get bit after Juniper's break?" Maya asked with an all-knowing smile. Even with a bite sleeve, the pressure from a K-9 could bruise a person.

"Sure," Josh said. "It's been a while since I've had a Malligator attached to my arm."

Maya laughed. "I have a feeling she's going to bite hard. Be ready."

"If your couch is any indication, I agree. How's the investigation going?"

Maya's stomach churned. While working Juniper, she had forgotten about Doug and the fact that he was the main suspect implicated. She hadn't told anyone else yet, but word was certain to get out soon. "The bombing investigation is closed for now."

"Did they find who did it?" Josh asked, raising an eyebrow.

Maya took a deep breath. "They think Doug set up the whole thing and that he was involved in running drugs. They found traces of Krokodil at his house. Might tie into your case. I was going to talk to you about working together on that part of the investigation."

A surprised look crossed Josh's face. "But what about the second person you saw? The one who actually detonated the bombs—aren't your investigators still looking for them?"

"Nope, in their minds, the case is closed since Doug is deceased. They think I was making up the second person or hit my head and was hallucinating or whatever. They don't believe me and there's no evidence that shows there was another person there. They even asked if I was involved. They thought *I* was the other person."

"Well...that's bullshit."

"Thanks," Maya said, grateful that Josh believed her. He reached over and took her hand. They interlocked fingers and stared at each other. She quickly let go and stammered on, trying to focus on what she was saying. "I'm still looking into it, even if they aren't. One person can't produce and run drugs."

"I'm having a hard time even believing that Doug was involved. He was a good guy. Not that type at all. There has to be an explanation."

"That's what I thought too, although..." Maya trailed off for a second. *Why am I saying all this to Josh? It does feel nice to talk to someone and Josh is a good listener.*

Maya continued and began filling Josh in about the money she found stashed. "Before Doug died, he told me some things. He said my grandfather knew the truth about the explosion and my grandmother's death. Maybe he was just talking in shock."

"I don't know. I still think there's a good explanation," Josh said. "I'll help you any way I can. I know your grandfather sits in his office and stares at the folder about your grandmother. I thought that he was just grieving in the weird way us cops grieve, but maybe he does know something more."

"What? Has he ever talked to you about my grandmother's death?"

"Never. Although I haven't asked," Josh said. "Can I ask you something, though?"

"You can ask, doesn't mean I'll answer," Maya said, smiling to let Josh know she was giving him a hard time.

They locked eyes for a moment. Josh had an amused look on his face, his lips curving into a slight grin. Maya thought about what it would be like to lean over and kiss him.

She glanced away, mad at herself for thinking such a thing and acting like a schoolgirl with a crush. "What's your question?"

"It's not really any of my business—"

"Just ask your damn question."

"Okay," Josh said. "What happened to your mom?"

Maya stared at him for a second. Out of all the questions she expected him to ask, that wasn't it.

Taking a moment to collect herself, she observed the beauty around her. The tall pine trees gave way to a view of the Snowy River Range to the north where snow still dotted some of the high peaks. Maya remembered sitting here with her grandmother in the summer guessing when the snow would melt. She took a deep breath. Josh brought up emotions in her that she thought she'd never feel again. She had to keep this relationship professional, but it was hard to not join in with all the women who found Josh charming and good-looking.

Maya concentrated on answering his question. "My mom was an only child and got herself into drugs and some sketchy things. She came back here and was supposedly trying to get clean, but when I was four, she died. I have vague memories of that day. She was murdered, but the case has remained unsolved. I've thought about looking into her death at some point. My grandparents adopted me, and were the best parents anyone could ask for. Why do you ask about her?"

Josh shrugged. "I saw your grandfather had pulled out another file. It was your mom's. He was looking over both her and your grandmother's cases. I asked him about the files, and he said he was just looking into a past case, but I saw a picture and at first I thought it was you. He closed the file fast. I was being nosy, so I pulled up the file later. Saw it was an OD like you said, but you look just like her, you know. Your biological mom."

"I have one picture of her that my grandmother gave me. It is kind of eerie how much we look alike. We never talked about her much when I was growing up. I realized at some point it was too painful, so I quit asking, but I kept that picture. I barely remember her. What I can remember is the night of the fire—the flames and the heat and Pops pulling me out and holding me in a blanket while our home burned. But I can't remember her. Sometimes I'm glad I can't, and sometimes I wish I could. I wonder why Pops is looking at her file again."

"I don't know," Josh said. "He might never tell us."

"Well, that would be my grandfather… Speaking of things my grandfather doesn't want to talk about, do you have any new intel on the Rays?" Maya asked, changing the subject and filling Josh in about the black truck at the funeral and the person she followed out the back of the church, including the threatening gesture.

"So that's what was going on. I know Wayne is keeping an eye on them. He's pretty certain they're doing something illegal, but he has no proof." Josh shrugged. "That's all I know right now."

"What about your case with the Krokodil?"

"That didn't go anywhere. The wife decided not to

charge her husband," Josh said. "And we didn't have enough evidence to charge him. The hospital cleaned up the guy's wounds and now he's back home. Not much of a lead."

"Okay. Well, ready to take a bite? Thought we'd just do one, so we don't overdo it."

"I'm ready," Josh said, standing up. Juniper lapped up some more water and then turned and stared at them. Maya swore a smile crept across the dog's face.

She handed Josh the bite sleeve, and they went out into an open area. She put Juniper on a down-stay, and then she and Josh worked out a scenario. Maya approached Josh like he was someone she had just asked for information, much like she would do approaching campers or hunters and asking to see a permit. Josh played the role of cooperating, and they shook hands and walked away.

Maya was happy to see that Juniper remained in her down-stay as she should. Some dogs might get excited seeing the bite sleeve and be ready to come flying in and apprehend someone when they shouldn't. The bite sleeve was as much a toy as a ball to a working dog.

"You ready for the fun now?" Maya asked, realizing that not only was Josh easy to talk to, but he made a fun training partner.

"Bring it on," Josh said.

Maya and Josh approached each other again, repeating the same scenario, only this time Josh didn't cooperate. He pretended to escalate and became angry, finishing by giving Maya a big shove. Maya stumbled backward as a streak of brown flew by. Josh made sure he had the sleeve presented so that he didn't get bit somewhere else.

Juniper latched on with force and speed. Josh pushed back and forth, encouraging Juniper to stay on the bite and shake harder. He made high-pitched noises, mimicking a squeaky toy.

Maya praised the dog and heard Josh saying something about the fact she could get Juniper to release now. Maya gave Juniper the command to let go, but Juniper ignored what she said. Maya corrected her and Juniper released.

"Guess we need to work on that," Maya said.

"You think?" Josh asked, waiting for Maya to walk Juniper a few steps away. "I haven't had a dog hit that hard and grip so well with her back teeth. She's awesome. No one is going to get this dog off a bite unless she wants to release."

"Yeah, she *is* pretty awesome," Maya said with a grin. Juniper gave a sharp bark in agreement. "You did good, girl. Now let's get Josh some more coffee. Time for you to rest."

Juniper groaned. Then she grabbed her teddy bear and lay back down.

Chapter Twenty-Four

Carson paced around the bunker, arms crossed, stopping to glance at Jenna. She sat on the new leather couch, staring off at the wall. Their eyes locked and Carson thought she looked like a rattlesnake ready to strike.

"This is my last batch. I want out," Jenna said, her voice tight and icy.

"I told you, you are part of this family and you're not leaving. Not yet. You're my daughter and you'll do as I say. I know you want to leave, but we need you. The family needs you."

"I could turn you in."

"You could," Carson laughed. "And then what? Tell them that you had nothing to do with it? No, you'll go to prison too and then all your little dreams of having a college degree will be done. No more. Finished. I'll let you go back to college, but first you have to help here."

"I'm not Mom." Jenna stood, her fists balled by her side. "I won't take your bullshit. And when Mom was sick, I was the one who came home. I helped nurse her. I helped you with this stupid business so you could pay off the bills. I understood it then, but now it's just stupid. This money has consumed you. I want out."

"You can go back to college next year. Help me out

now and you won't have any student loans. Things like that are why the money has consumed me. It's better this way."

The door opened behind Carson. He whirled around and saw Cody sauntering in, sunglasses on, a greasy ball cap stuck over dark hair that jutted out. A few of the men came in behind Cody. Some of them had on cowboy hats, some had on ball caps. Everyone had on jeans and boots, creating a loud marching sound as they headed toward their seats.

"We're done talking about this," Carson said to Jenna. "Don't get any ideas either or try anything stupid."

Jenna slumped back down into the couch, crossed her arms and stared at the wall again. Carson had won. He hated it when women spoke back to him. His authority should be the final word. He'd raised Jenna that way, making sure she knew there'd be consequences if she questioned him, but it looked like right now he needed to make sure she learned that lesson again. He supported her wanting to go to college and earning a degree. She should realize that she was lucky he was willing to allow her to do that. Seemed like she was taking that for granted.

Carson turned his attention to the men in the room. He was about ready to ask where Bobbi was when she strolled in. Once she was settled, Carson started the meeting. "I've heard from my inside source that the investigation into the bombing is closed at least for the FBI. Looks like the Forest Service fed was to blame for the explosion. If he weren't already dead, I'd kill him for what he cost us."

A few of the men murmured in surprise. Carson

waited for them to quiet down. "I do believe, though, that we have a loose end. There's still someone investigating us. Based on my sources he's kept the investigation to himself, so I think we can contain the problem. That person is our sheriff, Wayne Thompson."

Carson noticed that Jenna glanced up. Good, he had her attention too. "We need to neutralize this problem. Lana also wants someone to blame for the loss of product, so this could be a win-win for us."

"How's that?" one of the men asked.

"We are going to kidnap the sheriff, interrogate him and find out what he knows and if there are other agencies investigating us. Once we have the information, we'll give him to Lana so she can do what she wants with him. We'll make sure she knows that he's the one who destroyed the drugs. We'll tell her that he destroyed the lab to help his investigation. He couldn't get enough evidence against us, so he blew up the whole operation."

"That's the dumbest thing I've ever heard," Jenna said.

Carson was ready to slap her upside the head now, but he humored her. She was still his daughter, after all. "Why's that?"

"Because when the sheriff disappears, don't you think they'll investigate us more? You don't think there's at least one other deputy that knows what's going on?"

"Jenna, Jenna, Jenna. Haven't you learned anything?" Carson said, bringing some snickers from the men. Jenna scowled at them, but then swiveled her head back to Carson, maintaining eye contact. "Lana has become a problem. She's getting in the way of us making real money. If she takes the sheriff and kills him, we can make sure she's the one arrested. But first we need to find out what he knows."

Jenna didn't answer.

"I agree with Jenna. You need to rethink this plan."

Carson swung around. Bobbi. What the hell? How dare she disagree with him in front of the men? It made him look weak.

He held back the urge to go force her mouth shut. Women in the Ray family should know their place. These were the times when he missed his wife. She understood these things.

"There's no rethinking this plan. Wayne Thompson has been a thorn in my side for a long time. He's always wanted to arrest me. This kills two birds with one stone. It gets him out of my hair, and it means Lana will go away. Who here is tired of sharing their profits with foreigners?"

A loud chorus of agreement echoed throughout the bunker.

"That's what I thought," Carson said. "Now, the men and I will make plans. With the help of our insider in the sheriff's department, I can find out when and where the sheriff will be. When he's out alone fishing or riding as he so often does, we'll take him."

"If we cut Lana out, how will we get codeine?" Jenna asked. "We need that to make a good product."

Carson smiled. "I have my sources. I'm not worried about that. We don't need Lana anymore."

Bobbi spoke up. "Jenna's right. We need to be careful about cutting out Lana. She's been good about sharing the profits. She's treated you well."

"Yeah?" Carson asked, feeling his face burn. "I'm tired of not making all the money. I'm tired of always having someone in charge of me. I gave her a hell of a deal when we started. She had the product, but I had Jenna, the best chemist around. I want to go into business for myself."

"Okay," Bobbi said with an edge of frustration in her voice.

"I'd be a better chemist if I could finish my degree," Jenna muttered.

"Why don't you two leave? Get to work. I have things to discuss with the men," Carson said, barely able to contain his anger.

Bobbi shrugged and sauntered out the door, making sure Carson could see her tight behind sashaying in her blinged-out blue jeans.

Maybe he could forgive her for speaking out, but just this once. Next time, he'd have to make sure she knew no one crossed him.

Jenna stomped out, clearly pissed, but he couldn't remember a time when his daughter wasn't pissed.

"Jenna," Carson said. She paused at the door but didn't turn around. "We need more batches ASAP."

She didn't acknowledge him, but he watched and made sure she headed in the direction of the new lab he'd built for her. Then he turned back to the men.

"Now, let's discuss how we can catch ourselves a sheriff."

Chapter Twenty-Five

Wayne haltered Velvet and led the filly to the grooming area. After picking her hooves, he brushed her and then saddled up.

"Ready for your first ride out of the round pen today?" he asked as he stroked her soft copper coat. The day had dawned clear and bright, not a cloud in the sky. He combed his fingers through her mane and the little mare sighed. "You're a good girl. Probably the last young horse I'll have. Let's see how you do on an easy trail ride."

Wayne led the horse outside and put his left foot in the stirrup and swung up. The filly stayed steady and quiet. He gently pressed his legs on her sides and gave a little cluck, and the horse stepped off into a nice walk.

As they found the trail, Wayne couldn't help but think about Maya. His granddaughter was headstrong, stubborn, and feisty—just like him. As his wife, Karen, would tell him, "She's exactly like you, Wayne. You two need to get along because someday I might not be here."

When he'd found out Maya was drunk in a bar rather than at her grandmother's funeral, he was livid. Furious. None of that even covered what he felt. Maybe betrayed and deceived? He'd said things he regretted. Maya had said things he could only hope she'd regret.

The mare shifted underneath him picking her way up the mountainside as if she'd done this for a long time. He stroked her neck and soothed her, encouraging her—something he could rarely do with his granddaughter. It seemed like the only time he did soothe Maya was after her nightmares when she was a little girl. Since she'd grown up, he didn't know what to do with her or how to treat her.

Maybe it was because of Maya's biological mother. Their only child.

Wayne and Karen had raised their daughter with a firm hand, but she'd been wild from the start. Like a young filly who refused to be caught. Zoey ran away from home at sixteen and they had been unable to find her. Wayne had exhausted all his resources within the sheriff's department. He even called on friends in other law enforcement agencies for help, but she had disappeared.

He figured that someday he'd get the phone call every parent dreaded. He had steeled himself for the moment he would have to go identify his only daughter in the morgue. How many times in his job had he watched other families do the same thing? He had forced himself to quit feeling anything about her and ignored Karen's pleas to keep searching.

Then one day, about four years later, Zoey showed up on their doorstep with Maya in tow. Maya had bright auburn hair, large green eyes, freckles across her face and a look that seemed to peer into your soul. Wayne had fallen in love with his granddaughter instantly but was still angry with Zoey for all she'd put them through.

Zoey asked for help. Money. A place to stay.

He thought he should show her some tough love.

So, I turned her away. Karen had been furious. *My stubbornness.*

Zoey stayed in the area and told her mother she'd cleaned herself up because of Maya. She was going to regular NA meetings to stay off heroin. Maya was her inspiration, and she didn't want to lose her. Karen had loved being a grandmother and went to see their daughter and granddaughter almost every day. Wayne sometimes went along, admitting he was pretty enamored with his granddaughter.

Then one night, everything changed. During the night shift, a call came in while he was on duty. It was his daughter's address. The house she lived in was on fire. No one ever knew who made the 911 call.

Wayne had flipped on his lights and driven as fast as he could to the neighborhood where his daughter lived. When he arrived, flames were spilling out of the front windows and Maya was nowhere to be found. Wayne had covered his mouth and rushed in with the firefighters who were yelling at him to let them do their job.

His daughter sat in a kitchen chair. *Dead.* A needle in her arm with the rubber band still wrapped around her bicep. She'd also been shot in the head.

He thought he could hear Maya crying, but it was tough over the fire. Wayne remembered a secret Maya had shared with him—she was the best at hide-and-seek. Her favorite hiding place was in the hall closet where she could get behind jackets and the vacuum to conceal herself. He'd found her in the closet, scooped her up and got her out of there before the entire house went up in flames. The firefighters gave Maya oxygen and wrapped her in a blanket. Wayne couldn't leave her side. She'd grabbed his arm, and then snuggled into him, tears streaming down her face. At that moment he knew, he'd do anything for Maya.

They'd adopted Maya and raised her. Wayne's biggest fear was that Maya would be like her mom—headstrong and independent in a way that would lead to trouble. He suspected that Zoey had been involved in prostitution after she ran away from home. Wayne didn't know that for sure, but with her drug habit and needing money, it was a good possibility. If that had been the case, that might explain why they never knew who Maya's father was… Zoey hadn't put any name on the birth certificate.

They didn't talk with Maya much about her past or the fire, but the nightmares came with a fury. Over time they seemed to go away. As she grew up, Maya always told him she wanted to be just like him and join the military and then be a law enforcement officer. Wayne did his best to talk her out of it, but Maya did what Maya wanted. That was her mother coming out in her…*and maybe a little bit of me too.*

He'd been proud of Maya, but he'd never told her that.

Yesterday, he'd held something back too. The reason he didn't think his wife had killed herself was that the gun ballistics also matched the weapon used in the murder of Maya's mother. They'd never found the weapon that killed Zoey—until Karen's suicide. Wayne had discovered the gun was registered to his wife, but he couldn't believe that his wife had shot their daughter. The case remained open and Wayne kept all the evidence locked up and stored at the sheriff's department. Every lead into Karen and Zoey's deaths was a dead end. Wayne did know one thing for sure, though: he needed to protect Maya.

I can't lose Maya too. She's all I have.

Wayne had lost track of how far he'd ridden. He saw the turn in the trail where one direction would take you to a small lake formed from glaciers, the other way would take you to waterfalls.

Sweat rolled off the neck of the filly and her breathing came in hard puffs. Wayne pulled her up to give her a break. Then he dismounted and started leading her so she could have an easier time. They trekked for about another quarter mile before reaching his destination. Wayne took the water bottle out of the saddle packs and led Velvet over to the stream. She put her lips down to the cool water, taking a drink.

Wayne was pleased with how good the filly was behaving for her first long ride out of the round pen. This one was a gem and with some time and training he was certain she'd be ready for the mounted patrol by next spring. Maybe even next year's Fourth of July parade.

He let her catch her breath, then mounted back up, the leather saddle creaking as he sat down. They turned for home.

The filly picked her way on the trail through rocks and navigated turns with the ease of an experienced horse. Wayne shifted his weight to help her out.

All of a sudden, Velvet hunched her back and threw on the brakes. Her head flew up and her nostrils flared. She turned her head to gawk at whatever was spooking her. The whites of Velvet's eyes showed, and she started backing up.

"Okay, easy, girl," Wayne said.

But the filly continued to get more and more upset. Just when Wayne was thinking about turning her in a circle, he caught movement out of the corner of his eye.

He didn't have time to process it. Velvet reared up and he was caught off balance.

Falling off seemed to happen in slow motion. He remembered seeing the side of his saddle. Then the ground. Then the reins being pulled through his hands. Lying on the ground, he worked to catch his breath. The filly was galloping off toward home, bucking with reins flying and stirrups flapping.

Wayne pushed himself up to a sitting position, trying to suck in air. The fall had knocked the wind out of him. He peered around, trying to see what had spooked Velvet, but didn't see anything obvious. There could be a predator in the area.

He started to push himself to his feet when he felt it—the tingle developed by years in law enforcement. Someone was watching him.

He stood, trying to observe everything, but he missed the person in the bush behind him. The person rushed him. Still dazed by his fall, Wayne couldn't react quick enough.

A hand and cloth covered his mouth.

Then everything went black.

Chapter Twenty-Six

Maya had spent her morning on patrol checking campgrounds to make sure fires were properly put out. She'd covered a lot of territory and was ready to head back to the office for lunch. Juniper rested in the back as Maya went through her mental to-do list.

Up ahead a cloud of dust billowed. She slowed down as she approached the vehicle in front of her. The vehicle was a black truck with a camper top. Excited, she accelerated and pulled up closer, checking a sticky note on the dash with the plate number. Maya had been keeping an eye out for the pickup ever since the funeral incident.

The plates were a match. *Roberta Lind.* Maya's connection to the Ray family.

Maya wanted to pull the vehicle over, but she needed probable cause. The black truck pulled up to a stop sign, and as the driver slowed down, only one rear brake light lit up.

Maya grinned. *Perfect.*

She allowed the driver to make the turn and followed them down the road. Maya radioed dispatch that she was going to pull the vehicle over and then flipped on her lights.

Maya could hear Juniper circling in excitement.

"Sorry, girl, you don't get to do anything fun on duty until we get certified."

Juniper continued to pace. The vehicle pulled off the road onto the shoulder. Maya drove up behind the truck, parking at an angle. She radioed in to dispatch again and received information about the vehicle owner. Roberta Lind had a record for a few misdemeanors, but no outstanding warrants. Of course, Maya couldn't be certain who was driving until she approached the vehicle.

She stepped out of her SUV, and approached the truck, taking in every detail. There was a bumper sticker with the Don't Tread on Me rattlesnake. The truck had some rust over the wheel wells but otherwise seemed to be in good condition. The tire tread was thick and meant for off-roading. Maya peered in the camper window for weapons or anything associated with the drug lab. There wasn't anything obvious.

She touched the back of the vehicle, leaving her fingerprints and DNA. That way if anything happened, she could be connected to the vehicle later for evidence.

She approached close to the vehicle and observed the back seat of the truck, but it was empty. Maya made sure the passenger seat was empty too.

The window rolled down and a small blonde stuck her head out. Her hair was styled with gallons of hairspray. She had bright red nails and lipstick. Makeup coated her face in an attempt to hide wrinkles and crow's-feet. Maya recognized the lady from the bar. She was the same person who helped drag Cody outside.

She thought about the blond hair found at Doug's. Could Doug have been in a relationship with this person and hiding it because of the age difference?

"Problem, Officer?" the lady asked.

Maya stayed close to the vehicle and had herself in the best position possible to see into the vehicle and yet stay safe. "I noticed you had a taillight out."

"Is that a crime?"

"No, ma'am. In fact, I was just letting you know so that you can go get it fixed," Maya said, scanning the inside of the vehicle. The truck was clean. There was nothing that could give her probable cause to search the vehicle, but she wanted more information on this person. "I'll just need your license, insurance and registration."

The lady rolled her eyes and then reached over to the glove box. Maya watched her open it up and start rooting around. A black gun handle appeared under a stack of papers and maps. If Roberta was driving the truck at Doug's funeral, then she could be the one who threatened Maya and Juniper.

Maya put her hand on her Glock. "Stop what you're doing. Show me your hands."

"What?"

"Show me your hands. I need you to step out of the vehicle."

"What? Why?"

Maya now had her gun out of the holster. She could hear Juniper barking behind her. "I need you to step out of the vehicle. Take both hands, put them out the window and then open the door."

"Okay, okay. You're making a huge mistake," the lady said, following instructions.

"No, I'm not. Now please, step out of the vehicle."

Black leather cowboy boots decorated with silver and bling swung out. Maya was a little bit surprised. If this lady was involved with the Rays, she didn't look like the usual type. She appeared to be trying to fit in by wearing the western style of clothing that the store downtown sold to tourists.

Maya handcuffed her. She needed to run the gun through dispatch. "I'm going to have you sit in the back of my vehicle until I get more information on the gun and on you," she said.

The lady shrugged and continued to comply. "I don't know anything about that gun."

"I still need to run the number."

Maya put her in the back and closed the door. Juniper whined and continued to turn circles. Maya would have loved to have Juniper search the vehicle, but that couldn't happen until they passed certification. However, the gun gave her an opening to look through the truck until dispatch got back to her.

Maya radioed in the information and then searched more of the glove box. There was nothing more than the gun and paperwork. Some old dirty napkins from the local burger joint were on the floor, but nothing that seemed to connect this vehicle with Doug's death or running drugs.

"FS 28," Maya heard from dispatch.

"This is FS 28."

"The gun you asked us about is stolen."

"Okay," Maya said. She radioed that she would be arresting the person and then shut the door to the truck. She hadn't found anything out of the ordinary in the vehicle, but sometimes on the drive to jail people talked. Maya couldn't question her, but she could listen.

Chapter Twenty-Seven

Maya arrived at the sheriff's office, which also housed a small jail. Inmates would wait there until they could get a hearing with a judge that came up once a week. Other than telling Maya to call her "Bobbi," Roberta Lind hadn't said a word the entire drive. Maya was disappointed.

She opened the back door for Bobbi and escorted her to the back of the building. She handed her over to the jail deputy on duty. Josh was waiting for Maya. "She had a stolen gun in her truck. It was the truck, Josh."

"Did you find anything that ties her to the drug lab?"

"No." Maya shook her head, frustrated. "But maybe we can hold her on the gun charge and get some information from her. See what she knows. Let's call my grandfather and see what he wants to do. The sheriff's office can help with this."

Concern crossed Josh's face. Maya tilted her head to the side, sizing up his expression.

"What's wrong?" she asked.

"Sit down," Josh said.

"I don't want to."

"Please?"

Maya wanted to resist. People only asked you to sit

when something bad happened. She plopped down in the hard-plastic chair. "There, are you happy? Now what's wrong?"

"We can't reach your grandfather."

"It's his day off. He might be out hiking or fishing. Or riding..."

"Maya." Josh cut her off.

"What?"

"Just shut up and let me talk for a minute. We sent some deputies out to your grandfather's house. Even on a day off, he always keeps a cell phone or radio on him in case we need him."

"True," Maya said.

"When they got there, they found his young horse in the barn with no rider. The mare was spooked and upset. The deputies started looking for your grandfather right away, but they haven't been able to find him."

Maya leaned forward in the chair, holding her head in her hands. How often had she been so mad at her grandfather? Why couldn't she have forgiven him? Or better yet, apologized?

Then a thought hit her. "Tell them to stop looking."

"What?"

"Stop looking. Set up a perimeter. I'll take Juniper out and we'll track."

Josh didn't answer, but instead immediately went to his radio and made the call to the deputies. After he got off the radio, he said, "Let's go."

Maya was already out the door in front of him. She hoped the scent trail was still hot.

Bobbi made a phone call and less than an hour later, she was released. She stomped out of the jail and let the doors slam behind her. This was not how today was supposed to go. She was going to kill Cody. The stolen gun was probably in the truck courtesy of that stupid kid.

She was lucky the nosy officer hadn't pulled the damn K-9 out and run the vehicle. The dog probably would have alerted on the load of codeine hidden in the truck's secret compartment. They needed the codeine to make a new batch of Krok as soon as possible. Lana wasn't going to wait much longer.

Bobbi had to figure out how to get back to her truck. She could just strangle that redheaded Forest Service officer. What the hell was she thinking? Wasn't she supposed to be ticketing people for not putting out campfires and crap like that?

Damn it. Carson was going to be furious that she was this late. She didn't worry about the cargo. It was safe, but she'd have to come up with an explanation.

Bobbi marched down the street. It wasn't like she could call a taxi or an Uber out here. Small mountain towns without ski resorts didn't have amenities like that.

Down at the local hardware store, Bobbi's luck changed. She spotted a rancher who pastured cattle near her truck's location. She stopped for a minute and used her fingers to comb her hair down and then undid the top couple buttons of her shirt, so a glimpse of cleavage showed. She sashayed her way over to the rancher's truck. What was his name? She didn't need to worry, though, because the rancher paused from loading T-posts and other fencing materials.

"Can I help you?" he asked.

"Oh, if you don't mind, I do have a favor to ask." Bobbi plastered on her sweet smile.

"Shoot. What is it?"

"I need a ride to my truck. Would you mind taking me? I think it's parked near your ranch."

"My ranch is close to five thousand acres. Which part are you parked near?"

Bobbi hadn't expected this. She always forgot about the size of many Colorado ranches—something she wasn't used to being from the east coast. "The part that borders the national forest."

"Honey, that's half my ranch, but we've narrowed it down at least."

Bobbi sighed. When she'd secretly meet up with Doug, he'd always given her good directions. She'd learned some of the back roads, but she didn't know them like the locals.

Bobbi opened her purse, pulling out fifty dollars in cash. "Look, I'll pay you for your gas and time. I don't know the area well enough to tell you exact roads, but I can tell you how to get there."

The rancher laughed and shook his head. A toothpick rolled around in his mouth. Bobbi wished she had undone another button on her shirt, but there was no need as he opened up the driver side door and, nodding toward the passenger door, said, "Hop in. The door's unlocked."

Chapter Twenty-Eight

A gust of wind billowed through the trees and threatened to knock off Carson's black cowboy hat. He slammed his hand down on the hat, waiting until the wind died down. He was getting tired of this godforsaken place. Sometimes he thought about selling off everything and leaving.

He pushed that thought aside and went back to the main issue—where the hell was Bobbi? Carson kicked a stone with the toe of his boot. She'd been getting pretty uppity lately and now she was keeping him waiting. Could she be selling their stuff? She wouldn't do that, would she?

Jenna didn't trust Bobbi, and Carson hated to admit it, but his daughter had excellent intuition. She could spot problem people from a mile away. He stared out over the horizon. Jenna probably learned the hard way from having him as a father, but hell, didn't every parent mess up their kid? Wasn't that what they were supposed to do?

He knew she wanted to get back to college and at some point, he was going to have to let her go, but for now she needed to stay here, help out, and give something back to this family. Sure, she had come home and nursed her mother when she was dying of cancer, but Jenna owed him. He was her father, after all, and had done nothing but make sacrifices for her.

A billow of dust kicked up on one of the roads out to the east. Carson squinted and could see it was Bobbi's truck. His watch said 1:15. Over two hours late. What the hell had Bobbi been doing? All the codeine better be in that truck.

Carson waited for her to make her way up the dirt road. She pulled up next to him and hopped out. Her shirt was unbuttoned to the point he could see her black-lace bra and some cleavage. He didn't mind that, but Carson didn't like the thought of another man being able to see his property.

"Where were you?" he asked.

"Sorry I was late. Had a flat tire."

"Did you have to unbutton your shirt to change the tire?"

Bobbi's face turned red and she quickly started to button the shirt back up. "Oops. I got hot changing the tire."

"Is everything in the truck? You get everything okay?"

"Yes," Bobbi said. "The delivery was right on time. Other than the flat tire, everything went fine."

"Which one?"

"Which one what?"

"Which tire went flat?" Carson asked. "I don't see any tires that have been changed."

A glimpse of concern crossed Bobbi's face. *Is she lying?*

"I already had it patched. Put the original tire back on," Bobbi said.

Carson sauntered over to the truck. He tuned the

radio to a certain station, put the pickup in neutral, making sure the parking brake was on, and cocked the steering wheel to the right. The hidden compartment with the codeine popped open. Bobbi fidgeted from one foot to the other.

"You going to help me?" Carson asked. What was wrong with her? She was lying and nervous, but why?

"Yeah." Bobbi strode over to the truck and started helping Carson unload the drugs.

They worked in silence taking the codeine packages up to the new drug lab and placing the drugs in a gun safe. After they finished their work, Carson texted Jenna that she could start making the new batch anytime.

He closed the secret compartment on the truck. Bobbi's silence bothered him. He would find out more about what she was doing.

If she was lying to him, he'd make her regret it.

Chapter Twenty-Nine

Arriving at her grandfather's, Maya was relieved and happy to see Deputy Sam King. Maya hadn't seen him since the night Doug died. As a good family friend, Sam would do everything he could to help her and Pops. She flew out of the car and ran up to him.

Sam gave her a big bear hug. "We'll find him, Maya. I promise."

"Thanks, Sam. Hopefully Juniper will help us."

"I heard you were working K-9. Good for you."

"Is Velvet okay?"

"I think so, but you know me, I'm not much of a horse person. If you check her over, I can get her put up. That way you and your wonder dog can start searching for your grandfather."

Maya examined Velvet. There were no cuts, and the little mare didn't appear hurt. Velvet rolled her eyes around, exposing some white. At times she reached out with a front leg and pawed the air, displaying unease.

"I think she's fine, just needs to calm down," Maya said.

"Good. I'll be back to help when I'm done."

Josh came over to Maya as Sam led Velvet away. "The deputies have stopped searching for now. I told them we would have Juniper do a track. They've set up a perimeter and will show you where they stopped and hopefully where the scent won't be contaminated by them. You think Juniper is ready for this?"

"Yes." Maya didn't care if Juniper was ready or not. She had to find her grandfather and Juniper was their best chance of doing that.

Sam came back from putting Velvet in her stall and joined Maya and Josh. "You two have only done short tracks, right?" Josh asked.

Maya didn't want to answer. She knew as well as Josh that she needed more time to bond and form a working relationship with Juniper. Creating a solid partnership didn't happen overnight. "You're right, we've only done short tracks for practice. Nothing this intense, but Juniper's ready. We can do it."

"Okay," Josh said. "Let's go for it then."

"Now hold on," Sam said, turning to Maya. "You're like a daughter to me, and I'd do anything to help you and your grandfather, but if you don't think your dog is ready for a track, then let's not waste valuable time and resources."

Maya hesitated. *I can do this. I can trust my dog.*

Before she could answer, Josh spoke up. "Maya and Juniper are a solid team. If anyone can find Sheriff Thompson, it's them. Let's quit talking about this and get going."

"Thanks." Maya shot a grateful smile to Josh. *It helps having someone believe in me.* "I'll be right back."

She sprinted toward her grandfather's house and up the front steps. She needed something that belonged to her grandfather so she could give Juniper a scent article to track. That would help in case the deputies on scene had contaminated the scent from Pops.

Maya rushed through the kitchen. A cup of coffee sat on the table, cold from this morning. Next to it was Pops's notebook. The one all law enforcement keep on them to take notes during their shift. It was open to a page titled *Doug*. The date was a couple weeks before the explosion. Pops had probably been reading it while he ate breakfast. Maya knew that he often did that when he worked a case. Then he'd let his mind think about things while he rode. She grabbed the notebook and shoved it in her pocket to look at later.

She continued to her grandfather's bedroom and stopped short. The familiar scent of Pops's cologne wafted through the room. As a kid she always loved snuggling with Pops as he read her a story.

Nothing can happen to you, Pops. I can't lose you too.

She strode over to his closet and pushed back the door. The shirts hung straight and orderly. Maya saw a flannel shirt she'd bought online last Christmas and had sent to him since she was still deployed at the time. She'd looked forward to celebrating with him in person this year. *When I find him, I will tell him how much I love him. No more fighting.*

Next to the closet was the laundry basket. Maya saw a shirt in the pile that would have a strong scent. She put on gloves and bagged it up in a durable plastic Ziploc bag so she wouldn't get her scent on the shirt.

She ran back outside to her patrol vehicle and found Juniper's tracking harness and the thirty-foot-long leather lead. The dog started turning circles in the back seat.

"Settle, settle," Maya said, letting Juniper out of the

car. Juniper danced around, giving Maya quick licks on the hand. "You can't waste all your energy right now. You have a big task ahead of you. I need you to find Pops. You have to do this for me, okay?"

Maya put the harness on her and gave Juniper a chance to get a drink. Juniper lapped the water up and stared at Maya, intense eyes waiting for her command.

Josh came up and rested a hand on her shoulder, giving it a squeeze. "You ready?"

"Let's go up to the area where they stopped looking, and I'll cast Juniper out and see if she can pick up the scent," Maya said, thinking that location would be the best place to start casting or directing Juniper away from her so that the dog could get her nose in different areas and catch Pops's odor. Maya needed to make sure they weren't near the house or barn because Pops's scent would be everywhere there and could confuse Juniper. Going up the trail and starting where the deputies had stopped searching seemed the best place to start. "Hopefully, his odor is still hot."

Maya, Josh, and Juniper hiked up to where her grandfather's scent would be the freshest. Maya took a deep breath. This track was important. Would Juniper be up for this? More importantly, was *she* up for this?

Maya's hands shook and she closed her eyes, willing her heart rate to drop. Then she held out the bag with her grandfather's shirt to Juniper and said, "Let's find him, Juniper. Track. Track."

Juniper heard the change in Maya's voice and put her nose in the bag. She turned and air scented, catching the breeze, then sniffed the ground, working back and forth. Maya noticed that on the trail there were fresh hoofprints—some from Velvet heading out on the trail and more where the little mare had galloped back home.

Juniper suddenly sprang forward, almost pulling Maya off her feet. She struggled to catch up and get in rhythm with Juniper. The dog continued up the trail, tail poking straight up in the air, pausing for a split second and then continuing. The only sound was of Juniper sucking air in and out.

They worked together, finding a sync, and the old feeling of the dance came back to Maya. Reading each other, allowing the dog to work. Trusting her dog. Trusting herself.

They worked their way up the trail; the mountain air seemed still and hushed. Josh followed but stayed back far enough so he wouldn't distract the dog. Juniper flushed a gray squirrel out of a bush. The squirrel ran up the tree and chattered in an indignant manner. For a second Juniper eyed the squirrel, but then the dog put her nose back to the ground, continuing her work.

About twenty feet ahead, Maya could see some deputies at the split in the trail. Juniper didn't seem to mind them or get distracted, which made Maya happy. *She's an excellent dog.* She didn't want to admit it, but having a K-9 partner felt good again.

Juniper paused, sniffed around in a circle, and then whined.

"What's wrong with her?" one of the deputies asked.

"Nothing is wrong with her. You walked so much here you messed up the scent. She's having a hard time trailing."

"Let's give Juniper a break, get her some water and then see if she can pick the trail up again," Josh said.

Maya agreed that was a good idea. She pulled a portable water bowl off her duty belt and poured in some water from her backpack. Juniper happily lapped it up and, tongue hanging out of the side of her mouth, she wagged her tail.

"Ready to go again?" Maya asked her. Juniper started running a small circle, indicating she was ready to go back to work.

Maya moved to a new location, the trailhead that led to the waterfalls. She knew her grandfather loved that location, and there was a good chance that's where he would have been going. Maya started casting the dog out again to pick up the trail of her grandfather. "Okay. Track, girl. Let's find him."

Juniper put her nose to the ground sucking in air, tension traveling up the leash, hesitating, sniffing until her body stiffened, and then she shot away from the waterfall. This time Maya was a little more prepared and did less of a Superman impersonation.

Juniper pulled Maya through brush and over logs. She could hear Josh huffing and puffing behind her.

Picking her way through the forest, Juniper continued searching. They reached another trail that appeared to have been made by deer or elk. Juniper had her nose on the ground, in the bushes and back up in the air. Her nose twitched and Maya watched the dog, proud of how well she was doing with just a little bit of work after her injuries.

They came to an old Forest Service logging road that hadn't been used in years. Juniper worked a scent cone, which meant she was trying to pinpoint where she should alert. Maya knew odor would be coming off something hidden and Juniper would work that scent back and forth until she could determine the exact location.

Maya stayed patient and let her dog work. After a few seconds, Juniper sat and let out a small whine, asking for her toy while staring intently at the bushes to the side of the road.

"Good girl," Maya said, scratching her ears and rubbing around her neck.

"What does that mean?" Josh asked.

"It's her alert."

Maya praised Juniper and then rooted around in the bushes. The sun glinted off something small. Maya put on gloves and pulled out the shiny object. Her hand closed around the cold metal.

"What is it?" Josh asked.

Maya gave Juniper her toy, praising her and rewarding the dog, but fighting back tears at the same time. "It's Pops's St. Michael medal. Nana gave it to him. To protect him. Good girl, Juniper."

Maya shut down her emotions. *I have to stay on track, like Juniper. Stay focused.*

"You think she can keep tracking?"

"I don't know how much more she has in her," Maya said, desperately wanting the dog to track more, but knowing she'd already asked a lot. "Let me see if she'll do a little bit more."

Juniper wagged her tail and Maya used a higher-pitched voice to excite Juniper. She took Juniper past the bush where she'd alerted on the medal and started casting her out to see if she could find her grandfather's scent trail again. Juniper air scented, which meant she might have lost the scent on the ground. Maya worked her in the area and then Juniper took off again, nose on the ground, tail pricked up in the air. She trotted along for only a few more feet to a road and then stopped and started whining.

"Trail is cold here," Maya said. She reached down and praised Juniper. Her dog had worked well. *Where are you, Pops? How could you have just disappeared?*

"This gives us a better idea though of where your grandfather went," Josh said. "Looks like fresh tire tracks, so maybe he fell off and then caught a ride home from someone."

"This is an off-road Jeep trail," Maya said. "There's not a lot of traffic. I don't like it."

"I don't either," Josh said. "We're back on Forest Service land. Where does this road go?"

"It's an old logging road that really doesn't go anywhere except a few camping spots, but we're close to the Ray Ranch," Maya said.

"Okay, we'll check in with the local hospital and make sure Wayne didn't hitch a ride to the hospital."

"He would go check on his horse first," Maya said.

Josh nodded and got on the radio, telling the other deputies to go check the sheriff's ranch again.

"I think he was taken," Maya said.

"But why?" Josh asked.

"Because the other night at the bar, Cody Ray told me my grandfather and I should watch out. He was going to get us. I brushed it off, but maybe he wasn't kidding. I don't know. Something about all this seems off."

"Then I'll get our crime scene tech up here to take a cast of the tire treads. I'll see if I can get a search warrant for Cody Ray's vehicle. Maybe the tracks will be a match. Don't worry, we'll find him." Josh stepped closer to Maya and she leaned into him, hearing his heartbeat and feeling the strength of his arms as he wrapped them around her.

What am I doing? This is not the time to get close to someone.

Maya extracted herself from Josh's arms and went back to praising Juniper. She ran her fingers through Juniper's coat, working to get herself together.

"He'll be okay," Josh said.

Maya wished she could believe him.

Chapter Thirty

Wayne woke up to his head pounding and darkness surrounding him. He was blindfolded. His shoulders ached. His hips ached. It didn't help that he was tied up with his arms behind his back. Everything hurt from falling off Velvet.

Velvet. What had happened to her? She'd probably headed back to the barn and was okay. He hoped. Who had spooked her and then taken him? And why? *Where the hell am I?*

Wayne opened and closed his fingers, trying to loosen the knots on the rope around his wrists, but whoever tied him up did a damn fine job.

Good thing he always carried a small pocketknife in his front jeans pocket. Squirming around, Wayne worked to get his hands off to the right and into the pocket, hoping no one had taken the knife. He flopped around on the cold wooden floor that smelled of mouse urine and dust. He had to be in some old cabin or maybe a barn.

His fingers found the knife, but it clattered onto the floor.

"Shit," he muttered.

He scooted over to the knife and grasped it in his fingers as footsteps approached. Wayne palmed the knife, trying to push it up a little bit into his sleeve. The door creaked open. He stayed still.

"You awake?"

A female voice. He thought he should recognize it, but he couldn't quite place it. His throbbing head didn't help. Wayne didn't answer.

"I asked, are you awake?"

A boot came up and nudged him. Wayne stayed quiet.

"I know you're pretending to be sleeping, but I heard you. And it's pretty obvious you've moved."

The person crossed the room. "I heard you move or drop something. Don't get any ideas, Sheriff. You might live through this if you cooperate and stay useful."

There was a snicker, the sound of footsteps leaving and the door closing. Wayne let out his breath. He started mentally going through his cases, past and present. Who would take him and why? How would he be useful as a hostage? If he could answer these questions, he might be able to negotiate his way out of this situation.

His head pounded and he lay back down on the floor, this time hearing a critter scurry away. Mouse? Maybe a pack rat? The presence of the rodents probably meant this place wasn't occupied much. There was a good chance he was in a remote location, making it harder to find him.

He needed to focus on escaping. First he had to untie and free himself. Then he could figure out how to break out. Wayne let the knife slide back out of his shirt into his palm. The fun would be getting the knife open. He fumbled around, cussing under his breath until he felt

what he thought was the correct attachment. Pulling
and working it with his fingers, he flipped open the
piece, only to run his fingers over it and realize it was
the bottle opener. Why the hell did they have that on
the knife? Okay, maybe he had used it to open a few
beer bottles over the years, but right now that was not
what he needed.

Sweat started pouring down his face. His fingers
grazed the knife edge.

Dull.

Totally, completely dull. Damn it. Hadn't he always
lectured Maya about keeping blades sharp? Maybe he
should take some of his own advice.

His throat tightened at the thought of Maya. If anything happened to him, she'd be all alone. If he got
out of this alive, the first thing he'd tell her was how
proud he was of her. Why had he never said that? He
knew she'd been through tough battles, and yet he'd
been so furious with her that he'd quit saying the important things.

He didn't know why she'd come home after all the
things he'd said. Or why she'd shown up the other day
and been so good to him. Doug had tried to help mend
their relationship, but Wayne had pushed him away too.

Doug had been there for Maya when no one else had.
If only he'd been there for Doug like he should have.
Based on what Doug had confided to Wayne, the explosion had to be tied to the Rays, but he had found no
way to prove it.

Damn it, he needed to get out of here, if for no other
reason than to say the things he should have.

Wayne sawed at the ropes, the dull blade barely making a dent. He concentrated and finally felt the blade

slide through the first layer. Footsteps trudged outside the door, and Wayne paused, but they continued past.

He continued sawing, and after what felt like an eternity, the ropes released. He stretched, pins and needles running down his arms into his shoulders. He pulled off the blindfold and took in his surroundings. A dark room with log walls.

As his eyes adjusted, he realized the windows were boarded shut. That would make an escape route harder. He untied his ankles and stood. Stiff and sore, he ambled around, analyzing the cabin. His best bet out of here was picking the lock, but he didn't know what was on the other side.

Maybe he could take the boards off and pry open a window. How much noise would that make?

Wayne went to work, but the boards were stuck. He took his pocketknife and worked on scraping them to see if he could wiggle them loose.

He was working so hard he didn't hear the footsteps behind him until a voice said, "I thought you were awake."

He turned around, seeing his captor, but before he could say anything, he was shot with a taser. Electricity coursed through his body, dropping him to the floor.

He felt the pinprick of a needle and a rag over his mouth. His captor tied him back up, and before he blacked out, he heard the words, "Nighty night, Sheriff."

Chapter Thirty-One

Maya sat in her office flipping through the notes from Pops. Juniper, tired from trailing, sat on her dog bed, head on her paws, watching her.

Going through each page, Maya hoped she would find something that would indicate his kidnapper. Apparently, Doug had visited her grandfather about a week before the explosion. In her grandfather's writing, the notes read:

Bribes for past year; working with traffickers.
Drug production.
Informant in sheriff's office providing law enforcement information to suspects.
On patrol elsewhere when drugs were trafficked.
Verified by CAD.

All these notes did was confirm that Doug really was involved somehow, including the CAD, or computer-aided dispatch log. On the dates mentioned to move the drugs, Pops had verified the dispatch report showed Doug was always on patrol on the opposite side of the forest. He was deliberately staying out of the area so the drugs could be moved.

Maya wanted to punch something, but that wouldn't help, and she'd have to explain a hole in the wall to Todd. She stood up and started pacing. If only Pops had written down "the Rays" as the main suspects in his notes. That would make it easier to get a warrant. Right now, they didn't have anything concrete, just lots of circumstantial evidence.

And who could be the informant in the sheriff's office? There weren't that many deputies, and most of them had been around a long time. The only outsider was Josh, but he didn't seem like the type, and Pops had trusted him enough to promote him. *He's easy to talk to and has helped me out on this investigation. Of course, how well do I really know him? Maybe he's helping out for a reason.*

It appeared the Rays were smart about who they put on their payroll. In her mind there was no such thing as a coincidence. She wouldn't put it past Cody Ray to do something stupid like trafficking drugs or kidnapping the sheriff, but Maya also knew it was a long shot that a judge would give them a search warrant. Josh was right—there was no evidence other than a K-9 who wasn't even certified with her handler yet, tracking to a road that ran near the Ray Ranch. The fact that Josh would even ask a judge meant a lot to Maya.

A knock at the door made Juniper lift her head and give a low growl. Maya saw it was Josh and let him in. Juniper leaped off her bed, tail wagging as she pranced around.

Josh leaned down and petted Juniper, scratching her behind the ears. Juniper let out a low groan of happiness.

"Good grief," Maya said. "She is such a flirt."

"I told you, girls like me."

I'm beginning to see why girls like you. Seeing Josh glance at her, Maya blushed and then composed herself. "Yeah, yeah. What did the judge say?" She knew the answer as soon as Josh's smile disappeared and disappointment crossed his face.

"You knew it was a long shot," he said. "And the judge denied it. We need more evidence."

"I still think the Rays are behind this. And look at these notes." Maya handed Josh the notebook. She wanted to see his reaction to the note about the informant. She studied his expression as he read through the bullet points. His face remained neutral. She'd hate to play poker with him.

Maya couldn't stand the silence anymore. "What do you think? Don't you think it's the Rays trafficking drugs? You could call the judge again."

"I think these notes point to Doug giving your grandfather information, but nothing in here says it was the Rays. We still need more evidence."

"What about a deputy giving information to the suspects? Any idea who that would be?"

Maya watched for a reaction again, but Josh only shrugged. "No idea."

"Basic police work then. We need to do surveillance. We need to catch them in the act of loading and transporting drugs, or maybe we'll even see them holding Pops." Maya started to pace around her office again. Juniper followed her.

"That would be good, but from where? It's not like we can go park a car on the street and watch them."

"No, but we can sit on a mountainside," Maya said. She went over to her map of the national forest that hung on the wall behind her desk. "The Ray Ranch sits right here, but we can sit up on this mountainside, which is Forest Service land, and watch them from there. Nothing illegal and there's enough tree cover here that we should be able to hide pretty well."

"Works for me," Josh said.

"I know you're a city slicker from Chicago—think you can handle sitting out in the wilderness?"

"I guess we'll see," Josh said with a grin. "I'll try not to whine too much."

"Damn straight," Maya said. "Let's get our gear and go."

An hour later, Maya, Josh, and Juniper settled down onto the hillside, taking cover behind a thicket of evergreen trees. Even though the afternoon had warmed up, the shade under the trees remained cool. Maya put on her green Forest Service jacket, glad she could blend in with the woods. Josh had put on his dark blue sheriff's windbreaker. They were a good distance away from the ranch, but the Rays were experienced hunters and ranchers. They would notice the surveillance if they weren't careful.

Maya and Josh sat next to each other until Juniper shoved her way in between them. Maya gave Juniper a scratch on the head and Juniper gave her a lick on the hand.

"Down," Maya said.

Juniper gave a heavy sigh and slowly lay down, one paw creeping after the other. She stared at Maya with a look that seemed to be asking if she was satisfied.

Maya pulled a spotting scope out of her backpack. "Let's see what they're up to."

Josh had his binoculars and was already fixated on the ranch. "There seems to be a lot of activity, but no sign of your grandfather."

"I can see Cody and Carson. There's Roberta Lind, or Bobbi as she told us to call her. When did she get out?"

"About an hour after you brought her in."

"Seriously? How?"

"I guess she had a good lawyer."

"Go figure," Maya said. "I wouldn't have expected that. Maybe drug money means a good attorney on the payroll."

Josh grunted in agreement. Maya watched as Bobbi stomped over to Carson. She put her hands on her hips and started yelling. Carson stepped toward her and slapped her hard across the face.

"What a jerk," Josh said.

"I hate to say it, but no surprise there. Rumor always was that Carson slapped his wife around, but she just never reported it."

Bobbi stepped back. Even through the scope Maya could tell from Bobbi's body language that she was angry.

"Wish we could hear what they're saying and know what caused that," Josh said.

"No kidding. Maybe if we offer to help her and keep her safe, she'll talk to us."

"You never know."

"Domestic violence is so tough. I really feel for the women in this situation because it's a vicious cycle and so hard to leave, but maybe we can assist her in some way."

Maya scanned around the area, but still didn't see

any sign of her grandfather. She put the scope down for a second and rubbed her eyes.

Josh, continuing to look through his binoculars, said, "Don't worry, we'll find him. This is just the start of our lead and we've only been here a few minutes. You didn't think they would walk him out when we arrived, did you?"

"I was kind of hoping that would happen," Maya said.

"Surveillance takes patience and a lot of time."

"I know. I just don't have either. I feel like Pops's time is limited."

"Look over there," Josh said.

Maya knew he was avoiding her last statement. She peered through the scope at the location Josh was pointing out. A blue SUV was coming up the Ray Ranch drive. She zeroed in on the plates and saw they were red fleet plates, which in Colorado most likely meant they were rental car plates. She wrote down the number to run through the system. If she could find out which rental car company it belonged to, then she could possibly get the name of the person driving the car.

"You ever see that vehicle around town?" Maya asked.

"No, but it's not like I memorize every vehicle I see."

"I know, but Pinecone Junction doesn't have a lot of new rental cars, especially fancy SUVs."

"True, but I can't be suspicious just because someone rented a really nice car."

"Sure you can," Maya said. "And now that they're coming down the driveway of the Rays, we can be even more suspicious."

Josh laughed. "I see you learned Cop 101 in the military."

"It's the truth. The Rays are trouble. You know it. I know it. But no one has been able to prove it."

"I agree," Josh said.

Maya stared back through her scope. The blue vehicle parked near the Rays' renovated outbuilding. She hadn't been near the Ray Ranch in years, but she knew at one point, it needed many repairs and the Rays didn't have the money for the upkeep. Now it appeared to have been updated. The house and outbuildings all had fresh coats of paint. All the fencing was new, but there were very few cattle in the pens. The place appeared neat, tidy, and well-maintained. Perhaps running drugs had helped remedy that issue.

The driver's door opened and a tall blonde woman with no curves stepped out. She wore tight leather pants, high heels, and a white blouse.

"Who do you think that is?" Maya asked.

"No idea. I've never seen her around."

The lady approached Carson and shook hands. Bobbi stayed back, still rubbing her cheek where Carson had hit her. The black truck that Bobbi had been driving when Maya pulled her over was parked near the outbuilding.

Jenna came out of the building and spoke with her father and the stranger. Then she went back inside. A few minutes later she and Cody came out and drove the truck around to the back of the building, out of Maya's sight.

"What do you think they're doing?" Maya asked.

"I don't know."

"Damn, that doesn't help our case."

"Well, maybe not for finding your grandfather, but we need to find out more about this lady," Josh said.

Yet another blonde. Maya continued peering through her scope. *Could Doug have been involved with either Bobbi or this visitor? Maybe a love triangle, and Carson found out that Bobbi was seeing Doug and that's why he was killed? And then there's Jenna. She's also blonde.*

"You look like you're thinking about something. What is it?" Josh asked.

"How do you know that I'm thinking about something?"

"Basic body language. Spit it out."

"Doug was in a relationship, but I don't know with who. There were blond hairs at his house. I'm wondering if he could have been seeing Bobbi and Carson got jealous, and that's why Doug was killed. Maybe it has nothing to do with the drug trafficking."

"It's a possibility. How well did you know Doug?"

"We grew up together and I thought of him as my best friend, that we could tell each other anything. But I guess I was wrong," Maya said. "The more I learn about him, the less I think he considered me a friend he could confide in. I've realized I didn't really know him."

"I guess we all have our secrets. Doesn't mean he didn't love you or consider you a good friend."

"Thanks… Can I ask you a question?"

"As long as I don't have to reveal any of my secrets," Josh laughed.

Maya shook her head. "No secrets. I was just wondering, why did you become a cop? What made you want to do this job?"

Josh continued peering through his binoculars as he

answered, "I always played cops and robbers as a kid, and liked to antagonize my sister by handcuffing her stuffed animals. I wanted to keep doing that."

Maya giggled and nudged his shoulder with her elbow. "No, seriously. Why?"

"I wanted to help people. I wanted to help keep communities safe. I thought I could do that by becoming a cop...and I could still antagonize my sister," Josh said, with a laugh.

Maya's heart beat faster. She'd never noticed the dimple on his right cheek when he smiled. *I need to stop this. I should be careful. He could be the informant.*

Maya reached down and petted Juniper, avoiding eye contact. A few seconds later, feeling Josh's gaze on her, she looked back up.

"How about you, why do you want to do this job?" Josh asked.

"Because of Pops. I wanted to be like him. I loved going with him to work when I was a kid. I always knew I wanted to do something with law enforcement, and when the Marine recruiter came to our school and I found out I could join, become an MP and work a dog, I was all in. I loved the job, for the most part, except for losing my dog."

"What happened, if it's okay to ask?"

Maya shrugged. "I screwed up. That's all that you need to know."

"I doubt you screwed up," Josh said.

He reached over and tucked a loose piece of hair behind Maya's ear. His touch was tender. He reached down and picked up Maya's hand, letting his thumb graze across her fingers. Maya's stomach started to flip-flop in response. *Why does he make me feel this way? I don't know if I'm ready for this. It's easier to not let myself feel anything.*

She went to pull her hand away, but Josh held on. "You're strong and smart, Maya. You're a great K-9 handler. No one else could have bonded with Juniper the way you have. Don't doubt yourself."

"Thanks," Maya said. She liked having someone who believed in her. It made her feel like she could come back from her trauma. That maybe someday she could move forward.

Josh let go of her hand, but he leaned in closer. Maya found herself doing the same.

He gently touched Maya's cheek. She flushed at his caress. She hesitated for a second, but then Josh pulled her closer and she met his lips with hers.

The kiss started out slow and tender. Then Maya found herself tightening her arms around Josh, pulling him closer, wanting and needing him more than she realized. He made her feel safe and secure. Heat rose through her chest.

Josh responded by tightening his arms around Maya. His binoculars dropped out of his hand. Juniper, stuck between the two of them, whined indignantly and scooted back. Maya pulled away, her lips still tingling and her face flushed red.

"Is this how you do surveillance in Chicago?" she asked.

Josh grinned. "Nope. I think this might just be a Colorado thing."

The breeze changed direction and Juniper stuck her nose up in the air. She took in a couple deep breaths and then whined. Maya, glad for a distraction, studied Juniper's body language.

"I bet there are drugs down there," Maya said, making sure she had a good hold of Juniper's leash. "You stay, girl."

"Maybe that's what they're loading into their truck."

"I wish we could see better."

"Me too," Josh said.

She glanced over and saw that Josh wasn't looking through the binoculars, but instead straight at her. "Helps to do surveillance if you actually look through those."

"Good point." He went back to watching the activity below. Maya picked up her spotting scope.

Carson kicked a rock with the point of his boot and spat some tobacco on the ground. Then he stared back at Lana.

"You're early," he said.

"I like to be on time."

"You're not on time, you're early, and I don't like surprises."

A slow smile that seemed more like a grimace crept across Lana's face. She squinted as the sun shone in her eyes. "I gave you a lot of codeine. I needed to make sure it was being used properly and nothing was taken for personal use."

"I told you, that problem was taken care of." Carson glanced over at Cody and then regretted it after seeing Lana follow his gaze. He didn't need Lana taking things into her own hands right now.

Jenna stepped forward and said, "Dad, this batch is done. We can deliver it now."

Carson nodded and said, "Well, you heard her. You want it now? We can load it into your car."

"I do want it now." Lana's eyes narrowed. "But not in my rental car. You think I'm that stupid? I don't need your local sheriff bothering me. Speaking of your sheriff, I was never able to talk with him like you promised. You don't keep good promises, so maybe I should quit working with you."

"The sheriff is out of town." Carson lied because so far, his men hadn't been able to find him, but that wasn't something he wanted to let her know. He needed to keep her away from the sheriff. According to his insider, Sheriff Thompson had disappeared while out riding his horse. No one seemed to know where he went, but Carson was determined to find him first. He was irritated that his men hadn't done such a simple job. "We'll make sure you can have your meeting with him. And if you don't work with us, you'll lose your access to the national forest."

Carson knew that probably the only reason Lana had agreed to be in business with him was because his ranch provided national forest access and ways of transporting products that avoided major interstates and state patrol checks.

Lana also needed Jenna, who concocted the best Krok around. The drugs gave an immediate and desired high. Carson knew sales had increased when Jenna's superior product hit the street. Now he needed Lana out of the way so he could take over and run the business. He was tired of always having someone in charge, whether it was the government with grazing and logging restrictions or a person who thought they could tell you what to do.

"Well then," Lana said, taking a step closer to Carson. "Let's load the drugs into your truck and have your beautiful girlfriend meet our truck on the other side of the forest."

Carson didn't like that plan. He wanted to be in control, but for now he had to bide his time and wait this out. "Okay. Jenna, Cody, take the truck and start loading it up. Bobbi, you heard her. You're driving. Help Jenna and Cody out."

He could still see the red mark on Bobbi's cheek. If only she hadn't been so disrespectful.

Lana took another step closer, making Carson uncomfortable, but he refused to move out of the way. "You are being watched. Do you know that?" she said.

"What are you talking about?"

"Up there on the hillside. Don't make it obvious that you see them, but the sun is glinting off a scope. Perhaps your sheriff is hiding up there and watching from the trees. I can't do business with someone who doesn't pay attention."

Anger pulsed through Carson, and he wanted to grab Lana by the neck and show her that he could be tough too. Instead, he glanced over his shoulder and saw the glint Lana was talking about. "I'll take care of it."

"You better. And by the way, you have a mole too."

"What are you talking about?"

Lana stepped up and whispered in Carson's ear, "I have my sources. You know who I'm talking about. Take care of it. Or I will."

Then she turned and walked away. He discreetly glanced again to the hillside where the sun had glinted off the scope. He would take care of that, but Lana's words echoed in his mind. A mole?

Carson pulled out his phone and texted his informant in the sheriff's office. He would have to investigate this claim more. It was news to him.

Chapter Thirty-Two

Carson and his family went back inside, and the activity around the ranch died down.

Maya sat back and stretched her legs, moving her toes to try to gain feeling in them. There had been no sign of her grandfather and nothing that would give them enough evidence to get a search warrant.

"I was hoping we'd learn something new," she said, frustrated.

"Let's get back to town and see what the other deputies have found out," Josh said. His phone buzzed.

"You have reception up here?" Maya asked.

"Appears that I do, at least for texting." Josh punched in his pass code and checked his phone. As he read, his lips tightened and eyes narrowed.

"Is everything okay?"

"It is. Just something I need to deal with later."

"What is it? Maybe I can help."

"Nothing you can help with."

Great, now Josh is keeping secrets too. Maya, thinking about the fact Carson had sent a text message to someone, stood and gathered Juniper's leash. Could Josh be the recipient and that's why he didn't want to tell her what the message was about? Did he only kiss her to distract her? "Why won't you tell me about your text?"

"It's nothing, okay? Just leave it alone."

Annoyed and now suspicious, Maya and Juniper turned away from Josh and started on the path back to the vehicles. So far everything was a dead end and frustrating.

They hiked back over the mountainside to where they'd parked, and Maya loaded up Juniper. Josh got in his patrol vehicle, following as they took the back road into town. Maya wanted to find the truck Bobbi was driving, but there was no way to know which direction she was headed from the ranch.

Maya pulled up behind Josh's sheriff's vehicle at an intersection stop sign. The SUV with the rental plates flew by on the road. She picked up her radio. "You see what I see?"

"I do," Josh said. "I think they are definitely speeding."

She agreed. "Let's pull them over. I'll back you up."

"Ten-four."

Josh flipped on his lights and Maya followed suit. Juniper became excited and started howling. "You like running hot, girly?"

Juniper answered with a sharp bark. Josh pulled up behind the SUV and called the vehicle plates in to dispatch. Maya heard over the radio that the plates did come back to a rental agency.

The SUV pulled over to the shoulder of the road. Josh pulled up behind at an angle and Maya did the same. Juniper continued to whine and spin small circles in the back.

"I wish I could have you run this vehicle," Maya said

to her. "We'll get through certification and then you can go back to having fun."

Maya stepped out of the vehicle, approaching the opposite side from Josh. She could hear Josh asking for the driver's license, registration, and insurance. She took note of the back of the car and the back seat, looking for any kind of weapon or anything that could cause them danger. The car was clean, though. Not even much dust had settled on the outside. That meant they hadn't been in town for long.

Maya approached the passenger window, making sure she stayed close to the vehicle for safety. This made it more difficult for someone from the vehicle to shoot her.

The driver saw her and rolled down the window. "Two officers? Did I do something serious?" the woman asked in a Russian accent.

Maya peered over the seat and took note of any areas she could inspect for a weapon or anything to give them probable cause to search the vehicle. "You're from out of town?" she asked.

"I'm visiting from California."

"But I'm guessing from your accent that you are from Russia originally," Maya said.

"Good guess. How did you know?" the woman said sarcastically.

"I spent some time in the military and learned many different accents," Maya said.

Josh interjected, "Do you know why I pulled you over?"

"No, I do not," said the woman.

"You were going pretty fast on these back roads. The speed limit is thirty and I clocked you going about fifty."

"So in America it takes two officers to pull over a vehicle for speeding," the woman asked.

"Actually, I'm law enforcement for the U.S. Forest Service. While I am providing backup, I'm also looking for some poachers that supposedly shot a couple bull elk recently. Have you been around here for long? Have you seen any signs of hunters or anything suspicious going on?"

Maya caught the raised eyebrow Josh was giving her. "I'm going to go run all this information through dispatch," he said, heading to his vehicle.

The passenger turned back toward Maya and said, "I know nothing about this, what do you call them, poachers?"

"You haven't seen anything suspicious then?"

"No. Not at all."

"Would you mind if I took a quick look in your car? Just to cover my bases. Have to do my job," Maya said.

"Of course. I have nothing to hide."

She waited for Josh to return and they asked the woman to step out of the vehicle. Maya opened the front doors and started searching, not really expecting to find anything, but taking advantage of the opportunity to check out the inside anyway. She slid her hands under the seat, looking for signs of hidden compartments, and then worked methodically from underneath the seats to opening different compartments, even pulling down the visors and feeling around.

As she worked her way around the vehicle, she heard the woman say to Josh, "I wouldn't think a poached animal would fit in such a small spot."

"Officer Thompson just has to look for any evidence," Josh answered.

Maya finished her search and stepped back. The vehicle was the cleanest vehicle she'd seen in a long time, but it was a rental. Although drug traffickers often rented vehicles, this lady seemed too smart for that.

After doing a final check in the back, Maya stepped back from the vehicle. "Thank you," she said.

"See?" said the woman. "Nothing."

"I appreciate you letting me do my job."

"Of course. Anytime."

Josh wrote the woman a speeding ticket. Then he and Maya retreated to their vehicles and watched the SUV drive away.

"I thought about putting a tracker on the vehicle," she said, "but I think this lady is smart enough she would have minions working for her and we wouldn't catch her doing anything."

"I agree," Josh said. "But I have her information now. Name is Svetlana Egorov. I vote we go research her a little bit more. Maybe if we can figure out how exactly she ties in with the Rays, that will give us a better lead."

Maya went over to her vehicle and checked on Juniper. She was sitting in her compartment, body tensed up and tail wagging. She gave a few short, loud yips. Maya petted her on the head and scratched behind her ears. Loving on the dog eased some of her tension, but they needed a break in the case—and soon. Before something bad happened to Pops.

"Hang in there," she said under her breath. "We'll find you."

There was a full batch of Krok in hidden compartments in the black truck.

Things were getting rough. Bobbi needed to start

thinking about the future of this operation and completing it quickly. She headed for the access road into the national forest. When she was out of sight of Carson, she'd pulled over and grabbed her purse.

She opened the pocket that contained a cell phone and her badge.

Bobbi had placed several trackers in the bricks of drugs. She linked the trackers to her cell phone and the DEA, then texted her boss, This is my last load. Suspects are getting suspicious. I'm out.

Then she placed the phone back in the pocket and zipped it up. She grabbed her Sig Sauer and placed it in her holster. Once she delivered the drugs, she would leave. Carson suspected too much.

Last night in bed, she had come on to him and he hadn't responded. He'd been distant and aloof ever since she had shown up late with the codeine. Bobbi was beginning to suspect he had an in with the sheriff's department and knew she had lied to him about the flat tire.

Bobbi put the truck in Drive and started on her route. Sleeping with him had been a mistake. But she'd been undercover for so long now, she barely knew who she was anymore. Sure, other undercover officers probably crossed this line. Could she get out of this and still find her way back to a normal life?

Bobbi fought back tears. She was a tough agent, but this job was destroying her. Back in her real life, she had a son. He was the same age as Jenna, and she had completely lost touch with him. He had graduated from college and was married. Someday she would call him and ask for forgiveness for not being a part of his life.

When this assignment was over, Bobbi planned on turning in her badge. She couldn't do this anymore.

Bobbi downshifted the truck as she headed down a pass with rough roads. At the bottom of the incline, she would cross a shallow creek and drive another thirty minutes to the interstate, where she would meet Svetlana's courier.

Lana, or Svetlana, was the reason the DEA was interested in the Ray family. They had been investigating Lana for years. She was smart, and her father was a bigwig in the Russian mob. Lana, with her father's help, had started producing and trafficking drugs until she had one of the largest drug rings in the United States.

She'd always managed to elude law enforcement, but this time they were going to nail her. Bobbi's undercover time wasn't going to be wasted. She would bring this bitch down before she quit the DEA—and the Rays were her best chance of accomplishing that.

Bobbi just needed this last load delivered. Then the DEA could move in and arrest everyone while she moved far away and started her life over.

Chapter Thirty-Three

Maya pulled up next to Josh at the sheriff's building and opened the door to Juniper's kennel. The young dog had curled into a tiny ball of fur. She yawned and a little squeak came out.

Maya smiled and petted Juniper. She gave her a treat, shutting the door. "You have to stay here for now, but you'll be good."

She made sure the AC unit for Juniper's compartment was on and went inside to see what Josh had found out about her grandfather. Maya took in the lobby's '70s decor that included black-and-cream square tiles and worn old yellow cushy chairs. Above the chairs was an older photo of Longs Peak and Mount Meeker—the twin sisters, as the locals called them. The photo had faded over time. Her grandfather really needed to allocate some money to updating the station and a new picture of the majestic twin sisters.

The station hadn't changed since she was a little girl. At that time, her grandfather had been a deputy. Her grandmother would bring her in to visit. Pops would pick Maya up and twirl her around, making her giggle, and then give her a kiss before placing her on the floor. She missed those days when everything was simple and both of her grandparents were there. At the time, Maya had taken that for granted.

Tears threatened to well up. She balled up her hands into fists. They would find her grandfather. No matter what.

"Maya, good to see you." Sam strolled out into the lobby area.

"Hey, Sam. Thanks for your help earlier today."

He gave Maya a hug and then stepped back. "We'll find him, I promise. All the guys are working hard on it."

"Good to hear."

"What are you doing here?"

"I'm here with Josh. We're investigating a case together. It might tie in with Pops's disappearance."

Sam narrowed his eyes. "Be careful with Deputy Colten. I don't know why your grandfather hired him, but I don't trust him. He's got a checkered past."

Maya didn't know how to answer. She trusted Sam and knew if he was warning her, it was in her best interest, but Josh had done nothing to make her suspicious. Except kiss her. Maybe that in itself should make her suspicious.

There was also the text message he'd received. Why wouldn't Josh answer her questions—unless he had something to hide?

"I'll be careful, Sam," Maya said. "You and Pops taught me well."

"We did. Pretty proud of you, kid, but be careful with Colten. I saw his profile jacket. Didn't get a chance to read all of it, but he got his partner killed in the line of duty."

Josh had told her that, but Maya decided she needed

to learn more and find out the details about what had happened to his partner. She *did* trust Pops and if he'd hired Josh, then there had to be more to the story. Maya knew after being in Afghanistan that shit happened in tense situations.

"Maybe there's a good explanation. I don't think Pops would have hired him if there wasn't." Why did she feel the need to defend Josh? Sam cared about her and was watching out for her well-being. That was all. Maybe she should listen to Sam's warning, especially since she'd seen another side to Josh today with the text message.

"I just want you to be safe. Watch your back working with him. Okay?"

"Okay. Thanks," Maya said, not knowing how to react. *Am I capable of judging people anymore? First Doug and now Josh?* Maybe Josh was too good to be true and didn't have any feelings toward her, but rather was using her. She wouldn't let her guard down again or let Josh's good looks influence her.

First chance she had, she would get into Pops's office. She knew where he kept all his profile jackets with information about each deputy. She would read more about Josh's past and make up her own mind on him.

"I'm just watching out for you. I need to get back to work, but I feel better now that you know that."

"I know you mean well. I better get back to work too," Maya said as Josh came through the door to the lobby.

She thought about Sam's warning. Maybe she was trusting Josh too quickly. Could Josh be the informant working with the Rays? How much did she really know about him? If he was the informant, maybe she could manipulate the situation and have Josh lead her to Pops. He was helping out Maya quite a bit on the investigation. Was he being too helpful?

Josh held the door for Sam, who muttered a thanks.

"Hey," Josh said, shaking his head. "That guy Sam has had a chip on his shoulder ever since your grandfather promoted me."

"Yeah, I don't think you're his favorite person," Maya said. A headache was beginning to build behind her eyes, along with anger toward Josh as she thought about what Sam told her. First Doug, her best friend, had to go and betray her. Now Josh couldn't be trusted, and that only added to Maya's frustration.

I have my secrets too. Maybe I just wanted another friend and that's why I'm trusting Josh. Suck it up, Thompson. Keep your feelings to yourself for now. Pops is missing. Do what you need to do to find him.

"You okay?" Josh asked.

"Yeah, just tired. Any leads?" Maya asked, changing the subject.

"Nothing right now. I checked with Miranda, our crime scene tech. The tire tracks are a generic off-roading tire. Probably what every vehicle around here has on it."

"Dang." Maya tried not to show her disappointment. "I should get out to my grandfather's place and take care of the horses."

"I already have a deputy on it," Josh said. "What you need to do is get some rest and food so we can continue our search."

"But we need to get back to work and start making this circumstantial evidence become direct evidence. After wasting time surveilling today, we know the Rays are into something fishy, but that doesn't lead us to my grandfather and drug running. Or Doug's killer. Or anything."

"I know. Let's get some food and figure out our next step."

"Or let's get to work and stop messing around. Maybe you should quit telling me what to do. Maybe we can eat when Pops comes home."

"I know you're tired and I'm sorry if I'm coming across the wrong way. I just know I'm hungry and we'll think better with food. We'll figure out our next steps while we eat. Okay?"

"Okay." Maya gave in, knowing Josh was right. She was exhausted and needed to recharge. "Let's get something at the Black Bear Café."

"You mean the only restaurant in town? Sure. That sounds good."

"God, you're annoying. I'll meet you there."

"What's wrong with you?"

Maya ignored Josh. She strode out, letting the door slam behind her.

Bobbi bounced around in the truck as she navigated the back roads. She'd be glad to get to her destination and not have to deal with this Jeep trail anymore. She ground the truck gears as she downshifted and pulled the vehicle to the right to avoid a large boulder. She hoped the load wasn't getting bounced around too much—she didn't need any of the bricks breaking open, especially since she was running behind after placing all the trackers.

The trackers in the drugs would help give the DEA more information as far as Lana's distribution chain. They wanted to nail the person at the top, and if Carson thought that was really going to be him, he had a lot to learn about this business. Lana wouldn't go down without a fight.

Suddenly, an ATV shot out in front of her and parked near the side of the road. Bobbi was ready to yell at the person when the driver took his helmet off.

Carson.

Bobbi froze. This wasn't good. What was he doing here?

She felt under her jacket where the butt of the Sig Sauer sat. Reassured, she put the truck in Park and climbed out. "What's wrong?" she asked Carson.

"Just wanted to check in with you," Carson said. "I heard from Lana's person you hadn't arrived yet. What's taking you so long?"

"It's not like I can travel a normal speed on these roads."

"I need to know something."

"What?" Bobbi put her hands on her hips like she was pouting, but she wanted her hands near her gun.

"I want to know who you are."

Adrenaline surged through Bobbi. *Use your training and talk your way out of this.* "That's a silly question."

Before Bobbi could say anything more, Carson pulled his pistol and aimed it at her.

"Babe," Bobbi said. "What's wrong? Why are you doing that?"

"I think you know what's wrong. Keep your hands where I can see them."

"Why are you acting this way?"

"Seriously?" Carson asked.

Bobbi could see his hand shaking. "Just calm down."

"You deceived me."

"I don't know what you're talking about," Bobbi said.

"I know who you are. I just want to hear you say it."

Bobbi moved toward the truck. She should have stayed closer and used it to shield herself. If she could get over to the open door, she could possibly use it to help her stay safe.

"Stay where you are," Carson ordered.

Bobbi stopped. Years of training for moments like this flashed through her mind. *Keep him talking.* "Who do you think I am?"

"You're a pig. I trusted you. I slept with you. You used me."

"You think I'm a cop?"

"I know you're a cop. I just want to hear you say it. The other day when you were late, you didn't have a flat tire. You'd been arrested by that Forest Service pig. My informant told me you were in jail. You lied to me. You got out because you're a cop. Now explain that to me."

"I think you're hearing things. Who told you that?"

"I have my sources. You know that," Carson said.

Bobbi noticed that his hand had steadied. Her hand sat on her weapon. Once she pulled her gun, there was no going back. She had to shoot to kill. "Who's your source?"

"You think I'm going to tell you that? Why did you lie to me?"

"I didn't lie to you," Bobbi said.

"Do you know anything about the explosion? Did you do it?"

"Why would I do that?" she asked.

"I don't know. You pigs do crazy things."

"I'm not a pig and I didn't blow up the lab."

"I don't believe you. What about the sheriff? Did

you use your resources to get him somewhere safe? We needed him and you knew that."

"Look." Bobbi put her hands back on her hips, close to her gun. "I don't know what I have to say to convince you. I'm not a pig. I didn't blow up your drug lab and I didn't send the sheriff off to safety. What I do know is that I'll get this load delivered while you go home and keep working on the business moves we've discussed. Lana's guy is expecting me, not you. So let's do this the right way and not mess anything up. We don't need Lana asking more questions."

Bobbi thought she saw Carson waver for a moment, but then a look of resolve crossed his face. "Give me your purse," he said.

"What? Why?"

"You heard me. Give me your purse."

"Fine." She stepped, one foot after the other, to the truck, keeping her eyes on Carson. She didn't want to turn her back on him.

Bobbi snatched her purse off the seat and threw it at Carson, and then she grabbed for her weapon.

Chapter Thirty-Four

Still irritated, Maya checked on Juniper in the patrol vehicle. She was curled up sleeping. Josh was waiting to walk with her, but Maya stomped toward the Black Bear Café, ignoring him. He didn't need to be an ass.

Josh caught up to her, a patient look on his face and slight smile that only irritated Maya more.

She didn't know if she should believe Sam. Josh had become a friend to her over this past week. He'd been there for her when she needed someone the most. She needed to find out more about Josh. Maybe he was only being friendly because he needed to get information out of her. Two could play that game.

"Let's get our food to go and then head back to my office. It's quieter. We can think and I have a whiteboard we can use to hash out our plan," she said.

"Works for me."

Maya and Josh ordered some burgers to go.

"Doesn't Juniper get one?" Josh asked, grinning.

"You want to make her sick? Juniper gets dog food. We get burgers."

"I can't promise that I won't sneak her a small bite."

Maya put her hands on her hips. "You do that, and

I'll send her home with you tonight. You saw what she does to couches."

"I kind of like my couch. No sneaking the dog a burger. Got it."

Fifteen minutes later, a waitress brought over their dinners to go. She gave Josh a sly smile as she set the bags on the counter. Maya shook her head and said, "I'll meet you outside."

"Okay, I'll finish paying."

"I'm sure you will," Maya said, catching a confused look on Josh's face. Was he that oblivious to the way women threw themselves at him? Of course, was she any better?

They walked back to their vehicles and headed to Maya's office down the road. After arriving there, Maya let Juniper out to run around for a minute. Josh carried their dinner inside.

She and Juniper followed. "Did you get her phone number?" Maya asked.

"Who?" Josh said.

"The gal who brought our food. She liked you."

"I didn't even notice," Josh said.

She realized he was serious by the confusion on his face. "Guys. So oblivious, aren't they, Juniper?"

Juniper wagged her tail, then sat down by Josh and started begging.

"You have to lay down," Maya told her, pointing to the dog bed on the floor. Juniper flattened her ears and gave Maya a disappointed look. She slunk over and lay down, back facing them.

"That's pathetic," Josh said.

Maya studied her dog. She was already figuring out Juniper's personality traits, including when she sulked.

But when she worked, Juniper was on. Doug had told Maya tracking was Juniper's favorite part of working.

An idea began to form. "I was thinking—maybe we take her back to the spot she lost the track when we were looking for Pops and try again."

Josh set down his burger. "I thought about that too, but I think we're better off going through some current investigation files that involved your grandfather. We need to figure out who would want to harm him. I also have search and rescue out working just in case he simply fell off Velvet and is walking around with a head injury. They have a couple volunteer dogs working too."

"So, nothing yet?" Maya asked.

"Not yet, but I've told the deputies out with them to notify me if they find anything. I promise I'll keep you in the loop."

"Thanks for doing that."

"Sure," Josh said, taking another bite of his burger. "You going to eat or just stare at your food?"

"I can't eat knowing that my grandfather is out there somewhere. I know he could have fallen off, but I feel like something more happened to him. And if it happened near the Ray Ranch, then what if my grandfather's kidnapping and Doug's death are related? Pops was investigating the drug trafficking from information Doug gave him and someone wanted to make sure he didn't continue."

"If you don't eat, you won't have any energy to keep looking. Take ten minutes and eat something. Then we can hash out if the drug lab and your grandfather's disappearance are related."

Maya sighed. She knew Josh was right, but it still felt wrong. She took a small bite and thought about her deployment where if you had the chance to go to the chow hall, you took it. You never knew when a mission was going to take you out all day and night, and then you'd be stuck with MREs, otherwise known as Meals Rarely Edible.

"What are you thinking about?" Josh asked.

"Nothing." She set her burger down. "Okay, MREs."

"You're thinking about military food?"

"Just how you'd be out on a mission and that food was all you had. They were simple, like chicken and rice or chicken and noodles in some sort of sauce. None of us really knew what kind of sauce it was. It didn't matter because when you got really hungry, they worked. But overall, I'm glad to be home and have a burger right now."

"I think that's the first time I've heard you talk about anything with the military."

"Well, most of the shit over there isn't worth talking about," Maya said.

"You know, I deal with PTSD too."

"What?" Maya stared at him in surprise.

"That's why most of the guys don't trust me. Your grandfather gave me a second chance and they know it. Guys like Sam are old-school and don't want me around. They think I'm a ticking time bomb…uh, maybe a bad way to put it. But I'll give you a piece of advice."

"I didn't ask for advice or say I was dealing with PTSD," Maya said.

"Maya, sometimes it's pretty obvious. I've been through enough myself. I can see it in you."

Maya was about ready to interrupt, but Josh held up his hand and stopped her. "It's okay. Shit happens. We're allowed to have baggage in our jobs. All I'm going to say is that it's okay to ask for help. We don't always have to be tough."

"I don't need help," Maya said. "So why do you have PTSD? How did my grandfather give you a second chance?"

Josh leaned back in his chair. His expression changed, and Maya could see the story was still hard for him to think about, much less talk about.

"You don't have to tell me if you don't want to," she said.

Josh finished his burger and wadded up the napkin throwing it in the trash. "No, it's okay. After college, I joined the Chicago PD, much to my parents' dismay. My dad is a DA in Chicago and wanted his only son to go to law school. I, of course, didn't want anything to do with that, so I completed my degree in criminal justice and then joined the force. I loved my job. One night my partner and I were on a call, and I didn't do my job correctly. He was shot and killed. He left behind a wife and daughter. Their faces still haunt me every night. His wife forgave me, but I never forgave myself."

"I understand," Maya said. She wanted to know more about Josh after what Sam told her. She decided to try opening up to get more out of him. "Night is the hardest. I hate dreaming. So how did you end up here in small-town Colorado?"

"Your grandfather is a buddy of my grandfather's from the military, so I reached out. I told him the truth about the shooting and the fallout from it. Your grandfather was willing to give me a second chance, and for that I'll always be grateful."

"I'm sorry you went through all that, but I'm glad Pops hired you. You deserve it. Sometimes I wish he'd give me another chance. Coming home has been difficult. Everything is different now. Even a waterfall can trigger memories that I want buried," Maya said. She reached down and stroked Juniper on the head. "I think when I'm a mess it's hard for my grandfather to look at me because then I remind him of my mom. I just wish he could give me the second chance he gave you. Be proud of me, you know?"

"I came here about the time you were deployed to Afghanistan. He would show everyone pictures of you with your K-9 and talk about what an amazing handler you are. He's proud. Know that."

Maya fought back tears again. "Then I owe it to him to find him. We need to figure out where he went or who took him and why and how it connects with Doug's death."

Doug. Everything seemed to circle back to Doug and the Ray family. Find Doug's killer and maybe they'd find her grandfather too. There was still the unknown girlfriend Maya thought could shed some light on the case. Maybe it was Bobbi. If they could figure out who this mystery girl was, she might have answers.

Maya opened her top drawer and took out the ring case, setting it on the desk in front of Josh.

"I'm flattered, but don't you think we're moving too fast?" he asked.

She shook her head. "I hate to break your heart, but it's not for you. I found it in the patrol vehicle. Based on what I saw at Doug's house, I think he had a secret girlfriend."

"He never told you about this?"

"No, he never said anything. Seems like he kept the relationship well hidden. I didn't even hear rumors around town. If we can figure out who this was meant for, then we can talk to her and get more information about what Doug was into. Maybe this will be the break in the case we need."

Josh opened the case and let out a low whistle, which got Juniper to come over and climb up in his lap. He rubbed her behind her ears and said, "This is an expensive ring. Where did he get the money? You think he used some of the cash you found?"

"Maybe. Without access to his financial records to see if he used a credit card or something, I don't know for sure," Maya said. "But there was certainly a lot of money there."

"The last time Doug came in, he and your grandfather got into a huge fight. The office door was closed, but I could hear them yelling."

"Why didn't you tell me this before?"

Josh shrugged. "I didn't know what they fought about, and your grandfather didn't say anything, so I left it alone."

"It seems like everything leads back to Doug and the bombing."

Carson stepped over Bobbi's body and shot her two more times, making sure she was dead. It was a bittersweet moment for him. He had loved her, but no one betrayed him.

Grabbing Bobbi's purse from the truck, he started ransacking it looking to see what she had on him, if anything. Or if she'd notified someone about the drugs.

Inside the purse was a hidden compartment. He unzipped it and found another cell phone inside of it. When he pressed the button for the home screen, a pass-code notification popped up. Frustrated, he threw the phone on the ground and stomped it. The screen shattered into small pieces.

He opened her purse back up and started going through it again. At the bottom there was another compartment, where he found her badge. DEA. Shit. He put on his gloves and walked over to where Bobbi lay lifeless. He threw the badge onto her and dipped his gloved finger in blood. On her jacket he wrote the word *PIG*.

Then he dragged Bobbi's body behind a large boulder. He would come up with a plan to dispose of her later.

Stepping back from Bobbi's body, Carson threw some branches over her. He went to the truck and climbed in, tossing the purse over on the passenger seat. He would deliver the drugs himself and then get back to the ranch. Even dead, Bobbi complicated things. Lana had hinted there was a mole in his group. Did she know it was Bobbi?

A couple hours later Carson pulled into the ranch. He'd disposed of his gloves and changed into clean clothes. Then he'd burned his bloodstained clothes in the ranch fire pit. The ATV was still out by Bobbi's body, so he'd called Cody and told him to get one of his men, drive the ATV home, dispose of the dead body, and leave no evidence. He only hoped his inept son could do that.

As Carson parked, he noticed Lana's car outside the compound meeting area.

"Great, what does she want?" he muttered to himself, getting out of the truck and slamming the door shut. The gravel crunched underneath his boots as Carson strutted toward the compound. Lana needed to back off. He was sick of her.

The door creaked and groaned as he opened it, irritating him even more. He'd make sure someone took care of that.

"What do you want? The load has been delivered," Carson said.

Lana sat on the couch with her legs crossed, flipping through a gun magazine and chewing gum. She snapped the gum and peered over the pages. She didn't answer.

"If you don't have anything to discuss then you need to leave," Carson said, noting that some of his men had come in and were standing behind him. Good. Lana needed to see he was not afraid and had the men to back him up.

"Oh, we have things to discuss," Lana said, snapping her gum again. "But first I am reading about, how do you say it, these assault rifles your country is so afraid of."

"Well, finish reading. We have things to do."

"Yes, we do. We have a problem."

Carson crossed his arms. "Oh yeah? What's the problem?"

"I was pulled over after I left here this afternoon. A couple of cops harassed me. They searched my car. Asked me some interesting questions." Lana set the magazine down and stood up, her high heels clicking on the wooden floor as she approached Carson. "I'm wondering if you know anything about this?"

"Of course not. Why would I?"

"I thought it seemed strange that I left here after we saw someone watching us from the hillside and this happens. You told me that you have control over all your men here, but apparently not. Maybe one of them called me in."

"I doubt that, but I'll find out more. Anything else?" Carson asked. His men stepped up closer behind him.

Lana leaned into his personal space. "Yes, as a matter of fact. There *is* something else. We have a bigger problem."

"What's that?"

"There's money missing. I trusted you to hold some of the money until I could pay you your share, and that was obviously a mistake. When the money was counted there was at least $80,000 unaccounted for. So you need to get me that money as soon as possible or else."

"Or else what?" Carson said, taking a step closer to Lana. "We didn't take any money that wasn't ours, so it would be your people, not mine, that you need to talk to."

"I wish I could believe that."

Lana reached behind her and pulled her gun. Carson was staring down the barrel, but he didn't move. She was bluffing. If she'd wanted to shoot him, she would have done it when he first came in and no one else was in the room.

He heard his men pulling guns from their holsters. A few of the men had revolvers, and the click of the hammers being cocked echoed throughout the room.

"Looks like we have a situation here," Carson said. "It doesn't end well for either of us. You shoot me, my men will shoot you."

"Not before I shoot some of your men."

"That's a chance they're willing to take. Are you willing to take that chance?" Carson reached up and pushed the gun out of his face. "Now, I'll investigate things on my end, but I think you better also look into your business. Don't assume things. We all know what that word starts with, and you're acting like an ass."

Lana holstered her gun. "You are a dead man if you don't get me the money. You need to figure out who's stealing. First there were missing drugs. Now the money. You won't get a third chance."

"The problem is taken care of," Carson said, thinking of Bobbi. If money and drugs were missing, maybe she had stolen them as evidence. He would look around the property to see if anything was stashed.

"I hope so," Lana said. She turned on her heels and then paused, glancing back. "Because if you don't take care of the problem, I will. I'll be back to see what you find out."

Then she strutted out the door. Carson realized he'd balled up his fists. He'd wanted to make her shut up but had to bide his time. Right now, he still needed her for the codeine, but as soon as Jenna finished figuring out her recipe for synthetic codeine, he could cut ties with Lana. Make her disappear. People went missing all the time in the mountains.

He turned around to his men. "Thanks, now we have to figure out who's stealing from us. Is it one of us or someone in Lana's crew?"

The men nodded in agreement. They all holstered their weapons and headed to the meeting hall to discuss the next step. As they left the room, Cody trailed in. Carson walked over to him and put a hand on his shoulder. "All good?"

Cody tipped his hat back and smirked. "All good."

"Then let's go figure out how to run this business ourselves."

Chapter Thirty-Five

The morning sun glinted off the mountain peaks as Maya drove to her office, sipping her coffee and hoping the caffeine would hit her system soon. Juniper was curled up in the back. Apparently getting up at 0500 was early for her too.

Maya had spent the whole night tossing and turning. Trying to stay clearheaded, she hadn't had a drop of beer, which made sleeping even more difficult. When she did sleep, the nightmares came. They were a mixture of explosions, death, and her grandfather being tortured and killed.

I have to find him.

Josh was meeting Maya at her office and they were going back up to the Baker cabin. If her grandfather's disappearance was tied in with the explosion, going back to the crime scene made the most sense and might give them a much-needed break in the case. Josh would provide backup.

Maya had been ready to go last night, but Josh told her to go home and relax. She had been restless all night long. The cabin seemed too quiet and she dozed off and on. She had tried calling Josh before it got too late to see if he wanted to meet even earlier, but he didn't answer. Where had he been?

She'd thought through every person in the sheriff's department she knew. She couldn't come up with anyone who would give out inside information except for Josh. Maya thought about the information Sam had divulged about Josh's mistake getting his partner killed. She convinced herself she was being paranoid about Josh, but when she had a chance, she would go through the files in her grandfather's office. For now, she would watch her back.

At least I know I can trust Juniper.

As Maya approached the edge of town, she slowed down for a cow elk to cross the road. Its calf trailed behind it. Up ahead, Maya could see Josh parked by her office, waiting for her. She had brewed an extra cup of coffee for him complete with cream like he asked for at her cabin. After the elk scampered into the trees, she pulled up window-to-window so she and Josh could talk before leaving.

Juniper leaped to her feet, instantly awake, and started yipping. Her paws started making a tapping noise as she danced in the back. Maya told her to be quiet. Juniper grunted, but at least listened. As a reward, Maya opened up the door between the front of the vehicle and Juniper's compartment. Juniper stuck her head through along with a giant paw smacking Maya on the shoulder. Maya rubbed Juniper's ears and face. The dog responded with a few slurps on Maya's face and then Juniper retreated into her compartment, lying back down on her shredded blanket.

Maya handed Josh the coffee with cream. "How'd you know I take my coffee like that?" he asked.

"I spied on you."

"Seriously?"

"No. You asked for cream with your coffee when you came to my cabin and we live in a small town. The coffee shop barista shared the information with me. Apparently, you're one of her favorite customers."

"Oh, busted. I'm a coffee junkie and tip well."

"I'm not sure that's why you're a favorite, but it sounds good."

"I do stop there often. Glad we didn't get Juniper any caffeine," Josh said.

Maya agreed as her dog started yelping in excitement. She took a sip of her coffee, grateful for the caffeine. She could have used about ten coffees after her lack of sleep. "Tried calling you last night, but you didn't answer. Everything okay?"

"Everything is good," Josh said. "Just had to take care of some things."

Maya wanted to ask more, but held off, making a mental note to see if she could figure out where Josh was. This was a small town, after all. Someone had to have seen him.

"Ready to head up there?" Josh said. "Make sure you drink that before we head off on the Jeep road. You don't want to spill coffee all over that nice uniform. That would make the Forest Service look bad."

"Sounds like you have experience with this," Maya paused. "So, I've been thinking…"

"Uh-oh."

"We're going to drive up to the Baker cabin, right? Or pretty close?"

"Yeah," Josh said, taking a sip of coffee.

"I was thinking, why didn't we drive up there that day? Why did Doug insist we hike in?"

"Good question."

"At the time we responded to the call, I went with the fact that Doug was my FTO. Since he was training me I assumed there was a reason we were hiking in. I didn't question him, but I should have."

"Well," Josh said. "Let's get up there and take another look. You had a traumatic experience. Maybe getting back to the place where it happened will jog your memory."

"True. Okay, let's go." Maya rolled up her window and put the Tahoe in Drive. Juniper continued to run circles in excitement, but once the car moved, she settled down.

"Atta girl," Maya said. "Save some of that energy for work, will you?"

The better Juniper felt, the more her true personality was showing. She was a sweet dog with a good head and strong work drive, but without her regular job, she was getting bored, and Maya wasn't certain her cabin would survive much longer.

She drained the cup of coffee in time to turn on the road leading to the cabin and carefully negotiated driving over rocks and other obstacles. She would go from left or right, so she didn't bottom out the vehicle and cause any damage. If she broke down here, it would be a very unhappy tow truck driver who would have to come and get her out.

Maya glanced in the rearview mirror and saw Josh following her tracks. Aspen trees now fully leafed out lined the road, and off to one side several groves of evergreens stood tall. She couldn't wait to see what

Juniper's nose uncovered. Hopefully, there would be some evidence left behind from the mystery person, with enough scent left for Juniper to find it.

Handlers debated how long a scent lasted when it came to evidence. Some trainers would say only about twenty-four hours, but others had talked about how their K-9 found items days later. Maya wasn't sure what to believe as there were a lot of factors, like weather, but she knew running Juniper was worth a try.

The cabin, or what was left of it, came into view. Maya's heart started pounding as she parked the Tahoe and took in the scene. Juniper stood in the back and then started a low, heart-wrenching yowl. Maya opened the door between her and Juniper's compartment and reached through, giving her dog a pet. Juniper responded with a quick lick and then went back to whining.

"Hard to be back here again, isn't it, girl?" Maya said. Juniper pushed into her hand.

A piece of left-behind crime scene tape fluttered in the breeze. Parts of cabin walls remained standing, but others had been completely knocked down. Charred pieces of wood littered the ground. There was probably glass too. Maya made a mental note to stay clear of the cabin debris when she started working Juniper. She didn't need a shard of glass sticking into one of Juniper's pads.

Josh stood outside, waiting for her, seeming to understand that she needed a moment to herself. Maya eventually opened the door and stepped out. Juniper remained quiet.

"You okay?" Josh asked.

"I just need a minute."

"Take your time," Josh said.

Maya took in the surroundings. Aspen trees waved in the morning breeze. Sunlight created shadows from the tree trunks. She closed her eyes to remember the day of the bombing—hiking in and discussing her relationship with her grandfather.

"We came up from the other side," Maya told Josh. "Since we hiked in rather than drive, we discussed my relationship with my grandfather. Looking back, it was almost like Doug wanted to help patch things up. Maybe he knew he wasn't coming back."

"Do you think this was a suicide?"

"No." Maya shook her head. "He wouldn't have put Juniper in danger like that. I think every handler can agree that no matter what our mental state, we'd always put our dog first and make sure they're okay."

"Did you ever talk about your relationship with your grandfather before this?" Josh gently probed.

"No. I mean, we sort of did. We went fishing once and I told him about not coming home for Nana's funeral. He didn't say much. He just let me talk. And he was my FTO, so most of the time he was talking training stuff. I didn't think much of it that day, but now I wonder why he brought up all the stuff with my grandfather."

"Is that all you talked about on the hike?"

"All that I can remember."

"What was the original call you were responding to?" Josh asked.

"Suspicious activity at the Baker cabin."

"What if I told you that dispatch never received that call?"

"What do you mean?" Maya whipped around and stared at Josh.

"I've been doing some investigating on my own and there was never a call to dispatch. Did you hear it come through on your radio?"

"No." Maya let out a deep breath. "I had to use the restroom. You know, too much coffee." She left out the fact she'd had a long night of drinking too. "When I got back, Doug said the call had come in and we were going."

"You never saw it on the computer or heard dispatch radio?"

"No, I didn't look. Why would I doubt him?"

"Okay, so we know that he told you suspicious activity. Now you get up here and what do you see?" Josh asked.

"I saw a person. Over there." Maya pointed to where the suspect had been standing. "They were coming around the corner using the cabin to help hide their presence. Juniper sensed them first and started growling."

"What were they doing?"

"They were holding something in their hand. I couldn't see what, but more importantly they were covered from head to toe. Literally. They had a hat and a handkerchief with sunglasses that covered their face. I took cover, but Doug broke protocol and didn't. It was like he knew the person…" Maya trailed off. "He knew the person. Maybe he meant that this was his fault. Not just that he set the bombs, but that he didn't think the person would actually detonate them."

Josh shoved his hands in his pockets. "So why would he set the bombs in the first place? What was he trying to do? Did he seem surprised at all that this person was up here?"

"Not really. I had the adrenaline going and I was yelling at the person. The suspect pulled a knife. Doug sent Juniper to apprehend once that happened."

"Let's look around some more," Josh said. "Maybe there will be something that triggers another memory."

"The person ran away," Maya said.

"Okay," Josh said. He headed toward the cabin and was walking around. "Maya?"

"Yeah?" She stopped.

"Looks like there was a rainstorm up here last night."

She stared down at her boots squishing in the mud. "It does. Why? You know how Colorado is with small thunderstorms coming through at night. Hits one area and not the other."

"I know," Josh said. "But there's fresh footprints here. All the other prints from that day have been washed away, but someone has been up here looking around."

"I'll get Juniper," Maya said. "We'll track the person."

"Glad I'm here to back you up."

"Me too," she said, getting out Juniper's tracking harness. With Josh as backup, Maya could watch Juniper and her body language and not worry about the bad guy coming out and shooting her.

Unless Josh is the bad guy. Then I have a problem. It's a risk I'll take if it means finding Pops.

Maya opened the door to Juniper's compartment and put on her tracking harness. When she was done, she stepped back, and a fur missile came flying out. Juniper landed and then immediately turned around and started jumping up and down.

"You're not leaving paw prints all over my shirt again. Off," Maya said firmly.

Juniper stopped leaping, but then she started turning circles.

"Paw prints all over your shirt? That sounds interesting," Josh said.

"Yes, it was."

Maya heard Josh laugh. She worked on settling Juniper down. Some dogs needed to be jazzed up to focus and work, but she could already tell Juniper was more the type that needed to calm down.

She and Juniper went over to where Josh found the footprints. Maya started casting out her dog, telling her to "track." Juniper stuck her nose to the ground, sucking in air and taking in all the scents around her. She ran a couple circles, and just when Maya was ready to bring her in, settle her down and cast her out again, she snapped around, nose staying to the ground. Her tail went up and her body paused for a second. Then she took off.

This time Maya was ready for Juniper's sudden leap forward, sprinting to keep up.

Chapter Thirty-Six

Juniper tracked near the footprints. Maya made a quick note in her head that they appeared to be boots. They were close to her foot size. So maybe female?

As she followed Juniper, she thought back to the day of the explosion. The suspect at the cabin had appeared to be a skinny male, but maybe the person was instead a tall female.

Juniper kept her nose to the ground, sucking in air and sticking with the scent. The track ran parallel to the footprints, and Maya knew this was because of the way moisture affected the scent. Juniper wouldn't care about the footprints—she only cared about the smell of the person. Juniper saw the world through her nose.

Juniper wound her way through the woods, and at one point the mud changed to dirt where rain hadn't fallen. The footprints were no longer as visible. At a divide in the trail, Juniper stopped and put her nose up, air scenting. That could mean that she was losing the track, so Maya cast her back out in different directions until Juniper put her nose to the ground and followed the trail again. This part of the trail was rocky and a little harder to navigate, slowing the trio down. It also made it harder for Josh to cover them the way he needed to, and for Maya to keep track of him.

Maya pulled Juniper up. "You doing okay?" she asked Josh. "What do you think? Can you still cover me here?"

"It'll be fine. I'll stay off to one side and it won't be a problem."

"Okay," she said, glancing back. She wanted to be able to see Josh in case he was setting her up. "Juniper, track."

Juniper put her nose back down and continued. She took Maya by surprise by veering off to the left toward a chokecherry shrub. Juniper's body language didn't indicate a person could be hiding, but Maya kept an eye out. Juniper pulled on her harness and took Maya over to the bush. She started working a scent cone back and forth and then, toward the right side of the plant, she sat and stared at Maya expectantly.

"What is it, girl?" Maya asked, proud of the way the dog was tracking.

Lodged back in the bush, intertwined with some of the red berries at the end of a branch, money fluttered in the slight breeze. Maya took a closer look without touching anything. It was a hundred-dollar bill.

She praised Juniper and gave her the toy as a reward. As Maya inspected the bush further, she noticed the sun glinting off something shiny—a knife had been dropped on the ground.

"You got something?" Josh asked.

"Yeah, she found some possible evidence—a knife and hundred-dollar bill. You have gloves and a bag?"

"I do. Good girl, Juniper."

Juniper responded with a tail wag and squeaked her toy harder.

"Good. Let's bag both items. Maybe we can pull prints off it or something," Maya said. "Maybe this was the knife the person pulled on us."

"We can hope."

"I know." Maya stepped closer to the evidence. Could it be some of the money from Doug's house? She wished Juniper could talk and tell her the answer.

Josh gloved up and put the hundred-dollar bill in a brown paper bag and then sealed it. He repeated the process with the knife. Once he finished, Maya asked Juniper to track again. Juniper put her nose to the ground and shot forward.

After about a half mile, the trail opened into a clearing, but Juniper didn't waver. She continued, tail pricked high in the air, sniffing away. Maya allowed her out on the leash. They hiked through the clearing diagonally, and Juniper went off in a direction where there was no trail. She leaped over a log, and Maya scrambled behind. She heard Josh behind her do the same.

"You okay?" she asked him.

"Yep, just keep going."

"Okay." Maya continued to follow Juniper, who paused for a moment and then took a sharp left. The deeper off-trail they went, the more the danger increased. If Josh tried anything, Maya would be hard-pressed to protect herself or Juniper. Definitely no cell phone signal in this area, and they were probably out of radio range too. Juniper was tracking a strong odor, though, and maybe that would lead to Pops. *This is worth the risk.*

"I just hope we can find our way back out of here."

"Isn't that your job as the Forest Service person? To know your forests?" Josh said, his breathing a little ragged following them at the pace Juniper was setting.

"Sounds like you need less doughnuts and more hikes. And remember, this national forest is over a million acres and I'm the only law enforcement officer. I can't be everywhere at once and I don't know every inch. Makes it easy for people to hide and do what they want to do—legal or illegal." *Maybe I shouldn't have told him that.*

"That doesn't make me feel better," Josh said.

Maya was ready to answer when Juniper paused again. She worked a scent cone back and forth and then brought her head up, air scenting. Maya cast Juniper out again, directing her to areas where she had worked the odor to help her find it again. Juniper went between sniffing the ground and air scenting.

After working several different directions, her panting was becoming obvious. Maya was ready to pull her up and get her some water when Juniper took off again. After taking a couple sharp turns, they arrived at a dilapidated cabin. The windows were boarded up and some of the roof shingles appeared to be loose.

Juniper wanted to track up to the door, but Maya pulled her up at a safe distance. She praised Juniper, making sure she knew that the track she ran was perfect.

"What do you think?" Maya asked. "I don't think this is national forest land. I'd have to look at a map, but I think this is private. There are little pockets of private properties around the forest."

"Juniper took us here on fresh pursuit that pertains to drug trafficking and possibly the sheriff's disappearance. Let's clear it," Josh said.

"You want to try to get a warrant?"

"I don't think we have time for that."

"I agree. Since Juniper took us here, we have probable cause, although since we're not certified together that might not stand up in court," Maya said.

"But I would say this is an exigent circumstance. The sheriff is missing. I say we enter and check only for your grandfather. If he's not there, then I can work on getting a warrant for the rest of the house."

"Works for me." Maya gathered up Juniper's leash and they started toward the cabin. Her heart pounded as adrenaline pumped. She loved these moments. She loved the rush. She also feared these moments because of the uncertainty.

Approaching the door, Maya and Juniper moved toward the side, Josh behind them. They all stayed away from the front of the door in case anyone was in there waiting to ambush them. Law enforcement called doors the fatal funnel because they were the most dangerous spot when making an entry. Ready to unleash Juniper to clear the cabin, Maya announced, "Forest Service Law Enforcement. Anyone here?"

Josh also identified himself, but there was no answer to either of them.

Maya yelled again, "Forest Service Law Enforcement! If anyone is here, come out with your hands up or I'm sending the dog."

No answer.

Juniper sounded off. Maya yelled one more time over Juniper's barks and yips that if anyone was in there, they needed to come out or the dog was coming in. Usually the K-9 barking inspired suspects to come out.

Still no answer.

Maya nodded at Josh and tried to ignore how easy it was to work with him. She shoved her thoughts aside. *Don't disregard what Sam said.* She needed to know more about Josh before completely trusting him.

She unclipped Juniper's leash and Josh did a couple donkey kicks to open the door. Maya told Juniper to "seek and go get 'em," the command for clearing a cabin or building.

Maya and Josh stayed shoulder to shoulder as they entered behind Juniper, who was trained to follow her nose and search for the scent she'd been tracking. She would also go into each room and sniff for anyone else hiding in the house. Maya remained behind with her gun drawn, but made sure she kept Juniper in her sight. The hardest part of working a dog was that they went into danger first and could also be ambushed. But their nose and instincts usually beat a criminal.

She could hear the clicking of Juniper's nails on the wooden floor. The cabin seemed small. Maybe just a couple rooms. On average it took a K-9 twenty seconds to clear a house. Juniper would work this cabin quickly.

Maya cleared the area around the front door first. Her training had taught her to stop and assess each direction and to break up the area into slivers like a pizza—one slice of space at a time. She started to her left and cleared everything in front of her, including behind the door.

After clearing the rest of the cabin, Juniper's nail clicking stopped, replaced by a thumping noise. "What's that?" she whispered to Josh. He shrugged.

Thump. Thump.

"Footsteps?" she whispered.

"Maybe, but doesn't sound quite right."

Juniper was stopped in front of a door leading to what was probably a bedroom. She panted and whined. Then she started digging at the door, telling Maya she wanted in there. Now.

Maya noticed Josh watching Juniper. "Keep an eye on me. I'll watch my dog. Remember, you're my cover officer."

Maya gave Josh a hand signal that he should back her up. They remained shoulder to shoulder and once again announced themselves as law enforcement officers.

Thump. Thump.

Maya couldn't tell if the noise was footsteps or someone trying to open a window to maybe escape. She reached the door, every sense on high alert. Staying off to the side, she grabbed the smooth, cold metal of the doorknob. She turned the handle, threw the door open and told Juniper to "seek and go get 'em."

Juniper leaped forward, barking and scrambling to get good footing on the wood floor. She burst into the room, Maya behind her. The room was pitch-black and while Maya's eyes adjusted, she could only hear the sound of Juniper's nails clicking again on the floor, along with her sniffing.

Maya pulled out a flashlight, holding it underneath her gun with her left hand. She watched Juniper work the room clockwise. Juniper stayed on the perimeter and stuck her nose up against the wall. At times she went up on her hind legs to scent higher. Maya followed Juniper's search with her flashlight although that made her an easy target because she was backlit. Juniper too. Then she realized something.

Josh had slipped ahead and was between her and Juniper. A cover officer should never get between a dog and handler. It kept the handler from reading their dog's body language and risked the dog biting the cover officer.

"What the hell?" she muttered. Sam's warning of Josh not properly backing up his partner flashed through her mind. "Get back by me or behind me. I don't need Juniper biting or distracted by you."

Josh glanced over his shoulder and, realizing he'd stepped in front of Maya, followed her orders.

Thump. Thump.

Maya spun around to her right, gun out in front of her but still trying to watch Juniper. Josh stayed by her side. The thumping noise was a loose board covering a broken window. A breeze was blowing the board out and back. Josh headed over to inspect the board.

"Let Juniper work," Maya snapped. "Get out of the way."

"I'm clearing the area by this window and loose board."

"Let Juniper do it. That's why we have a K-9. And right now, since I'm the K-9 handler, I'm the officer in charge. You need to listen to me."

Maya thought she heard Josh mutter an expletive under his breath, but he backed away from the window. She didn't care. He needed to keep his ego in check.

"You going to back me up the right way?"

"Yes. Let's just get on with it. I got it. You're in charge. Now let's see what Juniper found."

"Okay," Maya said. "Just don't mess up again."

Juniper was sitting over by a corner, staring intently. Maya kept her gun out and stepped toward her dog. She shone the flashlight toward the area Juniper was alerting on and called her off. She asked Juniper to come sit by her side. "You can go see what Juniper found now."

"Gee, thanks," Josh said, getting down on his knees. An object was wedged back in the corner under the baseboard. He put on gloves and then began wiggling the object until it came loose. Her breath caught for a moment.

Josh must have heard her. "What is it?" he asked.

Maya didn't answer but threw Juniper her toy as a reward.

"That belongs to Pops," she said, staring at the engraved pocketknife Josh held in his hand. "My grandmother gave it to him. He never went anywhere without it."

"You think he left it for us to find?"

"Or he was trying to hide it. I'm not sure, but he was here, and his scent ties in with the track from Juniper."

"Okay, so this is all linked together. Let's get the money back to the lab for some fingerprinting and whatever else we can figure out. I can get some crime scene techs up here and start processing this cabin," Josh said. "Unless you want the FBI and your boss involved?"

"I'm guessing we are actually on private land right now."

"Really?"

Maya shot Josh a look. "Yes. Like I said before, I'd need to look at my map to tell for sure, but I think this is private. That means you have jurisdiction and I'm just along for the ride."

"Okay, I'll get a warrant since we know the sheriff was here and we haven't searched anything else. We'll tear this place apart and see if we can find more that will help us find your grandfather. Let's get this evidence to the lab. I'll put it on priority."

"Thank you," she said. Juniper came up and pushed her head into Maya's hands. She responded by scratching her ears and studying Josh's body language.

Did he really make honest mistakes as my cover officer? Or was he trying to get ahead of me and find evidence first? What are the odds Josh is working with the Rays?

Maya vowed to find out more about Josh. If he was behind the disappearance of her grandfather, then she needed to find out why and who Josh would be giving information to—quickly.

Chapter Thirty-Seven

Maya made a quick stop by her office to take a look at her national forest map hanging on the back wall. The cabin Juniper tracked to was indeed on private land. She didn't know who the property belonged to, but the sheriff's office could find out that information. She would head there next.

On the way out, Maya passed by her desk. She paused. The ring from Doug was back in the top drawer. She opened up the drawer and pulled out the black box, putting it in one of her pant pockets. Maybe somehow the ring would bring her luck. Or she would be able to use it to figure out the identity of Doug's mystery girl.

A few minutes later, she pulled up to the sheriff's office and let Juniper out to run around and stretch on the grassy area in front of the building. The dog sniffed around, enjoying the outside scents. The breeze picked up making the evergreen trees wave and dance. Near the entrance to the building, an American flag and Colorado State flag fluttered.

Maya smiled, watching the dog's joy. She hadn't realized how much she had missed having a dog, but she hated the stress of something happening to Juniper. What if someone had been in the cabin and Juniper had been injured? That was the part that worried Maya, but if she was going to do this job she had to toughen up.

Juniper wagged her tail, looking for a pat and for Maya to tell her what a great dog she was. Maya obliged. Then she opened the back compartment and Juniper jumped in, took a drink of water, turned in a circle and settled down for a nap. Josh had pulled up nearby and was waiting, evidence bags in hand.

Maya and Josh went inside the building and headed back to the evidence room. The sheriff's department was small, which matched the town, but she knew that her grandfather was pushing for building more evidence storage space as their town grew.

Josh started filling out the paperwork for each item, logging it in and writing up a chain of custody. Then he put the evidence into a locker. The locker could only be opened on the other side by the crime scene tech. "Let's go talk to Miranda really quick. Since this pertains to your grandfather, I want her to at least run prints tonight. Some of the other tests might take longer."

"Works for me," Maya said, following Josh through another set of doors into the room used to dust for fingerprints and that housed other equipment to collect evidence from crime scenes. The room was cool and a large evidence bench sat in the middle. Maya didn't know what all the different machines did, but she recognized a few of them including a specialized forensic drying cabinet, a fingerprint powder station and fingerprint development station. Different chemicals lined a shelf, including Luminol to check for blood and various types of fingerprint dust.

Another door swung open and a petite dark-haired woman strolled in. At first glance she appeared to be about twelve, but a few crow's-feet around her eyes gave away that she was probably a little older than Maya. She had large blue eyes accentuated by her purple-rimmed glasses and perfectly done dark red lipstick that somehow complemented her sheriff's uniform in a no-nonsense way.

"Hey Miranda," Josh said. "I'd like you to meet my friend and our local Forest Service officer, Maya Thompson."

"Nice to see you, Josh," Miranda said, turning to Maya. "Pleased to meet you."

"Likewise," Maya said.

"Thompson. You any relation to the sheriff?" Miranda asked.

"He's my grandfather."

"I'm sorry to hear that he's missing. Any news?"

Both Josh and Maya shook their heads no. "I have a favor to ask," Josh said.

"Am I going to have to stay late to fulfill this favor?"

Josh shrugged. "I don't know. Maybe. Probably."

"But it's to help find my grandfather," Maya interjected.

"In that case, I'm in. What do you need?"

"I have some evidence I put in a locker. I need prints lifted and run through the system," Josh answered.

"You got it. I have some evidence drying right now, so I was at a stopping point anyway with that case. I'll get on it."

"How about we get you some lunch?" Maya asked. "We were just heading over to the Black Bear Café. We can bring you something back."

"Deal," Miranda said, her eyes lighting up. "I'd love one of their BLTs with chips and a Coke."

"You got it," Maya said. "I'll buy."

Miranda smiled and then a look of concern came over her face. "If you don't mind me asking, did you find this evidence on federal land? Am I going to be stepping on any toes? I mean, I know we have agreements to help you, but for certain evidence, the FBI still likes to take the lead."

"The K-9 track started on federal land, but my dog took us to a cabin on private land. I confirmed that on my way here. I'd rather you run it here, especially since this pertains to my grandfather's disappearance."

"Okay," Miranda said. "Oh, and a chocolate chip cookie."

"Excuse me?" Maya said.

"A cookie with the lunch you're going to buy me." Miranda gave a wink. As she headed through the door she said, "Come back in an hour or so and I'll hopefully have some results for you."

"Thanks," Maya said.

"She's the best," Josh said. "We're lucky to have her."

"Don't forget that," came a voice from the other side of the door.

"And apparently she has really good hearing," Maya said. "Come on, let's go get some lunch."

They headed outside, and she stopped to check on Juniper. The young dog had her face pressed against the metal part of her carrier and was staring at Maya. "I guess she's rested," she said. "That was a quick nap. I forgot what a young dog was like."

Josh laughed. "Why don't you get her out and let her walk with us on leash? I'll go in and get the food. But you're still paying."

"Deal," Maya said, grabbing Juniper's leash. As soon

as Juniper saw that Maya had the leather lead, she ran circles and started yipping. "I'll be a minute. I'm going to wait for her to settle so this doesn't become a habit."

"You got it. I'll go get our order started."

A few minutes later, Juniper settled down enough for Maya to open the door and get her leash on. She stepped back and let Juniper jump down. Juniper landed, shook her whole body, and then began some small yips again. A few people walking by paused with concerned looks on their faces. Even though Maya knew the dog was being playful, a Malinois could be intimidating. There were many reasons law enforcement used the Mals and the shepherds. Intimidation was one of them.

Maya settled Juniper by taking the opportunity to work on obedience. Once Juniper was listening better, Maya asked her to heel. They left the sheriff's department and headed down the sidewalk. She was proud that Juniper's behavior was improving. One person even asked if she could pet Juniper. Maya gave her the command to relax and be "off duty." Juniper gave the lady a few licks in return.

Approaching the café, Maya saw Josh inside ordering. She signaled to Josh that she had the cash when he was ready and then she put Juniper on a down-stay in some grass. The door opened behind them, and Maya turned around expecting Josh to be there. Instead, Maya was staring at Jenna Ray.

It took Maya a moment to recognize Jenna. Even over the last couple of days, she'd lost weight and there were circles under her eyes. Jenna was a beautiful woman—she could almost be a model—but now she appeared haunted.

Jenna paused for a moment and stared at Juniper.

Before Maya could say anything, Juniper hopped up and raced toward Jenna.

Maya was ready to pull her up, but she noticed that Juniper's tail was wagging and she was dancing around Jenna the same way she did around Josh.

It was like Juniper knew Jenna.

"You can pet her if you want," Maya said, testing out her theory.

"No thanks." Jenna gave Juniper one last look and then headed down the street, hands in her pockets.

Jenna looked over her shoulder once, and Maya thought she saw a look of sadness cross her face. But Jenna continued, hunched over a little bit, not the same person Maya had seen even at the bar a couple days ago. Juniper continued to wag her tail and gazed longingly at Jenna.

"You seem like you know her pretty well, girl." Maya signaled for Josh to come out.

"Don't worry, I was going to get the money from you," he said.

She handed him a twenty. "Did you see where Jenna Ray was sitting?"

"I did."

"Go in there and grab her glass. Bag it for evidence just in case she's not in the system. I want to see if her fingerprints match the ones on the evidence we just gave Miranda."

"Okay. I look forward to hearing what brought you to that conclusion," Josh said, raising an eyebrow and shrugging. "I'll be right back."

"Hurry up. We don't want them to bus the table and lose the glass."

Josh shook his head. "I'm on it."

A few minutes later Josh came out with several paper bags. "Here's the evidence," he said, handing Maya a bag with a glass. "I think you bought a glass with lunch. You owe me five more dollars."

"It's worth it if it's a match."

"What makes you think Jenna is connected to this? Other than she's a Ray."

"Juniper acted like she knew her," Maya said. "She gave the same reaction to Jenna that she does to you or me. I let someone else who didn't know Juniper pet her a few minutes ago. Juniper was friendly, but not that excited. She broke a down-stay the moment she saw Jenna."

"So if Juniper knows Jenna that well, you're thinking Jenna is Doug's secret girlfriend and not Bobbi?"

"Maybe. And she's about the size and build of the person I saw at the cabin when we were bombed."

"But if she was dating Doug, why would he have set the bombs? His prints were the only ones on the explosives. Do you think he was trying to kill her? And from what you said, she set those bombs off deliberately, so maybe she beat him to it? Possibly a lovers' quarrel?" Josh said.

"I don't know. None of this makes sense, and I can't figure it out either. I don't think he would have killed her, but love can make people do strange things."

Josh's cell phone rang, and he handed Maya the bags with their lunches. Then he answered his phone. "Yep. Uh-huh. Okay, we'll be right there."

"Who was that?" Maya asked after Josh hung up.

"Miranda. She said she got some results, but she wants to tell us in person."

"That was quick. Let's go." Maya, Josh, and Juniper

sprinted back to the station. Maya put Juniper back in the car and they hurried into the sheriff's building to the crime scene lab.

Miranda was working on cleaning up some of the dust from the fingerprints. Maya had to admit she kept a very clean lab. "Here's your lunch," Josh said, holding up a bag.

"You can put it over there," Miranda said, pointing to an office.

Josh followed instructions and came back. "What did you find?"

"Believe it or not, there were a couple of good prints on the knife you found in the bushes, but there was no match in the system as of now. I also used Ninhydrin on the cash and found some good prints. Have a match for those. They belong to Officer Leyton. Those came back quick since he was definitely in the system."

Maya let out a breath and felt disappointment and anger at the same time. Doug *was* involved. What was he thinking? Did he start dating Jenna and let her pull him into this? Maya didn't want to accept that Doug might not be the person she thought he was, but it was a fact she had to deal with.

"You could take the print we can't identify to the feds and see if by any chance they get a hit in their system," Miranda said.

"Before I do that, would you mind running the print on this glass and seeing if it's a match to the print that's not in the system?" Maya asked.

"I can do that, but I have some other things to get done today. I may not get to it until tonight, unless it's a rush pertaining to the sheriff again."

"It's a rush," Josh said. Maya gave him a grateful

look and he said, "If this print matches Jenna, then we might be able to get a search warrant."

"Even though Juniper isn't certified and is the one who found the knife and cash?" Maya asked.

"I'll plead it to the judge. I'll explain that we used the K-9 in an unusual circumstance because of the missing sheriff and that we didn't have any other dogs available. It's worth a shot," Josh said, adding, "And the glass was obtained without using the dog, in a legal way, so that helps too."

"Agreed," Maya said.

"Okay," Miranda said. "I'll get this going and let you two know what I find and if the print matches."

"If it does, then we're one step closer to finding Pops," Maya said, feeling a little bit of hope for the first time.

Chapter Thirty-Eight

Wayne woke up, rolled over and struggled to sit up, his body aching. As he moved, he heard clanging and clinking. Chains. His captor had learned: don't tie him with a rope.

He forced his eyes open. It was almost like he was waking up from surgery. He must have been drugged. How long would it take to get his mind out of this fog?

He took in his new surroundings. He was in some sort of outbuilding. A barn or an old shed? He let his eyes adjust to the dark and breathed in and out slowly, working to get his brain to come out of the effects of the drug.

His left arm was sore and there was enough light to see a needle prick. He was lucky to still be alive since the person had injected him with who knows what. How long had he been out?

His lips were dry and cracked. If he got dehydrated, he couldn't live for long. What did she want with him? His brain was foggy, but he remembered her face. Not who he was expecting. Damn. He went to rub his face, but he hit the end of the chains and couldn't reach.

Wayne scooted back, trying to find a wall to lean against, fear welling up inside him—something he hadn't felt in a long time. He was going to die, and Maya would never know the truth about Doug and her grandmother. He should have told her everything. She deserved to know. He also wanted to say he was sorry about being so mad about the funeral. Didn't he always tell her that funerals were for the living? Had he stopped and thought about the pain she might be in? She wasn't the same. War did that to a person. He should know. He had served in Vietnam. Maya wasn't the only person with nightmares.

Wayne had been too wrapped up in his own grieving to tell her that he loved her and was proud of her, and most of all forgive her for not coming home for her grandmother's funeral. She'd been through so much in her life, including the snippets of memory she had from her mother's death, but he'd been selfish and hadn't seen that. Doug had tried to tell him. He hadn't listened.

He'd been so pissed when Doug had come to his office a couple weeks ago and told him the truth. He remembered Doug strolling in that day. Wayne was already in a bad spot, still grieving his wife and wishing she were there to help him talk to Maya.

When Doug had knocked on the door, Wayne could tell by his face that something was wrong. He'd assumed it was about Maya. That she'd finally unraveled. Maybe her drinking had earned her a DUI and now Wayne had to bail her out.

"Sit down," he remembered saying, gesturing to a chair. "What can I help you with?"

Doug had nodded and taken a seat. He stared at the floor, hands in his coat pockets. When he looked up, Wayne was surprised to notice signs of stress and even a few tears brimming.

"Doug, what's wrong? Is it Maya?" Wayne prodded. He stood up and shut his office door, sitting back down.

Doug stared down at his hands now on his lap, interlaced. "No, it's me," he finally answered. "I need to talk to you because I'm in deep shit and I don't know how to get out of it or what to do."

Wayne should have helped Doug more. He was like a father or grandfather to him, after all. After Doug's father died, Wayne and Karen had helped out Doug's mother. They became family. Family stood by your side no matter what.

But Doug wasn't a kid anymore. He should have known better. And Wayne wasn't young anymore either. He stretched his stiff joints again. As his body continued to ache, he also thought about his age. Next year he was back up for reelection, and at sixty-eight, maybe it was time to hang up his badge and take up more fishing and trail riding and most importantly, spending time with Maya.

First, he had to get out of here.

Think, Wayne.

Stop and think.

What had he always told Maya when she was little? *Don't panic.* He needed to take his own advice here.

Wind whooshed outside and the old building rattled. Sunbeams highlighted dust particles floating through the air. Wayne moved his feet and straw rustled underneath them. Picking up his hands, he tested the chains. Everything in here was old. Maybe he could pull the chains out of the wall. He strained against the cuffs and they bit into his skin.

Wayne shuffled around and worked to get a closer look at what was holding the chains. He was in some sort of old cow milking barn. The rings and chains were attached to concrete. If a cow couldn't pull that out, then no human would be able to either. The rest of the barn would probably collapse before the chains gave way. He had to wait until his captor came back.

If she ever did.

Keep thinking, Wayne.

Maybe he could unscrew the tie from the wall. His legs felt like rubber, but he managed to wobble to his feet. There were screws—rusted over. Even with a vat of WD-40 they might not ever move.

He studied the handcuffs around his wrists. If he could find the right tool like a small nail or paper clip, he could probably pick the cuffs loose. That seemed to be his best bet.

Wayne inspected the areas he could reach in the old barn. Most of the nails would be too big. He kicked around the straw, frustration building. What did he expect to find? Paper clips underneath? There was nothing useful here, but he refused to sit down and do nothing.

Wayne tipped his head. He thought he heard a truck. The closer it got, the louder the engine was. Most likely a diesel. He sat back down. He should look like he was waking up.

The truck shut off. After the deafening sound of the engine, the barn seemed eerily quiet. A vehicle door opened and closed. Wayne slowly breathed in and out. *Remain calm*, he kept telling himself.

The door to the barn creaked open, and for a moment the sunlight blasted through, blinding him. He shut his eyes and turned his head away.

"Nice to see you're awake again."

"Out of all the people I would think of who would take me, you aren't the one I was expecting," Wayne said.

"I know. It's time to move you again. I can't have anyone find you."

Wayne was ready to stand, but then the person rushed him. There was a prick in his arm, and a few seconds later, everything went dark again.

Chapter Thirty-Nine

"What next?" Maya asked Josh. They stood outside the sheriff's office, the sun beating down. Summer had arrived, but some thunderheads in the distance hinted toward afternoon storms. "We don't have anything to go on. All our leads have been a dead end. Even if Miranda matches Jenna's print, we can't do anything until we get a warrant."

"I know," Josh said. "You and Juniper could head back out on patrol and watch for the Russian visitor or any sign of Jenna. We can follow them. Maybe if the Russian or the Rays took your grandfather, they will lead you to his location."

Maya knew that Josh was giving her busywork to help her out. She wanted to figure out who the informant was from the department. Her grandfather might have more information in his office, but she didn't want to tell Josh what she was up to. "Going back to patrol sounds good, but keep me in the loop."

"I will. I promise."

"Okay." Maya turned to go when dispatch radioed in. She and Josh both stopped and listened to the call.

"There's a male subject on the line. He claims he has found a possible deceased person up Moose Track Pass.

Reporting party has agreed to stay on scene. Please respond."

"Shit," Maya said, hitting the button to her radio. Her hand shook. "Did the RP say if the deceased was male or female?"

"No, RP is very upset and didn't give me that information."

"Can you get back in touch and ask?" Maya said. *Could it be Pops?*

"I'm sorry, I keep losing contact with the RP. I'll see if we can switch to texting and if I can get more information."

"Just find out if the body is the sheriff. Radio me. I'm on my way," Maya said.

The sidewalk seemed to spin underneath her, and for a moment she thought she was going to toss up her lunch. She heard Josh radio that he would also go with her, but she was running to her patrol vehicle, not paying full attention. Her hands continued to shake as she tried to get the keys in the ignition. She couldn't lose Pops too.

Maya finally managed to start her vehicle when a knock at the window startled her. *Josh.*

"I'm responding to the call with you. You up for this? You look upset."

"Josh, what if it's Pops?"

"I'll look at the body first, okay?"

"Let's quit chatting and get going." Maya was now annoyed. She didn't need to be coddled—she needed to know the identity of the body. "You know where you're going?"

"I've heard of that mountain pass, but I'll follow you," Josh said, sprinting back toward his car.

Maya flipped on the lights and floored her vehicle in reverse. Juniper sensed the urgency and started to get excited in the back, giving loud yips. "Don't get too excited, girl. You may not be needed on this."

Juniper settled down for a moment, cocking her head to listen to Maya.

"Get ready for some bumpy roads."

Juniper lay down and gave a whine.

"Atta girl. Just stay there and you'll be good."

Maya floored her patrol vehicle to make up as much time as she could while she was still on paved roads. That and, she had to admit, driving fast was a blast. A job perk. Responding to a possible homicide? Not so much a job perk. Especially if the body was her grandfather.

She tried to push that thought away. *I can't handle losing him.*

About thirty minutes later, Maya parked near a clearing where two roads intersected. One road was meant more for ATVs, but many hikers liked to follow that path as well. The other road was a pass that served as a scenic shortcut through the mountains. Most people drove it in the summer or fall to enjoy the majestic mountains. In the winter, the Forest Service shut down the road due to heavy snowfall.

Maya put her vehicle in Park and could see a distraught guy pacing the area. He looked to be about nineteen. Maybe a college student up for the day from Colorado State University in Fort Collins, or maybe he was a ski bum that was trying to figure out what to do with his summer. He had on a baseball cap that said *420*, long shorts, and a shirt with Rocky Mountain High printed across his chest. Based on the marijuana references, Maya now wondered if he was out here to get away and smoke a little weed. If there hadn't been a dead body she would have asked since marijuana was still illegal on federal land.

Maya radioed to dispatch she had arrived at the scene. Josh was a little bit behind her, still making his way up the pass. She stepped out of her vehicle and approached the young man.

She didn't even have to ask him for information. The moment he saw her, he started blabbing. "I was, like, up here hiking and, uh, enjoying nature. Then I come around this bend and I see this."

"Where? I don't see the body. Male or female?"

"Yeah, it like totally freaked me out, so I don't know if it's a chick or a dude."

"Just show me where the body is," Maya said, irritated. Normally she'd be a little more understanding. Finding a deceased person was traumatic and she understood that, but she needed to know if it was Pops. She saw Josh pull up and step out of his vehicle. The man pointed to his left.

Maya was afraid to look but needed to know if this was Pops. She took a deep breath, tried to ready herself, and stepped forward towards the human remains. Josh had come over and was by her side. As they carefully treaded around the area to avoid damaging the crime scene, she couldn't tell at first if it was Pops. The body had been pulled behind a large boulder—either by a human or an animal.

"Maya," Josh said, stopping for a moment. "Why don't you let me look first? You know, just in case…"

"No, I'm fine. I need to know. Now."

She and Josh stepped over to the boulder and peered behind it.

Maya stared down, and shock registered through her body.

It was Bobbi.

The word *PIG* was smeared across her chest in blood. She was definitely dead, and by the looks of it had been here overnight, since it appeared some animals had come and chewed on her.

Maya sat back on her heels, relieved. *Thank God this isn't Pops.*

"Damn it," she muttered.

Her breathing became quick and she shut her eyes, trying to keep the flashback from happening. For a moment she remembered combat boots that were blown off the body they belonged to and had landed across the road. When she opened her eyes, the forest was gone and there was the desert, sand blowing in her face, shouts all around her, Zinger whining.

Maya shut her eyes again. When she reopened her them and saw tall pine trees, her whole body shook, and it felt like someone was standing on her chest. She fought to control her shaking and breathing.

"Maya, what's wrong?"

Josh. It was Josh. Josh hadn't been in Afghanistan. *Control yourself, Maya.*

She closed her eyes one more time. She heard footsteps, and when she opened her eyes, Josh was standing closer, a look of concern across his face.

She was in Colorado. She wasn't deployed. Juniper was in the Tahoe. Not Zinger.

"Sorry," she said. "I just need a moment."

"Dude, and I thought I was messed up about the body," the young man said.

"I'm fine," Maya said, coming back to reality. "First, tell us your name."

"Dustin."

"You have a last name, Dustin?" Maya asked.

"Flynn. Dustin Flynn."

"I need your phone number too, please," she said, glad to focus on something that kept her out of her flashback.

Dustin gave her the information she needed. "Do I have to stay here like much longer? That dead body is totally creeping me out, dude."

Maya and Josh gave each other a look. If they'd thought Dustin was a suspect Maya would have detained him, but there was nothing that pointed to him killing the person. He seemed to be telling the truth.

"Stay here for now in case we have any questions," Maya said.

"You can sit in the back of my vehicle," Josh said to Dustin. He went over to open the back door and then said to Maya, "I'll get crime scene techs up here."

"Not yours," she said. "Did you see the badge lying next to her? This has to go federal. She was working for the DEA."

"What?" Josh peered over at Bobbi again. "Shit. She must have been working undercover. No wonder she bailed out so quick. I'll start marking off the area then and we'll wait for hours for the feds to grace us with their presence."

"I know it'll take a while, although maybe once they know it's one of their agents, they'll get here faster. You get a deputy up here to secure the scene. That way we can continue investigating. Bobbi's death ties into the Rays, their drug business and the kidnapping of my grandfather. Her cover was probably blown, maybe even by me when I arrested her," Maya said. "I'll get Juniper out and see if we can do an evidence search or track again."

"We can't use that evidence since she's not certified."

"No," Maya sighed. "And that's a good point, because if I mess up the feds nailing someone for killing one of their own, they'll fire me."

Juniper stared out the window, and Maya heard a low whine come from her.

"Rad dog," Dustin said.

Maya tried not to roll her eyes. "Thanks. Listen, we need you to tell us the truth. Did you see anything? Anyone while you were out hiking today?"

"No, man. I was just out being one with nature, you know? I didn't see anyone."

Maya nodded, and then she and Josh walked away to chat where Dustin couldn't hear them. "I actually believe him," she said.

"I do too," Josh said.

"This ties into our case. You know it. I know it. It's just a matter of who killed her and why. Was it one of the Rays? Or is it our Russian tourist friend? Either way, this has to tie into my grandfather's disappearance too."

"We still don't know that all this ties into your grandfather's disappearance," Josh said. "But I agree that Bobbi's death was probably caused by the Rays or the Russian. I'm sure that's who she was investigating even though she never told us."

Maya looked at her cell phone. She had spotty service, which was why Dustin and the dispatcher had switched to texting. At least they had radio service. "Let's radio dispatch, see if we can get a deputy up here to secure the scene. When we get back into reliable cell phone service, we can call the DEA and let them know. Maybe we can get some information out of them about Bobbi's investigation and the Rays. Then I'm going out to the Ray Ranch and demanding that they let us look around."

"That'll go over really well." Josh raised an eyebrow.

"Okay, then Juniper and I will sneak in and I'll have her look for my grandfather. She'll let me know if he's at the Ray Ranch. You have any other suggestions?"

"Let's do the first part and then see if I can talk the judge into giving us a warrant. You know, stay legal and not lose our jobs? Especially if Miranda has a match to that print. She was going to call me, but as you mentioned, cell service is iffy here."

"What do we do with him?" Maya nodded toward Dustin.

"As soon as my deputy gets here, I'll take him back to town. Ask to get some more information and then let him go. I don't think he's our guy, but I want to make sure we can get in touch with him."

"It's a plan. I'm getting going. Daylight is a-wasting." Juniper barked in agreement.

Chapter Forty

Carson strode to the weapons room. Cody was trailing him like a duckling following its mother.

Carson had sent the men out on different tasks—the main one was following Lana. He needed more intel on her. He should have shot her when he'd had the chance.

He felt better now that Bobbi was dead. That had to be his leak, only one thing kept bothering him—he didn't think Bobbi stole the money or the product. There was someone else in his crew he couldn't trust. Carson had to figure that out before Lana came back. Was it someone close to him? Like Cody? Or Jenna? They knew what family meant and that you never betrayed family. Although sometimes he wondered about Jenna. She was so damn obsessed with getting back to college. As if that would change her life.

Then there was Cody. Lately Cody had been leaving at odd times, and after finding all the drug paraphernalia, Carson knew that he showed all the signs of using. Then there was that stupid stunt he'd pulled at the bar with the fed. At least Bobbi and Jenna had pulled him out of there.

He had to start with questioning Cody. Jenna would

be next. It would break his heart if his children were betraying him. But he would deal with it. He always did.

Carson pulled down a rifle and handed it to Cody. "You need to keep this with you. You'll need protection with Lana coming back."

"Got it," Cody said.

"You took care of things?" Carson said.

"What do you mean? Bobbi?" Cody asked.

"You buried the body? No one will find it?"

"Uh, yeah. It's all good."

"Don't lie to me, son." Carson stepped closer. "You know I don't like liars. You saw what happened to Bobbi when she lied to me, and I loved her. Tell me the truth—did you bury the body?"

"I didn't have time to bury it, but I hid it where no one would ever find it."

"If someone finds that body, so help me..."

"No, it'll be fine."

Carson stared at his son and then went back to contemplating which guns he would like to have with him. What gave him the best advantage against Lana? He had a nice selection that had increased from his earnings. His favorites were the assault rifles with the illegal thirty-round magazine. He also loved his Mossberg shotguns. His favorite handguns were the Sig Sauers, Glocks, and Berettas. He finally settled on the Sig P320.

Carson went over to the ammo supply. "See, the thing is," he said, "I think you've half-assed everything you've been doing lately, like not burying Bobbi."

Cody leaned back against the wall and crossed his arms.

"If you want to be a part of this business," Carson continued, "even take it over someday, then I need you to step up and show me that. Lying to me is not a way of doing that. Tell me how you disposed of Bobbi since you didn't bury her like I asked."

Cody looked away and then back at his father. "I hid the body and figured wild animals would take care of it. No one will know."

"Thanks for finally telling me the truth. We both know that at some point, despite your theory, someone will discover a bone or find the skull and that is when this will lead back to us."

"Then maybe you should start cleaning up your own messes, Dad."

"What's that supposed to mean?"

Cody stepped forward, and Carson saw anger cross his face. Good. The kid was finally growing a pair. "That means that when you shoot your pig girlfriend, then you should take care of it. Or have some other guy take care of it rather than let your son be the one who serves time. It means that you should have started your own business and never relied on Lana to help us out, and you should start treating Jenna and myself like the adults we are."

"Then stop lying to me like a little kid and start manning up."

"Fine," Cody said. "Now let's figure out how to get this Russian out of the way. I'll send some of the guys to where I left Bobbi. They can take care of it. I want to be a part of this business and be treated as an equal."

"Okay," Carson said. "Then I have a couple more questions. And I need the truth."

"Fine." Cody unfolded his arms. "What do you need to know?"

"There's some money missing that was meant to go

to the Russians. About eighty thousand. They're not happy, and rightfully so. While I don't like them and I plan on them leaving the business soon, we owe them that money."

"I don't know anything about it. How and when did that happen?"

Carson grabbed a toothpick and started rolling it around in his mouth. This time he believed Cody. His son was easy to read. "Back with a delivery. We were supposed to give her a percentage of our cut. Lana had increased that percentage and wanted some money back."

"That's bullshit," Cody said. "I didn't know she increased the percentage."

"I know, I know." Carson held up his hands. "It's one of the reasons I don't want to do business with her anymore. She's not honest. She doesn't deserve to be in business with someone like us. But it doesn't change the fact that we owed her the money. So I pulled some from our stash and sent it with one of our shipments a couple weeks ago. Someone had replaced the inner cash with twenties, so the outside had hundred-dollar bills and looked valid. Lana wants her money, and I don't blame her. What do you know about this?"

Cody shrugged and said, "Nothing. Which one of our guys made that delivery?"

"I've already looked into that and I don't think it was one of the delivery guys. I think it's someone close to us."

"You think I did that?"

Carson stepped up and cupped the back of Cody's head. "I don't think so, but I had to be sure. You see now why it's so important to tell me the truth? I'd hate to think my own son was betraying me."

"I love you, Dad. I would never betray you."

"I'm glad to hear that, because there's something else I need to know."

"What? I'll tell you anything."

"Good," Carson said. "Are you still using some of the product?"

Cody looked away, and Carson tightened his grip around Cody's head. "Look at me."

Cody's eyes flickered back and then he stared at his boots.

"You are using, aren't you?" Carson asked.

Tears sprang up in Cody's eyes. Shit, was his only son really such a pussy that he was going to cry over this? Carson thought he'd raised him to be stronger than that.

"Every now and then," Cody finally answered. "Just when things get rough."

"Are you stealing product from our shipments?"

"No, of course not. Sometimes Jenna has a little extra left over. You know."

"No, I don't know. How would she have extra?"

"I don't know," Cody said. "You'd have to ask her. I think she figured out how to make the codeine stretch out a little bit more. Purify the product or something like that. She offered me some a while back. I liked it. Every now and then I get some from her."

Carson lowered his grip to around Cody's neck. He gave a strong squeeze and saw Cody wince. Then he let go and unbuttoned Cody's cuff, rolling up the sleeve. Just as he suspected, there were some track marks and the start of sores.

"You're going to get clean. Stop this shit right now. We sell it. We don't use it. You start using it and you start making mistakes like not burying a body correctly. We don't want that, do we?"

Cody shook his head no.

"Good. At least this explains where you've been disappearing to and why you've been so out of it some days. I'll help you, son. You're going to go through some strong detox, but I'll get you through it."

"Okay, thanks, Dad." Cody wiped his nose with his arm. "I just want to make you proud. I know I need to do better."

"We'll do this. Together. Now, where's your sister? I need to talk to her."

"I'm not sure. I think she left a little bit ago. Something about starting another batch."

"I didn't ask her to do that. I'll figure out where she is. You get your shit together and then we'll figure out a plan from here."

"Okay," Cody said.

Carson sent him out of the room. How did he ever raise such a wuss? But at least he was loyal.

His daughter? That might be another story.

Chapter Forty-One

Wayne felt like he'd been beat with a sledgehammer. His captor must have given him some more of the drugs. His shoulders ached and he knew at this point his knees were so stiff it would make it hard to get to his feet. They were full of arthritis left over from the years in Vietnam as a young guy jumping in and out of helicopters. His doctor had wanted him to have both knees replaced. Wayne had put that off for as long as possible, but if he got out of this, maybe he'd consider it. The pain couldn't be much worse than what he was enduring right now.

He'd been moved again. Although, after being drugged, all the places were starting to look the same. It appeared he was in yet another barn or outbuilding. He could see into the next room where his captor was working in what almost looked like a chemistry lab.

She turned around. "I know you're awake."

Wayne looked up, carefully opening one eye and then another. "Yes, I'm awake. Don't suppose I could have some water?"

To his surprise, his captor walked over to him, crouched down, and pulled out a water bottle from her bag. She gave him a drink. The water hit his parched lips and slid down his throat. Cool and refreshing, it was the best thing he'd ever tasted.

"Thank you," Wayne said.

"You're welcome. You know, I'm not a horrible person."

"I know that, Jenna."

"I saved you from my father and brother."

"What do you mean?"

"They were going to kidnap you and hand you over to the Russian mob lady we've been working with. The mob was interested in torturing you for information."

"What kind of information?" Wayne asked. He was genuinely curious, and he wanted to keep Jenna talking. Her appearance came across a little ragged—her eyes were bloodshot, and her face was pale. She was a beautiful girl, but Wayne suspected based on her appearance that she'd been sampling a little bit of her own product. He didn't know if he could reason with her or not, but maybe if he kept her talking it would help.

"My dad wanted to know what Doug had told you and if there was an investigation into him. We had no idea how much you knew. The mob wanted someone to pay for losing the product to the explosion that day. Thinking Doug was responsible for the explosion, my dad was convinced you knew all about the drug trafficking operation. He thought kidnapping you was a good way to get his information and get the mob off his back by handing you over to them when he was done with you."

"You're not making total sense, Jenna. Slow down. Why did your father think kidnapping me would keep what Doug told me quiet?"

"Doug only told you about our family's illegal activities, no one else, so with you gone our secrets would be safe. Plus, my father's crazy. We all are. Haven't you noticed?" Jenna stepped back and gestured behind her. "I mean, who freaking makes drugs in one of their old outbuildings? Fire hazard at the minimum. Crazy people. My dad thinks he's so badass, like some drug kingpin or something. He thinks he'll rule the world because I've made the perfect product. Give his daughter a little education and see what happens. I never should have come home."

"Why did you? Come home, that is?"

Jenna stared at Wayne, and for a moment he thought he'd crossed a line. One that she wouldn't come back from. To his surprise she teared up a little bit and slumped back on a nearby hay bale. "It was my mom."

"If I remember right, she was sick. Cancer?" Wayne asked.

"Yes. And that bastard, otherwise known as my father, thought he could help her by taking codeine from someone in the Russian mob. Brilliant, don't you think? That's when I started making this shit." Jenna gestured behind her. "It helped with the pain and we didn't have to pay for expensive prescriptions. Krokodil is just desomorphine. Long ago it was used for anesthesia. Now it's been contaminated with lots of crap like lighter fluid. I figured out how to make it pure. It helped my mom feel less pain…and apparently users love the high."

"And your dad decided to have you make more and sell it."

"Yeah. That asshole. I would call from college and Mom would try to make it sound like things were good, but I knew better. So, I came home," Jenna said. "I took care of her to the end, not my dad like he tells everyone.

He likes to make it sound like he was a perfect, loving, devoted husband, but he wasn't. He didn't do shit."

"I'm sorry to hear that, and I'm sorry you had to come home, but I know you loved your mom and she loved you. I ran into her once at the café. She was proud of you and your accomplishments. The first person in your family to go to college is what she told me. Why didn't you go back to college?"

"Why do you think?" Jenna said, her face turning red with anger. "My father wanted to make big money, supposedly just to pay off the medical bills. Yeah, right. That was bullshit. I didn't want any part of that and told him I was leaving. He told me he'd turn me in to the authorities because what I'd done was wrong, illegal. He said he wouldn't turn me in if I made a few more batches. Or at least that's what he made me believe."

Wayne's head throbbed, but he had to keep Jenna talking. Get her over to his side. Not to mention he was learning some interesting information that matched what Doug had told him. He took a chance and said, "I can help you."

"No one can help me. Not now or ever. I'm on my own. It's the way it is. I have to take care of myself."

"That's not true, Jenna. It's not too late to make things right. If you let me go and promise to be a witness against your dad, then I can help protect you. Get you in witness protection."

"Isn't that a federal thing? Like the U.S. Marshals or something?"

"Yes, but this has gone federal. The DEA has been watching your father for a while. You're right, he's under investigation. Just not from me. They had the courtesy to let me know they were investigating but that

I needed to stay out of it. I can't give you any more information than that," Wayne said, knowing that wasn't the full truth, but trying to keep Jenna calm.

"So, what you're saying is that you really can't help, because the feds have cut you out? You don't really have any control then, do you?" Jenna said. "No, I'm taking care of my father my own way. I don't trust law enforcement. Even Doug was going to turn me in, and I thought he loved me."

"He loved you very much. He wasn't going to turn you in," Wayne said, rubbing his temple, where his head was pounding. If he could just get Jenna to let him go, he could take care of this whole situation his own way. He'd have to involve the feds, but he would do everything he could to protect her.

"I don't believe that," Jenna said, interrupting Wayne's thoughts. "Doug was going to see you. He was going to tell you everything. He told me that the morning before he visited. I pleaded with him not to do that, but he had to be a Boy Scout and make things right. See? I couldn't even trust him."

"He came to me to make things right, but he wanted you protected. He was taking full responsibility. He said he wanted you to go back to college and live out your dream. He'd serve his time in prison for what he did. He wanted you to be happy."

"That's not true," Jenna said. Anger and frustration crossed her face. She kicked the hay bale.

"It *is* true. And I'll honor his request. He was like a son to me." Wayne watched Jenna pace and realized it wasn't just anger on her face, but grief.

He closed his eyes. Had Doug set the bombs? He didn't tell Wayne that. Perhaps Doug hadn't trusted

Wayne to keep Jenna out of trouble, so was he going to destroy the evidence? That's why his fingerprints were all over the bomb pieces. He hadn't been expecting anyone up at the lab that day, but why didn't he leave Maya behind? Wayne didn't know. Maybe Doug was desperate and not thinking straight.

"It was you there, wasn't it?" Wayne asked.

"Shut up." Jenna kept pacing. "There's no help for me. But I'm not going to prison. I've been in prison. Here, at this ranch. My father won't let me go. You're the only way I'm getting out of this. You're my escape plan."

"No, Jenna. It doesn't have to be this way. Please let me help."

"I said shut up. Get to your feet. Now. You're going to help me take down my family. Then I can run the business while my father and worthless brother rot in prison."

Wayne kept his eyes closed. He heard Jenna stop pacing.

"Stand up. Now," she said, coming closer.

He held up his hand in surrender. "Okay. Just give me a second."

Wayne forced his body to move. He felt dizzy and his head hurt like hell. He managed to get to his feet. Jenna, to his surprise, put one of his arms around her shoulder and started to help him walk out of the barn. "I'm sorry to have to do this," she said.

"You still have a choice."

"No. I don't."

Chapter Forty-Two

Maya went to her vehicle to leave. She was relieved the body wasn't Pops, but to see another officer shot wasn't easy either. Not to mention Bobbi had been left out in the wilderness where animals had scavenged on her body. Even with the carnage, the murderer had shot her so many times that bullet holes were still visible.

Were Bobbi and Doug's murders connected? If so, how did they connect with Pops's disappearance? Bobbi led back to the Rays. The Rays were possibly trafficking drugs, which led back to Doug, and Pops's last known location was near the Ray Ranch. They really needed a warrant for the Ray Ranch, but the judge had made it clear much more evidence was needed.

Maya said hello to Juniper, who was running circles in her compartment. She had been in the car too long and needed to get out and work off some energy.

An idea started to form. They weren't certified, but that didn't mean that Maya couldn't take her for a walk outside the crime scene and see what Juniper might find. Say, put on the tracking harness and see if they could figure out where Bobbi had been killed. There wasn't enough blood behind the rock for it to be the spot where Bobbi was shot. There was probably a blood trail somewhere, but using Juniper to find the scent would be much easier and less time-consuming than Maya and Josh searching. If they could find the location of the murder, there could be more evidence that might help secure a search warrant for the Ray Ranch.

Maya grabbed Juniper's tracking harness and put it on her. They would go for a walk. Nothing wrong with that. They might catch a track back to the crime scene since the suspect would be nervous and give off a lot of scent. There might also be evidence along the way for Juniper to find.

"What are you doing?" Josh asked. He was finishing up giving directions to his deputy before he headed back to the office. Dustin was in the back of his car waiting for a ride to town.

"Juniper needs a walk. Way too much energy. I thought I'd get her out here for a little while."

"With her tracking harness on?"

Juniper stared back and forth between Maya and Josh and then let out a sharp bark.

"See?" Maya said. "She wants to do something. And I figured the tracking harness would be the best to use. Easier to hang on to. If we happen to find anything on our little jaunt around, I'll let you know."

Josh sighed. "How about I help you out and go with you? You know, just in case your walk turns up anything that pertains to the crime scene."

"Only if you back me up properly. I'm still not happy about earlier," Maya said.

Juniper, sitting on her haunches, wagged her tail in the dirt, sending small pieces of gravel flying around.

Josh shook his head. "I promise I'll do things right.

It's been a while since I've been a cover officer for a K-9 team."

"Then no more mistakes. Pops's life could depend on it," Maya said.

"I understand. Trust me, I'm not taking this lightly. I'll stay out of the way. Let me get Dustin a ride with another deputy who's heading back to town. I'll be right back."

While Maya waited for Josh, she took Juniper to the trail that led into this location. It seemed like the most plausible place for Juniper to be able to pick up an odor. She needed Juniper to find the hottest track without all their scents interfering. Hopefully, Dustin's scent didn't mess Juniper up either.

Josh came back and nodded to Maya, indicating he was ready. She said, "Okay, girl. Let's go. Track."

She ran forward after Juniper, letting a little slack out of the leash and casting her out in different directions until her telltale body language changed. Maya was finally getting to know her dog and their partnership felt stronger. This was good practice before they had to go to certification. Or so she told herself.

Practice. That's all they were doing. Okay, if her boss found out she could be fired, but if it meant finding Pops, it was worth it.

Juniper started back down the trail Dustin had said he'd hiked. She quickly took a hard left and headed up a hill. If Maya remembered right, they were headed for a road that went over a pass and would connect with the Interstate. She thought she saw some drag marks on the hill and maybe some blood spots. She yelled back to Josh.

"I'm on it," he said, setting the marks for the crime scene techs.

Juniper went a short distance and found the road. She sniffed around for a minute and then sat. Maya saw what was left of a cell phone on the ground, and tire marks. She pulled Juniper up and praised her, giving her the toy to play with as a reward for finding the cell phone.

Josh was right behind her and saw the same thing. Nearby they spotted a large pool of blood that had soaked into the ground.

"I think this is where she was killed," Maya said.

"I agree. I'll get another deputy up here and we can mark off the scene. I'll also see if we can get that phone to our tech guys—maybe there's something to salvage."

"You have any more deputies to protect the scene?"

"I'll admit, I'm running low, but the DEA will be here soon and take over. Bobbi was one of theirs, and you know how they get. I'll get another guy here until the federal crime scene guys arrive."

"True," Maya said. "They'll want that cell phone too."

"I know," Josh said. "I'll give it to them, but maybe we can get something off it that will tell us about your grandfather first. If the Rays really do have him, then Bobbi probably would have tried to get that message out. That could even be what got her killed. I'll leave out the part about you taking Juniper for a 'walk.'"

Maya heard a buzz, and Juniper stopped chewing on her toy for a minute and tilted her head. Her triangular ears perked straight up.

"You have cell reception here?" Maya asked.

"I guess I do," Josh said, pulling out his phone. "That must be why Bobbi was here. She was probably trying to send a message."

He hit a button and listened to the voice mail that

had been left. Maya and Juniper stared at him, waiting for information. Maya hoped it would be about her grandfather.

Josh's face registered concern and then surprise. Then he put the phone back in his pocket.

"What is it?" Maya asked. Juniper stood up and stretched. Sensing the change in Maya and hoping she was going back to work, she began to dance around. Maya settled her back down.

"You were right. Your inclination about Jenna. That was Miranda calling, and she said the unknown fingerprints on the knife matched the glass Jenna Ray used. There's a good chance she's the one who kidnapped your grandfather. We have enough to get a warrant. Also, I had asked another deputy to look into who owned the property with the abandoned cabin. He left a voice mail and said it belonged to a Lillian Ray. Who's she?"

Maya felt excited and sad at the same time. "Lillian was Jenna and Cody's mother. She died not too long ago. I think it was cancer. I heard that's why Jenna came home."

"I think we've got enough to approach the judge again."

At least there was a break in the evidence. Without Juniper they wouldn't have that.

Maya reached down and scratched her on the head. She thought about how Juniper reacted to Jenna. Jenna was built like the suspect at the bombing. She was also blonde. Could Jenna be the mystery girlfriend? Was she stashing the money at Doug's—was it drug money? But why would Doug take Maya and Juniper up to the cabin that he knew was rigged with bombs? How would taking Pops benefit Jenna?

There were too many unanswered questions. Searching the Ray property could be the only way to get answers.

"How long to get a warrant?" Maya asked.

"I'll call the judge before we leave this spot and see if I can have one ready by the time I get back to town."

"Call me as soon as you hear something."

When Maya was back in town, she went into the sheriff's office. She would go through her grandfather's files until she found Josh's profile jacket and see if Sam was right. She had to decide how much to trust him and she couldn't do that without more information.

Maya nodded to the front desk deputy who let her in and went down a hall lined with photographs from flood and forest fire rescues. She opened the door to her grandfather's office but left the light off. She didn't want anyone to know she was snooping around. Probably a little bit out of her jurisdiction. She turned on her flashlight, hoping it wouldn't tip someone off that she was in the office.

She took note of the pictures around the office. There was one of Pops and Nana many years ago on their wedding day, Maya's mom as a young girl fishing with Pops, and right on the desk where he could look at it every day was the picture Maya had sent home of her and Zinger. She didn't realize Pops had this on his desk.

She picked up the picture. That moment with Zinger seemed like years ago when Maya was much more innocent.

Setting it back down, she focused back on the task at hand. She went to the filing cabinet and scrolled through all the files until she found Josh's. After pulling it out, Maya started reading. Josh hadn't lied about how his partner had been killed, and he had been cleared.

As Maya read the details of the incident, relief flooded over her. Josh had made an honest mistake in the death of his partner and Sam blew it out of proportion. Josh had made an error any of them could make—he hadn't patted down a kid. Cops had to be careful frisking a juvenile when they weren't the suspects. The kid's parents were having a domestic dispute. There really wasn't any reason to check and see if there were weapons on him. But that had cost Josh's partner his life because it turned out the child had snuck a gun out of the house. The kid saw his parents being arrested, freaked out, and shot at the first cop he saw.

Maya knew some cops would hold this against Josh forever, and that's probably why he left Chicago. If Sam knew the whole story, he would be the type to hold it against Josh. Sam was a little bit old-school and maybe his ego was bruised by Josh's promotion—especially since he had been friends with Pops for a long time.

Then Maya turned the page and saw the next entry.

Relief turned back to anger. *Damn it.* Josh *had* been holding back. There was more to Josh's story than just his partner being killed. He left out the details of everything that happened *after* his partner's death. She understood now why Josh was happy to be in Pinecone Junction. Pops not only gave him a second chance—he took a big risk in hiring Josh. No wonder Sam wasn't happy. Josh had a lot of demons in his past.

Maya closed the profile jacket. She would confront Josh about this information. He should have told her the whole story.

Could he be the informant for the Rays? Maybe. I

saw Carson send a text when we were finishing our surveillance and then Josh received a text. And when I called the other night, he didn't answer. Where was he? Maya would find him and have a heart-to-heart with him, otherwise known as an interrogation, in her mind.

Putting the profile jacket back, she saw another folder in her grandfather's filing cabinet with the name *Roberta Lind* typed at the top. Maya opened the folder and saw that Pops had been given information about Bobbi being undercover. He would have had to keep it quiet from just about everyone. It was probably just out of courtesy that the DEA let him know Bobbi was in the area.

Maya quickly flipped through the file and saw a picture of the blonde Russian, Svetlana Egorov, from the traffic stop. Based on the information, she had strong ties to the Russian mob. Josh had mentioned he helped with a Russian mob drug case in Chicago. He also wasn't a rookie, and the mistake he made backing her up really could have been to hide evidence. *Maybe Josh really is the informant.*

As she slipped out the door and started back toward the front office, theories swirled in her head as she worked to put together all the pieces. A radio call from dispatch snapped her out of her thoughts.

"All available units to the Ray Ranch. The reporting party believes they saw the sheriff."

Chapter Forty-Three

Wayne was stuck in the truck while Jenna stood outside talking on the phone. He had no idea who she had called, but he had a bad feeling. She had handcuffed him, arms behind his back and locked the vehicle. There wasn't an easy way out. He had to think, but his thoughts were foggy. Probably from all the drugs she'd given him.

Hanging up, Jenna came back to the truck and climbed in. She had a wild look in her eyes. They were bloodshot and her hands were shaking. Whatever she was high on, it was coursing through her veins at full strength now. Hard to reason with someone who was doing who knows what, but Wayne was up for giving it a shot.

"You know, it's still not too late. Let me go and I'll never say anything to anyone that you were the one who took me. Just help me nail your father for the crimes he's committed."

Jenna barked a sharp laugh. "Yeah, right. You can feed me all the bullshit you want, but in the end you're no different than anyone else. My father would kill me, and you'll arrest me the first chance you get."

"Okay then, so what's your plan?"

Jenna put the truck in gear. "To use you as a decoy

so I can get the hell out of this godforsaken place. Then I have plans to go back to college, far away from here."

"There'll be a warrant out for you. You'll be running and hiding rather than attending school. You'll never be free. Help me out and I'll get you a deal. I'll talk to the DA."

"See? You're already changing your deal. Just a minute ago you said you'd never say anything. Now it's a deal. Screw that. I'll figure things out. Quit worrying about that, and quit talking. You're giving me a headache."

The truck bounced around on the back-mountain road. Wayne fought to ignore his aching head and concentrate on where they were going. He thought they were headed west. That would take them to Ray Ranch, which didn't make him feel any better.

Some thunderheads were building and moving in over the mountains. The clouds billowed and grew taller, twisting and spiraling up. There would be some good storms this afternoon and evening.

Jenna made a turn, and Wayne recognized the back of the Ray Ranch.

"Why are you taking me here?" he asked, trying one last attempt to get her to talk. "What's your plan? Maybe I can help you come up with a better one."

"I said shut up," Jenna said. Her knuckles were white from clutching the steering wheel so hard.

As they approached the ranch, a loud clap of thunder echoed through the valley. The storm was moving over the mountains and gaining strength. A bolt of lightning shot out of the sky. Wayne startled and Jenna laughed.

"Little jumpy?" she asked.

He shrugged. Even if he managed to get away from

Jenna at this moment, he would have a hard time getting away from the Ray Ranch. The ranch sat down in a valley trapped on all sides by steep mountainsides. There were only two roads in and out as far as Wayne knew. The only other way out was either on foot or by horseback.

She parked the truck and opened the door for him. He stepped out, taking mental notes about the location of buildings so he could remember the layout. That would be important to know just in case he had a good chance to escape.

Jenna pushed Wayne ahead of her and they marched into the outbuilding that had been turned into some sort of compound. They passed a room that was so full of guns a small military could work from there. He saw enough ammunition to last for years. But for what? Just drug running? Or was Carson dealing weapons too?

She forced him into a room that was not much bigger than a large walk-in closet. There was a metal chair in the middle. He tried to fight back, but several days without food and little water had taken its toll on his body, and Jenna easily shoved him back into the chair. She removed the handcuffs and secured his hands behind his back with several strands of baling twine she'd taken from the barn. Then she tied his legs together. The thin strands of rope cut into Wayne's ankles and wrists.

"Glad you have enough spunk in you to try to escape," Jenna said, pulling the twine tight. "But you need to stay here. I wish you luck, Sheriff. I'm outta here. And by the way, your final experience here should be explosive."

Wayne didn't answer. He was done talking to Jenna.

Negotiations with her at this point were futile. He would wait for her to leave and then work on escaping.

Jenna went over to a gun safe in the corner. She grabbed a large key ring hanging on the side.

When Jenna opened the door, Wayne saw stacks of cash and several handguns. There was enough money to feed and arm a small military for quite a while. And Wayne was certain that was probably what Carson Ray had in mind. Out in the boonies, if you had enough men and weapons you could almost certainly outdo any local police force. Any type of SWAT response would take forever to arrive. Probably forty-five minutes to an hour since the closest SWAT team was in Fort Collins. With the weapons the Rays had, any conflict would be long over before SWAT even showed up. Wayne had no doubt that Carson had thought that through.

Jenna pulled out several stacks of cash, putting them in a duffel bag. Smart. She could get quite a distance and start over with that amount of money, buying things like new IDs and passports.

She shut the safe door and slung the bag over her shoulder. "Well, Sheriff, it's been fun. See you later."

Wayne grunted, but still refused to answer. He was already peering around his surroundings to see how he could get the twine undone.

"Not so fast, sister."

Cody. Wayne knew he was mean and nasty. His arrival didn't make this situation any better.

Cody sauntered into the room, his arms crossed, deliberately blocking the doorway. "What you are doing?" he asked.

"Nothing," Jenna said.

"Who's back there? Is that the sheriff?"

Jenna pulled her gun out of her holster and pointed it at Cody. "Just stay out of my way."

Cody stepped into the room. "Well, well, it *is* the sheriff. Nice, Jenna. Where did you find him? Or did you have him all the time?"

"Shut up, Cody. Let me go and the sheriff is all yours. You can take credit for finding him and bringing him here. Dad will love you for that."

Wayne thought about speaking up, but instead he stayed quiet. He began looking around the room for a knife or something he could cut the baling twine with. Baling twine was strong, but with the right knife or sharp edge he might be able to saw through it. He moved his chair an inch, but Jenna heard him and swung around, pointing her gun at him.

"Stay where you are, Sheriff," she said.

"I will, I will," Wayne said, trying to reassure her.

Jenna turned back to Cody. "Just let me go, Cody. All I want to do is go back to college and finish my degree. I want some sort of a normal life."

"I can't let you do that," he said, a smirk on his face. "I might have the sheriff, but when Dad finds money missing, he won't be happy that I let you go."

"You won't let me have anything, will you? I couldn't even have Doug."

"What're you talking about," Cody asked. "That stupid fed?"

"Yeah, I was in love with that stupid fed, but you had to go and ruin that too."

"Well, who knew?" Cody's grin grew bigger. "Wait until Dad hears this."

"I always suspected you were in love with Doug. I'm so disappointed in you, Jenna."

Wayne recognized that voice—Carson. He pushed past Cody, who was still near the doorway, and strolled into the room. Wayne took note that Carson was armed with a couple handguns.

"Are you? So sorry to upset you. Now step aside and let me out of here. I'm leaving and if I have to shoot you, I will," Jenna said.

"I can see that," Carson said. "But let me tell you how this is going down. I love you, but I know what you've been doing. I know you've been stealing from me, you little bitch. I have no problem shooting you."

Jenna stepped closer to her father. "Then do it already. Go ahead, pull the trigger. I don't care anymore. But know that in a short time, this whole place is going to be gone."

Chapter Forty-Four

Jenna stood face-to-face with her father. She wasn't much shorter than her dad and didn't seem intimidated at all. In fact, if Wayne didn't know better, he would say Carson was the one who appeared to have a flicker of concern cross his face.

"Where do you think you will go and what do you mean this place will be gone?" Carson asked.

"Anywhere you can't find me, and I've rigged up a little surprise for you. Turns out I'm pretty good with explosives too. I'm done making drugs and I'm walking out of here now. If you let me go, I'll maybe consider not blowing up your hard work."

Wayne saw Jenna put her finger on the trigger of the gun she held. He had no doubt that she would be willing to pull the trigger, but before she could do anything, Carson grabbed Jenna by the hair, and she screamed.

Carson snatched at Jenna's weapon. She jumped back and pulled her pistol in closer to her, trying to keep her father from grabbing it. Cody lunged toward Jenna. The shot echoed throughout the small room, making Wayne's ears ring.

"I can't believe you did that!" Carson screamed.

"You caused this! This is your fault!" Jenna said.

Cody clutched his stomach. Blood spread out, contrasting with his white shirt. He screamed in pain. The cries quickly diminished to groans as he collapsed to the floor.

Carson grabbed Jenna and marched her back out of Wayne's sight, but the door remained open. Cody still lay on the floor, no longer moving. Loud moans echoed throughout the room. As the storm clouds rolled in, they blocked the sun. The room darkened.

Cody continued wailing like a hurt animal. Wayne scooted his chair back again, desperately trying to find a spot where he could rub the baling twine until it broke. There was no way the Rays would leave him alive. He'd witnessed Cody being shot and that put a target on him. Not to mention Jenna kidnapping him. She never meant to do anything but bide her time and use Wayne as a pawn when it best suited her—she didn't care if he lived or died.

He had no doubt Carson would be back soon to shoot him. Anyone who left their son bleeding on the floor with a gut shot wouldn't think twice about killing a sheriff. Cody needed immediate medical attention. Wayne could help him if he wasn't tied up.

I need to get out of here. Fast.

"Cody. I'll help you, but you need to free me," Wayne said.

Cody quieted for a moment.

"Just help me cut this baling twine. Come on. Put pressure on that wound too."

"Am I going to die?" Cody asked. Tears streamed down his face. Wayne saw another side to Cody—the scared side.

"I don't know," he answered. "But if you can keep

pressure on where it's bleeding, that will help. Try to use your hands or see if there's a towel anywhere around you. The fact that you're still conscious is a good sign. That means the bullet didn't hit something like your abdominal aorta. You'd be dead by now if that was the case."

"I'm not ready to die," Cody said, pushing down on his belly.

Wayne was hopeful that Cody was listening to him. Maybe they could get out of this.

"Good," he said. "No one wants you to die, and I'll help you, but first you're going to have to help me. It'll hurt like hell to move, but your sister left the safe keys on the counter. Do you think you can make your way over there and get them? Open up the safe? I think there's a knife in there. You cut me loose and I'll help you."

"Yeah, I'll try."

"Good." Wayne waited, and when Cody didn't move, he thought that maybe he had passed out. "Cody?"

"I'm sorry, I can't move. I'm trying, but my legs aren't responding."

Wayne leaned back and closed his eyes. The bullet had probably paralyzed Cody. If he even lived there was a good chance he'd never walk again.

Carson had ahold of Jenna by her ponytail, pushing her ahead of him, when Lana appeared. Her timing was terrible. He was tired of her showing up unannounced.

Carson forced Jenna out into the drive, holding her gun in his right hand while pushing her with his left. Lana stood in front of her Tahoe. She'd brought one of her men with her.

Jenna stopped suddenly, throwing Carson off balance. She reached in her duffel bag and grabbed a fistful of money, waving it in front of Lana.

"My father has been stealing from you!" she yelled.

Carson had been so mad at Jenna after shooting Cody that he didn't notice the bag of money she had carried out. He shoved her to the ground, giving her a kick in the ribs. Jenna responded with a small yelp, but much to his surprise, she scrambled to her feet and stepped a good distance away from him.

Before Carson could stop her, Jenna started yelling again. "My father has the sheriff too! He's in the back room. My father had him the whole time and is a liar."

"Jenna," Carson said. "Shut up. Why are you doing this?"

Lana took a step forward and pulled a gun from her holster, aiming it at Carson. "Is what your daughter telling me true?" she asked. "Is the sheriff here and you've been holding out on me all this time?"

Carson aimed Jenna's Sig Sauer at Lana. "You'll have to excuse my daughter," he said. "She's lying."

"No," Jenna said. "Go look in the back room. The sheriff is there, and this money is some of what my father stole from you."

Lana nodded to the man and told him to go check the back room. Carson swung the pistol toward Jenna, fury coursing through his body. He would shoot her. He didn't care anymore.

Both of my kids are worthless.

He would run the business alone.

Chapter Forty-Five

Maya and Josh pulled up near the Ray Ranch. They would assess the scene from an area where they could see the ranch, but not be seen. That way they could still respond if needed, but it would be better to wait for backup. Josh had called in the closest SWAT team. The response time would be about forty-five minutes.

That could be too long. This might all be over before SWAT arrived.

Maya still wanted to confront Josh. He should have told her everything. This wasn't the time to interrogate him, but if he was the informant, she had to be careful too. She and Juniper could be in danger.

She had learned in battle that strategy and surprise could go a long way. She had Juniper, and the K-9 could give them the upper hand. Sometimes people gave up once the dog was present. Somehow, though, she didn't think the Rays would just surrender.

Maya jumped out of her vehicle and started grabbing important equipment, including her shotgun, M4, and portable radio. She wanted all these items accessible in case the Rays had a way to destroy the patrol cars. She put on Juniper's leash and brought her out. All three of them gathered in an area not too far from the patrol vehicles and hidden by a stand of pine trees.

Josh took out his binoculars and began scanning in the direction of the Rays' ranch.

"What do you see?" Maya asked.

"We have ourselves a situation. I see Jenna Ray on the ground, Carson is aiming a gun at her. The lady we pulled over also has a gun. She's pointing her gun at Carson. Nice standoff going on."

"Shit," Maya said. "We may need to move in."

"We need to wait for backup. I think if they were going to shoot Carson, they would have. And it's just the two, I mean three of us," Josh said, nodding at Juniper, "against who knows how many. We need to wait."

"Any sign of Pops?"

"No."

"Damn it," Maya muttered.

"He's probably inside somewhere. If he's here."

"Where else would Jenna have him?"

"I don't know," Josh conceded. "Look, let's see if we can hike in closer and get a better look. I have a couple deputies responding. They should be here soon."

"This whole thing could be over by then."

"True, but let's be smart about this."

"We can sneak in and set ourselves up for a better response. Let your deputies know that they can meet here and start setting up a command post. Maybe we can get a phone in for negotiations," Maya said.

Josh put his binoculars down. "Yeah, you're right. If you flank them from the west with Juniper and I come in from the east, behind the building, we can back each other up. What we don't know is how many militia members are there waiting and watching. We could be ambushed and outnumbered."

Or if you're the informant, Juniper and I could be ambushed.

The sound of a gunshot echoed through the valley. Maya grabbed the binoculars and stared through them. No one appeared to be shot, except for a tree that had taken the brunt of the bullet's impact. "Shot fired. We should move in. Are you sure you don't know how many militia members are down there?"

"How would I know that?"

"Just asking."

"Let's at least get in closer and disable their vehicles. That's a good start. Especially the rental car. We need to start thinking about containing this scene. No one is down, so we need backup or else this is a suicide mission," Josh said.

Maya stayed quiet. The less she said to Josh, the better, since she didn't know if she could depend on him. She would figure out her own plan—one that kept Josh from surprising her. She agreed they needed backup, but she also wanted to know if Pops was inside. If he was, the longer he was there, the more his life was at risk.

Thunder echoed down the valley, sounding like battle drums. A few drops of rain started to fall. Maya wiped away the beads of water on her face. Her body shook with a chill. Whether it was from the cool rain or the situation, she wasn't sure. Bad weather wouldn't help them right now. Visibility could be difficult, and lightning posed another threat.

"I know you're right. I'll get Juniper's vest while you radio your deputies. Tell them to get here fast."

She moved back to her vehicle, staying low to make

herself difficult to see. Juniper stayed close to her side. Maya reached the door to Juniper's compartment and grabbed the Kevlar K-9 vest. It was made from the same ballistics material as Maya's protective vest. The design included complete range of motion for Juniper so she could apprehend and move any way she needed. The brown color helped camouflage her, and there was a pocket for a GPS tracker. That way Maya could always find Juniper.

Juniper saw the vest and immediately started to leap around in excitement. She wanted to work. Maya told her to heel and, to her surprise and satisfaction, Juniper listened.

Another round of lightning flashed and hit the ground on the opposite mountainside. Electricity jolted through Maya's body and her arm hair stood on end. She made sure Juniper was okay, but the dog seemed unfazed by the situation.

Being up on the hillside in this storm was the worst possible spot for their safety. But Maya would take the risk for Pops.

"That shot was a warning," Lana said. "Don't think that I won't kill you. Right now, you are a liar and a thief in my eyes. Your daughter is the only worthwhile one in your family. She knows how to cook up the best drugs and she is the only one to tell me the truth."

Jenna clutched her ribs but managed to say thank you. Then she turned toward Carson and smirked. He wanted to go smack the look off Jenna's face, but he refrained. Lana would execute him if he killed Jenna. Then Lana would have everything, and he couldn't stand that. He would get back at Jenna later. She would pay for this.

Carson relaxed the gun. The sound of the compound door opening came from behind him. He heard the shuffling of feet, more than one pair.

"Look who I found," said the Russian, staying in the doorway of the compound.

Carson glanced over his shoulder but didn't really need to. He knew who Lana's man had dragged out. The sheriff.

"Well, well," Lana said. "Looks like Jenna was telling the truth after all."

"She's using you. Manipulating you," Carson said.

He had to make one last-ditch effort to get the situation under control. He noticed that Jenna was starting to back away from all of them. If she was able to get enough distance, then an escape through the valley and up into the mountains was possible. Jenna had grown up hunting and packing in those mountains. She could survive for days on her own, and no one would ever find her.

"Jenna's going to take off. She's been taking money and stashing it away. She's been sampling your product. You need to get her before she escapes."

"I don't believe you. You're the one who dated a narc. You'll pay for this," Lana said, stepping forward and putting her gun against Carson's temple. She nodded toward her man. "Take the sheriff back inside. I'm looking forward to having a little chat with him."

Chapter Forty-Six

After hurrying back to Josh with Juniper, Maya picked up the binoculars and peered through. The storm clouds and rain cloaked them in darkness, as the wind howled and violently shook the trees. Another flash of lightning allowed Maya to see Jenna stepping slowly away from her father and the Russian.

If Jenna headed up the mountainside, she could possibly escape into the national forest and they would have a hard time finding her. Maya could get through the valley and possibly cut Jenna off before she headed into the mountains. Even if Jenna was a little farther ahead, Maya had Juniper to help track her.

She stared down at Juniper, who wagged her tail and gave a doggy grin. She was just waiting for Maya's signal.

"Jenna just split off from the standoff. I'm going to go after her," Maya told Josh.

"What?"

"You heard me. She took off, that way." Maya pointed. "She's going to flee into the mountains. We'll never find her. Juniper and I are going after her."

"You need backup. You need to stay here," Josh said. His voice had an edge of anger.

"No, I don't. Plus, your backup tactics are less than stellar. Juniper and I can take care of ourselves."

"Are you going to hold that over me forever?"

"Probably."

"I backed you up just fine when you and Juniper tracked at the crime scene with Bobbi."

"You did, but sorry, we're going after her." Until Maya knew if Josh was the snitch, she was better off on her own. "Jenna's the key to all of this. She took my grandfather and she's the only one who knows where he is."

She heard Josh mutter some expletives as she and Juniper sprinted off.

Wayne was back in the room behind a locked door, but the man with the thick Russian accent hadn't thought to tie his legs back up to the chair. He breathed a sigh of relief. This gave him a better chance to stay alive and escape.

He was guessing that the man was an associate of Svetlana Egorov's. Probably one of her hit men who liked the dirty work. He was pretty certain that Svetlana was the one outside starting a standoff with the Rays. He'd been on the lookout for her for a while when the DEA let him know she might be in the area.

Wayne peered around the room, looking for something sharp. Having his arms behind his back made everything more difficult. In his younger years, Wayne might have been able to contort himself and get his hands back in front, but he wasn't that flexible anymore.

Seeing nothing obvious to cut through the binding, Wayne finally noticed an empty beer bottle sitting on a shelf above the safe. If he could find something to stand on, he might be able to knock the bottle off and break it. Staring around the room, he spotted a bucket in the corner. Wayne kicked it over and then rolled the bucket over to the counter. Using his feet, he managed to tip the bucket up so he could stand on it.

Wayne stepped up, wobbling a bit. His balance wasn't great and not having his hands free only made things harder. He steadied himself and then slowly turned around so his back was to the shelf with the bottle. His fingers grazed the smooth glass a couple times and, just as frustration was setting in, Wayne managed to move the bottle. It teetered on the shelf edge and, after what seemed like an eternity, fell to the floor. The satisfying sound of glass breaking made him smile.

Wayne stepped back off the bucket, crouched down and managed to grab a sharp piece. It took him a few minutes, but he eventually sliced through the rope. He shook his arms, relieved to be free.

He stooped over Cody and felt for a pulse. There was still a faint one, but he needed medical attention soon. Wayne rummaged around the room trying to find a medical kit or anything that would help with Cody's wounds. He didn't want to move him since Cody had said he couldn't feel his limbs.

Wayne found a blanket stuffed back in the corner and some rags to help stop the bleeding. They were dirty, but at this point, that was the least of Cody's worries. It was the best he could do. He covered Cody with a blanket. The young man was pale and unresponsive.

Wayne double-checked the door handle, but it was locked, with no way to unlock it from the inside. He had to figure a way out of the room—for his sake and Cody's.

Cody groaned. At least he was still alive. For now. If he lived, what life was left for him? He'd be going to prison for his role in all this—a life wasted, rotting in a cell. Wayne felt sorry for the young man.

The storm outside must have stalled out over the mountains. Lightning lit up the room and thunder rolled down the valley. Rain pelted the metal roof creating a deafening roar.

Wayne went over to the safe. The keys lay on the counter next to it. There were about twenty keys total, but he didn't care—he'd try each one until the safe opened. If he could get in the safe, he could get a gun. If he had a gun, he could get out of this place. After the next flash of lightning, he could shoot the door open when the thunder echoed. With any luck that would hide the sound of the gunshot.

What was Maya doing right now? Was she scared? Looking for him? God, he missed her. He would get out of here if nothing else than to tell her how much he loved her. He didn't care if that was the last thing he did.

One of the keys finally slid in and the lock turned. Wayne saw several different types of pistols in the back. He grabbed a Glock 23 .40 caliber and ejected the magazine to check it.

It's full. Thirteen rounds. I'll need every round.

He racked the slide and heard the click as a bullet loaded into the chamber.

Outside the wind picked up as the rain cascaded down. He had to wait for the right moment to pull the trigger and then hope to hell that no one heard the shot.

A flash of lightning lit up the room again. Wayne started counting to see when the thunder would crash.

He got to five and heard thunder echo through the hills. The lightning was close.

He waited for the next flash, counted to five, and discharged the weapon, shooting the lock. The timing was perfect as the shot coincided with the clap of thunder.

Wayne slowly opened the door and stayed behind it for cover. He started clearing the hall, methodically making sure no one was hiding. The building appeared to be empty. He continued on through the compound. No one was around.

He took cover behind the final door.

Then he took a deep breath, pulled it open, and stepped outside.

Chapter Forty-Seven

Maya and Juniper found a good tree to stop and slip behind. Putting Juniper on a down-stay, Maya scanned the hillside for movement. She had a good vantage point to view Jenna sneaking away.

Maya didn't see Jenna at first, but then a flash of motion in the trees caught her eye. Jenna was wearing a light-colored shirt and it stood out in the darkness from the storm. Maya guessed that Jenna was following a game trail that went up the mountainside. On the other side of the mountain there was a trail that would eventually lead into the national forest and out to a parking area. If Jenna were smart, and Maya knew she was, she would have a car stashed there to get away.

She and Juniper would need to cover a lot of ground to catch up, and when they went downhill they would lose sight of Jenna. That didn't matter, though. Juniper would be able to find Jenna's scent and track her.

Maya allowed slack in the tracking leash and together she and Juniper took off into the woods. They went off the trail on a more direct route across the mountainside, Juniper loping ahead of her. Jenna's path cut toward their route.

We'll catch her.

Reaching the area Maya last saw Jenna, she cast Juniper out. "Track. Go find her. Let's go get her."

Juniper kept her nose to the ground, taking in the odors around her and following the trail. Jenna's scent was fresh since no one else had been in the area.

Jenna. Find her and I'll find Pops. Come on, Juniper. You're working like a champ. Jenna doesn't have a chance of escaping with you in pursuit.

Juniper had her tail straight up and sucked in air, working the odor. Maya sprinted to keep up, slipping in the mud and loose rocks. She jumped over logs, and dodged tree stumps and stones that jutted out from the mountainside. The rain started to let up, but with the long lead, Maya had a hard time seeing Juniper. Juniper's fur and vest blended into the dark forest, but Maya could hear sniffing. Trusting her dog, she fought to keep pace with Juniper.

A branch breaking stopped Maya and Juniper for a moment. The dog pulled off the scent and stood rigid, air scenting in the direction the sound came from. Maya could see Juniper was about ready to bark.

"Quiet," Maya whispered to her dog, hoping she'd respond and not sound off. Juniper stared at her handler and didn't make any noise, but she remained on alert.

So did Maya. Dark clouds and rain closed in on her—her mind traveling back to Afghanistan, in the mountains out on a night raid with her team. You never knew where the enemy hid, and you relied on your dog. She and her team had depended on Zinger's skills for their lives, and now was no different. The enemy could be hiding anywhere. Or be anyone. A small child asking for help might be a suicide bomber sacrificed by his own family.

Maya shifted to her left and stepped on a small tree branch. The crack of the branch popped like rifle fire. She grabbed Juniper and hunkered down behind a tree, her breath coming in short, hard gasps. Lightning struck nearby and the sharp crack that followed boomed like an explosion.

Blood everywhere.

Blood from Zinger.

Blood from Doug.

The cold rain picked back up again. Maya's teeth chattered together. She cleared the area, looking around the tree to the left and to the right. Her soaked shirt clung to her skin. Some of the VA counselors had coached her on some things to do, but the main tool Maya remembered from her few counseling sessions was grounding. Closing her eyes, she took a deep breath and fought her mind taking her back to war.

She opened her eyes back up and took in her surroundings. She was home. In Colorado. She could smell the pine trees and could hear the rain hitting the ground. Juniper's fur was soft and wet under her fingertips. Her flashback started to dissipate and her breathing slowed.

Keep moving.

Find Pops.

You have the dog, Maya. Use her. Trust Juniper.

Come on, soldier.

Maya slid her hand up the leash, feeling the strength of a K-9 at attention wanting to protect her handler and do what she was trained to do. Vibrations came back to her from Juniper as she shook with excitement. She snapped the quick pin release on Juniper's leash and pulled her gun out of her holster. She didn't know if

Jenna was armed. She had to assume she was, but Maya would be ready.

Juniper responded to Maya and stayed with her, ready and alert, waiting for the command to find their person and take a bite. Together they began to work as a team.

"Track, Juniper. Track. Go find her."

Juniper took the command and went back to searching, her whole body rigid. Maya kept from making noise herself and tried to keep an eye on her surroundings while working the dog.

Juniper put her nose to the ground and continued following the scent, but at times she'd stop and put her nose up in the air as the breeze would pick up and whoosh by.

"Don't get windy," Maya muttered. "Come on, weather. Cooperate." If the wind picked up, Jenna's scent would be blown all over the place and Juniper would have a hard time tracking and pinpointing it.

For a second the trees stood still, but then there was a whoosh of wind that came down the mountain and roared through the area they were tracking, almost like the sound of an avalanche.

"Shit," Maya said. "Juniper, wait, girl."

The dog hesitated, still attempting to air scent as the wind whipped down the mountainside. Juniper remained tense, not backing off from the weather.

When the worst of the wind died down, they continued to climb up the mountainside. Unsettling sounds of cracking ricocheted through the forest. Old pine trees swayed around as a few widowmakers creaked and made noise.

Great. Just what we need right now.

Then Maya saw Jenna bobbing in and out between

the trees not far ahead, her blond ponytail swinging like a pendulum. Juniper also saw the person and turned on the speed, rushing forward.

Jenna stopped, turned to face them, gun aimed and ready to fire. Maya could sense some hesitation on Jenna's part. She hoped that meant that Jenna didn't want to shoot Juniper, which would give the dog time to apprehend.

"Go get 'em, girl!" Maya shouted to Juniper.

The sound of a creaking tree branch overshadowed her words. A widowmaker came loose.

Maya screamed at her dog to stop as the tree branch crashed down.

Chapter Forty-Eight

Maya's stomach churned as she listened for yelps or other signs that Juniper was hurt. There was only silence. The gust of wind had settled just as quickly as it came up.

Not seeing Juniper or Jenna, she stepped toward their last location. Her gun drawn, she worked to stay quiet and not trip—something hard to do with branches littering the ground. These old pine trees were ravaged from the beetle kill and several had already fallen over, creating another hazard.

Maya stopped every few steps, listening for Juniper. A whine. A growl. Anything to let her know where her dog was.

But there was nothing.

Come on, Juniper. Where are you?

Maya kept her gun out in front of her and managed to avoid tripping over a stump and some jagged rocks. She wanted to pull out her flashlight and look around for Juniper, but that would only make her a target. She tiptoed as best she could and reached the giant branch that crashed down. The ragged dead limb stuck out like fingers. She searched the area, holding her breath, hoping Juniper wasn't underneath it.

Nothing.

Maya breathed a sigh of relief. *Thank God Juniper isn't trapped under there.*

Finally, she heard growling, and as she ran toward the sound, she saw Juniper's tail straight up in the air. Maya peered around a pine and saw that a widowmaker had crashed down and landed on Jenna's legs. With Jenna pinned down by the giant branches on her legs, Juniper had managed to apprehend her, biting Jenna on the bicep. Relief flooded through Maya's body.

"Get her off me!" Jenna said.

"I'll release her, but I need to see your hands. If you reach for anything, I'll tell her to bite again. Once I get her off you, you need to put your hands behind your head and interlace your fingers."

Jenna screamed in pain as Juniper continued to hold with a solid grip.

Maya gave Juniper the command "out" to ask her to release. Juniper rolled one eye toward Maya. She thought at first that Juniper wasn't going to release, but she eventually let go and continued to stand guard as Maya pulled out her handcuffs.

"Can't you just cuff me with my hands in front?" Jenna asked. Sweat started to bead up on her forehead.

"I'm sorry, Jenna. I don't trust you. I need your hands behind your head. Once I get you handcuffed, I'll help you get out from under this tree."

She was beginning to wonder if Jenna was going to comply when she sat up and put her hands behind her head. "Good," Maya said. "Now I need you to inter-lace your fingers."

Jenna obeyed and Juniper continued to stand guard. Maya walked behind Jenna and pulled one arm at a time behind her back putting on the handcuffs. Maya didn't release her hold on the pressure points until the cuffs were on and secure.

The gun was on the ground not far from Jenna, so Maya picked it up and cleared the weapon. She needed to frisk Jenna, but the branch was in the way. She told Juniper to guard, which meant that if Jenna tried anything, Juniper would come in and apprehend again.

Maya did her best to pat Jenna down.

Then she walked in front of Jenna and began to evaluate how to get Jenna out from under the tree. The old fir was thick and heavy, but luckily Jenna hadn't been pinned too far under the trunk or else Maya might not have been able to help her on her own. "I'm going to pull this as much as possible and I know it will hurt like hell, but I need you to scoot back."

Jenna nodded. Maya grabbed a few of the old branches and began to tug. She could see that Jenna's leg might be broken. It was more likely the fibula, which meant she could help Jenna walk and get her to the command post to be taken to jail, where she would receive medical attention.

"Okay, now," Maya said as she pulled on the tree with all her strength.

Jenna managed to wiggle back and free her leg. Juniper continued guarding, making Maya proud.

"Good," she said. "I'll help you to your feet and I'll help you walk back, but you have to behave, or else Juniper will bite you again. I'll wrap your arm up too until you can get medical attention for where Juniper bit you."

"Why did she do it?" Jenna asked.

"Do what?"

"Attack me. I've always loved Juniper and we'd hang out together at Doug's."

Maya saw Juniper's tail wag for a moment, but otherwise she never moved.

I knew Juniper was acting friendly toward Jenna in town. I was right—Jenna spent a lot of time with Juniper because she was Doug's girlfriend.

She thought about ignoring Jenna as anger coursed through her. *Jenna is my best suspect for Doug's killer. I should play the game. This may be my only opportunity to get answers.*

Maya took a deep breath, hoping to settle some of her emotions. "It's Juniper's training. We work on situations like this in training so that they bite when they need to protect their handler. Doug did a great job with her training."

"Yeah, I guess."

Maya helped Jenna hobble to her feet and cited her Miranda rights, so she could legally be questioned. But would Jenna give her answers? "How long were you and Doug together?"

"None of your business."

"It must not have been that serious," Maya said. She hoped to get Jenna upset and maybe talking more. "I mean, I was his best friend. He told me everything but never mentioned you."

"Maybe you two weren't as close as you thought," Jenna said through clenched teeth as she continued to hobble down the mountainside.

"Oh, we were. Doug and I were in love. Did he tell you that? We talked about getting married at one point," Maya said. *I need to keep her talking. Lying about my relationship with Doug may be the key to getting information out of Jenna.*

"Yeah, but then you went off and joined the military. You broke his heart. I fixed it."

"I don't know about that, but I do know he was going to pop the question to me." Maya pulled the ring from her pocket. She'd been carrying it with her for good luck. *If I can get Jenna mad at me, she might confess to being Doug's killer too.* "See? That was for me."

Jenna stopped abruptly and Juniper cocked her head, looking to Maya, muscles tense waiting to see if she needed to assist. Maya was grateful for Juniper's presence and she urged Jenna to keep moving, but she was frozen in place.

"A ring!" she said.

"Yeah. A ring. He was going to pop the question."

"Did he tell you that?" Jenna whispered.

"No. I put the pieces together when I went and picked up Juniper's things from his house."

"What makes you think that ring was for you? It was for me."

"No, I don't think so. I'm quite sure Doug was going to ask me."

"Screw you," Jenna said, pushing herself into Maya.

Maya slightly lost her balance but fought to stay on her feet. She couldn't give Jenna the upper hand. Juniper growled and locked her eyes onto Jenna, giving Maya a chance to get her footing. "See? I have everything from Doug. The ring. Juniper. You'll have nothing. You'll be rotting in prison thinking about how you killed Doug."

Jenna didn't say anything. *Maybe I pushed too hard.*

Just as Maya was getting ready to take another tactic,

Jenna broke the silence. "It was his idea. The bombs, that is."

"What? What are you talking about?"

"Doug. He set the bombs."

Wayne pointed the gun straight out in front of him, but kept his elbows pulled in tight to his body so that no one could ambush him and grab his arms.

He could hear the voices off in the distance. Yelling. Some of the accents sounded Russian. Probably one of them was the man who had grabbed him and stupidly put Wayne back in the room without tying him back up to the chair. With any luck they would continue to make stupid mistakes like that.

One of the voices was the female Russian. That voice was cold, with no emotions, and sent chills down Wayne's spine.

He continued to creep up to the side of the building to peek around the corner and see the situation brewing. As he went to stare around the side, a movement from his right side caught his eye. A person was coming down the hillside.

Wayne turned, keeping his back against the wall, looking for a spot to take cover. He was a sitting duck with the person on the hillside. He pulled his gun up and aimed.

The figure slinked down the mountainside and used rocks as cover. Wayne couldn't get a good look. Hopefully, they hadn't seen him yet. He moved back toward the door he had just come out of and waited. Watching.

The person crouched behind a rock, then stood up slightly, glancing over the top of the boulder. The thunderstorm had moved out, allowing a sunbeam to shine down and provide better light. The person ducked down again, but this time Wayne recognized Josh.

Thank God.

Maya continued to help Jenna down the mountainside. Juniper stayed right beside them. Jenna leaned into Maya as they navigated several boulders that created a tricky path. Maya stepped down first and then let Jenna prop onto her shoulder to get through the tight area created by the rocks.

Jenna's last comment disturbed Maya. If Doug set the bombs, did that mean Jenna had roped him into it?

"I know Doug was involved and, according to you, set the bombs. What I don't know is why," Maya said, working to keep her anger under control as she helped Jenna.

"I don't think I should tell you anything more."

Maya didn't want Jenna to clam up. She could talk to the prosecutor and let him know that Jenna had cooperated. Maybe it would help reduce her prison sentence. "I can try to help you get a lighter charge, but you have to tell me everything."

Jenna remained silent for a moment, and Maya thought she wasn't going to say anything, but then she spoke up. "You promise you'll help me?"

"I promise."

"Doug told me he was going to destroy the evidence so that I wouldn't be convicted of making the drugs. He was going to help me get away and wanted my father to go away for a long time. But then he went and spoke with your grandfather, and after that he was quiet. I figured he was going to turn me in, and I had to do something. When he showed up with you and Juniper,

I knew he was going to pretend like he didn't know anything about the lab and start an investigation. Otherwise, he would have come on his own. I made sure I took the remote from his house that morning and detonated everything."

"So why didn't you just leave then? Escape? Get out of here?" Maya asked, trying to hide the bitterness in her voice.

"My father would have hunted me down and found me. He was never going to let me go. Doug was no different. He said he loved me and that he supported me going back to college. That was a lie. Total bullshit. He knew what I'd been doing. He wanted out and he knew that wasn't going to happen while I was in his life. Then I saw him talking to Bobbi. I think they were having an affair."

"Bobbi?"

"Yeah, Bobbi. Roberta? You know, the blonde sleeping with my father."

Maya stopped. Juniper came up next to her and nudged her with her nose. "Doug was talking to her?"

"Yes."

"When did you see this?"

"The night before I blew everything up. They were talking passionately."

"Passionately?"

"Yeah. I pulled up to Doug's house and could see them through the window. They were in a heated discussion."

"That doesn't mean they were having an affair. It's probably not what you think," Maya said. "Did you know Bobbi was undercover? For the DEA?"

"What?"

"I think Doug was telling her everything, and I think he was trying to protect you."

Jenna stood stunned.

"Doug wanted to help you," Maya said, tugging on Jenna's arm to get her moving forward again. "That's all. You killed the one person who was looking out for you. Now you have to live with that."

"According to you, Doug was in love with you and going to ask you to marry him."

"Of course he wasn't going to ask me to marry him. That ring was for you." Maya pulled it out of her pocket and opened the case. "This is how much he loved you. This is how much Doug cared for you. And you murdered him."

She snapped the box shut and shoved it back in her pocket. She was ready to help Jenna move again, but noticed tears rolling down her face as she started to sob. Juniper went to her and nudged her with her nose.

"Even Juniper loves you," Maya said.

Jenna continued to cry.

"Come on, let's get going," Maya said. "I feel sorry for you. I know you lost everything, and your father is a complete jerk. You can help me out, though. Make up for some of this."

"How's that?" Jenna asked, her cheeks flushed red from crying.

"Tell me who your father is getting information from in the sheriff's office."

"I have no idea. My father would never tell me."

"Then tell me, where's my grandfather? What did you do with him? I know you took him."

"I'm not a monster."

Maya gritted her teeth. "I never said you were. I

just want to know why you took my grandfather and where he is."

Jenna sighed. "Your grandfather is at the compound. I left him there when I was trying to escape."

Many choice words came to mind. Maya didn't know where to start. Her fists balled up, but she quickly opened her fingers. Punching Jenna wouldn't change anything, and Maya would be in big trouble...but she wanted to. She wanted to let go of her grief. Her anger.

Use these feelings to go to battle and find Pops.

Maya was ready to ask Jenna more specifics about the exact location of her grandfather at the compound, but she was interrupted by the sound of gunshots echoing through the valley.

"There's one more thing," Jenna said. "I rigged the compound with bombs. I wanted to make sure my father had nothing left."

"You *are* a monster," Maya said, as a mixture of anger and fear flowed through her, increasing her already high adrenaline.

"No. I'm someone who has nothing left and nothing to lose."

Chapter Forty-Nine

Maya started sprinting, dragging Jenna faster. Juniper trotted by Maya's side.

"Son of a bitch, slow down," Jenna said, with ragged breaths.

"I'm done listening to you now that I know your plan is to kill Pops."

"At least I told you."

"Yeah, you're a real hero. Thanks a lot. Now quit talking and move faster."

"You'll never make it in time."

"Shut up and get your ass moving," Maya said. She needed to get to her grandfather. Josh would've waited for backup and be responding with the other deputies, but her grandfather could still be in the compound. Jenna had rigged bombs, probably on a timer, so they would explode after she had escaped. That had been her plan all along.

Jenna had intended to kill her entire family. And Pops.

"Tell me where the bombs are and how to stop them," Maya said.

"No." They came over the rise and Maya forced Jenna down the hill. Gunshots echoed off the mountainsides.

The gunshots only added to Maya's irritation and worry. Would Josh hear the shots fired and go in? Was he the informant and if so, would he kill Pops? She had to get back and find Pops. She didn't care how injured Jenna was. Jenna had brought this on herself. Running on a broken fibula wouldn't kill her.

"Hurry up," she said.

"I'm doing my best," Jenna said. Maya heard impatience in her voice, but she didn't care.

Juniper stuck to Maya's side as they all came into the area where the temporary command post was set up. A young deputy stepped out of his vehicle. She scanned the area for Josh but didn't see him. Crap. He was probably already responding because of the shots fired.

"Help me out here," Maya called out to the deputy. He came jogging over when he saw that Maya had Jenna handcuffed. "I need to get her into a cruiser, and she needs medical attention. Nothing life-threatening, but she will need to go to the hospital. Who's in charge right now?"

The deputy grunted in acknowledgement and waved over a couple paramedics to help him out. He pointed out another deputy over at the makeshift command post. Maya stepped back as the deputy and paramedics took over and began taking care of Jenna. She hoped Jenna would continue to cooperate and maybe they could strike a plea deal. But, for now, they needed to evacuate the area and end this standoff.

Before they could take Jenna away, Maya grabbed her shirt. "You better hope my grandfather lives or else prison will be the least of your worries."

Jenna smirked. "You don't have enough time. In about thirty more minutes, this place will be gone."

The deputy dragged her away. At least Jenna had given her a time—if she could be trusted.

Juniper pushed her nose up into Maya's hand. Maya reached down, feeling Juniper's fur and her soft undercoat. This was something she had done with Zinger before they went on any missions. She would feel the rigidity of the muscles, the tension, and the excitement of a dog ready to join her in battle.

She stared down at Juniper and was met with golden eyes. She swore Juniper smiled and gave her the look that said *Let's go. We're a team.*

Her dog was meant for this work. All the training, years of breeding the perfect K-9 and all of Juniper's instincts combined into a weapon that was on Maya's side, but time was running out.

Chapter Fifty

Maya spoke quickly with one of the deputies at the command center. "Where's Josh? Radio him and tell him to get everyone out of there. Now."

"Just sit tight," the deputy said. "SWAT should be here any minute. And we've lost some radio contact. The repeaters out in this area are not that good."

"Shit, that'll be too late. This compound is lined with bombs. It's all rigged to blow. We need everyone out. I'm going in, so tell me Josh's plan." Maya stepped closer. Juniper stood in front of her, both staring at the deputy.

"Holy shit." The deputy pointed down toward a map. "Here's what Colten told us. He's going in this way and there's a couple deputies coming down the backside of the valley…"

"Got it," Maya interrupted; the deputy was going too slow. "When SWAT arrives, let them know about the bombs and that the entire ranch needs to be evacuated. What channel are they on?"

The deputy told Maya and she changed her radio. She had to be careful that she didn't set off any bombs when she used the radio, but she had to take that chance.

Maya set a timer on her watch. Based on her calculations she had about twenty-five minutes left.

She had a mental picture of the map in her mind and where the other officers were located. Josh was putting himself in the worst danger by going directly into the compound, but he had heard the shots fired and Maya knew that meant he went for the immediate response. She and Juniper would be his backup. She gathered up Juniper's leash and headed for the mountainside.

Maya and Juniper ran along the trail that went above the ridge of the compound and wound their way around. They stayed behind the tree line in hopes they wouldn't be seen, but they needed to get down there quickly. She would probably only have minutes to find her grandfather and get him out.

Maya checked her watch. Twenty minutes.

They snuck in closer to the compound. There were some large boulders that gave her good cover, and there were recent footprints in the dirt. Most likely this was the same route Josh had taken. She put Juniper on a down-stay and then peeked around the rock. The scene down below made her catch her breath.

Pops! He's with Josh. They're alive.

Pops doesn't appear to be injured.

I have to warn them. They need to get out of there.

From her vantage point, Maya had a perfect view of the compound's layout and everyone involved in the standoff. Carson and the Russian lady had realized that law enforcement was moving in on them. They'd quit pointing guns at each other and teamed up. Just around the corner, Josh and her grandfather were getting ready to make their move. They must have thought they had the element of surprise, but Carson and Svetlana were waiting to ambush them.

Another person scurried up near Carson and Svetlana. Maya squinted trying to see who it was, but shadows made an identification difficult. Based on how the figure moved and how he held his weapon close into his chest, she could tell this person had law enforcement training. The figure moved and stepped out of the shadows. She gasped when she recognized Sam.

What's he doing? He was dressed in civilian clothing, and Maya realized he wasn't one of the responding officers. *Is Sam the informant?*

She needed to distract Josh and her grandfather. *Now.*

If she pulled her gun and fired off a shot, Juniper would respond by trying to apprehend someone, and Maya didn't want that yet. She had to do something different.

She whistled the way she had been taught by her grandfather. A small, high, shrill clicking sound that mimicked mountain bluebirds.

She saw her grandfather pause and signal to Josh, but before they could react, Carson started moving forward. He was going after Josh and Pops.

Maya couldn't just stand and watch. She closed her eyes and said a prayer for her dog. Once she stood up and started yelling commands, there was a good chance Carson would shoot at her and Juniper would go after him.

Maya took a deep breath and then leaped up and moved toward a tree to help give her cover. It wasn't much, but she'd take it. "Freeze! Forest Service Law Enforcement! Put your weapon on the ground or I'll send the dog!"

Maya saw her grandfather stare at her, confused. Carson swung toward Maya and Juniper. The sound of a bullet shattered the silence as he fired in her direction, but he had a pistol and they were out of range. The shot went wide and smacked the hillside.

Maya knew she was still yelling, but she almost couldn't hear herself. Everything became quiet and happened in slow motion.

Dirt flew up and hit her in the leg from Juniper leaping forward and rushing at Carson. This was what the dog was for. She had to let her do her job. And Maya needed to do hers.

She heard the weapon fire again, and she stepped out to fire back, but before she could get the shot off, she realized her grandfather had rushed Carson, knocking him off balance and landing on the ground, fighting for his weapon. Juniper went for the bite but missed as Carson and Pops fell to the ground.

Carson overpowered her grandfather, and Maya sprinted toward them. Josh tried to rush forward, but Sam and Svetlana surprised him by coming around the corner. Maya pushed herself to run faster as Sam aimed his gun at Josh.

Holy shit. Sam's going to shoot Josh. Where's Juniper? Can I get there fast enough?

Still in slow motion, Maya fired off two shots at Sam. She missed, but succeeded in distracting him before he could shoot at Josh. Carson pushed her grandfather to the ground, grabbed his gun and aimed it at him. She had just put her finger on the trigger when a rush of brown fur flew in front of her.

Juniper took a flying leap and knocked Carson down. She attached to the back of Carson's bicep and started shaking as hard as she could. The gun went flying. Carson screamed and tried to get Juniper off him.

Maya rushed toward Carson. She wanted to go to Pops, but the priority would be getting Carson under control and handcuffed. Juniper maintained the bite, hanging on, growling, shaking her head and entire body. Seeing Juniper taking a bite, Svetlana fled toward the compound entrance and out of Maya's sight.

We'll find you. I have the best dog—you can't escape her. But where's Sam?

Maya noticed he had also retreated around the corner. She didn't like him leaving, but they had to get one person at a time. Once Carson was under control, she and Juniper would go after Sam and the Russian.

Josh jumped in to help Maya. They gave Carson instructions to cooperate, and Maya would get the dog off. Just as she was ready to give Juniper the instruction to release, she heard another gunshot. Her first instinct was to take cover, but she had to stay with Carson and her dog. Juniper rolled her eyes toward the gunshot as the woodpile behind them shattered from the bullet hitting the logs. Maya glanced back over her shoulder and realized it was Svetlana shooting at them.

Pops stood up, limping on a leg that appeared to be broken. He dragged the leg and took aim at the Russian. Maya ducked down, and together she, Josh, and Juniper pulled Carson back toward the woodpile. Spent cartridges came flying out of her grandfather's gun as he fired round after round. Maya saw him flinch. His leg had blood running down it, but he didn't quit firing. Maya remembered him telling her before she left for the military that you had to decide how you were going to survive in war. Would you give up? Or would you fight harder no matter what was happening and how many times you had been hit?

She thought she had chosen to always fight harder, but she realized now that her grandfather was showing her what that meant. She saw his gun rack stay open. He was out of ammo and getting ready to do a tactical reload when Sam came around the corner, gun aimed at her grandfather.

Maya pulled her gun, aimed, and fired several rounds. Sam dropped to the ground.

Her chest constricted. She'd always tried to tell herself that killing someone in war didn't take a piece of you. They were the enemy. But that was a lie, and seeing Sam lying on the ground, a family friend she had loved and trusted, was only that much harder.

She stared back down at Juniper, who still had ahold of Carson. Carson was yelling and writhing in pain. She gave Juniper the command to release and she did. Josh took Carson's arms and pulled them behind his back, handcuffing him, and then motioned for a deputy who had come on the scene to take Carson away.

Maya reached down and pushed her hands into Juniper's fur, giving thanks for the dog. Then she rushed to her grandfather. Juniper followed, ready to protect her. Maya knelt by Pops, taking him in her arms and hugging him as blood spread across his outer thigh. She did her best to reach down and hold pressure to stop the bleeding.

I'm going to get you out of here. Maya checked her watch. *Eight minutes.*

"I'm so sorry, Pops. I love you. I love you. I need to move you and I know it's going to hurt, but you have to trust me."

She felt him grip her with his hand. "I trust you, Maya."

She smiled and leaned over him to apply more pressure to the wounds. "Thanks, Pops. I love you." Her necklace from Nana slid out from underneath her shirt and vest, hanging near Pops.

"I love you too," Pops said. He reached up and gently took the necklace in his fingers. "Nana is looking out for us, isn't she?"

"Yes, Pops, she is."

Pops smiled and then his eyes fluttered shut.

Shit, he's lost too much blood.

"Pops. Stay with me."

Maya checked her watch. *Seven minutes.*

Chapter Fifty-One

Maya crossed her grandfather's arms so she could pull him to safety. They couldn't be anywhere near this place when it blew.

"Juniper, heel."

The dog stepped next to Maya, tilting her head, waiting to see where they were going.

Maya started dragging Pops, but she couldn't go quickly enough. There was no way to know how many explosives Jenna had rigged, but Maya would bet it was enough to flatten the compound.

Where's Josh?

"Josh!" Maya yelled. She saw him giving directions to the deputies who were arresting Carson. Josh didn't know about the explosives. He peeled off from the group and ran toward her, picking up speed when he saw her trying to drag Pops.

Josh sprinted, his long stride quickly covering the ground over to them. "Don't move him. We'll get the paramedics to come down here."

"No, we have to get out of here. This whole place is rigged with explosives."

His face was blank at first, and then Maya could tell what she had said registered with him. Josh yelled at the other deputies to get everyone out. Then, together, they started pulling Pops again, hearing him make noises of agony as he bumped along the ground.

"We need to get back to the giant boulder on the hillside," she said. "I think that's our best shot. We need distance and shielding."

"Okay," Josh said. "How much time do we have?"

"About two minutes."

Instead of answering, he began pulling harder. Maya's adrenaline surged and she found more strength. Together they gained speed. Juniper jogged along with them.

One minute.

The large boulder was only a few more feet away.

I won't fail this time. I'm saving Pops. It won't be like Doug.

Maya strained to move Pops the last few feet. Josh helped her, and they managed to get her grandfather behind the large boulder.

"Juniper. Come. Down," Maya said. Juniper listened and lay down next to Pops. "We need to help shield each other. This is going to be a big explosion."

Josh nodded in agreement, and he and Maya lay over Pops. She made sure Juniper was tucked underneath her.

This sucker's going to blow any second now—

The air around them suddenly whooshed back, like a giant tidal wave.

The explosives kicked off, each boom sending more debris raining down on them.

Maya kept her head down. Juniper shifted underneath her, but she clung to her collar harder. "Juniper, down. Stay," she said.

Juniper still wriggled underneath her.

"Pfui," Maya said, using the command that was reserved for letting the dog know she needed to listen. *Now.* Juniper quieted.

The bombs sounded like a freight train thundering down the tracks toward them. Rocks pelted her body with the force of baseballs thrown at high speed.

Then silence.

Maya's ears were ringing. *Did I shatter my eardrums?*

Darkness. More silence. *Am I still alive?*

She couldn't move. *Is Pops okay?*

Juniper shifted underneath her. *Is Juniper okay? What about Josh?*

Maya's eyes closed. *Did I lose consciousness? How much time has passed?*

Her head pounded. Her fingertips rubbed dirt and small pebbles on the ground. The smell of burning flesh assaulted her. *Am I on fire? Is that my flesh burning?*

A bitter metallic taste made Maya want to spit, but she couldn't move.

Is this what it feels like to die?

Darkness wrapped around her.

A hand shook Maya's shoulder. She opened one eye. Then the other. Her fingers moved. Her legs still worked.

"Officer?"

I don't think I'm dead.

Maya stared at the face scrutinizing her. The man looked like a fellow Marine she'd served with. He'd died from a roadside bomb. Maybe she *was* dead. "Matt?"

"No, I'm not Matt. I'm a paramedic. I need to make sure you're okay."

"I'm fine, but Pops…"

Maya scrambled to get off her grandfather. Juniper

jumped to her feet and shook off, an indignant look on her face. Josh, feeling Maya move, sat up too.

"I'm okay. My grandfather, the sheriff—he needs help, and Deputy Colten—"

"I'm good," Josh said. "But I think the sheriff is unconscious."

They stood, both wobbly on their feet, and stepped back so the paramedic could do his job. She hugged herself with her arms until she felt Juniper come up and nudge her. She stooped down and put her arms around her dog, tears streaming full force. All the emotions of war, losing Doug, and now the possibility of losing her grandfather came out at once.

A hand started to rub her back, and Maya was ready to shake it off and pull herself together. She didn't need the SWAT guys to see her lose it, but as she turned her head to say something, Maya realized it was Josh. He didn't do anything more than just keep his hand on her as he watched the paramedics work on her grandfather. She was glad that he didn't try to tell her something crazy like everything would be okay. That was something neither of them knew.

Juniper leaned up against Maya's legs, pushing into her, which helped, but she felt powerless. Some more paramedics arrived on scene with a carry litter. They loaded Pops on and started carrying him toward the ambulance that was parked back by the command post. Maya, Josh, and Juniper followed behind.

She glanced over at Josh. He had a cut across his cheek and his clothes were shredded around his vest. A large gash started up at his shoulder and took a crooked path down his arm. Blood flowed down and trickled onto the ground leaving a path of droplets in the dust. Dirt and other debris stuck to the wound.

"Josh, you're bleeding," Maya said, taking the last wrap from her trauma kit. She stopped him and wrapped the arm up. "You'll probably have to get that looked at. It might need stitches."

He shrugged. "We'll see. I don't think it's that bad."

"You don't have to be tough for me. At least get the wound properly cleaned." She paused. "You protected us. Thank you."

He smiled. "I'll always protect you."

Maya reached up and touched Josh's cheek where some dirt was smeared across his face. She wiped away the smudge. "Thank you. It's good to have a friend."

She turned and continued walking toward the command post, where her grandfather was being loaded in the ambulance. Maya was ready to go join him, but the back doors shut with a final click. She stopped and wrapped her arms around herself.

A few men who had escaped the compound before the explosion were being handcuffed and taken away. The SWAT team was setting up a perimeter and heading down to finish clearing what was left of the Ray Ranch. Firefighters surrounded the area, working to make sure the explosion didn't torch any of the dead trees in the forest.

"Come on," Josh said. "Let's get you to the hospital and find out how your grandfather is doing."

"It's the same nightmare. Like with Doug. What if he doesn't make it? I don't think I can handle that," Maya said. She leaned into Josh and his arms circled around her. For a moment she let go and enjoyed the strength of his arms. The smell of aftershave and sweat mixed together with the metallic odor of blood and gunpowder stung her nose.

"Your grandfather is a tough guy. If anyone can make it through all this, it's him. Let's go," Josh said.

"Okay," Maya said, holding back tears as he let her go. A part of her wanted to ask him to hold her again, but Juniper was standing by her side, tail down but still wagging. Maya reached down and rubbed her head. "You're the best dog, Juniper."

Juniper responded with a quick leap up to slurp Maya's face.

About forty-five minutes later, Maya and Josh walked through the hospital doors.

After giving Juniper a thorough exam to make sure she didn't need to see a vet, Maya had set her up in the patrol vehicle to rest. She turned on the air-conditioning, gave her fresh water and provided a new blanket to curl up in and take a nap. Most likely the blanket would be shredded into confetti-size pieces when they returned.

The smell of disinfectant mingled with the sounds of people in the waiting area. The vending machine still had the dent left by Maya. She approached the volunteer at the front desk. "I'm here to see about my grandfather, Wayne Thompson. Is there any news about him?"

"I'll call back and find out." The volunteer picked up the phone and punched in some numbers, then waited.

Maya prayed that her grandfather would be okay.

The volunteer hung up the phone. "Your grandfather is in surgery. He is stable right now. The doctor will be out when he's done and talk to you. You can take a seat over there, and please, stay away from the vending machine."

He's alive. He's a fighter. He'll get through this. Maya said, "I promise the vending machine won't get hurt today."

She and Josh sat down in the gray chairs next to a coffee table. Magazines were spread out on the table, and while other people waiting were reading, Maya couldn't do anything but think about Pops.

She was grateful Josh was here with her. A twinge of guilt came over her thinking about reading his file and thinking Josh was the informant. She never would have suspected Sam. She'd believed him.

She didn't want to think about another person betraying her. She wanted the truth…straight from Josh.

"How come you didn't give me the full story?" Maya asked.

"The full story?" Josh fixed his dark eyes on her.

"You know, about your drinking and using drugs? Crashing a car? Getting fired from Chicago PD?"

Shock registered on Josh's face. "How'd you find out about that?"

Maya didn't want to admit that she'd been snooping, but she also believed in honesty. "Sam warned me about you. He said I needed to be careful and not get involved with you. I snuck into my grandfather's office and looked at your profile jacket. I knew there was an informant in the department; I thought it could be you."

Josh shook his head. He stared out the window, not making eye contact for a few minutes. Maya didn't know what to say. She'd pushed too hard and didn't want to lose him. Josh had become not only a friend that stood by her, but someone she cared deeply about. She didn't want to hurt him.

"Sorry. I shouldn't have asked or read through your

file. I thought you might be giving information to the Rays. I guess that was Sam. I never thought he'd do something like that."

"No, it's okay." Josh looked back at her. "I didn't think Sam would work with the Rays either, but I guess we don't always know everyone. We all have our hidden sides."

"We do. Can I ask you something? It's none of my business, but I'm curious."

"You can ask me anything you want, Maya. I'll always be truthful with you."

She took a deep breath. "One of the reasons I thought you might be involved with the Rays was because of the timing of that text when we were on surveillance. Was that text for work?"

"No. That message was actually my AA sponsor contacting me. With everything going on I'd missed a few meetings and he wanted to make sure I was okay."

"Oh." She shouldn't have been so quick to make assumptions.

"Hey," Josh said. "It's okay. I can see how that looked. As police officers, we're wired to think things like that."

Maya braved looking back at him. "I supposed when I called you and couldn't get you, that also has a good explanation?"

"If you call going to an AA meeting a good explanation, then yes."

"Gotcha." Her face flushed red. This would teach her to jump to conclusions.

"You know, if you ever want to go with me to an AA meeting, you can let me know. Give it a try. See if it helps. Or I could go with you to a veteran's support group. Don't know that I could attend one of those meetings since I'm not a veteran, but I'd drive you there. As a friend helping a friend. I can tell you have demons—I know what it looks like—but I can also tell you it's so worth dealing with them. The other side of sobriety is beautiful, and while we will always be addicts and always battle, it's a battle we can win."

"I'll think about it," Maya said. Part of her doubted she could ever heal from her trauma, but she had to admit, part of her wanted to try. For the first time in a long time, there was a little bit of hope inside of her.

"You'll know when you're ready."

"How did you know when you were ready to change? I know it's none of my business, but I'd love to know your story in *your* words. And maybe it will help pass the time."

He reached over and took her hand, holding it softly. "As you know, my partner and I were out on patrol one night. Got called to a domestic. Husband and wife were screaming at each other. Their ten-year-old son called it in. We went inside, broke up the fight and took the wife outside. I took their son outside too. It was winter so I didn't think twice about him wearing a thick jacket. I left him with another cop, but never frisked him. I never asked the other cop to frisk him either. My partner came out with the father in handcuffs and the kid freaked out. Started yelling about how his daddy wasn't going to jail. He had a gun under his jacket, pulled it out and shot my partner. I screwed up and my partner paid the price."

"Josh, you couldn't have known."

"I should have frisked the kid."

"You and I both know you better have a damn good reason to frisk a kid. It's no different than children coming up to us in Afghanistan. They're innocent. You think they would never do anything to you, but then you realize they're suicide bombers. Their families sacrificed them. This kid in so many ways is no different."

Josh shook his head. "Tell that to the guys in the department. No one wanted to even come near me after that, much less work with me. I couldn't handle it and went down a road of drinking too much and even started using some cocaine and other drugs. I only did the coke off duty and drank when I got home, so I told myself I was in control and could still do my job.

"One night I was on a date, and we were both high and drunk, driving too fast, and I crashed. We walked away somehow with only minor injuries and it was a single-car accident, so no one else was hurt. My dad pulled some strings and made sure no charges were pressed, but of course my chief fired me.

"It was only a matter of time before I did something on duty. I knew I had to get my shit together, but the nightmares and anxiety continued. I sat in my apartment and drank and snorted lines until I ran out of money and got kicked out. I remember trying to go home, but my dad refused to have me stay there. He offered to pay for rehab, and I figured it was a place to crash for a while, so I took him up on it. The night before I went, I sat out by Lake Michigan and got as messed up as I could. One last bender, you know?"

Maya nodded. She understood although she couldn't picture Josh so messed up.

"That night some homeless guys sat next to me, and we shared disgusting vodka and who knows what kind of drugs all night long. I got up and thought about walking into the lake. I wanted the pain to stop, so why not end it? Right then, right there. I had my clothes just about off and was heading toward the shore, but then I saw a ghost.

"My partner stood there on the shore, the moonlight illuminated him. He appeared so peaceful. I could have been hallucinating after all the shit I'd done, but either way, I stopped. He told me he forgave me and to get better, then he walked away up the shore and disappeared into the night. I've never seen him again… of course, maybe it's because that was my last night of being high. I went to rehab, got sober, but knew I had to leave Chicago. So now, here I am."

"Thanks for sharing that with me." Maya paused for a moment, thinking about the ghost Josh saw. She had plenty of ghosts, Zinger included. They often invaded her dreams. "I'm glad your partner stopped you from walking into the lake. Before I was deployed, I would have told you that you only saw your partner because you were high, but ghosts come home with you after war or after an experience like yours. Ghosts are real. They come uninvited into our dreams and haunt us, but sometimes they change us for the better. No one understands PTSD unless they've dealt with it. I tried telling a friend of mine once what was happening to me and she said, 'You look fine.'" She sighed.

"That's the problem," Josh said. "We do look fine, but no one can see inside us. My family, they didn't understand and still don't. The few friends I had left, they just figured if I drank enough, I'd get over it and get better. That didn't happen."

"Do you know why Pops and I fought?" Tears welled up in Maya's eyes.

"No."

She had never told anyone about the night of her grandmother's funeral. Not even Doug. It had been one of her darkest moments, but she trusted Josh.

"Tell me more, if you want," Josh said.

"I came home stateside for my grandmother's funeral. The military gave me emergency leave, but I never made it out of San Diego. I couldn't handle it. I wasn't prepared to lose Nana. She was my main support.

"When I left for boot camp, I was so excited. But then I got homesick. I didn't think I'd be able to finish. I called Nana and she helped me through it all. She helped me believe in myself. When I finished boot camp and found out I was on my dream career track of becoming a K-9 handler, Nana was my first call. She was so proud of me. She was my everything. So, when she died, I couldn't come home and face it.

"I went to a bar and drank myself into a stupor. Somehow, I got myself in a cab and back to a hotel. I sat there for about an hour with a gun to my head telling myself to end it. That all the mistakes I'd made would be over. But I kept thinking about my grandfather and how I couldn't leave him alone, so I set the gun down and passed out. When I woke up the next morning, I decided that when I got out of the military, I would go home. I thought home would be healing, but it wasn't. My grandfather was furious that I missed the funeral, and that's why we fought. I don't blame him. I'd be mad too. I've never been able to tell him how close I was to ending it all. He'd be so disappointed in me."

Josh nodded and squeezed her hand. "One thing I've learned going to NA and AA, we all make mistakes in life. It's how we pick ourselves up and move forward that makes all the difference. Your grandfather loves you. He's already forgiven you. You just need to forgive yourself. I'm glad we're both still here. If I'd walked into Lake Michigan, I never would have met you, and you're the best thing that's happened to me in a long time."

Maya didn't know what to say. She gave Josh a tentative smile and squeezed his hand back. "Thank you. You're the best thing that's happened to me too. Except for Juniper. Juniper has you beat."

"As she should," Josh said.

"You going to get that wound looked at?"

"You going to keep bossing me around?"

"Yep," Maya said.

"I'll get it checked out when we find out how Pops is doing. I don't think it's life-threatening and I'd rather stay here with you, if you're okay with that."

"I am."

Then they waited.

Chapter Fifty-Two

Two weeks later

Maya stepped over Juniper, who was lying on the rug in the sun near her grandfather. He liked to sit in the living room, where he had large picture windows that provided breathtaking views of the mountains and the meadow behind the house. Velvet and Daisy were grazing in the pasture. Pops watched out the window, sipping the coffee Maya had brought him.

"You need anything else right now?" she asked.

Juniper opened one eye and then let out a large sigh and went back to snoozing. Pops had been home for about ten days, and in that time, Juniper had become attached to him. Maya had enjoyed the time with Pops too. In a couple days she and Juniper would be back at her place and she would start working on building a yard and run, but she vowed to visit Pops as often as possible.

"No, I'm good."

"Okay." Maya paused and then said, "Pops?"

"Yes?"

"There's something I've been thinking about. That I'd like to do with you."

"What's that?"

"I'd like to go see Nana's grave. I know it doesn't take the place of going to her funeral, but I'd like that. Maybe we can get flowers...for Doug and my mother's grave too."

Her grandfather set his coffee down, and she tried to gauge what his reaction was going to be. He took a few moments before speaking. "I'd like that. You know, I'm starting to feel better. And as much as I've enjoyed the company of you and Juniper, I would like to get out of the house. Go do something. Why don't we go this afternoon?"

Maya hesitated and then said, "That sounds perfect."

A little while later, she went outside and pulled her car up to the porch, parking close so her grandfather wouldn't have to move too far. The doctor thought he would have to do lots of physical therapy and walk with a cane for a while. The gunshot to his outer thigh was healing well, but still needed time. Pops had also broken his fibula, but that was quickly healing.

She thought she'd load Juniper first, and as she opened the front door a fur missile came shooting out of the house. Maya whistled and Juniper ran around the car several times, but then hopped in. Another blanket had been shredded. Maya would have to get a stash of blankets.

The door creaked open and she heard what had become the familiar sound of her grandfather's cane and footsteps on the porch. She hurried up the stairs to assist him, but he waved her off. "I won't get better if you keep helping. The occupational therapist taught me how to do stairs, so I'll do them."

"Okay," Maya said. She stayed back far enough to

give him independence, but close enough she could support him if needed. Pops limped down the stairs, taking each one carefully, but he did them on his own and climbed into her vehicle.

"You're getting stronger every day, Pops," she said. She closed the door and hopped in on the driver's side.

"Flowers?" he verified.

"Yes." Maya put the car in Drive and headed for the grocery store.

"Josh call lately?" Pops asked. "Heard you read his files. You know he's made mistakes, but he's a good guy."

Maya tried not to flush at the mention of Josh. She guessed Pops was trying to figure out their relationship. Problem was, she wasn't certain about their relationship either, so she dealt with it by avoiding questions.

Maya and Josh had talked almost every day, and she knew he was a special person. She had joined him at one AA meeting and had managed not to go to the bar or the liquor store since the standoff at the compound. But she didn't know if she was ready for something more. Right now, she needed a good friend and someone to talk to. Josh seemed to need the same, and Maya found they could talk for hours.

"I haven't talked to Josh today," she said.

"Any news on the investigation?"

"You know where the investigation stands."

"Remind me."

She tried not to roll her eyes. "The DEA has Carson locked up. The Russian, Svetlana, was killed in the explosion. Dental records proved it was her. Sam's remains were recovered." Maya hesitated as her chest constricted with the memory of shooting Sam. After a moment, she continued.

"Seemed like Bobbi was able to get quite a bit of evidence to them before Carson killed her. The crime scene techs found enough evidence to put Carson away for life for Bobbi's murder, including some bloody clothes he thought he burned. Luckily, he didn't do the best job though of destroying the evidence.

"Jenna, once she recovers, will spend some time in jail on drug charges, but it seems she has cut a plea deal to testify against her father. She will still have to stand trial, though, for Doug's death…" Maya's voice caught, and then she continued. "No one seems to know for certain who killed Cody. You were there, though. Any ideas?"

Wayne shook his head no. "The Rays were all fighting for the gun and it went off in the scuffle, so I don't know who actually pulled the trigger and killed Cody."

"That's all I know, but I have a question for you," Maya said.

"What's that?"

"You didn't seem surprised that Sam had sided with the Rays. Did you know he was feeding them information?"

Wayne gazed out his window, and just when Maya thought he wasn't going to answer, he said, "Sam had changed over the last few years. He and Carson were buddies from high school, and I suspected he was giving them information. I mean, it's a small town. You see things and hear things. Like when Sam last went hunting, he told me he went alone. I found out later that he actually went with Carson. If he hadn't deceived me, I probably wouldn't have been suspicious. I caught him in a few more lies too. I decided I wanted someone from the outside who didn't have ties to folks in this area. That's why I promoted Josh instead. I was hoping I was wrong about Sam, but I guess I wasn't."

"I'm sorry to hear that. I always liked Sam. He was like family. I don't understand why he did the things he did."

"I don't either. I supposed he got caught up in everything and couldn't get out. Or maybe that's who he really was all along."

"That's true. I'm still sorry to hear that."

Wayne nodded and then went back to staring out his window. Maya pulled into the grocery store parking lot, ran in, bought three bouquets of red roses and came back out. Wayne had opened the door between Juniper's compartment and the front of the car. He and Juniper were snuggling, and Wayne was feeding her dog cookies.

"Looks like you've completely spoiled her," Maya said.

"She deserves it."

"Yeah, she does."

Maya headed out of town toward the cemetery. She pulled into the parking lot and helped her grandfather out of the car. Juniper stared at her, and Maya decided that since no one else was there, Juniper could use the exercise. She opened the door, and Juniper bounded out, running around in a large circle and pouncing on some grasshoppers before coming back to Maya's side.

They visited Doug's grave first. Juniper went and lay down near the headstone. Maya put the roses near her, gave Juniper a rub and a kiss on the head, and stepped back beside her grandfather.

"I'm so mad at him and yet I miss him so much," she said, breaking the silence. Juniper lifted her head and tilted it toward Maya.

"I understand. If I could go back in time, I would have arrested him when he came and talked to me… when he told me everything. I wouldn't have kept that from you either. I'm sorry I put you in danger. I'll never forgive myself."

"I understand why you didn't tell me, though. You were protecting both of us. I just couldn't see it."

"You've been through a lot, Maya. I know that and I should have been more supportive. When I came home from Vietnam, I was a mess too. It took time to get back to whatever normal is. If it hadn't been for your grandmother, I don't know if I could have done that."

"Are you ever going to tell me the whole story? What Doug came in and told you?"

"I'll tell you whatever you want to know. I should have done that from the start."

"I know Doug was taking bribes from the Rays, but did he say why? How did it start?"

Her grandfather hesitated. "I don't know why he started taking money from the Rays. Maybe he had debts. The money was good and that can be hard to ignore. He never really said, but what he did say is that he fell in love with Jenna and that's why he kept doing it."

Maya stared at the mountains. She knew that Doug had loved Jenna, and as his friend, she wished they could have gotten married and had a normal life together. But what was normal anymore? Regret washed over her. She had to forgive Doug and let him go. "Was he protecting her?"

"He was. When he came to me, he was ready to turn

himself in, but he didn't want her to go to prison. He wanted to take the fall for her. I lost my temper then and started yelling at him. I told him I would help him, but he had a week to turn himself in. Then three days later the explosion happened."

"I wonder why he created a fake dispatch call. He put Juniper in danger. And me. I didn't think he would do that."

"I don't know for sure. We didn't talk about that, but I have a feeling he was going to tell you everything. You wouldn't have believed him if you didn't see it for yourself. He was probably going to have you arrest him, but we'll never know for sure. Jenna made sure of that."

"I was so mad at him when I started finding the evidence against him. But I miss him too. I miss his friendship." Maya squeezed Pops's hand. "We have each other, though. I never want to be mad at each other again or keep anything from each other. I love you, Pops."

"I love you too, Maya Bear. But there's something else I need to tell you."

Maya hadn't heard him use his pet nickname for her in years. She gave him a smile. "What's that?"

Pops's tone changed to concern. "There's a good chance the DA will be opening up an investigation into my lack of action when Doug came and told me everything. I broke the law enforcement code of ethics and there will be consequences."

"I understand why you did it, though. I'll help you. We'll deal with this together," Maya said, trying to sound confident, but her heart pounded. Not only could Pops lose his job, but he could serve time.

"Thank you, Maya. This may be my battle, but I don't want to push you away."

"I'm here for you, Pops."

Together they strolled over to her grandmother and mother's graves. Juniper got up and followed them.

Maya placed the flowers at her grandmother's headstone, and then her mother's. She stepped back. "I wish I could remember my mother better," she said.

"You look a lot like her. She was a good person. Had a kind heart, but a wild one too. I should have been there more for her."

"Don't be so hard on yourself, Pops."

"I'll give you the files," Wayne said.

"What files?"

"The files pertaining to your grandmother's death. I know you wanted to see them and there's no reason why you shouldn't. Just know that there are pictures of the crime scene. It may not be how you want to remember your grandmother. You're an amazing law enforcement officer and I trust your judgment. I would love to have you look over the investigation. If you tell me that it looks like suicide, then I'll leave it alone. There are a few discrepancies I've noticed about the crime scene. I've spent hours staring at the photos. I want to see if you see the same things. There's another thing you should know."

"What?"

"The gun she used matches the ballistics to the gun that killed your mother."

Maya stared at Pops. Dizziness washed over her and she closed her eyes to stop the sensation. When she felt better, she opened them again. "Tell me more."

"I didn't want you to know that, but your mother didn't just OD. She was shot too. We never found the weapon. The coroner ruled your grandmother's death a suicide, but I've continued investigating on my own. I don't think your grandmother killed herself, especially with the ballistics matching, but I want you to look over the file and tell me what you see."

"I don't think she would have taken her own life either. I think that was one of the reasons I didn't come home. Nothing about her death seemed right." Maya took a deep breath. "And thank you. Thank you for letting me help."

They stood together until the sun started to set. She knew her grandfather was getting tired, and she helped him to the car to drive back to his house. As soon as she could, Maya would read the files.

Maya assisted her grandfather going into the house. He went and lay down on his bed, and a few minutes later he was asleep. She fed the horses and then put wood into the outdoor fire pit. She lit the fire, pulled up a chair, and let Juniper out of the house. They sat down and watched the flames slowly crawl up the wood.

She shivered in the cool night air, and put on her jacket and rubbed Juniper on the head. Maya reached into her pocket and pulled out the letters from Doug that she had read so many times. The letters had brought so many emotions with them—anger, fear, and regret. If she wanted to start the healing process, she had to start letting go of the past. These letters would only keep the past alive, but she needed to move on.

One by one, she tossed them into the fire. She watched as the flames engulfed the paper and the words disappeared.

I'll always remember you, Doug. We both changed, but I forgive you.

With that, Maya threw the remaining letters in the fire.

She tilted her head back and took in the night sky with the moon shining down through the aspen grove while petting Juniper on the head. Picking up the file about her grandmother, her hands shook. She had to pretend that this wasn't about her nana, but rather look at it as another case. Plain and simple.

Maya had to find her killer.

Juniper slapped Maya on the arm with her paw and whined.

"I know, girl. I need to ask for help with this, but you know that's tough for me."

Juniper barked.

"Not so loud, you'll wake Pops. Do you think I should call *him*?"

Taking her paw off Maya, Juniper spun a circle, whined and stared at Maya longingly with her golden eyes.

"Okay. Okay." Maya pulled her phone out and unlocked the screen. She paused and then called the one person she could trust to help her—other than her grandfather. She needed a friend. She missed him. She needed strength to be able to open the file.

"Hi, Josh. It's Maya. Will you come over?"

* * * * *

Acknowledgments

Writing a book is a journey and I'm lucky to have had some wonderful friends join me along the way. I'm so grateful for everyone who took the time to share their experiences and expertise with me. Any and all mistakes are mine.

A big thank-you to Forest Service Law Enforcement officer Chris Magallon for taking the time to answer all my questions about the unique job of being a K-9 handler and officer in the national forests. I loved learning about Chris's K-9, Ice, who was also a finalist for the Hero Dog Competition. Now retired, Ice helped inspire Juniper's character. Thank you for your service, Chris and Ice!

I am lucky enough to have some good friends who served in law enforcement and the military. They were all willing to share their stories and knowledge with me. Thank you to retired chief of police Dave Lewandowski. I appreciate your time and always answering my phone calls and text messages. And a big thank-you to Dave's wife, Jamie, for always encouraging me on this writing endeavor.

I'd also love to thank MSgt Dr. James A. Burghard, USA/USCG/USAF, Retired, for all your military and emergency response insight and knowledge. You helped me shape Maya's career and background. Also, you have the most amazing wife, and I'm lucky to call her my best friend. Thank you, Marie, for your friendship and all the beta reads. I couldn't have done this without you!

Also helping me with Maya's background was Tara Darlene Smith, former U.S. Army Sergeant. Tara, you are a phenomenal person and I appreciate the time you took to sit with me and share your military experiences. I am honored to have learned more about your story and I can't wait to read your memoir. Please take the time to learn more about Tara and her extraordinary work at her website www.taradarlenesmith.com.

While I work K-9s with a private company, I was able to create a better law enforcement K-9 character with the help of retired officer Dee Deyen. Thank you, Dee, for putting up with my questions, reading an early copy of the book, and sharing your amazing stories of working your dog. Your help was invaluable!

Also helping me with K-9 questions was our trainer, Mackey Kelly of Canis Major Dog Training. Mackey, thanks for sharing so much about how these amazing dogs are trained and helping me become a better handler over the years.

As I finished this book, I met Patrick O'Donnell, who has a great Facebook group and podcast called "Cops and Writers." Thanks so much, Patrick, for the information and insights! I'm lucky to be part of a fantastic critique group, Broad Horizons. Your support, honest feedback, and encouragement means the world to me.

I had some awesome beta readers and help with critiques from Anne Hunsinger, Margaret Mizushima, Kristin Horton, and Michelle Kubitz. Thank you all so much!

I also appreciated the scholarship from Lisa Jackson to attend Killer Nashville, where I met Clay Stafford. Thank you to Clay for the wonderful conference. Killer Nashville helped me find my "tribe" and opened up a whole new world for me that helped me on the path to publication. At Killer Nashville I had the opportunity to receive a critique from author Baron Birtcher. Thank you, Baron, for your help and encouragement. A big thank you to best-selling author Grant Blackwood for teaching a great course. You taught me how to put all the pieces of novel writing together, not to mention, patiently answering every single one of my questions.

Having an amazing publishing team around you is inspiring. I couldn't ask for a better agent when it comes to Ella Marie Shupe of the Belcastro Agency. Thank you for believing in this book! My editor, Mackenzie Walton, helped shape this book, encouraged me and made the story so much better. Thank you! I'm thrilled to be working with the awesome team at Carina Press, including Kerri Buckley and Ronan Sadler. I'm so lucky to have all of you! Thank you all for taking a chance on a debut author.

I'm grateful to my whole family for the love and support they have shown me as I pursued this dream. My parents instilled the love of reading and writing and I'm so glad they did. Thank you, Mom and Dad, for always believing in me! I have the most patient and loving husband in the world who puts up with dinner conversations about characters and plots. I love you and I'm lucky to have you by my side! And to my aunt June and uncle Maury, thank you for always having faith in me! I couldn't ask for a better "Ant" and "Unc."

My final thank-you goes to the dogs I've worked over the years. There's a little bit of each of them in Juniper's character. They've taught me what partnership, love, and trust means. Here's to all the K-9s out there doing a job they love!

About the Author

Award-winning author Kathleen Donnelly is a K-9 handler for a private narcotics dog detection company. She
enjoys using her K-9 experience to craft realism into
her fictional stories. Kathleen loves the beauty of the
mountains, which inspired her choice of setting for her
series. She lives near the Colorado foothills with her
husband and her four-legged coworkers.

Visit Kathleen on her website at www.kathleendon-
nelly.com, on Facebook at facebook.com/AuthorKath-
leenDonnelly, follow her on Twitter @KatK9writer or
find her on Instagram @authorkathleendonnelly.

*From award-winning author Sandra Owens
comes the first book in a suspenseful new series
full of adventure, sparks-flying romance,
and companionship between a Navy SEAL,
a local artist, and their dogs.*

Read on for an excerpt from
Operation K-9 Brothers *by Sandra Owens,
out from Carina Press!*

Chapter One

"Stupid me. I trusted you," said the voice on the other end of the phone.

Jack Daniels, Whiskey to his SEAL teammates, blinked sleepy eyes at his bedside clock. Three in the morning sucked for getting angry calls from women. What the hell had he done to this one?

"Who's this?" That was the wrong thing to say. Jack held the phone away from his ear in an effort to save his hearing. He didn't recognize the number on the screen. Her voice wasn't familiar either.

"Sweetheart," he said, interrupting her tirade. "You sure you have the right number?" Even though her voice and phone number didn't ring any bells, he couldn't say for sure he wasn't the douchebag—along with some other impressively creative names she was calling him—in question.

Ah hell, now she was crying.

"How could you?" she said, her words slightly slurred. She hung up on him.

After thirty minutes of trying to go back to sleep, Jack let out a long sigh. How could he what? That question was going to bug him until he got an answer. Although her voice hadn't been at all familiar, he'd liked

it, even when she'd been calling him names. He grinned.
Sewer-sucking slimeball and twatwaffle were good,
but his favorite was doggy doo. That one had a nice
ring to it.

He got out of bed and padded to the living room
where he'd left his laptop. Dakota sighed in resignation before hoisting herself up from her dog bed, her
nails clicking on the wood floor as she followed him.
She liked her sleep, something he interrupted too often
for her taste because of his nightmares. At least they
weren't occurring every night anymore. She sat near his
leg and peered up at him with worried eyes.

"Not a nightmare this time, girl. We got a mystery
on our hands. What do you think of that?"

She knew him inside and out, knew from the tone of
his voice that he wasn't weighed down by his memories this time. Once she determined he didn't need her
comfort, she made two circles, got her damaged leg
under her, then curled up on the floor at his feet, apparently liking her sleep more than mysteries. Jack was
intrigued, though, his interest in something flaring for
the first time since coming home.

It only took a few minutes to find a name and address
attached to her phone number. Nichole Masters, cur-
rently living in Asheville. Nope, not ringing even one
little bell in his memory bank of female acquaintances
or hookups. It was possible he'd forgotten one but not
likely. He had a good memory, especially for women,
and she had a sexy voice he was sure he wouldn't have
forgotten.

Jack stared absently at the half moon framed by the
window. Coming to a decision, he nodded. "All right,
Nikki girl, you have me curious." As his teammates

would tell anyone who asked, get on Whiskey's radar and all bets were off.

He showered, and after staring at himself for a minute in the mirror, he shaved off his beard, seeing his face for the first time in months. He felt naked.

At sunrise Jack made a recon run on one Nichole Masters. Her house was a cute little bungalow near the River Arts District of Asheville, North Carolina. As soon as he downloaded her Facebook profile picture to his phone, he knew that he'd never met her. There was no way he'd forget that face.

He should let it go, but she'd fucking cried, believing he was the cause. That couldn't stand. And yeah, he recognized that his reasoning was skewed. She'd thought he was some other douchebag, but Jack couldn't get her voice out of his head. Then there were her eyes, a warm golden brown. Were they as beautiful in person as they were in the photo? But it was her smile that drew him. It was an honest smile, and he sensed that Nichole Masters was a happy person. That some faceless man had made her cry didn't sit well.

It creeped him out a little that he was stalking her—and it sure as hell would her if she knew—but he needed to learn where she worked. Once he knew that, he'd come up with a plan to meet her in a way that wouldn't freak her out. Besides, he had nothing better to do.

He was on medical leave after getting too up close and personal with an IED. Dakota had saved his life by putting herself in front of him and pushing him back, in all likelihood preventing him from being blown to bits. She'd been severely injured, had almost lost a hind leg. Thank God she had survived, though, and was now recuperating, along with him. He would be returning to his team. She would not. She'd served her time, had saved the lives of many of his brothers, along with his, and had earned her retirement.

But it was preying on his mind. Dakota needed him, but he'd have to leave her behind when he was healed enough to go back. The problem was that he didn't know who to give her to. It had to be someone both he and Dakota trusted, and the only names that came to mind were his teammates. Because he'd given himself a deadline—two more months to get his arm and shoulder in shape—he was running out of time to make a decision.

Since there was a VA hospital in Asheville, he'd come home as soon as he'd been released from Walter Reed Bethesda Medical Center. After a month in the hospital—first in Germany and then at Walter Reed—he'd been ecstatic to leave that place behind. Physical therapy on his arm and shoulder was a bitch, but the sooner he was healed, the sooner he could get back to his team.

The first thing he'd done after getting out of the hospital was to track down Dakota. He almost hadn't recognized her. She'd been curled up in a corner of the kennel, rib bones showing, eyes dull, and fur lackluster. At the sight of him, she'd tried to stand, only to fall over when she put weight on her damaged leg. Since she belonged to the military, he'd had to call in some favors to get her released to him, but he'd been relentless in making that happen. When he'd first brought her home, she had been depressed and lethargic, and Jack thought she'd as much as given up. Thankfully she'd come a long way, and except for her leg, she was back to the dog she'd been before the bomb.

At precisely eight, Nichole Masters appeared, wearing a blue-and-white striped dress and white sandals. Jack blew out a breath as she walked down the steps of her little porch, a mug in one hand and the end of a leash in the other.

She was gorgeous. Her shoulder-length hair was a riot of curls in a fascinating mix of colors—reds, golds, and browns. A man could happily get lost in all that hair. She was tall, which he liked, and a little on the thin side, which he didn't like. Made him want to feed her.

He wasn't close enough to hear what she was saying to the puppy straining at the other end of the leash, but the dog was completely ignoring her. Jack could have told her that the little beast was going to keep winning their test of wills unless and until she positioned herself as the alpha dog in their relationship.

The puppy finally lifted a leg and watered a bush. The woman disappeared back inside with her little friend, and then a few minutes later walked out with a purse over her shoulder and the dog still on his leash.

Jack followed her to the River Arts District. After she parked and exited her car with her dog, he waited a few minutes before heading for the renovated warehouse she'd entered. As soon as he walked in, the aroma of coffee caught his attention and he headed for the small concession stand. While he waited for his order, he scanned the area. Artists on both sides of the aisle were setting up their tables and booths for the day.

It was a mix of arts and crafts. Next to the coffee stand, an older couple had a display of landscape paintings: waterfalls, mountain sunsets, and a few of downtown Asheville. Directly across the aisle was a booth filled with stained-glass pieces.

It was a cool place, one he'd have to come back and investigate when he wasn't on a mission. A puppy bark caught his attention, and coffee in hand, he headed for it. In the middle of the building, he found his target standing in front of a long table loaded with pottery, tangled up in the leash her puppy had wrapped around her legs.

"He taking you prisoner?" Jack said.

She glanced over at him with laughter in those golden-brown eyes, and his heart thump-skipped in his chest. That had never, ever happened before, and he almost turned and walked away. A female-induced twitchy heart wasn't his thing.

Then she leaned precariously, looking like a tree about to topple over. Jack dropped his coffee onto the table next to her and was at her side in time to catch her before she landed face-first on the cement floor. Damn, she smelled good, like vanilla and maybe almonds. Whatever it was, it made his mouth water.

"Um, you can let me go now."

And there was that throaty voice that had kept him awake last night. "Do I have to?" He winked to let her know he was teasing—not really—and then he made sure she was steady on her feet before crouching down in front of the puppy.

"Hey, buddy," he said, putting one hand on the dog's rear end. Jack lifted his gaze to his new fantasy. "What's his name?"

"Rambo."

"Here's the deal, Rambo. When I say sit, you're going to plant your butt on the ground." He pushed down on

Rambo's rear end while pressing the palm of his other hand to the puppy's nose. "Sit." Still keeping his hands on the dog, he had to repeat the command a second time when the little guy tried to climb onto his lap.

Rambo wasn't stupid. He recognized Jack was the alpha and kept his butt glued to the ground this time, although he did wiggle his rear end, all that puppy energy making it impossible to sit completely still. But he kept his gaze on Jack, as if waiting for his next instructions.

"Good boy." Jack gave him a chin scratch as a reward.

"Wow, how did you do that?"

As soon as the puppy heard her voice, he tried to jump up her legs, his tail furiously wagging. She laughed, a musical sound that Jack liked a lot.

"A combination of things. Using my hands to signal what he needs to do for one, but mostly the tone of my voice."

"Can you show me?"

That would be an affirmative. Jack took a moment to rein in his lust before lifting his eyes to hers. "I could help you train him."

He took the end of the leash from her hand and unwound it, freeing her legs. Wasn't his fault if the leash was so tight that his fingers brushed across her skin as he performed his chore. Not that it was a chore in any way, shape, or form. The goose bumps that rose where he touched her pleased him. She wasn't immune to him.

"Are you a professional dog trainer?"

How much truth to tell her? Most of it, just not the stalking part. That was entirely too creepy. He stood, keeping the leash and tightening it so that Rambo had to stay by his legs.

"Jack Daniels," he said, holding out his hand.

She raised a finely arched brow. "For real?"

"Yeah. My parents had a weird sense of humor. My SEAL teammates call me Whiskey, if that works better for you." A lot of people thought SEALs weren't allowed to reveal their identity, but that wasn't true. They just didn't go around advertising the fact. He hoped knowing would make her feel more comfortable with him.

He smiled—impressed that he remembered how—and waited to hear her answer.

Nichole eyed the blond-haired, blue-eyed man who was apparently a dog whisperer. Wow, an honest-to-God SEAL, and he was as hot as the SEAL heroes in her romance books. Maybe even hotter. Definitely hotter.

"Nice to meet you, Jack. I'm Nichole Masters." She held out her hand, and it disappeared inside his massive one. His touch was gentle, but she was sure he could crush her bones if he wanted. His voice sounded vaguely familiar, but she was positive she'd never met him before. Jack Daniels was not a man a girl would forget.

"And you, Nichole." Rambo barked, and Jack let go of her hand. He smiled down at her puppy. "Yes, we haven't forgotten about you, Rambo." He glanced up at her. "That's a big name for the little man to live up to."

"I'm hoping he'll grow into his name. He's a rescue, part German shepherd, part anyone's guess. The vet said maybe some sheltie." Her hand was warm from being in his, her fingers tingling a little from his touch. The last time she'd had tingly anything from touching a man had been with Lane, before he had shown her his true self. But she wasn't going there, not when a hotter-than-hot hero was sharing her breathing space.

He handed her the leash. "Two intelligent dog combinations and very trainable. He'll test you, but he'll also want to please you."

She blinked, trying to catch up with their conversation. She ran his last words through her mind. Right. They were talking about Rambo. "Believe me, he's doing a great job of testing me." She'd never had a dog before, and honestly hadn't had a clue how rambunctious or destructive a puppy could be.

He glanced around. "Maybe this isn't the best place for him. At least not until he's trained."

As if to prove his point, Rambo tangled his leash around her legs again, then stuck his nose under her dress, lifting the hem halfway up her thighs. She bent over to grab the skirt before she flashed not only a hot SEAL but all the strangers around them, whose attention suddenly seemed to be on her.

Rambo dropped to his feet, gave a happy bark, and then tried to run in the opposite direction. With her legs bound together by the leash, preventing her from getting her balance, she toppled forward, her face heading directly for Jack's crotch.

She put her hands out to keep her mouth from landing on the most private part of him, but when she realized that would result in her groping him, she panicked and ended up windmilling her arms. A mere inch before her mouth got entirely too up close and personal with a man she'd only met minutes ago, a pair of hands slid under her arms and lifted her back to her feet. That would have been great if her new position wasn't breast to SEAL chest. An extremely hard chest. Desire spiked through her, adding to her embarrassment. Her cheeks and the back of her neck felt like they were on fire.

"Ah…ah." She realized her arms were sticking out in a pretty good imitation of a scarecrow, so she dropped them to her sides. He kept his hands on her arms, trailed his fingers over her skin, down to her wrists, leaving goose bumps in his wake. She lifted her gaze to his. Lord have mercy, his eyes were a hundred times darker than they had been before she'd smashed her breasts into his chest. She wondered if he would mind if she climbed him like a tree.

A slow—sexy as all get-out—smile curved his lips. "Hello," he murmured.

"Hi," she chirped. *Really, Nichole, you've taken to chirping?* He let go of her and stepped back, then dropped to his knees. Her heart slammed into her rib cage at seeing him in that position while her mind was stuck on the breasts-to-chest thing and her skin tingling from his touch.

As if he could read her thoughts, he lifted his eyes—still a darker blue—and gave her that sexy smile again. "I'm just going to free you."

"Oh." That came out sounding disappointed, and he chuckled. What in the world was wrong with her? She'd never reacted to a man like this before, not this fast and this…well, tingly.

"There, all better," he said once he had her unwrapped from the leash. He tapped the puppy's nose. "You're a handful of trouble, aren't you?" Rambo tried to lick him. Jack stood and handed her the end of the leash.

"This is the first time I've brought him here with me. I guess I jumped the gun, but he's learned to recognize when I'm leaving and starts to cry. I felt guilty for sticking him in his crate all day. Eventually I want to be able to bring him, but obviously I need to wait until he loses some of his puppy energy."

"That will happen, even faster if he gets some training, but yeah, this isn't a good place for him right now. Too many interesting things and people to check out."

"Live and learn, right?" A couple walked up to her booth. "Um, I need to get to work."

"You have your phone on you?"

"Yes. Do you need to make a call?" Heaven help her, the man really did have a killer smile.

"No. I was going to put my number in it. You know, in case you decide to take me up on my offer to help you train Rambo."

"Oh. Right." He probably thought she was a scatterbrain, but it was entirely his fault for being so sexy that it was hard to think around him.

As if to prove he needed training, her dog was straining at the end of his leash, trying to get the couple's attention with begging yips, hoping for a little petting. "Rambo, no." She pulled him back toward her, and of course, he planted his paws so that she ended up dragging him.

She glanced at Jack, expecting to see disapproval, but the only thing in his eyes was amusement. "Here." She unlocked her phone and handed it to him. "You'll definitely be hearing from me if you can teach him some manners."

"I can."

When he handed her phone back, their fingers brushed against each other, and there was that tingling again.

"Take care, Nichole." He squatted in front of Rambo. "I know you have a lot of energy, buddy, but try to behave for your mistress." Rambo tossed himself onto his back, his tail scraping across the floor.

"I don't think *behave* is in his vocabulary."

Jack glanced up at her as he gave her dog a belly rub. "Part of teaching him that word will be to teach you how to master him."

There was something in the way he said that, in the flash of heat in his eyes, that had her almost fanning her face. "Um, master him, right." *Jeez, Nichole, get your mind out of the gutter.*

That was easier said than done with this man, and when the heat returned to his eyes and one side of his mouth curved up, she knew he knew right where her mind had gone. Again.

She glanced at the couple, who were still browsing. The woman picked up a mug. "I love how you embedded a maple leaf in these. I'll take the set."

"I'll be right with you." She glanced at Jack. "Gotta go." Before something else came out of her mouth... Like *my bed is only a few minutes from here. Want to go play?*

He rose in a slow unfolding of his body that had her eyes tracking every movement and flex of his muscles. Oh, yeah. Sex. On. A. Freakin'. Stick. She'd been burned so badly by her last boyfriend that she'd gone through an I-hate-men stage. That phase might have just ended.

"Hope to hear from you, Nichole," he said before picking up his coffee.

"I think you will," she murmured as she watched him walk away. "And real nice butt, Whiskey," she added.

Her morning had started off as one of the crappiest ever. She'd woken up tired and out of sorts after drinking enough wine to get up the nerve to call Trevor the Bastard Allen at three in the morning and tell him what she thought of him for sabotaging her commission. She'd figured that if she was up at that time of night, stewing over what he'd done, that it was only right for his sleep to be disturbed. The jerk had pretended not to know who she was.

Rambo hadn't helped her mood when she'd found her favorite running shoes chewed up. Her fault for leaving them out, but weren't all the toys she'd showered him with enough? Considering everything the world had rained down on her recently, she deserved a hot SEAL to play with, right? But she refused to appear too eager—because, really, the man probably had eager-to-get-into-his-pants women at his beck and call—so she'd wait a bit to contact him.

Don't miss Operation K-9 Brothers *by Sandra Owens, available wherever books are sold.*

www.Harlequin.com